ALEXANDER BOTTS

Great Stories from
THE SATURDAY EVENING POST

ALEXANDER BOTTS

Great Stories from
THE SATURDAY EVENING POST

by William Hazlett Upson

THE CURTIS PUBLISHING COMPANY INDIANAPOLIS, INDIANA

Third Printing, March, 1979

CONTENTS

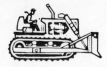

INTRODUCTION

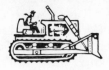

Few fictional characters become as real to their readers as Alexander Botts, over the years. Botts even acquired an official biography, neatly printed, which was mailed out on request. Here are the facts, as set forth by Botts' creator, William Hazlett Upson, in the 1950's:

Alexander Botts was born in Smedleytown, Iowa, on March 15, 1892, the son of a prosperous farmer. He finished high school there; then embarked on a series of jobs—none of them quite worthy of his mettle. In these early days the largest piece of machinery he sold was the Excelsior Peerless Self-Adjusting Automatic Safety Razor Blade Sharpener. He became interested in heavy machinery in 1918 while serving in France as a cook with the motorized field artillery. In March, 1920, he was hired as a salesman by the Farmers' Friend Tractor Company, which later became the Earthworm Tractor Company.

On April 12, 1926, he met Miss Mildred Deane, the attractive daughter of an Earthworm dealer in Mercedillo, California. Seven days later they were married. Mildred, later nicknamed Gadget, had attended the language schools at Middlebury College (Vermont) and acted as interpreter for her husband when he was sent to Europe in 1928 to open new tractor outlets there.

Mr. and Mrs. Botts returned from Europe in early 1929 to await the birth of Alexander Botts, Jr., who arrived in February along with a twin sister, Little Gadget. Mr. Botts now has been a grandfather for some years.

INTRODUCTION

There were, in all, 112 Alexander Botts stories in *The Saturday Evening Post*. The first appeared in 1927; the last in 1975, shortly before Mr. Upson's death.

As might be expected, there are parallels between Botts' life and the life of his creator. Mr. Upson was born in 1891, in New Jersey. He was graduated from Cornell in 1914 and worked for the service department of the Caterpillar Tractor Company in Peoria, Illinois, up until his service in World War I, in France. In the postwar '20s, Upson, like Botts, married and had two children, a boy and a girl. But while Botts continued in the tractor business, in the Midwest, Upson settled down in Middlebury, Connecticut, to become a writer of enormously popular fiction.

Upson once said about himself: "I was born lazy, I still am. And I probably always will be. I hate brisk walks before breakfast. And, as far as I am concerned, the whole idea of calisthenics is positively revolting."

Amusing, perhaps, but hard to believe. A lazy man would never have written 175 carefully constructed, tightly plotted and richly varied stories like the ones in this collection.

ALEXANDER BOTTS

Great Stories from
THE SATURDAY EVENING POST

I'M A NATURAL BORN SALESMAN

STONEWALL JACKSON HOTEL
MEMPHIS, TENNESSEE

March 15, 1920.

The Farmers' Friend Tractor Company,
Earthworm City, Ill.

Gentlemen:

I have decided you are the best tractor company in the country, and consequently I am giving you first chance to hire me as your salesman to sell tractors in this region.

I'm a natural-born salesman, have a very quick mind, am twenty-eight years old, am honest and reliable, and can give references if required. I have already had considerable experience as a machinery salesman, and I became familiar with your Earthworm tractors as a member of the motorized field artillery in France. I can demonstrate tractors as well as sell them. When do I start work?

Very truly yours,
Alexander Botts.

FARMERS' FRIEND TRACTOR COMPANY
MAKERS OF EARTHWORM TRACTORS
EARTHWORM CITY, ILLINOIS

March 17, 1920

Mr. Alexander Botts,
Stonewall Jackson Hotel,
Memphis, Tenn.

Dear Mr. Botts:

Your letter is received. We have no opening for a salesman at present, but we are badly in need of a service mechanic. As you say

1

you are familiar with our tractors, we will try you out on this job, at $100 per month plus traveling expenses.

You will report at once to our Mr. George Healy, salesman for Tennessee and Mississippi, who is now at the Dartmouth Hotel, Memphis. You will go with him to Cyprus City, Mississippi, to demonstrate a ten-ton Earthworm tractor for Mr. Jackson, a lumber operator of that place. Mr. Healy will tell you just what you are to do.

We enclose check for $100 advance expense money.

Very truly,
Gilbert Henderson,
Sales Manager.

STONEWALL JACKSON HOTEL
MEMPHIS, TENNESSEE

March 19, 1920.

The Farmers' Friend Tractor Company,
Earthworm City, Ill.

Gentlemen:

As soon as your letter came, I went around to see Mr. Healy, and it is lucky for you that you hired me, because Mr. Healy has just been taken sick with appendicitis. They were getting ready to take him to the hospital, and he was pretty weak, but he managed to tell me that the tractor for the demonstration had already arrived at the freight station in Cyprus City.

He also explained that this Mr. Jackson down there owns about a million feet of cyprus timber which he wants to get out and sell right away before the present high price of lumber goes down. It seems the ground is so swampy and soft from the winter rains that with his present equipment of mules and wagons he won't be able to move any of his timber until summer.

But Mr. Healy was down there a couple of weeks ago, and he arranged to put on a demonstration to show Mr. Jackson that an Earthworm tractor can go into those swamps and drag out the timber right away. Mr. Jackson said he would buy the tractor if it did the work, and Mr. Healy was feeling very low because he was sick and couldn't go down to hold the demonstration.

"You can rest easy, Mr. Healy," I said. "When you look at me you're gazing on a natural-born salesman. I will go down there and

2

do your work as well as mine. I will put on a swell demonstration, and then I will sell the goods."

As Mr. Healy did not seem to know just what to say to this, I gathered up all his order blanks, selling literature, price lists, etc., and also the bill of lading and the check to pay the freight on the tractor. Then I wished him good luck, and left.

From this you can see that I am quick to grasp an opportunity, and that you made no mistake in hiring me. I am leaving for Cyprus City tonight.

Cordially yours,
Alexander Botts.

FARMERS' FRIEND TRACTOR COMPANY
SALESMAN'S DAILY REPORT

Date: March 20, 1920.
Written from: Delta Hotel, Cyprus City, Miss.
Written by: Alexander Botts, Service Mechanic and
Pinch Hitter Salesman.

I found this pad of salesman's report blanks among the stuff I got from Mr. Healy. I see by the instructions on the cover that each salesman is supposed to send in a full and complete report of everything he does, so I will give you all particulars of a very busy day.

I arrived at 7:51 this morning at Cyprus City—which turns out to be pretty much of a hick town in what they call the Yazoo Delta. The whole country here is nothing but a swamp, and the main street of the town ends in a high bank that they call a levee, on the other side of which is the Mississippi River flowing along about twenty feet higher than the town.

After alighting from the train, and after noting that it was a cloudy day and looked like rain, I engaged a room at the Delta Hotel. I then hurried over to the freight station where I found the big ten-ton Earthworm tractor on the unloading platform. They had dragged it off the car with a block and tackle. And when I saw that beautiful machine standing there so big and powerful, with its fine wide tracks like an army tank, with its elegant new shiny paint, and with its stylish cab for the driver, I will admit that I felt a glow of pride to think that I was the salesman and service mechanic for such a splendid piece of machinery.

(*Note:* Of course, as I said in my letter, I am an old machinery salesman. But the largest thing I ever sold before was the Excelsior Peerless Self-adjusting Automatic Safety Razor Blade Sharpener. I did very well with this machine, but I could not take the pride in it that I feel I am going to have in this wonderful ten-ton Earthworm tractor.)

After paying the freight, I hired several guys from the town garage to put gas and oil in the tractor, and then I started them bolting the little cleats onto the tracks. You see I am right up on my toes all the time. I think of everything. And I figured that if we were going through the mud we would need these cleats to prevent slipping. While they were being put on, I stepped over to the office of Mr. Johnson, the lumber man.

(*Note:* This bird's name is Johnson—not Jackson, as you and Mr. Healy told me. Also it strikes me that Mr. Healy may have been fairly sick even as long as two weeks ago when he was down here. In addition to getting the name wrong, he did very poor work in preparing this prospect. He did not seem to be in a buying mood at all.)

As soon as I had explained my errand to this Mr. Johnson—who is a very large, hard-boiled bozo—he gave me what you might call a horse laugh. "You are wasting your time," he said. "I told that fool salesman who was here before that tractors would be no good to me. All my timber is four miles away on the other side of the Great Gumbo Swamp, which means that it would have to be brought through mud that is deeper and stickier than anything you ever seen, young feller."

"You would like to get it out, wouldn't you?" I asked.

"I sure would," he said, "but it's impossible. You don't understand conditions down here. Right on the roads the mules and horses sink in up to their bellies; and when you get off the roads, even ducks and turtles can hardly navigate."

"The Earthworm tractor," I said, "has more power than any duck or turtle. And if you'll come out with me, I'll show you that I can pull your logs through that swamp."

"I can't afford to waste my time with such crazy ideas," he said. "I've tried motor equipment. I have a motor truck now that is stuck three feet deep right on the main road at the edge of town."

"All right," I said, always quick to grasp an opportunity, "how about coming along with me while I pull out your truck?"

"Well," said Mr. Johnson, "I can spare about an hour this morning. If you'll go right now, I'll go with you—although I doubt if you can even pull out the truck. And even if you do, I won't buy your tractor."

"How about going this afternoon?" I asked.

"I'll be busy this afternoon. It's now or never."

"Come on!" I said.

We went over to the freight platform, and as the cleats were now all bolted on we both climbed into the cab.

(*Note:* I will explain that I was sorry that Mr. Johnson had been unable to wait until afternoon, as I had intended to use the morning in practicing up on driving the machine. It is true, as I said in my letter, that I became familiar with Earthworm tractors when I was a member of a motorized artillery outfit in France, but as my job in the artillery was that of cook, and as I had never before sat in the seat of one of these tractors, I was not as familiar with the details of driving as I might have wished. However, I was pleased to see that the tractor seemed to have a clutch and gearshift like the automobiles I have often driven, and a pair of handlebars for steering very much like those of a tricycle I had operated in my early boyhood.)

I sat down on the driver's seat with reasonable confidence, Mr. Johnson sat down beside me; and one of the garage men cranked up the motor. It started at once, and when I heard the splendid roar of the powerful exhaust, and saw that thirty or forty of the inhabitants, both white and otherwise, were standing around with wondering and admiring faces, I can tell you I felt proud of myself, I put the gear in low, opened the throttle, and let in the clutch.

(*Note:* I would suggest that you tell your chief engineer, or whoever it is that designs your tractors, that he ought to put in a standard gearshift. You can understand that it is very annoying—after you have pulled the gearshift lever to the left and then back—to find that instead of being in low you are really in reverse.)

As I said, I opened the throttle, let in the clutch, and started forward. But I found that when I started forward, I was really—on account of the funny gearshift—moving backwards. And instead of going down the gentle slope of the ramp in front, the whole works backed off the rear edge of the platform, dropping at least four feet into a pile of crates with such a sickening crash that I thought the machine was wrecked and both of us killed.

But it soon appeared that, although we were both very much shaken up, we were still alive—especially Mr. Johnson, who began talking so loud and vigorously that I saw I need have no worry about his health. After I had got Mr. Johnson quieted down a bit, I inspected the machine and found that it was not hurt at all. As I am always alert to seize an opportunity, I told Mr. Johnson that I had run off the platform on purpose to show him how strongly built the tractor was. Then, after I had promised I would not make any more of these jumps, he consented to remain in the tractor, and we started off again.

(*Note:* Kindly tell your chief engineer that Alexander Botts congratulates him on producing a practically unbreakable tractor. But tell him that I wish he would design some thicker and softer seat cushions. If the base of the chief engineer's spine was as sore as mine still is, he would realize that there are times when good thick seat cushions are highly desirable.)

As we drove up the main street of Cyprus City, with a large crowd of admiring natives following after, I seemed to smell something burning. At once I stopped, opened up the hood, and discovered that the paint on the cylinders was crackling and smoking like bacon in a frying pan.

"Perhaps," suggested Mr. Johnson, "there is no water in the radiator."

I promptly inspected the radiator, and, sure enough, that was the trouble.

(*Note:* I would suggest that if your chief engineer would design an air-cooled motor for the tractor, such incidents as the above would be avoided.)

I borrowed a pail from a store and filled the radiator. Apparently, owing to my alertness in this emergency, no damage had been done.

When we started up again, we had not gone more than a few yards before I felt the tractor give a little lurch. After we had got a little farther along I looked back, and right at the side of the street I saw one of the biggest fountains I have ever seen in all my life. A solid column of water about eight inches thick was spouting high in the air, spreading out at the top like a mushroom, and raining down all around like Niagara Falls.

I heard somebody yell something about a fire plug; and, as I have a quick mind, I saw right away what had happened. The hood of the tractor is so big that it had prevented me from seeing a fire plug right in front of me. I had unfortunately run right into it, and as it was of very cheap, inferior construction, it had broken right off.

For a while there was great excitement, with people running here and there, hollering and yelling. The sheriff came up and took my name, as he seemed to think I was to blame—in spite of the fact that the fire plug was in such an exposed position. I was a bit worried at the way the water was accumulating in the street, and consequently I was much relieved when they finally got hold of the waterworks authorities and got the water turned off. You see the fire mains here are connected to the Mississippi River, and if they had not turned the water off the whole river would have flowed into the business district of Cyprus City.

(*Note:* I would suggest that your chief engineer design these tractor hoods a little lower so as to avoid such accidents in the future.)

After the water had been turned off, we got underway again, clanking along the main street in high gear, and then driving out of town to the eastward over one of the muddiest roads I ever saw. The tractor, on account of its wide tracks, stayed right up on top of the mud, and rolled along as easy and smooth as a Pullman car. Behind us a large crowd of local sightseers floundered along as best they could—some of them wading through the mud and slop, and others riding in buggies pulled by horses or mules.

Mr. Johnson acted as if he was pretty sore—and I did not blame him. Although the various mishaps and accidents we had been through were unavoidable and not my fault at all, I could understand that they might have been very annoying to my passenger. Perhaps that is one reason I am such a good salesman; I can always get the other fellow's point of view. I livened up the journey a bit by telling Mr. Johnson a number of Irish jokes, but I did not seem to get any laughs—possibly because the motor made so much noise Mr. Johnson couldn't hear me.

By this time I had got the hang of driving the machine very well, and I was going along like a veteran. When we reached Mr. Johnson's truck deep in the mud at the side of the road about a half mile from town—I swung around and backed up in front of it in great style.

The road, as I have said, was soft and muddy enough; but off to the right was a low, flat stretch of swamp land that looked much muddier, and a whole lot softer. There were patches of standing water here and there, and most of it was covered with canebrake—which is a growth of tall canes that look like bamboo fishing poles.

Mr. Johnson pointed out over this mass of canebrake and mud. "That is an arm of the Great Gumbo Swamp," he yelled very loud so I could hear him above the noise of the motor. "Your machine may be able to navigate these roads, but it would never pull a load through a slough like that."

I rather doubted it myself, but I didn't admit it. "First of all," I said, "we'll pull out this truck."

We both got out of the tractor, and right away we sank up to our knees in the soft sticky mud. The truck was a big one, loaded with lumber, and it was mired down so deep that the wheels were practically out of sight, and the body seemed to be resting on the ground. Mr. Johnson didn't think the tractor could budge it, but I told him to get into the driver's seat of the truck so he could steer it when it got going.

By this time a gentle rain had started up, and Mr. Johnson told me to hurry up as the truck had no cab and he was getting wet. I grabbed a big chain out of the truck tool box, and told Mr. Johnson to get out his watch. He did so.

"In just thirty seconds," I said, "things are going to start moving around here."

I then rapidly hooked one end of the chain to the back of the tractor, fastened the other end to the truck, sprang into the tractor seat, and started the splendid machine moving forward. As the tractor rolled steadily and powerfully down the road, I could hear the shouting of the crowd even above the noise of the motor. Looking around, however, I saw that something was wrong. The truck—or rather, the major portion of it—was still in the same place, and I was pulling only the radiator. As I had a quick mind, I saw at once what had happened. Quite naturally, I had slung the chain around the handiest thing on the front of the truck—which happened to be the radiator cap. And as the truck was of a cheap make, with the radiator not properly anchored, it had come off.

I stopped at once, and then I had to spend about ten minutes calming down Mr. Johnson by assuring him that the Farmers' Friend Tractor Company would pay for a new radiator. I backed up to the truck again, and Mr. Johnson took the chain himself, and by burrowing down in the mud managed to get it fastened around the front axle. Then he climbed back into the seat of the truck and scowled at me very disagreeably. By this time the rain was falling fairly briskly, and this may have had something to do with his ill humor.

When I started up again, everything went well. The motor roared, the cleats on the tracks dug into the mud, and slowly and majestically the tractor moved down the road, dragging the heavy truck through the mud behind it.

At this point I stuck my head out of the tractor cab to acknowledge the cheers of the bystanders, and in so doing I unfortunately knocked off my hat, which was caught by the wind and blown some distance away. At once I jumped out and began chasing it through the mud. The crowd began to shout and yell, but I paid no attention to this noise until I had reached my hat and picked it up—which took me some time, as the hat had blown a good ways, and I could not make any speed through the mud. When at last I looked around, I saw that a very curious thing had happened.

In getting out of the tractor I had accidentally pulled on one of the handlebars enough to turn the tractor sidewise. And in my natural excitement—the hat having cost me $8.98 last week in Memphis—I had forgotten to pull out the clutch. So when I looked up, I saw that the tractor, with Mr. Johnson and his truck in tow, was headed right out into the Great Gumbo Swamp. It had already got a good start, and it was going strong. As Mr. Johnson seemed to be waving and yelling for help, I ran after him. But as soon as I got off the road the mud was so deep and soft that I could make no headway at all. Several of the bystanders also attempted to follow, but had to give it up as a bad job. There was nothing to do but let poor Mr. Johnson go dragging off through the swamp.

And, although I was really sorry to see Mr. Johnson going off all by himself with no protection from the pouring rain, I could not help feeling a thrill of pride when I saw how the great ten-ton Earthworm tractor was eating up that terrible soft mud. The wide tracks kept it from sinking in more than a few inches; the cleats gave it good traction; and the motor was so powerful that it pulled that big truck like it was a matchbox—and this in spite of the fact that the truck sank in so deep that it plowed a regular ditch as it went along.

As I am a natural-born salesman, and quick to grasp every opportunity, I yelled a little sales talk after Mr. Johnson. "It's all right," I hollered; "I'm doing this to show you that the Earthworm can go through any swamp you got." But I doubt if he heard me; the roar of the tractor motor was too loud. And a moment later the tractor, the truck, and Mr. Johnson had disappeared in the canebrake.

While I was considering what to do next, a nice-looking man in a corduroy suit came over to me from one of the groups of bystanders. "This is only an arm of the Great Gumbo Swamp," he said. "If that tractor doesn't mire down, and if it goes straight, it will come out on the levee on the other side about a mile from here."

"An Earthworm tractor never mires down," I said. "And as long as there is nobody there to pull on the handlebars, it can't help going straight."

"All right," said the man, "if you want to hop in my buggy, I'll drive you back to town and out the levee so we can meet it when it gets there."

"Fine!" I said. "Let's go." I have always been noted for my quick decisions, being similar to Napoleon in this particular. I at once climbed in the buggy with the man in the corduroy suit, and he drove the horse as fast as possible into town and then out the levee, with all the sightseers plowing along behind—both on foot and in buggies.

When we reached the place where the tractor ought to come out, we stopped and listened. Far out in the swamp we could hear the roar of the tractor motor. It got gradually louder and louder. We waited. It was still raining hard. Suddenly there was a shout from the crowd. The tractor came nosing out of the canebrake, and a moment later it had reached the bottom of the levee, with the big truck and Mr. Johnson dragging along behind. As the tractor was in low gear, I had no trouble in jumping aboard and stopping it—and it is just as well I was there to do this. If I had not stopped it, it would have shot right on over the levee and into the Mississippi River, probably drowning poor Mr. Johnson.

As it was, Mr. Johnson was as wet as a sponge, on account of the heavy rain, and because he had been too cheap to get himself a truck with a cab on it. But he was a long way from being drowned. In fact, he seemed very lively; and as I got down from the tractor he jumped out of the truck and came running at me, waving his arms around, and shouting and yelling, and with a very dirty look on his face. What he had to say to me would fill a small book; in fact, he said so much that I'm afraid I will have to put off telling you about it until my report tomorrow.

It is now midnight and I am very tired, so I will merely enclose my expense account for the day and wish you a pleasant good night. Kindly send check to cover expenses as soon as possible. As you will see, my $100 advance is already gone, and I have had to pay money out of my own pocket.

Cordially yours,
Alexander Botts.

EXPENSE ACCOUNT

Railroad fare (Memphis to Cyprus City)	$ 6.10
Pullman ticket	3.20
Gas and oil for tractor	8.50
Labor (putting on cleats, etc.)	9.00
36 doz. eggs at 50 cents per doz.	18.00

(*Note:* It seems the crates we landed on when we dropped off the freight platform were full of eggs.)

1 plate glass window	80.00

(*Note:* I forgot to say in my report that in the confusion following the breaking of the fire plug I accidentally sideswiped a drugstore with the tractor.)

Radiator for truck, and labor to install	46.75
Cleaning hat and pressing trousers	3.50
Total	$175.05

(*Note:* I will list the hotel bill, the bill for the fire plug, and other expenses when I pay them.)

I'M A NATURAL BORN SALESMAN

FARMERS' FRIEND TRACTOR COMPANY
SALESMAN'S DAILY REPORT

Date: March 21, 1920.
Written from: Delta Hotel, Cyprus City, Miss.
Written by: Alexander Botts.

I will take up the report of my activities at the point where I stopped yesterday when Mr. Johnson had just gotten out of the truck and was coming in my direction. As I stated, he had a great deal to say. Instead of being grateful to me for having given him such a splendid demonstration of the ability of the Earthworm tractor to go through a swamp, and instead of thanking me for saving his life by stopping him just as he was about to shoot over the levee into the Mississippi River, he began using very abusive language which I will not repeat except to say that he told me he would not buy my tractor, and that he never wanted to see me or my damn machinery again. He also said he was going to slam me down in the mud and jump on my face, and it took six of the bystanders to hold him and prevent him from doing this. And although there were six of them, they had a lot of trouble holding him, owing to the fact that he was so wet and slippery from the rain.

As I am a natural-born salesman, I saw right away that this was not an auspicious time to give Mr. Johnson any sales talk about tractors. I decided to wait until later, and I walked back to the tractor in a dignified manner, looking back over my shoulder, however, to make sure Mr. Johnson was not getting away from the guys that were holding him.

After they had led Mr. Johnson back to town, I made up my mind to be a good sport, and I hauled his truck into town and left it at the garage to be repaired. The rest of the day I spent settling up various expense items—which appeared on my yesterday's expense account—and in writing up my report. When I finally went to bed at midnight, it was with a glow of pride that I thought of the splendid work I had done on the first day of my employment with the great Farmers' Friend Tractor Company, Makers of Earthworm Tractors. Although I had not as yet made any sales, I could congratulate myself on having put on the best tractor demonstration ever seen in Cyprus City, Mississippi.

This morning, after breakfast, I had a visit from the nice-looking man in the corduroy suit who gave me the buggy ride yesterday.

"I am a lumber operator," he said, "and I have a lot of cypress back in the swamps that I have been wanting to get out. I haven't been

11

able to move it because the ground has been so soft. However, since I saw your tractor drag that big heavy truck through the swamp yesterday, I know that it is just what I want. I understand the price is $6,000, and if you will let me have the machine right away I will take you over to the bank and give you a certified check for that amount."

"Well," I said, "I was supposed to sell this machine to Mr. Johnson, but as he has had a chance at it and hasn't taken it, I suppose I might as well let you have it."

"I don't see why you gave him first chance," said the man in the corduroy suit. "When your other salesman, Mr. Healy, was down here, I gave him more encouragement than anybody else he talked to. And he said he would ship a tractor down here and put on a demonstration for me."

"By the way," I said, "what is your name?"

"William Jackson," he said.

As I have a quick mind, I saw at once what had happened. This was the guy I had been supposed to give the demonstration for in the first place, but I had very naturally confused his name with that of Mr. Johnson. There ought to be a law against two men with such similar names being in the same kind of business in the same town.

However, it had come out all right. And, as I am a natural-born salesman, I decided that the thing to do was to take Mr. Jackson over to the bank right away—which I did. And now the tractor is his.

I enclose the certified check. And I have decided to remain in town several days more on the chance of selling some more machines.

Cordially yours,
Alexander Botts.

TELEGRAM

EARTHWORM CITY ILL 1015A MAR 22 1920
ALEXANDER BOTTS
DELTA HOTEL
CYPRUS CITY MISS
YOUR FIRST REPORT AND EXPENSE ACCOUNT RECEIVED STOP YOU ARE FIRED STOP WILL DISCUSS THAT EXPENSE ACCOUNT BY LETTER STOP IF YOU SO MUCH AS TOUCH THAT TRACTOR AGAIN WE WILL PROSECUTE YOU TO THE FULLEST EXTENT OF THE LAW

FARMERS FRIEND TRACTOR COMPANY
GILBERT HENDERSON SALES MANAGER

THE INDIRECT METHOD

FARMERS' FRIEND TRACTOR COMPANY
MAKERS OF EARTHWORM TRACTORS
EARTHWORM CITY, ILLINOIS

June 1, 1920.

Mr. Alexander Botts,
Muller Hotel,
Kansas City, Mo.

Dear Mr. Botts:
   We are informed that the road commissioners of Silica County, Kansas, are considering buying a tractor for grading and general road work. We want you to go at once to Sandy Forks, the county seat, and sell these commissioners an Earthworm Tractor.
   Salesmen from other companies will probably be there. In addition, it is possible that you may encounter a little sales resistance, due to the fact that Mr. Joseph Ripley, a wealthy farmer of Silica County, has been having trouble with his Earthworm Tractor—due entirely to his own negligence—and has been blaming everything on the company.
   However, we have every confidence in you and feel sure you will put over this deal. Advise us fully in your daily reports as to what progress you make.

Very sincerely,
Gilbert Henderson,
Sales Manager.

THE INDIRECT METHOD

FARMERS' FRIEND TRACTOR COMPANY
SALESMAN'S DAILY REPORT

Date: June 3, 1920.
Written from: Sandy Forks, Kansas.
Written by: Alexander Botts, Salesman.

I got your letter yesterday, and it is a good thing you are putting onto this job a real high-powered salesman like me, rather than one of your ordinary men. When I explain the situation, you will see that any ordinary man would have quit cold. Not Alexander Botts.

I left Kansas City bright and early this morning in my new flivver roadster, and about the middle of the afternoon—when I had gotten to within about two miles of the town of Sandy Forks—I saw something that I can only describe as a sickening sight. Right beside the main road as you approach Sandy Forks is a little bluff looking out over a very pretty lake. And right on top of this bluff, in plain sight of anybody coming along the road, was a large ten-ton Earthworm Tractor with a big sign on it reading:

I WILL SELL THIS EARTHWORM TRACTOR VERY CHEAP OWING TO THE FACT THAT IT IS ABSOLUTELY NO GOOD, NEVER WAS NO GOOD, AND THE COMPANY THAT MADE IT WON'T STAND BEHIND IT.—JOSEPH RIPLEY

Parking my car by the road, I walked up and looked at the tractor. It was old, weather-beaten and rusty, and the carburetor and magneto were gone. One of the side plates was off the crankcase, so that I could look in and see that the bearings were all loose and wobbly. Running my hand up into the cylinders I could feel that they were scored and pitted in a scandalous manner.

As I sadly returned to my car there came walking along the road a young man in overalls.

"Yes," he said, in answer to my questions, "Old Man Ripley has had a lot of grief with that tractor, and he sure is sore at the company that made it. He has just got himself elected to the county board of road commissioners so he can make sure that when the county buys a tractor it will be something else besides one of these Earthworms."

"Won't the other members have something to say about that?" I asked.

"Well," he said, "old Joe Ripley is the richest and most influential farmer in the county. Most of the other members have worked for him at one time or another and they'll probably want to work for him again. They aren't apt to go against what he says."

"Where does this Mr. Ripley live?" I asked.

"Straight ahead. First house on the right."

"Thank you," I said.

After the young man had left I pondered the situation, and as I have a quick mind I soon realized that you were right when you said in your letter that Mr. Ripley has been having trouble with his tractor. Apparently you hadn't heard that he was the main guy on the board of road commissioners, or that he was putting on this pretty little tractor show out beside the state road. But I decided you were right when you said I might possibly encounter a little sales resistance. And that is why it is lucky you sent the kind of man that it takes to overcome sales resistance.

I didn't waste any time. I decided I would take this bull by the horns; I would beard this lion in his den. Accordingly I drove on up the road to the first house on the right, which turned out to be a nice-looking white farmhouse with trees all around it and big red barns behind. In the front yard stood an old gentleman who appeared to be gazing down a well. In his hands he held a large mirror.

"Howdy, neighbor!" I said cordially, as I drew up beside the road. "What seems to be the trouble?"

"There seems to be something the matter with this well," he said, "but I can't find out what it is. It's so dark down there I can't see a thing."

"Well," I said, "it just happens that I am an expert on wells, so perhaps I can help you."

(*Note:* As a matter of fact, all I know about a well is that it is a hole in the ground with water at the bottom. I have never even been able to figure out just how it gets there. But I felt it would be wiser to approach this guy by the indirect method and to introduce myself as a well expert rather than as a salesman for Earthworm Tractors.)

"My name," I said, "is Alexander Botts, Expert on Wells."

"My name," said the old gentleman, "is Joseph Ripley."

"Pleased to meet you," I said. "And now we will see what is the matter with this well. First of all, what is the idea of that mirror?"

"Everybody knows," said Mr. Ripley, "that the way to look down a well is to hold a mirror at the top and shine the sunlight down into it. But this tree, right over the well here, makes such a dense shade that there isn't enough sunlight to do any good."

"Yes," I said, "that tree complicates matters. I will have to think it over and see what we can do."

At first I was going to suggest cutting down the tree, but I doubt if the old gentleman would have approved. Then, all at once, like an inspiration, I got one of the most brilliant ideas that has come into my mind for a long time.

"Have you another mirror in the house?" I asked.

"Yes," he answered.

"Fine," I said. "Go in and get it."

Somewhat doubtfully he went into the house and came out with another large mirror. I then had him go out by the road in the bright sunshine and reflect a beam of light over to where I was standing at the top of the well. With the other mirror I reflected this beam of light down into the depths. The results were extraordinarily gratifying. The inside of the well was brilliantly illuminated, and far below, I could see a large cat.

"Beautiful!" I said. "Splendid! I have discovered what is the matter with your well."

I then walked out into the sunlight with my mirror and had Mr. Ripley look down into the well with his. He agreed with me at once that we had discovered what was the matter with the well, and declared that the unlucky animal was no doubt a cat by the name of Cicero, which he had kept at the barn and which had disappeared some two weeks before. He said he would call a couple of men from the fields to get busy and clean the well.

"No," I said, "I am an expert on wells, and I will go down for you and take out this unfortunate cat."

(*Note:* I will admit that I did not particularly enjoy the idea of going down into a well after a cat, but it seemed to me that this was an opportunity to get in strong with the old guy.)

I immediately let the bucket down into the bottom of the well and, after removing my coat, I went down the rope hand over hand. As I am fairly agile and as the force of gravity was working in my favor, it did not take me long to descend to the level of the water. Standing with my feet on projecting stones at opposite sides of the well, I reached down, placed all that was left of poor old Cicero in the bucket and yelled to Mr. Ripley to pull it up.

This he did. And as Cicero was mounting upward there suddenly came to me, just like an inspiration, a plan by which I could extend my visit with Mr. Ripley and have a better chance to get in strong with him. Acting upon this inspiration I at once climbed down into the water of the well, bracing my feet against the projecting stones at the sides, until I was up to my neck in the icy water. Many men would have shrunk back from the terrible coldness of that water, but not Alexander Botts. As soon as I was completely covered by the water I began splashing and yelling as loud as I could that I had fallen in and was drowning. Mr. Ripley at once let down the bucket, and I proceeded to scramble up the rope, assisting myself by stepping on the projecting stones on the sides of the well.

When I reached the top I tumbled out on the grass and lay on my back, gasping, coughing, choking and rolling my eyes, imitating as nearly as I could a person who is half drowned. Mr. Ripley set up a great hollering, and a couple of farm hands came running from the barn. He had them carry me into the house, and after they had laid me on the bed in the spare room he gave me a drink of some liquid which produced a pleasant feeling of warmth over my entire body. By the time I had had two or three drinks of this excellent stuff I was feeling very comfortable, and I was able to accept very gracefully Mr. Ripley's invitation to spend the night. He saw that my car was put in the barn, and I remained in bed for the rest of the afternoon while old Mrs. Ripley dried and pressed my clothes. Meanwhile Mr. Ripley had his men pump all the water out of the well and give it a thorough cleaning.

So far I had not mentioned tractors, but after supper I brought up the subject in a casual and indirect way—without spilling the news that I was a salesman for Earthworms. Mr. Ripley was very willing to talk. He said that he bought the tractor last year and that after he had used it only two weeks it quit on him. He had then asked for a service man from the factory, and the service man had told him it was all his own fault for not putting oil in the machine, and the company had refused to repair it for him free. That made him so mad he had run it out by the road and put that sign on it so as to knock the company as much as he could.

"Did you really run it for two weeks without oil?" I asked.

"I can't remember for sure," said Mr. Ripley; "very possibly I did. But that doesn't let the tractor company out. That machine was guaranteed for a year, and it went bad after only two weeks. So it was their business to fix it up for me free. What if I did forget about the oil? Anybody is liable to forget a little thing like that. I know that I gave it plenty of gasoline and plenty of water, and anybody is liable to forget a little minor thing like oil. No, sir, these Earthworm Tractor people are nothing but a bunch of crooks."

"Well," I said, "you certainly have had a most unfortunate experience."

"Right you are," said Mr. Ripley, "and the worst of it is all the people around here are kidding me about it. I suppose I got bit once, but I ain't going to get bit again. I am a member of the board of county commissioners and we're going to buy a tractor for road work, but you can bet your bottom dollar it won't be one of those damn Earthworms. Salesmen for several other makes of tractors are going to do some demonstrating for us down around town, and we'll take whichever one of them shows up the best. There was a man here trying to sell us an Earthworm, and we told him we wouldn't even consider it."

"I didn't know there were any Earthworm salesmen around here," I said.

"This man," said Mr. Ripley, "is a contractor by the name of Casey. He's just finished up a dirt-moving job over in the next county at Johnsonville. He's moving out to Oregon for his next job and he has a secondhand Earthworm tractor that he is willing to sell cheap. But I told him I wouldn't take it as a gift, so that's all there is to that."

"And what are you going to do with that old tractor of yours," I asked; "just leave it out there beside the road?"

"Sure," he said, "unless somebody comes along and wants to buy it. But I haven't had any offers for it yet. I paid $6,000 for it, and I'll let it go for $1,000 just as it stands, including the carburetor and magneto, which I've got up here in the barn."

"Sold!" I said. "You mean you want to buy it yourself?" he said.

"Exactly so."

"But I don't want to stick you."

"I'll risk that."

"It's absolutely no good," he said. "I have had several mechanics from town come out and look at it, and they tell me it is completely shot to pieces."

"Don't worry about me," I said. "In addition to being an expert on wells, I am also an expert on tractors, and I figure I can fix it up and maybe sell it at a profit. You said you would sell it for $1,000. You certainly aren't going to be a cheap sport and back down on your promise, are you?"

"No."

"Fine," I said. "The deal is closed."

I at once got out my checkbook and wrote him a check for $1,000 on the First National Bank of Earthworm City.

"I am dating this check June tenth—a week ahead," I said, "to give me time to transfer that much money into my checking account, but I won't take the tractor away until the check has been cashed. That will be all right with you, won't it?"

"Absolutely," said Mr. Ripley.

Shortly after this I said good night and came up to my room, where I have been spending the rest of the evening writing up this report.

From what I have related you can see that you made no mistake in sending me to handle this very difficult job. Instead of blurting out the news that I was an Earthworm salesman, and thus getting myself thrown off Old Man Ripley's farm, I have proceeded by the indirect method, and—thanks to my energy in taking advantage of the fortunate incident of Cicero in the well—I have already gotten in very strong with this old gentleman, who is the main guy on the board of road commissioners. Furthermore, by purchasing this old tractor I have taken the first step toward carrying out a very deep plan which I have evolved for the purpose of carrying through this matter in my usual brilliant manner.

I will now close and get myself some sleep, but tomorrow I am going to start some real action around this neck of the woods.

Cordially yours,
Alexander Botts,
Earthworm Salesman

P.S.—In looking over the stubs in my checkbook, I find that my balance in the First National Bank of Earthworm City is $21.30. As I have no funds of my own to bring up this account, I must ask you to have the cashier of the tractor company place $1,000 to my credit in this bank at once. Otherwise the highly important operations which I am conducting in this region are liable to be somewhat hampered.

A.B.

FARMERS' FRIEND TRACTOR COMPANY
SALESMAN'S DAILY REPORT

Date: June 5, 1920.
Written from: Sandy Forks, Kansas.
Written by: Alexander Botts.

I was so busy all day yesterday, last night and today that I haven't had time to write you any report until just now. But when you read what I have been doing, you will realize that I have been right up on my toes all the time. I have got things moving along something swell.

Bright and early yesterday morning I got my car out and told Mr. Ripley I was going to get some tools to repair the tractor, and that I would be back the next day. He gave me the magneto and carburetor, which I placed in the car, and then I started toward town. As soon as I had rounded the first curve I chucked the carburetor and magneto into some thick bramble bushes beside the road. Then, instead of getting any tools, I drove twenty miles over into the next county, and just outside the town of Johnsonville, I found the camp of this contractor, Casey. Most of the equipment of the camp seemed to be packed up ready to move. The only man there was a young guy with red hair who told me that Mr. Casey had gone to town and would be back in about half an hour. So I had to wait, but while waiting I did not let any grass grow under my feet. I talked most pleasantly with this young redheaded guy, and I got him to show me the tractor, which turned out to be exactly the same model as the one owned by Mr. Ripley. I was also pleased to see that it had been out in the weather long enough to make it just about as rusty-looking as Mr. Ripley's old wreck. The redheaded guy told me, however, that it was in A1 condition, and he proved it by cranking it up and driving around a bit for me. Then I thanked him and gave him a few cigars and patted him on the back, and talked to him so pleasantly that he finally blurted out the good news that Mr. Casey was so anxious to sell the tractor he would let it go for $2,000, although he was asking and hoping for $4,000.

Pretty soon after that an automobile came driving up and out stepped a rather nervous-looking guy, who proved to be Mr. Casey himself. I don't know why it is, but pretty near all these contractors are nervous-looking guys—they seem to have a whole lot on their mind.

I at once offered Mr. Casey $600 for his tractor, at which he let out a loud laugh and told me he wouldn't take one cent less than $4,000. So we jawed around a while. I came up a little and he went down a little, until finally I told him that if he would include a big chain that was hanging on the tractor, and if he would have his man drive the tractor over to the town of Sandy Forks for me, I would pay him $2,000. As he saw that he couldn't make any better bargain, and as he had already—according to the redheaded guy—decided to let her go for that, he accepted. But when I started to write out a check on the First National Bank of Earthworm City he began to look even more nervous than before.

"How do I know," he said, "that your check will be good?"

"Oh, don't worry about that!" I said. "Anybody around Earthworm City could tell you that Alexander Botts is good for a hundred times as much money as this paltry $2,000."

"That's all right," he said, "but is there anybody around here that knows you?"

"No," I said, "I am afraid there isn't. But listen," I said, "this check will go through in a few days, and in the meantime I am taking this tractor only as far as Sandy Forks. You are a reasonable man and you ought to know that I couldn't skip out of the country with a great big thing like a ten-ton tractor."

"Well," he said, "I guess maybe that's right."

"Sure it's right," I said; "but, of course, if you want to call off the sale——"

"No," he said, "I'll take a chance."

So he took the check and made me out a bill of sale.

(*Note:* As Mr. Casey was so suspicious about my check, I did not like to ask his permission to date it ahead. Consequently it is very important that the cashier of The Farmers' Friend Tractor Company place an additional $2,000 to my credit at the First National Bank of Earthworm City. Be sure and have him do this AT ONCE, as Mr. Casey will probably send in the check right away, and it is possible that if this check came back marked No Funds it might very seriously cramp my style in my present undertakings and result in considerable embarrassment and detriment to myself and to the best interests of the Farmers' Friend Tractor Company.)

The young redheaded guy filled up the tractor with gas and oil, and we started out for Sandy Forks with me leading the way in my car and him following with the tractor. I had him drive very slow, and we stopped a long time for lunch at a little village, so we didn't get to Sandy Forks until dark. I led the way along a road that went around the town so as not to attract too much attention, and I had him drive the tractor into a field about a mile from Mr. Ripley's farm. Then I drove him back to Casey's camp at Johnsonville in my car, after which I returned to Sandy Forks.

I had supper at a little restaurant, and about midnight I drove out to where I had left Casey's tractor. I cranked it up and then I drove it along the road until I came to Mr. Ripley's old tractor. It didn't take me more than five minutes to remove the big sign, hook onto the tractor with the big chain, and drag it down to the shore of the little lake. Then I unhooked, drove around behind it with the Casey tractor and gave it a good healthy push that sent it over the steep bank and into the deep muddy water beneath. Next, I drove back and stopped Mr. Casey's tractor exactly where the other one had been, and I put Mr. Ripley's sign on top of it. After this I walked back to where I had left my car, drove to town, got myself a room at the hotel and went to bed about two a.m.

Bright and early this morning I drove out to Mr. Ripley's farm and found him inspecting his well, which, after being cleaned out, was now once more full of fine fresh water. "Good morning, Mr. Botts," he said as I drove up. "What is the news with you?"

"Very good news," I said. "I have just been down the country a ways to my brother-in-law's farm, and my brother-in-law has promised me that if this tractor runs as well as I expect to make it, he will buy it from me for $5,000."

21

(*Note:* I will admit that this statement was somewhat exaggerated. As a matter of fact, I have no brother-in-law, and even if I had I doubt very much if he would have $5,000 to spend on a tractor. However, I felt that the delicacy of my maneuvers in the matter of all these various tractors justified the use of a certain amount of strategy.)

"If you can get $5,000 for that bunch of junk," said Mr. Ripley, "you're welcome to it."

"That's fine," I said. "I was sure you'd be a good sport about it. You know that when I bought that tractor I took an awful chance, and I was ready to stand the loss in case it turned out worse than I thought it was. But now that it turns out to be in really swell condition, I figure that I am entitled to whatever profit I can make on it."

"Sounds fair enough to me," said Mr. Ripley. "But I think you are fooling yourself. The best automobile mechanics in town have told me that the machine is a wreck."

"The best automobile mechanics," I answered, "are sometimes none too good on tractors. But I am a tractor expert. I stopped off this morning and put on the carburetor and magneto, and filled the old baby up with gas, oil and water. And I find that lack of oil was really the only thing the matter. Now that I have filled her up with plenty of good fresh oil, she's practically as good as new."

"Important," said the old guy, "if true."

"If you have any plowing or any other work you want done," I suggested, "we'll crank up the tractor and try it out."

"All right," said Mr. Ripley, "I want to plow that forty-acre patch across the road. There is an eight-bottom gang plow in the barn, and if you can get that tractor up here, you can hook on and start in. But I doubt if you can make the tractor run three feet. The only way I could get it to where it is now was by hooking onto it with all the horses on the place."

"Let's go," I said, "and see what we can do."

We walked down to the tractor, and I removed the handsome sign. Then I gave the crank one flip and the motor started with a roar. I climbed in and drove up to the barn as fast as I could, with Mr. Ripley trotting along behind—the most surprised-looking old geezer I have ever seen in my life. By the time he reached the barn I had already hooked up to the plow, taken it across the road, and started a back furrow down the middle of his forty-acre field. At the end of the first round I stopped and cut off the motor, and I was very much pleased to note that I was making quite an impression on old Joe. He came up and stood behind the machine, and for a while he couldn't say a word or do anything except open and shut his mouth in a foolish sort of way.

"I never seen the like," he said after a while. "I wouldn't have believed it possible. Those mechanics all told me that the machine was a wreck."

"Those mechanics must have been trying to fool you," I said. "The idea of telling a smart, intelligent man like you that you were a dumb tractor operator! From the looks of this machine I would say that you were one of the best tractor operators in the country. You have kept it in fine shape."

"Do you really think so?" he asked.

"Sure I do," I said. "Stick around and wait until we make a few more rounds."

Mr. Ripley looked at his watch. "I wish I could," he said, "but I just happened to think I have to get to town to see a tractor demonstration that these other guys are putting on today. There are three different machines down there and they are all going to demonstrate what they can do on road grading and moving dirt."

"Where is this demonstration going to be?" I said.

"Oh, just up and down some of the main roads," he said.

"Listen," I said. "I don't want to butt in on anybody else's business, but I am an expert on all kinds of tractors, and I can give you a tip on how to find out which one of these machines is the best."

"How is that?" he asked.

"Any of these machines," I said, "can pull a grader on a nice dry road, but when you get a tractor for road work, you want one that will go through all the deep mud holes that come in the bad weather in the spring and fall. So if I were you I would pick out a nice wet swamp and make them all go through that."

"Sounds like a good idea," said Mr. Ripley. "There's a nice soft swamp just north of town."

"Make 'em go through that," I said. "And in the meantime I'll see if I can't get a little plowing done for you."

I cranked up the machine and started across the field again, and looking over my shoulder I saw Mr. Ripley climb into his car and drive off toward town.

All the rest of the morning I kept that tractor running wide open, and I certainly have got to hand it to Casey and his redheaded operator for keeping the old baby in fine shape. She went sailing back and forth across that field as smooth and steady as a ferryboat.

The ground was loose and sandy and turned over just as easy as could be. I took half an hour off at noon to eat some lunch that Mrs. Ripley gave me, and then went back and plowed all the afternoon. And at half-past five I finished up the last headland and dragged the plow back to the barn.

At six o'clock, when Mr. Ripley got back from town, I was all washed up and sitting comfortably in a rocking chair on the porch. When he saw how I had plowed forty acres in one day with a machine that he supposed was nothing but a bunch of junk, I thought the poor old gentleman was going to faint. It also seemed to me that he looked just a little bit sore, so I started in to talk right away. And I will admit that I am a good talker.

"It certainly is lucky, Mr. Ripley," I said, "that you are such an intelligent, fair-minded man. Some people would be low-down enough to be mad because I am going to make such a nice profit on this tractor deal. But I know that you are a gentleman and a real good sport."

"Yes," he said, "of course I want to be a gentleman and a good sport. But at the same time I almost wish I hadn't sold you that machine. I'd almost be willing to buy it back from you for twice as much as you paid for it."

"I wish I could let you have it, Mr. Ripley," I said, "but I really don't see how I can without going back on my promise to my brother-in-law. You see I told him he could have it for $5,000, and, of course, you are too fine a man, Mr. Ripley, to want me to break my word to my brother-in-law."

"I suppose you're right," said Mr. Ripley, shaking his head very sadly, "but this business has gotten me all confused. I don't know whether I am going in or coming out."

"There is one thing to be thankful for anyway," I said. "You know now that you were a good judge of machinery when you bought this machine, and you also know that you are a perfectly competent tractor operator. And by the way, how did the big tractor demonstration come off down in town?"

"The tractor demonstration," said Mr. Ripley, "was a joke."

"Did they go through the swamp?"

"They went into the swamp," said Mr. Ripley. "At first none of them would try it, but I told them that we wouldn't buy any tractor that couldn't go through soft ground. So they all started, and all three of them are mired down so deep in the swamp that it looks like it will take a week to get them out."

"But which one of them are you going to buy?" I asked.

"I don't know," said Mr. Ripley. "We have a meeting of the board of county commissioners tomorrow afternoon to decide what to do, but I don't know as I want to buy any of those machines."

"I'll tell you how you could have a lot of fun," I said, "and show up a lot of those town people for the boobs that they are. You know that they have been saying around town that you are a bum tractor operator. Now is your chance to show them all that you are the best there is."

"How can I do that?"

"In the morning," I said, "we will both get in that old Earthworm tractor and you will drive. We will go down there and drive right through that old swamp and pull these three machines out of the mud. I guess that will show them what a real operator like you will do when you are driving a real machine like this Earthworm."

"Do you honestly think we could do it?" "Sure we can," I said. "These three machines are nothing more than ordinary tractors; and of course they sink right down in the mud just the same as an automobile would. But this Earthworm has tracks on it like a wartime tank, and it can stay right up on top of the mud as nice as you please. And I would be glad to let you use the tractor, because I promised you I wouldn't take it away until that check came through."

"It sounds like a good idea," said old Mr. Ripley. "I believe we will do it."

"Fine," I said.

Soon after that we had supper, and as Mr. Ripley had invited me to spend the night I came up to my room and I have been writing this report ever since.

From what I have told you, you can see that everything is going swell, and that you made no mistake in sending me to handle this very delicate situation. By the use of the indirect method I have now gotten Mr. Ripley eating out of my hand. Tomorrow morning I intend to sell him back his own old tractor—which, as I have explained, is not really his own old tractor at all. And tomorrow afternoon I will go before the road commissioners, tell them that I have just taken over the Earthworm agency, and I will then count on Mr. Ripley's help to sell them a machine for the county.

Please let me know right away whether or not you have deposited that $3,000 to my account in the First National Bank of Earthworm City.

Cordially yours,
Alexander Botts.

THE INDIRECT METHOD

FARMERS' FRIEND TRACTOR COMPANY
SALESMAN'S DAILY REPORT

Date: June 6, 1920.
Written from: County Jail, Johnsonville, Kansas.
Written by: Alexander Botts.

As you may guess from the heading of this letter, my operations in this region are not proceeding in as felicitous a manner as I had hoped they would, but when I explain matters, you will see that it is not my fault. I will admit that I was very much shocked and disappointed when I visited the post office this noon and received such a chilly letter from Mr. Gilbert Henderson, Sales Manager of the Earthworm Tractor Company. I notice that Mr. Henderson says that the salesmen of this company are expected to sell tractors and not buy them, and that the company cannot finance unauthorized purchases of secondhand tractors. Also I see that he has turned down my request that $3,000 be deposited to my account at the First National Bank of Earthworm City. I suppose Mr. Henderson thinks he knows how to run a sales department, but I nevertheless wish to point out that his action in this matter has probably cost the company the sale of a tractor, and has also put this particular salesman in a somewhat embarrassing position—as you may judge from the heading of this report. This is particularly unfortunate in view of the fact that I had already managed—by employing all my energy and intellect and sales experience—to bring matters almost to the point of a brilliant and highly successful conclusion.

When I think of the splendid things I accomplished this morning, it almost makes me weep to think of the depths to which I have sunk this evening. Immediately after breakfast I cranked up the good old tractor, told Mr. Ripley once more what a splendid operator he was, and had him take his place on the driver's seat. I then climbed in beside him, and we started for town. Mr. Ripley—although probably one of the worst mechanics in Kansas—is nevertheless perfectly capable of going through the simple procedure of starting and stopping a tractor, and also steering it to the right, left, or straight ahead, as the case may be. We rolled down the road very nicely and before long we had reached the swamp where the three tractors were mired down.

The salesmen and mechanics in charge of these tractors were all out with shovels and timbers trying to get them out, and there were also a great many of the townspeople, who had come to observe the excitement. I have never seen a prouder man than old Mr. Ripley as he drove that splendid Earthworm tractor out over the soft swamp in front of all the admiring townspeople. I coached him up on just what to do, and we put on a beautiful show. The salesmen for these other tractors were none too pleased to have us come out there, but they could not afford to refuse the assistance that we so kindly offered them.

First of all we drove out to the nearest tractor—a big hulk of a machine. I told Mr. Ripley to take our machine up to the front of it, and then I hooked on the big chain and told him to go ahead. It was a hard pull, but we finally got it out of its hole and dragged it up onto the firm ground at the edge of the swamp. Then we went after the other two. And just as I had predicted, the old Earthworm stayed right up on top of the soft ground and performed in a really splendid manner. After about an hour's work we had all three of these clumsy machines out of the swamp and up on the high ground.

By this time it looked as if practically all of the town was out to see the show, and when we had at last finished they all began waving their hats around and shouting with the greatest enthusiasm. Old Mr. Ripley was tickled absolutely pink. He stood up and bowed gracefully to the crowd, and when he finally sat down I told him once more that he was one of the best tractor operators in the entire United States, and also a very good sport.

"Yes, sir," he said to me, "I guess I have shown you and all of the rest of them that I am a pretty swell operator, and now I am going to show you that I am also a very good sport. I will buy this tractor back from you and I will pay you exactly what you said you could get from that other guy down in the country. I will pay you the full $5,000."

"No, Mr. Ripley," I said, "you are such a good friend of mine that I could not think of asking you that much. I am making a profit on this tractor myself, and I am such a good sport that I am going to let you also make a profit of $1,000 on this transaction. I will make it up to my brother-in-law in some other way, and I will sell you this tractor for only $4,000. I know that you are offering me $5,000, but you are such a good friend of mine that I am willing to let you take it for only $4,000."

It was really touching to see the gratitude with which old Mr. Ripley received my very generous offer. He shook me by the hand, and there actually seemed to be tears in his eyes as he accepted the proposition. I persuaded the old gentleman to get down out of the tractor at once, and I took him over to the bank in town while the cheers of the crowd were still ringing in his ears. With a smile on his face he wrote me out a check for $3,000 and handed me over my own check for $1,000 which he had been carrying around in his pocket. I then handed him back the bill of sale on the tractor, which he had given me, and we shook hands once more in the most cordial spirit imaginable.

(*Note:* I wish to point out—in view of my somewhat unfortunate situation this evening, as indicated in the heading of this report—that my financial operations in respect to this tractor were rather good, if I do say so myself. You will have to admit that it takes a guy with a quick mind—and a good talker too—to buy a man's tractor for $1,000 and then sell back to him what he thinks is the same machine for $4,000, and make him think you are doing him a favor. And in a way I was doing him a favor—I could have soaked him $5,000 easily.)

As soon as our little transaction was completed, Mr. Ripley started back to look after his tractor, and I at once turned his check into the bank, opening an account in my own name for the $3,000. I felt that if Mr. Ripley calmed down from the warm glow which had been induced by the applause of the crowd, and if he then changed his mind, it would be just as well to have the check cashed so he could not stop payment.

After leaving the bank I stopped in at the post office and received Mr. Henderson's most unwelcome letter, which seemed to indicate that I had no funds at the First National Bank of Earthworm City to back up the $2,000 check I had given Mr. Casey. As I am a very good businessman, it at once occurred to me that it might be wise to get in touch with Mr. Casey to prevent the possibility of there being any misunderstanding. Consequently I called his camp at once on the long-distance telephone. Unfortunately Mr. Casey was out, and the redheaded tractor operator with whom I talked did not know when he would return. As I am very conservative, I decided to take no more chances than I could help. So I told the redheaded operator to inform Mr. Casey when he came back that I was coming over to Johnsonville at once to see him. I then went back to the bank and had them give me a certified check for $2,000, after which I hired a car to take me out to Mr. Ripley's place, where I got into my own machine and drove at once to Johnsonville.

As I am always the soul of honor in all business transactions, I was resolved to avoid even the appearance of evil in my dealings with Mr. Casey. If he had not yet sent in the check on the First National Bank of Earthworm City I would redeem it with the gilt-edged certified check on the Sandy Forks bank. In case he had already sent in the check, I was prepared to place the certified check in the care of the cashier of the Johnsonville bank, to be paid over to Mr. Casey when my other check should come back.

But unfortunately all my good intentions went for nothing. When I arrived at Mr. Casey's camp I was met not by Mr. Casey but by a tall gentleman with a very disagreeable face. As soon as I had told him my name he pulled back the flap of his coat and showed me a cheap-looking nickel-plated star, which was pinned to his vest, and which bore the words Deputy Sheriff. He then drew a large paper from the side pocket of his coat and informed me that it was a warrant for my arrest.

"I would advise you to come quietly," he said, "and I must warn you that anything you say may be used against you."

"But why," I said, "would anyone want to arrest a law-abiding citizen like me?"

"This warrant," he said, "was sworn out by Mr. Casey, who charges you with passing a bad check for $2,000."

"It is all a mistake," I said. "Take me to Mr. Casey and I will straighten everything out."

"Mr. Casey," he said, "left about a half hour ago for Kansas City to see his lawyer. He said he would be back in the morning, at which time you will have a hearing before the judge."

"But I have to be back in Sandy Forks this afternoon for a very important meeting." I said. "I can't stay until tomorrow."

"Oh, yes, you can," he said.

I then gave that man all the arguments I could think of. I told him it was all a mistake. I showed him the certified check. I threatened to sue him for false arrest. I even gave him two very good cigars—which he took—and asked him as one gentleman to another to let me go for the afternoon on my word of honor to come back the next day. I talked with that man for a good half hour—and I am a pretty good talker, if I do say so myself—but it seems as though these guys with the stars on their vests are pretty hard birds to talk to. I didn't seem to get anywhere at all; and finally he even had the nerve to make me drive the both of us back to town in my own car, after which he locked me up in the Johnsonville jail.

In all fairness I must admit that this is a very handsome jail. It seems to be brand new, and the bars of my little cage seem to be of as good quality steel as anything used even in such a high-grade machine as the Earthworm tractor. I have been scratching away on one of the bars for half an hour with a piece of a hacksaw blade which I happened to have in my pocket and which they missed when they took my money and everything else away from me, but I haven't been able to make any impression on it.

So I have been sitting around in this dump all the afternoon, and now, after supper, I am writing this report with pencil and paper

29

which the jailer's wife was kind enough to let me have. I am fairly comfortable in here, but it just makes me sick to think that I got the chief county commissioner over at Sandy Forks all worked up and ready to buy an Earthworm tractor, and then I was unable to attend the meeting and put over the deal. As no Earthworm salesman was present at that meeting this afternoon, I suppose they have probably bought one of those other tractors.

Yours,
Alexander Botts.

FARMERS' FRIEND TRACTOR COMPANY
SALESMAN'S DAILY REPORT

Date: June 7, 1920.
Written from: Sandy Forks, Kansas.
Written by: Alexander Botts.

Well, I am out of jail again.

When Mr. Casey showed up at the hearing this morning I learned that right after he had taken my check some days ago, he had become even more nervous than usual. And as he seems to have a peculiarly low, suspicious type of mind, he had pulled a very dirty trick indeed. Instead of sending my check through in the regular way, he had had his own bank telegraph at once to the First National Bank of Earthworm City to inquire whether my account was good for $2,000. When the word came back that it was not, he had at once sworn out a warrant for me. However, when I explained that it was all a mistake and produced the certified check, he at least had the decency to say he would drop the charges if he was sure to get his money. So as soon as they had telephoned to the bank in Sandy Forks and found that the certified check was O.K., they turned me loose.

I drove back to Mr. Ripley's house outside Sandy Forks with a heavy heart. I was somewhat reassured when that gentleman met me with a smiling face, and I was greatly pleased when I heard what had happened at the meeting.

It seems that the commissioners had unanimously turned down the three other tractors. And, as there was no Earthworm salesman present, they decided—on Mr. Ripley's motion—to write in to the Farmers' Friend Tractor Company and order two ten-ton Earthworm Tractors to be used in county road work. Their letters will, no doubt, be in your hands by the time this report reaches you. I am leaving tonight for Kansas City, and I wish to point out that although I have used the indirect method in this transaction so that my name does not appear on the county order, and although nobody around here suspects that I am a salesman for the Earthworm Company, nevertheless I am entitled to my regular commission on this sale.

As I look back on the events of the last three days I am very much impressed with the energy and resourcefulness I employed in bringing this transaction to such a successful conclusion.

Very cordially yours,
Alexander Botts.

P.S.—I have been wondering what I ought to do about that extra $1,000 in the bank that seems to be left over. If the Earthworm Company had put $3,000 into the financial operation I would feel that this $1,000 profit belonged to the company. But as long as the company did not do so, I have decided, after long thought, to keep the money myself.

BIG BUSINESS

FARMERS' FRIEND TRACTOR COMPANY
MAKERS OF EARTHWORM TRACTORS

Western Office,
Harvester Building,
San Francisco, Calif.
April 19, 1924

Mr. Alexander Botts,
Biltmore Hotel,
Los Angeles, Calif.

Dear Mr. Botts:

We have just received a letter from Mr. Spencer K. Yerkes, President of the Bianca Beach Development Corporation, requesting information about Earthworm tractors. Mr. Yerkes states that he is starting the development of a resort property near Los Angeles, and will have to do a great deal of grading. We have written him that you will call on him, and we are depending on you to secure his order for as many tractors as his proposed work requires.

Very truly yours,
J.D. Whitcomb,
Western Sales Manager.

FARMERS' FRIEND TRACTOR COMPANY
SALESMAN'S DAILY REPORT

Date: Monday, April 21, 1924,
Written from: Biltmore Hotel, Los Angeles, Calif.
Written by: Alexander Botts.

Your letter came yesterday. I called on Mr. Yerkes this afternoon. And I have every reason to suppose that I am about to put across one of the most important deals that I have ever handled since I first became a salesman for the Farmers' Friend Tractor Company. Mr. Yerkes is a big businessman in the largest sense of the word, and it is therefore lucky that you entrusted this job to a man like myself, who is able to handle big things. When I tell you exactly what I have done so far you will realize what a tremendous proposition this is and you will see that I am handling affairs with great skill and gradually working things around to the point of getting a big order.

I did not call on Mr. Yerkes in the morning. These big businessmen usually spend the time before lunch in reading mail, dictating letters, and similar activities, reserving the afternoon for callers. It is, therefore, a great mistake for a salesman to call on an important prospect in the morning. Furthermore, I find that I am always in better shape to handle the subtle details of a selling talk if I have slept fairly late and not hurried myself at breakfast.

Accordingly I did not make my call until three o'clock in the afternoon. The office of the Bianca Beach Development Corporation is very large and handsome, and in every way worthy of the high-grade business which it carries on. The outer office was large and airy. The young lady at the telephone switch took my card in to Mr. Yerkes, and returned in a moment or two to usher me through a small gate, across a large outer room, and into Mr. Yerkes's private office.

Never before have I seen such a splendid room. There was a thick oriental rug on the floor. There was a tremendous carved mahogany desk that must have cost at least a thousand dollars. There were mahogany chairs and mahogany filing cases. In one corner was a small office-type electric refrigerator and water cooler of the latest design. And on the walls were several genuine oil paintings of California scenery, and Spanish-type stucco houses. Everything was quiet, refined and richly luxurious. And the whole room seemed to be murmuring, "I cost money." Naturally I was very favorably impressed.

Mr. Spencer K. Yerkes turned out to be a lean and efficient-looking man between thirty and forty years of age. He shook hands with me most cordially, and I was at once struck by his great natural charm and pleasing personality. And, before I left, I came to realize that he is also a person of intellect and imagination—a truly big man, capable of handling big things in a big way.

"Sit down, Mr. Botts," he said. "Have a cigar."

"Thank you," I said, taking one.

"I am a businessman; my time is valuable. You are also a businessman and your time is valuable. Let us get down to brass tacks at once."

"If you will tell me," I said, "what sort of work you are planning, I will be pleased to recommend the machinery necessary for doing it. Until I know exactly what you are going to do, I cannot talk intelligently."

"Quite right," said Mr. Yerkes. "I have a feeling, Mr. Botts, that we are going to get along very well."

"I am sure of it," I said.

"What I am planning to do," said Mr. Yerkes, "is to build a town. I have purchased a tract of twenty-five hundred acres. It includes two miles of ocean beach, and it extends back about two miles into the hills. At present the land is entirely unoccupied, but it is within easy driving distance of Los Angeles, and I am going to make it into the city's most beautiful suburb. I have bought water rights up in the mountains, and I am going to build a five-mile aqueduct which will give Bianca Beach the finest water supply of any town its size on the coast. I am going to lay out streets and boulevards, parks and golf courses. As the ground is hilly, I will have to do a lot of grading. I will have to move a lot of dirt, and I will probably need a lot of tractors to do it."

"When it comes to moving dirt," I said, "the Earthworm tractor is the wonder machine of the century. I have pictures and testimonials here in my briefcase, and I am prepared to prove to you that the Earthworm tractor is exactly the machine you want."

"Never mind all that," said Mr. Yerkes, holding up his hand, "I already know the reputation of your company. In fact I have already figured out that I will probably want twelve of your ten-ton machines."

"I have my blanks right here," I said, "and you might just as well sign an order for them right away. We can ship them out of Oakland tomorrow."

At this Mr. Yerkes smiled. "You are a fast worker and a splendid salesman," he said, "and it is a pleasure to do business with you. But I am not quite ready to sign an order."

"If there is anything more you wish to know about our tractors," I said, "I would be most happy to inform you."

"No," said Mr. Yerkes, "I have no doubts about your tractors. But I am a very conservative and cautious businessman, and I have doubts about the buying public."

"What do you mean?"

"I am undertaking a very large enterprise," he said. "I have already spent two hundred thousand dollars for the land and fifty thousand dollars for the water rights. And I am planning to spend an even five million in development. I have every reason to suppose that the project will be a great success. There will be five thousand lots from a quarter to a half acre in size. If I can sell these lots at an average price of five thousand dollars each, I will take in twenty-five million dollars. If I sell only half the lots I will still make a handsome profit."

"It certainly looks like a good proposition," I said.

"Yes," said Mr. Yerkes. "But I am conservative. My friends say I am insanely conservative. I do not wish to go ahead until I have tested the reaction of the public. I am therefore offering two hundred lots at the absurdly low price of one thousand dollars each, five hundred dollars down and the rest on easy terms if desired. If I can dispose of this offering I will have proof that the buying public is in the mood to support my scheme. But until I get this proof I will not move one grain of dirt; I will not spend one cent in development."

"I should think," I said, "that at that price the lots would go like hot cakes."

Mr. Yerkes's reply showed that he is a deep student of psychology. "You might think so," he said. "But the average man is very dense and matter-of-fact. He has no imagination. When you show him a tract of land that is covered with greasewood and cactus, without a street or a house in sight, he refuses to buy a lot at any price. He is a doubting Thomas. But the man of imagination sees more. With his mind's eye he gazes into the future and visualizes the scene as it will be in a year or two. He sees hundreds of beautiful white stucco houses with their red tile roofs, set in lovely rose gardens. He sees smooth concrete streets and sidewalks, a luxurious country club, a velvety green golf course, and crowds of bathers swimming in the glorious ocean surf or wandering up and down the pure white sands of the beach. The man with imagination buys his lot now for only a thousand dollars. Two years hence the common man will pay five or ten times as much for his. Would you like to see the plans and pictures of the development?"

"Certainly," I answered.

Mr. Yerkes then spent a half hour showing me maps and architect's drawings, and by the time he finished I will have to admit that I was completely sold on his proposition. He is going to have a five-hundred-thousand-dollar country club that will be as magnificent as anything anywhere in the west. And the plans for the new hotel, the Pompeian swimming pool, the Florentine fountain, and the civic theater indicated that they will be artistic masterpieces of the first magnitude.

"It almost makes me want to buy a lot myself," I said.

"Evidently," said Mr. Yerkes, "you are one of the people with imagination. But I am not trying to sell you a lot today. However, I would like you to come out and look at the property. I am taking out a party of prospective buyers tomorrow. I would like you to come along, look over the ground, and check up on the grading and dirt-moving work which I am planning. With your expert knowledge you ought to be able to tell me whether I am right in my estimate that twelve ten-ton tractors is what I need. I am also contemplating the purchase of six elevating graders, and a lot of wheel scrapers, fresnoes, dump wagons, and other equipment. I would like your ideas on this also."

"Nothing would give me greater pleasure," I said. "I am glad to help you in any way that I can."

"Splendid," said Mr. Yerkes. "Meet me here tomorrow morning at nine o'clock."

"I will be here," I said. "Good afternoon."

Then—as I am always very careful not to trespass upon the time of a busy executive—I took my departure at once. I have described my call on Mr. Yerkes very fully so that you can see what a very big man he is and what a very big order he is going to give us. With a man like Mr. Yerkes it does not pay to be in too much of a hurry. But I am going to camp on his trail until these two hundred lots are sold and I get his order for the twelve ten-ton Earthworms.

Yours,
Alexander Botts.

FARMERS' FRIEND TRACTOR COMPANY
SALESMAN'S DAILY REPORT

Date: Tuesday, April 22, 1924.
Written from: Los Angeles, California.
Written by: Alexander Botts.

This has been a thrilling day. And when I relate everything that I have done you will see that I have been on my toes all the time, that I have handled things in exactly the right way, and that on account of my efforts we are likely to get an even bigger order from Mr. Yerkes than I had hoped. In fact, it would not surprise me at all if we sold him twenty ten-tons and about six five-tons.

At exactly two minutes before nine this morning I walked into the office of the Bianca Beach Development Corporation. I sent in my card, and at exactly nine o'clock Mr. Spencer K. Yerkes himself came out and greeted me.

"Good morning, Mr. Botts," he said. "I see you are punctual. You are a man after my own heart. We will start at once."

"I am ready anytime you want to go," I replied.

"Good," said Mr. Yerkes. "I am putting on a real selling drive today. I have advertised in the papers, and I am sending out several busloads of prospective buyers. Besides this I have gathered in three very important prospects whom I will take out in my private car. These men are all reasonably wealthy and I hope to sell them a dozen or more lots apiece. I am expecting that you will ride along with us."

"I should feel highly honored," I replied politely.

"Very good," said Mr. Yerkes. "And there is one thing more. I take it you are pretty well sold on this little development project of mine?"

"I think it is a wonderful thing, Mr. Yerkes," I said. "I am sure it will succeed."

"Splendid," he said. "Then I shall probably call on you to help me a little in my selling campaign. I can tell that you are a natural salesman, and it wouldn't hurt things at all if you were to talk up this proposition of mine with these prospects. Furthermore, I would be very glad if you would tell them that I have bought a lot of tractors from you, and that the work of grading is going to start at once. It is just as much to your interest as mine to sell these lots. The sooner we get them sold the sooner you will get your order for the tractors."

"That's right," I said; "you can be sure that I will do everything in my power to help you."

"Thank you," said Mr. Yerkes. "I know I can count on you."

He then took me into his private office and introduced me to the three important prospects. They were ordinary-looking, uninteresting, middle-aged businessmen.

"I want you to meet Mr. Alexander Botts," said Mr. Yerkes. "He is the representative of the Farmers' Friend Tractor Company, and he has just sold me twenty ten-ton Earthworm tractors."

(*Note:* As you can imagine, these words fell upon my ears with a most pleasing sound. The day before, Mr. Yerkes had spoken of only twelve, but now he had evidently changed his mind and was thinking of twenty.)

After we had shaken hands all around, Mr. Yerkes served us some refreshments out of his little trick electric refrigerator, and we then went down and climbed into Mr. Yerkes's car.

It was a splendid eight-cylinder Italian creation, as fine as any I have ever seen. It must have cost at least ten thousand dollars, and it caused my esteem for the owner to mount even higher than ever. Mr. Yerkes is quite evidently a man who considers that the best is none too good for him.

We were soon rolling smoothly along through the Los Angeles traffic. Mr. Yerkes sat at the wheel, and beside him was one of the three prospects. The other two sat with me in the rear seat. The man beside me was a rather stolid, German-looking person by the name of Joseph Schwartzberger. I at once engaged him in conversation, and gave him a very good sales talk on Mr. Yerkes's real estate proposition. In doing this I was, of course, indirectly helping myself and the Earthworm Tractor Company, for as Mr. Yerkes had pointed out, the sooner these lots were sold the sooner we would get the order for the twenty tractors.

Unfortunately Mr. Schwartzberger seemed very dumb and unreasonable. He kept gazing at the scenery as we drove along, and seemed to take very little interest in my glowing descriptions of the splendid development work which Mr. Yerkes was going to do. His mind kept wandering off the subject, and he kept talking about orange growing—which had nothing to do with Bianca Beach development at all, as the ground there is too rough for orchards. Several times he asked me whether Earthworm tractors were any good for working in orchards. If I had let him ramble on, probably he would have talked about nothing but orange growing. However, each time he brought up the subject I very skillfully changed the discussion to the consideration of the new Bianca Beach five-hundred-thousand-dollar country club, the Pompeian baths, or some other feature of Mr. Yerkes's project.

It took us about an hour to reach Bianca Beach, and here I got a very pleasant surprise. Mr. Yerkes had certainly put on his selling drive in splendid fashion. For a quarter of a mile the main road was lined with rows of American flags, flapping bravely in the breeze. There were several dozen enormous billboards announcing the sale of lots in the new Bianca Beach development. And artistically placed amid these billboards was a large tent containing pictures and descriptive literature, and also a large plaster-of-Paris relief map of the project, showing Bianca Beach as it would look when completed. This map was a veritable work of art. The ocean was painted blue, the beach white, and the hills green. And there were hundreds of little model houses stuck around among thousands of little artificial trees and shrubs. Just outside the tent was a large brass band of at least fifty pieces, which, as soon as we arrived, struck up the "Star Spangled Banner."

There were a dozen or more salesmen and other assistants preparing for the crowds which were expected later. Mr. Yerkes spent ten or fifteen minutes checking up in his efficient businesslike way to make sure that all arrangements had been attended to. Then he took the three important prospects and myself for a short walk to see the principal points of interest in the future town.

The property looked very much as Mr. Yerkes had described it to me in the office. There was a beautiful wide beach washed by the blue waters of the Pacific Ocean. Behind the beach the land was rough and hilly, rising irregularly toward the high mountains five or six miles away. The ground was dry and sandy and covered with bushes and tough grass and a little cactus.

The whole place had been surveyed, and the proposed streets had been neatly marked with little white painted wooden stakes. At the street corners were neat little signs with names such as "Rose Lane,"—"Desdemonia Boulevard,"—"Nightingale Road,"—"Delphinium Drive," and so on. I was interested to learn that Mr. Yerkes had selected these names himself—which shows that he has the soul of a poet as well as the mind of a businessman.

There were also stakes showing the position of the five-hundred-thousand-dollar country club, the Pompeian swimming pool, and other features.

As we looked around Mr. Yerkes showed us the plans and pictures of the future improvements and described them so vividly that I could almost see them, rising up in all their beauty and grandeur from the sandy wastelands. Mr. Yerkes must have been right when he said that I was evidently a man of imagination. The three important prospects, however, seemed to be very unresponsive, and this was particularly the case with Mr. Schwartzberger. It took his dense intellect at least ten minutes to comprehend what Mr. Yerkes meant by the Pompeian swimming pool. Apparently Mr. Schwartzberger had never heard of Pompeii and thought that the word "Pompeian" referred exclusively to some sort of cosmetic.

During the course of our walk Mr. Yerkes had me check up on the grading which was to be done in putting through his street program. Owing to the rough hilly nature of the land there will be a tremendous amount of cut and fill work, and a tremendous amount of dirt will have to be moved to make the park and the eighteen-hole golf course. Besides this there will be a great deal of dirt moving in connection with building a dam back in the hills, making an open ditch to bring the water down to the reservoir just above town, digging the smaller ditches for the water supply mains and the sewage system. As Mr. Yerkes was insistent that all this work be completed before the end of the year, I told him privately that I thought he would need about six five-tons as well as the twenty ten-tons he was contemplating purchasing.

"Well," said Mr. Yerkes, "if I need that much machinery I will have to get it. We are doing a big thing here in a big way, and we can't afford to economize on equipment."

Naturally I was overjoyed to hear him say this. And I was also very much pleased a little later when he told the three important prospects very positively and without any reservations that he was buying twenty ten-tons, six five-tons, and a lot of other miscellaneous equipment.

One of the prospects—a man by the name of Smith—seemed particularly impressed with this fact.

"That piece of information," he said, "is the one thing necessary to make me decide to buy. A man is naturally leery about buying lots before the property has been improved. But now that I know you are actually getting this large amount of machinery, I feel very much reassured, and I have every confidence that the improvements will go through according to schedule."

Mr. Schwartzberger, however, was skeptical. On the way back to the tent he spoke to me privately.

"Are you really selling this man that much machinery?" he asked.

"Certainly," I replied. "That is, I am selling him the twenty-six tractors, and he is getting the other equipment from the respective manufacturers."

"Have you got your money yet?" asked Mr. Schwartzberger.

"Really, sir," I replied, "I do not feel that I ought to discuss my customer's financial arrangements, but I might say that naturally the Farmers' Friend Tractor Company does not expect payment until the machines are delivered—and that will not be until next week."

"Well," said Mr. Schwartzberger, "I hope you get your money. You know practically all of these real estate fellers are crooks. I very much doubt if I'll buy any lots here. The proposition sounds good, but there must be a catch in it somewhere. And by the way, sometime I want you to tell me whether your tractors are any good for work in orange groves."

"Why talk about orange groves now?" I said. "The best thing for us to do here is to find out all we can about this wonderful development scheme. I only wish I could get you to take a little more interest. I really believe, Mr. Schwartzberger, that if you do not buy as many lots as you are able to, you will be throwing away the opportunity of a lifetime."

"Maybe so," he said, "but I hate to take a chance."

By this time we had gotten back to the tent, which was now full of people. Four large busloads of prospective buyers had arrived from Los Angeles, and a great many more had come in their own cars. Mr. Yerkes at once took charge of these people and led them around the same route which we had taken. At each important point he stopped and gave a short explanatory talk. When this tour of inspection was finished a light lunch was served to everyone in the tent, while the band played stirring music.

After lunch Mr. Yerkes mounted a small platform and delivered one of the most remarkable orations I have ever heard. I am a pretty good talker and a pretty good salesman myself, but from now on I am going to take Mr. Yerkes as my model and master. The man is a wonder. He is a super-salesman and a modern Demosthenes.

He started his talk on a very high plane. He described in great detail and with a wonderful warm flow of language the magnificent building operations which would soon commence. He painted such a convincing and vivid word picture of the lovely Pompeian swimming pool that he made us all feel as if we were standing beside it ready to plunge into its cool and inviting waters. He then shifted to the golf links and the five-hundred-thousand-dollar country club, and at once we were transferred to the velvety greens with our golf clubs. And a moment later we were sitting on the spacious veranda sipping cool drinks and gazing out over the lovely green landscape. By his consummate artistry and mastery of words he took us for a walk down the beautiful palm-lined avenues, and past the cozy white houses, set in gardens of fragrant roses. He showed us the cool and delightful park, the crowds of bathers on the beach, and the happy throngs going to the moving picture show in the civic theater.

And then he suddenly became quite businesslike. With hard facts and remorseless logic he drove home the great truth that the people who bought lots today would be able to sell them in a year or two for ten times what they had paid for them.

"But," he said, "I hope that you will not want to sell. I hope that you will all remain in this paradise on earth. Bianca Beach is to be a city of homes, where you may all dwell in peace and contentment with your gracious wives and your darling children. Picture to yourselves what this place will be like in only one or two short years. Crowds of happy youths and maidens will be sporting in the surf or cleaving the waters of the Pompeian swimming pool. Young and old will be spending many happy hours on the golf links in the glorious

California sunshine. Others will idle away the balmy afternoons under the shade of the palms in the park. There will be splendid schools, churches and a library, moving pictures, high-grade stores of all kinds, beauty parlors, barber shops, garages, and filling stations. But greatest of all will be the homes, where happy families will dwell amid the most modern conveniences, making use to the fullest extent of our up-to-date electric light service, our copious water supply and our splendid sanitary sewage system. It is a beautiful thought—men and women—a beautiful thought.

"And in conclusion I wish to state that the young man at the table by the entrance to this tent is prepared to sell you as many lots as you desire to take. And I would advise you not to delay. This is a limited offer at an absurdly low figure, and if you do not act at once your opportunity to profit by these prices will be gone forever. I thank you."

I have repeated Mr. Yerkes's exact words, as near as I can remember them, so that you can see I am profiting by this opportunity to improve myself. The basic principles of all selling are the same— whether it be real estate or tractors, insurance or anything else. I am making a thorough study of Mr. Yerkes's methods. I have always been pretty good myself, but in Mr. Yerkes I recognize a real genius in the higher art of selling. And by taking him as my ideal I confidently expect to become an even greater tractor salesman than I have been in the past.

As soon as Mr. Yerkes had finished his masterly address the people—several hundred of them—began crowding around the table where the lots were being sold. The effect of Mr. Yerkes's talk was so stupendous that it took fifteen minutes to get the crowd under control and make them line up in an orderly manner, and it was two hours before everyone could be attended to. There were a few people, of course, who bought nothing, but most of them bought at least one lot, and many bought more. I, myself, have no use for a lot, but I was so impressed by the investment possibilities of the scheme that I decided that I must have one. Upon consulting my checkbook I found that I had only three hundred and twenty-five dollars available, but Mr. Yerkes as a special personal favor consented to let me take a lot with only three hundred dollars instead of five hundred dollars as a down payment.

Of the three important prospects who had come out in Mr. Yerkes's private car, two of them purchased thirty lots apiece, but Mr. Schwartzberger remained stubborn and bullheaded to the end. In view of the fact that Mr. Schwartzberger had been riding in Mr. Yerkes's car and had eaten his food, it seemed to me that this was a very small way for him to act. Some people are so mean and so suspicious and have so little trust in human nature that they won't do any business at all for fear somebody will slip something over on them. If you took a guy like this Schwartzberger to the bank and got out a five-dollar gold piece, which was guaranteed by the cashier to be genuine, and offered it to him for fifty cents he would probably turn it down unless you agreed to give him his money back if he wasn't satisfied, and at that he would probably want 10 percent off for cash.

After the last customer had been satisfied Mr. Yerkes gathered up the records and receipts, left his assistants in charge of the tent and equipment, started up his elegant motorcar, and drove us all back to Los Angeles. On the way he made a last attempt to get Mr. Schwartzberger interested. But even a master like Mr. Yerkes is powerless in the face of complete stupidity. Mr. Schwartzberger had various absurd and evasive replies. First of all he said he would make no down payment until he had the actual deed to the property, with a title abstract, and an insurance policy from some reputable title guaranty company. Mr. Yerkes pointed out most reasonably that this procedure would be impossible in this case, as the sales had to be made on the spot and that it would take several weeks of clerical work before the final papers could be made out. In the meantime a signed receipt of the Bianca Beach Development Corporation was sufficient proof that the sale had been made.

Mr. Schwartzberger was still stubborn. He admitted that Mr. Yerkes's point was well taken, but he then proceeded to run in a lot of foolish technical stuff by saying that he would be willing to take a few lots if the money could be put in escrow—whatever that means. But he would not put up any money outright.

Mr. Yerkes's only reply to this proposition was to state that if a man didn't want to risk anything, he couldn't expect ever to make any profits. And there the matter was dropped.

When we reached Los Angeles Mr. Yerkes left me at my hotel. In parting he told me that he had not completely checked up all his sales, but that he had sold enough to make him decide to go ahead. He asked me to call on him at his office tomorrow afternoon to close the deal on the tractors.

And so before tomorrow's sun has set I expect to bring to a successful conclusion the largest and most brilliant sale in all my years of service as a salesman for the Farmers' Friend Tractor Company.

Yours,
Alexander Botts.

FARMERS' FRIEND TRACTOR COMPANY
SALESMAN'S DAILY REPORT

Date: Wednesday, April 23, 1924.
Written from: Los Angeles, California.
Written by: Alexander Botts.

Today I have received two sickening jolts—either one of which would have been sufficient to completely discourage most ordinary people. But it is pretty hard to keep Alexander Botts down, and I wish to announce that I am still going strong—or as strong as anyone could under the circumstances.

The first jolt came this afternoon when I called at the office of The Bianca Beach Development Corporation. In the outer room I found a small group of nervous and excited people. The place seemed to be in charge of a rather tough-looking man whom I had never seen before.

"Where," I asked this man, "can I find Mr. Spencer K. Yerkes?"

"That is what I would like to know myself," he replied, "and so would all these gentlemen who purchased lots from him." With a wave of his hand he indicated the people who were standing around. "I suppose," he added, "you also bought a lot at Bianca Beach?"

"Yes," I admitted, "I bought a lot. And I am here to see Mr. Yerkes on very important business."

"Mr. Yerkes has gone," said the man, "and I doubt if he plans to return."

"But what has happened?"

"Haven't you read the afternoon papers?"

"No. What is it all about, and who are you?"

"I am a United States marshal, and I am temporarily in charge of this office."

"Do you mean to say that there was anything crooked about Mr. Yerkes's business?"

"It looks a little bit that way," said the marshal. "We got a tip yesterday from Mr. Schwartzberger, the big orange grower, who thought there was something wrong about this whole Bianca Beach proposition. As soon as we looked into things we found that Mr. Yerkes did not own the land at Bianca Beach at all. All he had was an option which expired last night."

"But he sold several hundred lots," I said.

"Exactly," said the marshal. "And late yesterday afternoon he cashed all the checks he got on down payments and drove out of town in his car. We think he crossed the border at Tijuana."

44

"It doesn't seem possible," I said.

"Apparently," the marshal went on, "he owes pretty nearly everybody in town. He hasn't paid for his car, or for his office furniture. He owes the band, and all the people that worked for him yesterday, and the engineers that surveyed his land, and pretty nearly everybody that had anything to do with him. The main thing we are after him for, though, is using the mails to defraud. I hope we catch him. I'd like to meet him. He must be a very slick talker."

"Yes," I said sadly, "he is quite a talker."

At this point the average salesman would have given way to despair. But I am different. I decided there was no use crying over spilled milk. I at once dismissed the nefarious, low-down, slimy Mr. Yerkes from my mind. I resolved to forget my poor, unfortunate three hundred dollars. And I at once turned my active mind onto the problem of what to do next.

"By the way," I asked the marshal, "did you say this Mr. Schwartzberger was a friend of yours?"

"I know him fairly well."

"You say he is a big orange grower?"

"He owns about four thousand acres."

"Can you imagine that!" I exclaimed. "The big bum never told me he actually owned any orange groves. What is his address? Where does he live?"

"Out at Pomona."

"Thanks," I said, and started back to the hotel.

I had already mapped out a plan of campaign. My logical mind had at once grasped the situation. Mr. Schwartzberger had been asking about using tractors in orange groves only the day before. And now it appeared that he actually owned tremendous orange properties. Putting two and two together I decided that he might possibly buy a few Earthworms. If I couldn't sell tractors to Mr. Yerkes, I could to Mr. Schwartzberger. It was too late to go out to Pomona this afternoon, but I resolved to make the trip first thing in the morning.

When I reached the hotel, the clerk handed me a telegram from Mr. J.D. Whitcomb, Western Sales Manager of the Farmers' Friend Tractor Company. And when I read it I received the second big jolt of this most disagreeable day. Part of the telegram wasn't so bad. It was all right for Mr. Whitcomb to mention that he had received my yesterday's report. It was all right for him to inform me that Mr. Joseph Schwartzberger is a big orange grower, and that the Farmers' Friend Tractor Company and a lot of other tractor companies were after him last year, but failed to get any orders. I was amazed, however, at Mr. Whitcomb's closing words: "You must be sound

45

asleep stop if Schwartzberger asked for information about tractors he must be getting interested at last and if you had had the brains of a half-wit you would have followed him up stop see if you can't wake up and get his order before some other company gets ahead of you."

Why Mr. Whitcomb felt it necessary to send such a message I do not know. But I cannot pass over his remarks in silence. Mr. Whitcomb completely ignores the fact that I was not asleep. I was working on a very big proposition, and I was succeeding. I had handled matters so well that I was right on the point of selling twenty-six tractors—and I would have closed the deal, too, except for the fact that Mr. Yerkes was suddenly compelled to leave town.

Furthermore, I object to Mr. Whitcomb's insinuation that my brains are less than those of a half-wit. As I explained earlier in this report, I had shown great intelligence by finding out all about Mr. Schwartzberger before I ever received Mr. Whitcomb's telegram, and I had already decided to go out to see him.

Mr. Whitcomb need have no fear that any other company will get ahead of me. I will call on Mr. Schwartzberger tomorrow morning. And if it is humanly possible I will get his order for as many tractors as he needs—and, considering the size of his properties, that ought to be a good many.

To reassure Mr. Whitcomb, and to show him that he is entirely unjustified in his fear that some other company may beat me to it, I wish to state here and now that if Mr. Schwartzberger actually decides to buy any tractors, and he gives his order to any other company, I will save you the trouble of firing me; I will send you my resignation at once. That is the kind of a guy I am.

Yours,
Alexander Botts.

FARMERS' FRIEND TRACTOR COMPANY
SALESMAN'S DAILY REPORT

Date: Thursday, April 24, 1924.
Written from: Los Angeles, California.
Written by: Alexander Botts.

Today's report will be a very hard one to write. But I will go ahead in my usual straightforward way and I will tell you everything exactly as it occurred.

I reached Mr. Schwartzberger's house in Pomona about the mid-

dle of the morning. The old geezer met me at the door, and I will
have to admit that he treated me very politely. He said he was sorry I
had lost the money I paid out for my lot at Bianca Beach, and it was
too bad he hadn't been a little quicker about getting the authorities
after Mr. Spencer K. Yerkes. "They'll never catch him now," he said.
"He is too smart for them." Mr. Schwartzberger then took me into
his sitting room and introduced me to a young man that was in there.

"Shake hands with Mr. Jensen," he said.

"Pleased to meet you, Mr. Jensen," I said, shaking hands.

"Mr. Jensen is in the same line of business as you," said Mr.
Schwartzberger. "He is with the Steel Elephant Tractor Company."

"By the way, Mr. Schwartzberger," I said, "you haven't been
thinking of buying any tractors, have you?"

"Yes, I have," he said. "I was even considering getting some of
your machines, but when I asked you the other day you didn't seem
to know whether they were adapted to orchard work or not. So I
decided to do business with Mr. Jensen here."

"You haven't signed an order yet, have you?"

"Yes, I have," he replied. "I am getting fifteen small machines."

"You don't need any more, do you?"

"Not now."

"No chance of your changing your mind?"

"No," he said, "not a chance." And the worst of it is the stubborn
old bozo apparently actually meant it. I talked around and argued
and pleaded for fifteen or twenty minutes, but there was nothing
doing at all. So finally I got up to say good-bye. Restraining a natural
impulse to sock Mr. Schwartzberger in the stomach, and put my foot
in Mr. Jensen's face, I shook hands most politely with both of them,
and took my departure.

So that was that. And there is not much more to say at the present
time, except that I seem to remember promising you in my yesterday's report that, if Mr. Schwartzberger was to buy any tractors
from any other company, I would save you the trouble of firing me
by resigning.

I see now that I was a bit hasty in making this promise. And I
realize—in view of the fact that this Schwartzberger affair is an
exception, and in no way typical of my habitually successful operations—that my resignation would be a heavy blow to the company.
But a promise is a promise. I am not the man to back down. So I
hereby tender my resignation as salesman for the Farmers' Friend
Tractor Company.

Yours,
Alexander Botts.

BIG BUSINESS

TELEGRAM
SAN FRANCISCO CALIF 1105 A APR 25 1924.

ALEXANDER BOTTS
BILTMORE HOTEL
LOS ANGELES CALIF
YOUR RESIGNATION NOT ACCEPTED STOP MUCH RELIEVED TO
HEAR YOU ARE NOT AS GOOD A SALESMAN AS YOU THOUGHT STOP
FORGET WHAT YOU SAID IN FORMER REPORT ABOUT TAKING
YERKES AS YOUR MODEL STOP IF YOU EVER START SELLING STUFF
YOU DON'T OWN TO PEOPLE THAT DON'T WANT IT YOU WILL BE TOO
GOOD FOR THIS COMPANY AND WILL BE FIRED SURE ENOUGH
J D WHITCOMB WESTERN SALES MANAGER

EUROPE IS DUE
FOR A SURPRISE

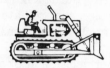

EARTHWORM TRACTOR COMPANY
EARTHWORM CITY, ILLINOIS

January 19, 1928.

Mr. Alexander Botts,
Deane Supply Company,
Mercedillo, California.

Dear Botts:

At a meeting of the officers of the company this morning, it was decided to ask you to go to Europe for several months as our sales representative.

Since the merger last spring of the Farmers' Friend Tractor Company and the Steel Elephant Tractor Company into the new Earthworm Tractor Company, we have, as you know, greatly increased our business. And, as ample capital is available, we are planning an even greater expansion.

Up to this time our European business has been practically nothing. Economic conditions since the war have made it almost impossible for us to sell any tractors, either in England or on the Continent. But conditions have recently improved so much that we are seriously thinking of going into the European market.

Our plan is to send you and another man over at once to see what you can do. Your trip will be more or less experimental; possibly you may not be able to accomplish anything. But if you succeed in selling a reasonable number of tractors, we will know that the market is there, and we will open a number of European branches. If everything goes well, it is even possible that within a few years we may start a European factory.

We have arranged to send Mr. George McGinnis, whom you will remember as the former star salesman of the Steel Elephant Company, to England, Germany and the rest of Northern Europe. We want you to see what you can do in Southern Europe, particularly France and Italy.

We have not forgotten your splendid record when you were a salesman with this company, and we have noted with great satisfaction your fine work as tractor sales manager for the Deane Supply Company at Mercedillo.

Please let us know your decision at once. Your salary will be five hundred dollars a month plus expenses.

> Cordially yours,
> Gilbert Henderson,
> Sales Manager.

DEANE SUPPLY COMPANY
MERCEDILLO, CALIFORNIA

January 23, 1928.

Mr. Gilbert Henderson, Sales Manager,
Earthworm Tractor Company,
Earthworm City, Illinois.

Dear Henderson:

Well, well, it seems like old times to get a letter from you saying that you want me to go out on a trip. The idea appeals to me very much. I have a good assistant here who can handle my job while I am gone, so there is no reason why I can't go. Of course, five hundred a month is nothing at all as compared with what I get from my share in the business here, but I realize that you can't afford to pay big money on what you regard as a speculative, experimental trip. Of course, I always look at these vulgar money matters in a very large way. I suppose I am something like Mr. Andrew Mellon in this respect—always ready to take on an interesting, worthwhile job, either as a cabinet member or as a tractor sales ambassador, regardless of the financial sacrifice involved. However, as soon as I start making sales in a big way over in Europe, I will expect you to pay me adequately.

I was rather amused at your statement that I might possibly make no sales at all. Of course, it is perfectly possible—in fact, probable—that this man McGinnis may make no sales in England and Germany.

But you don't have to worry about me. There must be people in Europe who can either beg, borrow or steal the price of a tractor; if so, I will sell them. And it is with a feeling of the greatest pleasure that I look forward to this experience.

Selling tractors around this place has become too easy. The people of California are so intelligent, and are so well informed regarding tractors, that they just come in and buy them of their own free will. I have had so few difficulties for the past year and a half that I am getting soft and out of condition mentally. If there is as much sales resistance in Europe as you indicate, it will be just what I need to tone me up. Consequently, I will accept your offer on two conditions:

1. Mrs. Botts is to go with me, and the expense account will cover the expenses of both of us. It is absolutely essential that Gadget go along. (Note: My wife's real name is Mildred, but I always call her Gadget, because she is one of the most valuable accessories I have ever picked up.) She has a fine education and a wonderful brain, and since our marriage I have come to rely absolutely on her excellent business judgment. The combination of my energy and resourcefulness with her brilliant intellect makes a team that cannot be beat. Furthermore, she can act as interpreter. In spite of the fact that I am familiar with France, having spent more than a year over there in the A. E. F., I am forced to admit that my knowledge of the French language is a trifle weak. Gadget has never been to Europe, but she has studied at a splendid summer school in Vermont and she can talk it better than most of the French people themselves. She also knows Italian and German. Consequently, she must go along.

2. There must be no hollering, yawping, or nagging about small sums on my expense account. I am very insistent about this. The greatest annoyance connected with my otherwise pleasant association of former years with your tractor company was the continual bickering about my expense account. If I am to be at my best on this foreign trip, I must not be hampered and constricted in my style by petty money considerations. I am willing to be broad-minded. It is perfectly reasonable that you should check up closely on expense items running to a hundred dollars or more, but all trifling amounts, such as only twenty or fifty dollars, must be passed without question and in a gentlemanly way.

If you agree to these two conditions, I will accept your offer with the greatest joy. When do we start?

Sincerely,
Alexander Botts.

EUROPE IS DUE FOR A SURPRISE

EARTHWORM TRACTOR COMPANY,
EARTHWORM CITY, ILLINOIS

January 27, 1928.

Mr. Alexander Botts,
Deane Supply Company,
Mercedillo, California

Dear Botts:

Your letter has come, and we are very glad to welcome you back as an Earthworm tractor salesman. We accept your two conditions. We have engaged passage for you and Mrs. Botts on the steamship Beaucaire, sailing from New York on February eighteenth, and due in Marseilles on March third. We are shipping on this same boat eight demonstration tractors—four of them billed to Marseilles to be used for your work in France, and four of them billed to Genoa—at which port the Beaucaire also touches—for your work in Italy. We are also including a combined harvester and an assortment of plows, blade graders, wheel scrapers, dump wagons and other machinery.

We are mailing foreign advertising matter to chambers of commerce and agricultural associations all over France and Italy. We will supply you with additional advertising matter, and with a number of reels of talking motion pictures showing tractors in action, with running sales talks in French and in Italian.

We are giving you the greatest latitude on this trip. We expect you to make inquiries and find out about conditions when you get there. We want you to sell tractors at any place, or in any way that you can, with a view to opening up the South European market for future sales. You will keep in touch with me at all times, and I shall expect full reports of your progress.

Very sincerely,
Gilbert Henderson,
Sales Manager.

ALEXANDER BOTTS
EUROPEAN REPRESENTATIVE FOR THE
EARTHWORM TRACTOR ON BOARD S. S. BEAUCAIRE,

February 20, 1928.

Mr. Gilbert Henderson,
Earthworm Tractor Company,
Earthworm City, Illinois

Dear Henderson.

We are now two days out from New York. So far it has been pretty rough, but Gadget and I are feeling fine, and already I have much to report. You don't know how glad I am that I am taking this trip. Already I am all steamed up and working hard. An ordinary salesman, on going to Europe, would probably wait until he got there before he tried to do any business. But I started in as soon as I got to New York—two days before the boat sailed. First of all, I had this letter paper made up. If you run your finger over the printing you will see that the letters stand out in a very expensive way. Furthermore, the paper is the highest-grade bond, in every way worthy of the European representative of such a high-grade machine as the Earthworm tractor. I have also had some high-grade business cards printed.

All this, of course, is of no great importance. I merely mentioned it so that you could see that I am right up on my toes, and attending to all details—even the most trifling—with my old-time vigor and efficiency.

While attending to the smaller matters, I have not neglected the larger, and you will be delighted to learn that I have evolved and commenced to put into action an idea that is as large and splendid as anything I ever put across in the good old days.

This idea came to me when I first reached New York. At the steamship office I learned that on this boat, the Beaucaire, there would be a delegation of forty or fifty French grape growers, who were returning to France after a visit to the United States. The steamship officials did not know the exact purpose of their visit to America, but it at once occurred to me that they had probably come to investigate modern American methods of vineyard culture. And if they had visited the splendid vineyards in California they would, of course, have seen hundreds of our small Earthworm tractors at work plowing and cultivating. They would have seen how far superior these machines are to any other method of culture. And if they had talked to the California vineyard owners, they would have learned that Earthworm tractors are the world's cheapest, easiest, and best method of taking care of grapevines. I saw at once that these French grape growers were my meat. I had a feeling that when I approached them I would find them already about half sold on the idea of Earthworm tractors.

An ordinary salesman, when he feels that a prospect is already half sold, usually slackens his efforts, hoping that he can swing the sale without much more work.

With me, however, it is just the opposite. When things begin to look favorable I always work twice as hard and exert every possible effort to make sure that nothing shall prevent matters from coming to a triumphant and favorable conclusion.

In this case I decided to catch these Frenchmen off their guard on the boat, while I had them where they couldn't get away, and put on a terrific high-powered selling campaign.

At once I rushed down to the pier, where the good ship Beaucaire was being loaded. I was delighted to find that the eight tractors which we are shipping had not yet been put on board. They were all standing on the pier, neatly boxed for export. I told the man in charge of the loading that only seven of these machines were to go in the hold; the eighth one—a small ten-horsepower model—I told him was to be placed on the promenade deck where it could be used for demonstration purposes.

The man seemed very much surprised and puzzled at this request. He said he had never heard of such a thing. So I started in and explained everything to him as patiently and politely as I could. I impressed it on his mind that this was a very reasonable request, that I would not hurt the ship in any way, that I would bring along a set of rubber pads to bolt onto the tracks so that the deck would not become scratched, that I would be very careful not to run over any of the passengers, and that most of these passengers were French vineyard men who would be deeply interested in the tractor and would want to see it working. After I had elucidated this matter for more than half an hour, the man said he had no authority to load the tractors anywhere but in the hold, and that I would have to see one of the officials of the company.

Accordingly, I got him to promise to leave the small tractor on the pier for the time being, and went back to the company office. Here I found a Mr. Brown, who seemed to be in charge of the company's freight business. I had to talk to him about an hour, explaining everything in great detail. Then he said I would have to see another guy—whose name I have now forgotten. I talked and argued with this other guy for almost two hours, and then he told me that it was a matter which would have to be decided by the captain of the ship.

As the captain was French, I took Gadget along to act as interpreter—which was unnecessary, as it turned out that he spoke very good English. However, it was lucky that we both went, because the captain was very stupid and stubborn, and it took the best efforts of the two of us—talking alternately for about three hours—to convince him that we were right.

He finally agreed to put the tractor on the after end of one of the upper decks, where it would be lashed down to prevent it from sliding around in rough weather. For two hours every afternoon— provided the weather was fair—he would have the end of the deck roped off and let us drive the tractor around and show what it could do. I had to sign a paper releasing the steamship company from all responsibility in case anything happened to the tractor, and assuming full responsibility for any damage the machine might do. He absolutely refused to give me the run of the whole deck with the machine. And for these restricted privileges I had to pay three hundred dollars—which I suppose is for deck rent or something. This seems like a pretty stiff price, but it is worthwhile, in view of the tremendous impression we are sure to make on these Frenchmen.

So far it has been too rough to do anything. Gadget and I are feeling great, but practically all of the Frenchmen seem to be cooped up in their staterooms. Apparently they are seasick—which, of course, is of no importance, because the boat is rolling so heavily that we could not demonstrate the tractor to them anyway But I am all prepared to put on a swell demonstration as soon as we get some fair weather. I have rubber pads installed on the track shoes, and these ought to give me good traction on the boards of the deck. I have a number of railroad ties which I can pile up in various ways so that the tractor can climb over them and show these Frenchmen how it negotiates rough country. Also, I have fixed up a system of pulleys with large weights for the tractor to lift. This will give them an idea of what we can pull. Toward the end of the voyage I expect to put on a moving-picture show, showing the tractors doing actual farm work. The projector on the ship is equipped with the latest sound system, and that should help a lot. I am much encouraged. Never before, as far as I know, has there been a tractor demonstration on a great transatlantic liner. It is sure to make a tremendous impression. Already I can see a flood of orders pouring in.

February 21, 1928.

Three days out.

Still too rough to do anything with the tractor. But it is a little smoother than yesterday, and the Frenchmen are commencing to come up out of their holes. Some of them have their wives with them. Gadget and I have made the acquaintance of several couples. And Gadget, owing to her superb knowledge of the French language, has unearthed some information which indicates that our projected demonstration will be of even more importance than I had supposed. Apparently we shall have to start at the very beginning in our education of these people. They know nothing of American methods, and they care less. They say that Frenchmen have been growing grapes since before the Year 1, and know all about it; and it would be absurd to think they could learn anything from California, where the large vineyards are less than a hundred years old.

They had not come to America to learn; they had come to instruct. They had been to Washington, and their mission was to persuade the American Government that the prohibition law was all wrong. In the first place, they said, it deprived them of one of their best markets, and thus seriously cut into their profits. In the second place, it deprived the American people of the world's most pleasing and healthful beverages.

To prove this latter point they had brought along a full line of samples. They had supposed that the official nature of their visit, and the fact that they had a letter from the President of France, would let them take this stuff into the United States through some sort of diplomatic courtesy. But the customs authorities had been hardboiled and had decided against them. And the wines are now on their way back to France on this very boat.

In spite of the lack of samples, however, they had pointed out to everyone they met that the French light wines are a natural God-given drink, completely harmless, an aid to digestion, a promoter of good fellowship and good feeling, and, when properly used, do not cause intoxication. They had, therefore, suggested—in the friendliest and most helpful spirit, and making it plain that they had no wish to meddle in our affairs—that it would be a great benefit to all concerned if the law were amended in such a way as to admit French wines to the United States. If this were done, prosperity would settle once more over the fair vineyards of France, and the American people, instead of being tempted to indulge in white mule and other vile distilled liquors, could return once more to the smooth and satisfying juice of the grape. They had spread this message among all the senators, representatives and officials they met, and everywhere they had been received with such politeness and good will that they felt sure—in spite of the fact that no one had promised them anything definite—that the laws would soon be changed in their favor.

Gadget and I, of course, had our doubts about this, but we were too polite to mention them to the Frenchmen. I did, however, discuss the matter with an American by the name of Bowers that I met in the smoking room.

"It seems incredible," I said, "but these grape growers actually think that all they have to do is tell Senator Heflin and the rest of them what wonderful stuff this French wine is, and right away they will drop everything else and push through a law so that it can be brought into the country. For pure, childlike simplicity you couldn't beat that anywhere."

"Well," said Bowers, "it doesn't seem to me anywhere near as simple-minded as your idea that you can go over to Europe, tell the Europeans what wonderful machines your Earthworms are, and then sit back and watch the orders come rolling in. I doubt if you sell a single one."

"Why not?" I asked.

"The Europeans don't like machinery. They hate it—especially if it's American. I've traveled in Europe a lot and I know."

"You seem to be pretty sure of yourself," I said.

"I am," he said. And then he told me a long yarn about an American he knew that went broke trying to sell some kind of motor to the gondoliers in Venice. It seems this guy had it all figured out how he would speed up traffic in the Grand Canal several hundred percent, and he had thought out a system of traffic control with red and green lights on the Rialto Bridge and at other strategic points. But the Venetians couldn't use it at all; they passed a law prohibiting that kind of motor anywhere in the city, and the poor man didn't make a single sale.

"Probably," I said, "he was a poor salesman. But I am different. And if you want to see a selling campaign handled right, you just want to stick around when I put on my magnificent tractor demonstration on the promenade deck. If you want to see names being signed on dotted lines, that will be your big chance."

"I'll believe it when it happens," he said.

"Wait and see," I said.

February 22, 1928.

Washington's Birthday, and a special dinner, with flags on the tables. The sea is getting smoother all the time. It won't be long now.

Sunday, March 4, 1928. 8 A. M.

Since the last entry in this letter we have had a most distressing time. On the evening of Washington's Birthday it started to get rough. The next day we were in the midst of a regular storm, which continued the rest of the way across the ocean, and even after we got into the Mediterranean. I never supposed a ship could heave and bang around the way this one did. The French passengers—and, in fact, almost everybody else—remained cooped up in their staterooms day and night. Part of the time even Gadget and I felt a bit wabbly. It has been impossible for me to do any business at all.

But today I believe that my great hour is at hand. Yesterday afternoon it began to clear up a little, the wind died down, and this morning is as fair and beautiful a day as I have ever seen. There is still a little ground swell, but not enough to do any harm. This is the first and only day of the entire voyage that the sea has been smooth enough to make possible a tractor demonstration. The Frenchmen are all up on deck looking at the beautiful blue sky and the beautiful blue water, and enjoying the balmy, warm spring breezes. We are due to land at Marseilles late this afternoon—one day late.

I wanted to start demonstrating the tractor first thing this morning, but the captain would not permit it. He quoted our arrangement, which provided that I should drive the tractor for two hours in the afternoon only, on such days as the weather permitted. I told him that, in view of the fact I had lost out on all afternoons except this one, I ought to be given a morning period, but he is a stubborn old cuss, and I couldn't make him see my point of view at all.

However, a short, snappy, intensive demonstration is often better than a series of dull, uninteresting and long-drawn-out ones, so I have the highest hopes of making a sensational impression. Gadget is already mingling with our charming French friends, and I will join her in a moment. The canvas cover has been taken off the tractor, and we will spend the rest of the morning letting these French people look at it and telling them its good points.

At noon the French delegation is giving a dinner for all the passengers. This dinner is dedicated to the honor and glory of French wines, and they are going to serve some of the excellent samples which they carried to America and which—fortunately for us—they were unable to get into the country. After the meal, I have arranged to show my talking moving picture of tractors in action, following which we will all assemble on deck, where I expect to astound them all by letting them see what a real tractor can do. Following the demonstration, Gadget and I will circulate through the crowd with order blanks so that the Frenchmen can put their names on the dotted lines. I have a feeling that you are going to be greatly pleased and surprised at the final installment of this letter, which I shall probably not have time to write until after we have landed.

Marseilles, Monday morning,
March 5th.

I have just been reading over the last few sentences which I wrote yesterday, and I hardly know how to begin my narrative of the events which took place on our last day aboard the good ship Beaucaire. You will, no doubt, be surprised when you hear what happened, but I fear you will not be as pleased as I had hoped you would be.

I am not pleased myself. As I sit here in this hotel room, weary and bruised in mind and body, my only pleasant thought is a sense of gratitude that dear old Gadget is here with me to cheer me up, and to change from time to time the bandage on my eye. This is the first time in my life that I ever had what might be called a real 100 percent black eye, and I find that it is as painful as it is disfiguring.

The events of yesterday were most complicated. The day started most auspiciously, as I wrote you, with beautiful weather, a smooth sea, and everybody feeling fine. Gadget and I spent the morning talking tractors to dozens of Frenchmen. They were all very polite and very much interested, although perhaps a trifle noncommittal.

At noon the French delegation gave their dinner, which was graced by copious samples of the finest of wines. Various members of the delegation made speeches expressing their friendship and high regard for the American people, and their hope that these splendid beverages would soon have free entry into the greatest and most glorious of all the countries of the earth. There was a tremendous amount of applause for these sentiments, and everybody seemed to be in a remarkably pleasant and friendly frame of mind.

Unfortunately, however, these high-grade French wines are so delicate, and slide down the esophagus so smoothly and easily, that persons who are used to our more corrosive American bootleg stuff fail to realize that there is a considerable amount of kick concealed in these gentle liquids. The French people, of course, knew exactly what they were doing, but I fear that some of our American friends may, perhaps, have been a little unwise.

As for myself, I drank only water, as I wanted a clear head and a steady hand for the demonstration which was to follow. After the banquet was concluded, I arose—according to the program which had been arranged—and announced that the curtains would be drawn over the portholes and the room darkened so that we could have the talking motion pictures of the great Earthworm tractor. I made a few remarks to the Frenchmen who could understand English, requesting them to translate the gist of what I had to say to those who were so unfortunate as to know only French. I told them what a wonderful machine I had, how admirably adapted it was to vineyard culture, and I laid great stress on its simplicity of operation.

"After the pictures," I said, "we will adjourn to the deck and I will show you what the tractor can do. And to prove to you how simple it is to operate, I will permit you to drive it around yourselves, if you so desire."

At this point, one of the American passengers arose and started to speak. He was a very large man with a florid face and red hair. I have since learned that his name is Mr. Tilton. He had been seasick and had stayed in his room practically all the way across, so I had never seen him before. At this time, however, he seemed to be full of life.

"I want to drive the tractor," he announced in a loud voice.

"Very well," I said. "Nothing would give me greater pleasure. As soon as the demonstration is under way, you may take your turn with these other gentlemen."

"I want to drive the tractor," said Mr. Tilton. "I want to drive it right away."

I noticed that the gentleman was swaying about a bit more than seemed justified by the very gentle motion of the boat, and I began to suspect that probably he had been indulging himself not wisely, but too well. Subsequent events showed that I was right in this surmise.

"I want to drive the tractor," he repeated. "I want to drive it right away."

"I am sorry," I said, "but we are going to see the moving pictures now. After that we will drive the tractor."

"I want to drive the tractor. I want to drive it right away. Listen," he went on. "I know all about those machines. I used to drive one of them when I was in the Army. And I just love those machines. They're wonderful—positively wonderful. It's ten long years since I've had a chance to drive one of them. And now that I have a chance, you won't let me do it. I am surprised at you."

"If you would only wait," I began, "until after the moving picture——"

"I'm surprised at you," he went on. "Here we are at this splendid banquet, given by our splendid French friends, where everything ought to be peace and good feeling and friendship—and what do you do? You come in and start an argument."

"But I didn't start an argument," I said.

"You're a liar," said Mr. Tilton. "You've been arguing with me here for five minutes. It's an outrage. I won't stand for it."

He brought his fist down on the table with a bang, and I noticed several stewards moving in his direction. As I did not want a painful scene, I walked over to him myself to try to quiet him.

"I want to drive the tractor," he said.

"Very well," I said. "Come with me." He followed me out of the dining saloon and up to the deck, where I prevailed upon him to sit down in a steamer chair. "You stay right here," I said, "and after the moving pictures I'll come back and we'll see what we can do about the tractor."

I then returned to the dining saloon and told the moving-picture operator to shoot. He did so, and I was immediately subjected to what I can only describe as a very painful surprise, caused by some very sloppy work at the New York office of the Earthworm Tractor

Company. When I got those moving pictures at the New York office, they told me they showed the Earthworm tractor performing a great variety of tasks—agricultural and otherwise—with a running explanation and sales talk in the French language. There were five reels, each in a large tin can, bearing the trademark of a well-known moving-picture company, and the label, "Earthworm Tractor Pictures. French." Naturally, I took these films in good faith, little dreaming that somewhere—probably at the motion-picture offices—someone had made a careless mistake and put in the wrong film.

You can imagine my astonishment when the picture opened with a loud burst of jazz music, and the title was flashed on the screen: "Red-Hot Tamales. A Rip Snorting Musical Spasm in Five Reels—All Talking, Dancing, Singing." Then, instead of an Earthworm tractor pulling a plow, there appeared a bevy of scantily clad young ladies stepping and kicking high, wide and handsome.

As fast as I could, I rushed around to the moving-picture booth and asked the operator what he thought he was doing. He protested that he was only running the pictures which I had given him, and this proved to be the case. Believe me, when I get back to the New York office I will tell those birds what I think of them. At once I stopped the show and explained to the people what had happened. Instead of being disappointed, however, they immediately set up a cry for the picture to go on. So, as I was most anxious not to offend anyone, I had to run the whole five reels. I think it was probably a pretty good show. The audience seemed to like it, but I was in no shape to enjoy the entertainment, and my annoyance was increased by Mr. Bowers, the pessimistic American, who sat down beside me and began telling me how all the American salesmen he had ever met were complete failures when it came to selling machinery to Europeans. He had a long sob story of a man that tried to sell electric refrigerators in Spain, and did no business at all. The Spaniards didn't even know what an old-fashioned ice refrigerator was. Another guy wore himself out trying to sell oil burners for furnaces to the Italians.

"And the Italians wouldn't even look at them," said Mr. Bowers. "They didn't even know what a furnace was; let alone a fancy oil burner."

"All of which," I said, "doesn't interest me in the slightest."

That shut him up for the time being. At last the moving picture came to an end, and I stood up and announced: "We will now go on deck for the big tractor demonstration."

As Gadget and I mounted the stairs, with the rest of the audience trooping along behind us, my heart beat high with hope. Although I was keenly disappointed that the moving pictures had contributed nothing to our tractor-selling campaign, I felt that we could make up for this lack as soon as we got the tractor in action. Little did I think, as I mounted the stairs, that the tractor was already in action.

My first intimation of disaster came when Gadget and I reached the door leading out onto the forward part of the promenade deck. This door was suddenly pulled open. There were loud shrieks of terror and dismay, and five or six elderly ladies came scrambling in. These ladies, we learned later, considered themselves rather old and feeble. They had not been feeling very well, so, instead of attending the banquet and moving-picture show, they had been resting in their steamer chairs. But when we saw them they were resting no more. As they came in that door they showed an amount of energy and agility that was positively remarkable.

I stuck my head out the door. I heard the roar of a motor. And looking toward the stern I was horrified to see my demonstration tractor approaching along the deck. In the driver's seat was Mr. Tilton, waving his hat with one hand and steering with the other. The gears were in high, the throttle was wide open, and the machine was coming at top speed. Naturally, I was much displeased to observe Mr. Tilton taking such liberties with my tractor, and I was particularly annoyed at the course he was steering.

I might explain that the promenade deck was very wide. On the inside next to the cabin was a long row of about a hundred steamer chairs, all of them at this time vacant. Between these chairs and the rail was an open space, plenty wide enough for the passage of the tractor. But, instead of following this obvious path, Mr. Tilton had seen fit to veer over next to the cabin wall, and he was clattering along at a fearful speed, right down the middle of the row of chairs. If I live to be a hundred years old I will never forget that sight, with its fearful accompaniment of sound effect—the roar of the motor and the steady, sickening crash of rending wood, as one steamer chair after another was crushed under the whirling tracks of the machine.

As Mr. Tilton approached the door, I drew my head safely inside, and as soon as he had passed, I rushed out and pursued him. Ordinarily, I could have caught him very quickly, but in this case I kept stumbling and tripping over the fragments of the steamer chairs. In fact, I did not draw even with him until he had reached the forward end of the deck, swung around under the bridge, and started down the deck on the other side of the boat.

"Stop!" I yelled, and reached out one hand to try to turn off the ignition.

"A-ha!" said Mr. Tilton. "So it's you, you big bum!" And with a mighty swing of his large and powerful right arm he brought his fist around and landed what was by far the heaviest jolt I have ever received. It got me right on my poor unprotected left eye. And that was the last I saw of Mr. Tilton and the tractor.

Apparently I was knocked out cold. And I must have stayed out for some time. When I finally woke up, I was in my stateroom and good old Gadget was taking care of me. And as she insisted that I keep quiet, I did not learn what had happened until after we were inside the port at Marseilles, and most of the passengers had left the boat.

Finally Gadget consented to tell me that Mr. Tilton had made three complete circuits of the boat, wrecking every chair on the promenade deck, before they had been able to grab him and haul him off the machine.

After this it had been impossible to get any of the Frenchmen to listen to reason. Gadget had bravely rushed around and talked and pleaded with them, thrusting order blanks under their noses, and working upon them as hard as she could. But they were all in such a state of excitement that it was impossible for any mere human—even so remarkable a human as Gadget—to make any impression on them. All they would do was wander about, looking at the pitiful fragments of the steamer chairs, and commenting upon what a dangerous thing an Earthworm tractor was.

"Look what that terrible machine did," they said.

At this some of the American ladies came to Gadget's defense.

"It was not the fault of the machine," they said. "It was the fault of your cursed wine. The man was drunk."

Upon hearing this, one of the Frenchmen said, "That is an insult to the fair name of France, and to her honorable grape growers. If the man was drunk, it is the fault of the American prohibition law, which made it impossible for him to learn how to drink like a gentleman."

Then another Frenchman, for no reason at all, stood up and said, "You Americans are all crazy anyway, and you absolutely ruin the stewards by tipping them too much."

These statements started a long, bitter and completely idiotic argument between and among practically all the passengers on the boat. Gadget, of course, tried to quiet things down, as she is familiar with the well-known business principle that you never make any sales while engaging in a fight. But she had no luck. Everybody was too excited. And finally all the Frenchmen left the boat without placing a single order.

"But never mind, Alec," said Gadget. "We may be licked for the moment, but as soon as we get going on shore we will show these foreigners what kind of stuff we are made of, and we will get some real results."

"In the words of the immortal John Paul Jones," I said, " 'we have only begun to fight!' And by the way, what happened to this guy Tilton?"

"That," said Gadget, "is the one bright spot in this whole mess."

"What do you mean?"

Gadget's answer shows that it is indeed a lucky thing I brought her along on this trip. "They took him down to his stateroom," she said, "and gave him a cold bath. He sobered up very quickly and came around and apologized to me most profusely. He really seems like a very nice man."

"When he is sober," I said.

"Yes. He had already settled with the captain for the damage he had done to the ship, and he offered to do anything he could for us to make up for the trouble he had caused. So I talked to him and found out that he is a big contractor from Omaha. I asked him if he could use any Earthworm tractors in his business, and he said he could. So I sold him three machines. One of them is the tractor he was driving this afternoon—he had offered to pay for that anyway—and the other two are sixty-horsepower machines, to be delivered to him in Omaha next June. Of course, this sale doesn't count for anything on the foreign business that we are trying to get. But after all, it is something."

"It certainly is," I said. "But what is this guy going to do with the tractor over here?"

"What tractor?"

"Why, the one he was driving this afternoon. Didn't you say he just bought it?"

"Yes, he bought it," said Gadget. "And he paid for it. But there isn't much he can do with it. You see, when they grabbed him and hauled him off the seat of the tractor, they didn't succeed in getting the motor stopped. The machine ran right down the deck all by itself, broke through the rail and dropped into the water. So in one way, I guess I have made something of a sales record. In all the history of the business I don't believe there is another case of anybody selling a tractor which was on the bottom of the Mediterranean Sea."

THE NEW MODEL

ALEXANDER BOTTS
EUROPEAN REPRESENTATIVE FOR THE
EARTH WORM TRACTOR

Grand Hotel Miramare & De La Ville.
Genoa, Italy, Wednesday, May 16, 1928.

Mr. Gilbert Henderson, Sales Manager,
Earthworm Tractor Company,
Earthworm City, Illinois.

Dear Henderson:

I have great news for you. I believe that I am about to open up a new and tremendously important field for the sale of Earthworm tractors. Since my arrival in Europe more than two months ago, I have, as you know, done pretty good work. I have sold an even dozen machines—a truly remarkable number, considering the difficulties which have confronted me. But all my previous achievements are about to pale into insignificance as compared to the tremendous proposition I am now undertaking.

It was last Monday morning that a gentleman called at the hotel, sent up a card bearing the name of Vladimir Krimsky, and asked to see me on important business. Gadget and I at once descended to the lobby, where we found a tall and very impressive gentleman awaiting us. He was about forty years old, smooth-shaven, and dressed in a neat and rather expensive-looking business suit.

"Pleased to meet you, Mr. Krimsky," I said. "I am Mr. Alexander Botts himself." I then presented Gadget. "This is Mrs. Botts," I said. "She speaks French, German and Italian. All you have to do is pick your language, and she will translate it so I can understand it."

"It is an honor to meet you, Mrs. Botts," he replied, with a low bow. "And you, too, Mr. Botts. I fancy we shall get along very well speaking English. I know it reasonably well."

"You sure do," I said. "You speak it swell."

"Thank you," he said.

"And what can I do for you today?" I asked.

"I wish to see you on a matter of business. I understand that you are the European representative for the Earthworm tractor."

"That is correct," I said.

"I am the representative," he said, "of the Ukrainian Cooperative Society, which handles most of the buying and selling for the farmers in Ukrainia."

"Where is that?" I asked.

"It is in southern Russia. I have been sent here to Italy by the Soviet Government to handle any business which my cooperative society may have in this region."

"Well, well," I said, "are you one of these Bolsheviks that I have been hearing about?"

"I am a member in good standing of the Communist Party," he said, smiling pleasantly.

[Note: I will have to admit that this surprised me a good deal. I had always supposed that Bolsheviks and communists were strange, uncouth creatures with bushy whiskers, who went about throwing bombs in all directions. This bozo was, as I have said, very well dressed; he had no whiskers at all, he seemed perfectly harmless, and his manner was polished and suave. It was, therefore, something of a jolt to hear him calmly tell me he was a communist. However, as I am naturally polite, I did not kid him about it.]

"You say you are interested in tractors?" I asked.

"I am," he said. "I was in Venice some weeks ago, and happened to observe a machine at work clearing up the ruins of a large tower which had recently fallen down. This machine was doing the work so much more easily and quickly than any other tractor I had ever seen that I interviewed the owner."

"Whose name," I interrupted, "was Luigi Bontade. Yes, Mr. Krimsky, I sold that tractor to Luigi myself—with a little help from my wife here. What did he have to say about it?"

"He said that I was correct in thinking it was a very superior tractor. He told me that it was called the Earthworm, and that it came from America. He gave me your name and address, and said that you were the European representative of the company that makes it."

[Note: As you see, all this new business is sprouting directly from that sale in Venice. I don't want to rub it in too much, but I cannot help delicately reminding you that not so long ago you wrote me a letter bawling me out for spending so much time in Venice, "because," as you said, "it is obviously such a poor market for tractors that any sale in Venice can never help build up future business." Well, all I can say is that my native sense of courtesy prevents me telling you what I think of your opinion.]

I assured Mr. Krimsky that I was indeed the European representative of the great Earthworm Tractor Company. "If you want to buy any of our machines," I said, "I am the guy that will sell them to you."

"Very good," he replied. "I have authority from my superiors to offer you a most favorable proposition. I want you to come with me to Ukrainia with one or two tractors and demonstrate them in our farming villages. If they prove satisfactory, they will be bought by the local branches of the Ukrainian Cooperative Society, and orders will probably be placed for several more. If they are not satisfactory, you will lose nothing, as I am authorized to pay all your expenses, coming and going."

"That sounds fair enough," I said. "Do you really think there is any market for tractors in Russia?"

"I know there is. Russia is a tremendous country, with a tremendous population. There are enormous tracts of fabulously rich farm lands which are capable of raising more grain than all the rest of the world put together. All we need is modern methods and modern mâchinery. If your tractors prove to be as good as I think they are, it is possible that before the end of the year our society may buy several hundred of them."

"Pardon me," I said. "Did you actually say several hundred?"

"I did," said Mr. Krimsky. "But that is only a beginning. These few hundred machines would be merely for some of the Ukrainian peasants on individual farms who wish to make group purchases of farm machinery through our society. But when the collectives get going we will begin to do some real heavy business."

"Collectives?"

"Yes," said Mr. Krimsky. "Within a year or two the Soviet Government—which is the most progressive government on earth—will have all the land organized into large collective farms operating on a quantity-production basis. These collectives will all be controlled by a single administrative head, and will form the most stupendous, most efficient and most beneficent agricultural system ever known to man. When this scheme gets started we shall need thousands of tractors—yes, tens of thousands."

"You don't know how you interest me," I said. "You seem to have a reasonably large proposition here, and as long as you want to let me in on the ground floor, I will accept your offer. Business in Italy is at the moment a bit dull, so there is no reason why my wife and I can't both go."

"I am delighted to hear you say so."

"We will take along a new and much improved thirty-horsepower Earthworm which, by great good luck, has just arrived from America. We will also take one of the old-model sixty-horsepower machines. And we will take a plow. When do we start?"

Mr. Krimsky suggested that we embark on the Santa Lucia, an Italian freight boat, which leaves next Saturday for Odessa. Gadget and I said we were willing, and it was so arranged. Mr. Krimsky gave us credit references and explained to us various details, such as passport and visa requirements, and so on. Then he bade us a very courteous good morning and told us he would see us on the boat.

We are leaving Marco Manzione, the young Italian whom we recently hired as a salesman, to look after any business that may come up here in Italy. And on Saturday we are sailing for the fabled land of the Muscovites in high hopes of accomplishing new and dazzling feats of large-scale selling.

As ever, your vigorous and efficient salesman,
Alexander Botts.

ALEXANDER BOTTS
EUROPEAN REPRESENTATIVE FOR THE
EARTHWORM TRACTOR

On Board Steamship Santa Lucia,
Sunday, June 3, 1928.
Fifteen Days Out From Genoa.

Mr. Gilbert Henderson,
Earthworm Tractor Company,
Earthworm City, Illinois.

Dear Henderson:

We are due in Odessa tomorrow morning. It has been a long, slow voyage, but I can assure you that Gadget and I have not been wasting our time. We have, in fact, been improving each and every shining hour by feeding Mr. Krimsky large doses of sales talk on the subject of the Earthworm tractor; laying particular stress on the advantages of the new thirty-horsepower model. Mr. Krimsky—although a highly intelligent man—is a red-hot Bolshevik, and whenever we start talking tractors, he tries to twist the conversation to the subject of communism, so that he can give us an inspirational sermon on what a good thing it is.

Why he should want to talk about mere political affairs when he can listen to us discussing tractors, I don't know. But that seems to be the way he is.

Only this morning I had occasion to refer to the fact that our new thirty-horsepower model is a real masterpiece of engineering art. "Every useless part is eliminated," I said. "Every needed part is so placed and so coordinated with every other part that it can work to greatest advantage. As a result of all this, the new model is probably the world's finest example of harmony of design."

"An even finer example," interrupted Mr. Krimsky, "is the communist state. We have eliminated all useless and parasitic elements, such as the predatory bourgeois classes who wrongfully exploit the labor of others. And we are organizing the industrial and agricultural life of the country into a single rationalized system, which is destined soon to lead the world in efficient production."

"Did we tell you about our new gasoline tank?" asked Gadget. "It is set in such a position on the machine that we get rid of all troublesome elements, such as——"

"Speaking of troublesome elements," said Mr. Krimsky, "Lenin has well said that religion is the opium of the people. Now, in the communist state——"

"However," continued Gadget, "we have not stopped with eliminating useless parts. In our new-model Earthworm we have greatly improved the remaining necessary parts. Wait till you see our latest-type precision-movement super-delicate steering mechanism. One touch from a baby's hand, and the entire machine—weighing more than five tons—turns around in a space no larger than a silver ten-kopeck piece."

"Another good point," I continued, "is the new system of velvet-grip brakes." And I then proceeded to give him a highly interesting and instructive half-hour lecture on the advantages of this feature of the new model.

From the above you can get an idea of what has been going on throughout this entire voyage. Mr. Krimsky is constantly attempting to discuss his favorite topic of communism. But Gadget and I, working as a team, have always been able to overwhelm him with an irresistible flood of tractor sales talk. We have got him so saturated with our ideas that after we have made our demonstration he will just automatically start urging his associates to buy as many tractors as they possibly can.

I have high hopes for the future.

Yours,
Alexander Botts.

ALEXANDER BOTTS
EUROPEAN REPRESENTATIVE FOR THE
EARTHWORM TRACTOR

Hotel Londonskaya, Odessa, U.S.S.R.
Monday, June 4, 1928.

Dear Henderson:

Early this morning we landed at Odessa, which is a beautiful town on a high bluff, overlooking the sea. It has wide, well-paved streets, handsome buildings and a very fine harbor, with stone and concrete piers. There are many grain elevators and big oil tanks. The railroad tracks here run right out onto the piers, just as they do at Genoa and other European ports. Mr. Krimsky explained that this makes the handling of freight very easy, and is a great improvement over the medieval methods still used on many of the piers at New York.

We got the two tractors unloaded very promptly, and we have put in a busy and exciting day. Mr. Krimsky had, of course, notified his friends that we were coming, and it had been arranged that the new-model thirty-horsepower tractor was to be shipped this evening to an outlying village called Usk, where we are to put on a demonstration.

As this plan left us the day unoccupied, and as I am always eager to advertise the Earthworm tractor, I decided to inaugurate a combination parade and demonstration for the benefit of the citizens of Odessa. Unfortunately, this demonstration was not a complete success, but I will give you a brief account of it, so you can see that I did everything all right, and that the trouble we ran into was in no way my fault. In fact, my skillful driving was the only thing that prevented a holocaust.

As usual, I made my plans with the greatest skill and forethought. And I executed them with all my usual energy and efficiency. As soon as we had attended to the formalities at the port and had our passports and papers properly fixed up, Gadget, with the baggage, took an automobile to the hotel. Mr. Krimsky and I grabbed a venerable horse-drawn cab and speeded up to a hardware store on the Uliza Lenina, where we bought a large can of high-gloss, quick-drying, red enamel. Then we shopped around and got a number of banners and pictures, threw them all into the cab, and raced back to the port. Here, for a few kopecks, I was able to hire a number of dock laborers to repaint the new model. By the end of the morning the work was completed, and the tractor was indeed a remarkable thing to look at. Never have I seen such a swell paint job. The entire machine fairly glowed a rich warm crimson. This color, of course, was intended as a delicate compliment to the Soviet Government.

As soon as the paint was dry, I fastened on the banners and other paraphernalia. On top of the radiator I had a large red flag. At the rear I had a beautiful banner with a lot of Russian letters on it meaning, "Long Live the Revolution." On the side of the machine I put a number of smaller red flags and banners of various kinds. And as the crowning artistic touch I affixed two large colored pictures of Lenin and Karl Marx, who seem to be the chief patron saints of the country. As Karl Marx had by far the best-looking whiskers, I gave him the place of honor up in front. By the time I had finished the decorating, Gadget had returned from the hotel. She was, naturally, delighted with what I had done, and we at once asked Mr. Krimsky to take a ride with us.

"We are going to drive all over town," I said, "and let these bozos see what a real tractor looks like."

At first he was a little doubtful as to whether it would be legal for us to have a parade without securing a permit from the police, but I finally persuaded him that one tractor wasn't a parade and it ought to be just as lawful as three people riding in an automobile. He finally agreed; we all three climbed up into the broad and handsomely cushioned seat and I gave her the gas. With a splendid roaring and clanking I drove over the granite pavement of the pier, and then continued along the waterfront and past the coal port, looking for a street to take me up the hill into the town.

Almost at once, however, I discovered something far better than a street. Directly in front of me I was delighted to observe a most magnificent flight of steps. These steps are broad and beautiful. They are made of stone; there must be several hundred of them; and they lead straight up the bluff to the town.

"This is a historic spot," said Mr. Krimsky. "During the evil reign of the Czar a company of soldiers fired from those steps into a crowd of rebellious citizens. It was a terrible massacre."

"That is most interesting," I replied, "because the place is about to be the scene of another historic event—the first Russian demonstration of the climbing abilities of the great Earthworm tractor."

"What are you going to do?"

"I am going to give the people of Odessa a show," I said, "and I'm going to give them a good one."

I drove to the bottom of the steps. I shifted into low. I started up.

"Stop!" yelled Mr. Krimsky. "You can't do this!"

"Sure I can!" I yelled back. And I kept on.

It was a rough ride, but the tractor rolled along up powerfully and surely, and I would have made it easily if it had not been for two very unfortunate occurrences. The first of these was the sudden appearance of a half dozen gentlemen in uniform. Apparently they were policemen. They stood at the top of the steps, directly in my path, and held up their hands as a signal for me to stop. I couldn't go on without running over them. So I threw out the clutch, pulled on the brake and shifted the gears into neutral.

And then came the second unfortunate occurrence. The new-fangled velvet-grip brakes refused to hold, and we started rolling backward. Mr. Krimsky let out an ear-shattering screech and leaped from the machine. Gadget let out an even louder yell, but stuck by me. And I would have made more noise than both of them, except that I was too busy. I pulled and heaved at the gear-shift lever, but the gears were already spinning so fast that I couldn't get them meshed. Faster and faster we rolled. The emergency brake seemed to be doing no good at all, but, by bearing down with all my strength on the two foot brakes, I found I could slow up our progress a little and do a certain amount of steering. Looking back over my shoulder, I could see the port, apparently very far away, and at a dizzy distance beneath me. A large crowd, which had gathered very rapidly at the bottom of the steps, was now dispersing even more rapidly. And it was just as well, or the famous steps of Odessa might have been the scene of another massacre. As it was, I almost hit a dozen or more fleeing pedestrians and came within inches of demolishing three dogs and a baby carriage. Down, down we went, for what seemed like hours, although I don't suppose it was really more than thirty seconds. At last we reached the bottom, rolled out over the flat pavement for a short distance, and came to a stop.

Fortunately, nobody was hurt, and, fortunately, the tractor was all right. The motor was still running, so I started back for the pier. But I was soon blocked by the crowd which had gathered. I stopped. Mr. Krimsky came running down the steps and climbed aboard just as another lot of policemen accosted us. They seemed very angry indeed, but Mr. Krimsky talked to them most effectively and showed them his official papers. They finally stepped back and shooed the crowd away from in front of us, and I was able to continue to the pier.

Here Mr. Krimsky bawled me out good and plenty for attempting to go up the steps. And for once in my life I was pretty near speechless. I couldn't say anything except to admit that the tractor was at fault.

"These improved brakes," I said, "are the finest in the world. But they are so new that apparently the boys at the factory don't understand them yet. They left them too loose. But I will readjust them right away, and we will never have an accident like this again."

"I am sure of one thing," said Mr. Krimsky, still somewhat sore; "you won't have any more accidents on those steps. If I ever see you driving in that direction again, I'll knock you over the head with one of your own big track wrenches."

"And I wouldn't blame you," I said.

At once I got busy and tightened up the brakes, after which I loaded the tractor and the plow onto a freight car. They will go out tonight, and Gadget, Mr. Krimsky and I will follow on the passenger train tomorrow morning. And by tomorrow afternoon we hope to be starting our great demonstration in the little village of Usk, which is on the banks of the River Bug, about a hundred and fifty versts—a hundred miles—northeast of here.

In conclusion, I wish to ask you to present my compliments to the final inspection department at the plant, and tell them that they are a disgrace to a respectable company. If they let any more machines come through without adjusting the brakes, I will go out there when I get home and fix them so their necks will need adjusting.

Yours,
Alexander Botts.

ALEXANDER BOTTS
EUROPEAN REPRESENTATIVE FOR THE
EARTHWORM TRACTOR

Usk, Ukrainia, U.S.S.R.
7 p.m., June 5, 1928.

Dear Henderson:

Here we are, and everything is going fine. We have had a few minor accidents and mishaps, but nothing serious enough to interfere with our great selling compaign.

Gadget and I and Mr. Krimsky took the train out of Odessa this morning. The railroads here seem very good, in spite of the fact that the rails are clumsily spaced considerably farther apart than in America. We reached Usk about noon and found that the tractor had already arrived, or rather part of it had. Somewhere on the way somebody had stolen the carburetor and the magneto. Naturally, this made me very sore, particularly as Mr. Krimsky had been lecturing us most of the morning on the splendid loyalty of all the people to the Soviet Government. According to him, all the working class was doing everything possible to cooperate with the government in its efforts to improve the industry and agriculture of the country.

"It seems to me," I said, "that there is at least one guy in this country that has an awful funny idea of cooperation. He certainly has helped us a lot by swiping our carburetor and magneto."

"This is indeed most regrettable," said Mr. Krimsky, "but, of course, the crime could not have been committed by one of the working class. It was probably done by a former member of the so-called upper or middle classes as an expression of his counterrevolutionary bourgeois ideology."

"Oh, I see," I said. "That makes it all right, I suppose."

At this moment a couple of railroad officials arrived, leading a huge lout of a peasant who had a face like a chimpanzee. I was interested to observe that this uncouth creature was carrying in his hairy paws the missing magneto and carburetor. At once there was a long argument in Russian, or Ukrainian, or something—which, of course, neither Gadget nor I understood—and then Mr. Krimsky explained the matter to us.

It appeared that the strange-looking missing link who had taken our stuff was a good communist by the name of Ivan Tschukovsky. His act was due not to any counterrevolutionary bourgeois ideology but rather to a mistaken attempt to assist the Soviet Government in making a success of National Junk Week.

"And what," I asked, "is National Junk Week?"

"The government," explained Mr. Krimsky, "in order to promote the well-being of the nation, has designated certain weeks which are to be devoted to concentrated efforts on behalf of various worthy activities. We have had National Defense Week, National Health Week, and many others."

"Yes, yes," I said. "We have them in America. We have Be Kind to Animals Week, Eat More Cheese Week, and I don't know what all. It is a wonderful idea."

"It is, indeed," said Mr. Krimsky. "And it happens that this is National Junk Week, which is to be devoted to the prevention of waste all over the Soviet Union. All good citizens are urged to gather up and bring in to designated depots all junk which would otherwise go to waste, such as scrap iron, old brass, rags, bottles, and so on."

"And Comrade Tschukovsky," I said, "like the good communist

he is, was trying to perform his daily good deed by converting my perfectly good tractor into junk?"

"Apparently that was it," said Mr. Krimsky. "He made a mistake. But he meant well, so everything is all right."

"Yes," I said, "but I hope there won't be too many of these errors."

As Comrade Tschukovsky shuffled away, I put the stuff back on the tractor. I unloaded the machine and the plow, and then we all climbed into the seat and drove down the main street of the village. Gadget and I were both much surprised at how primitive the place was. The village consisted of perhaps a hundred little shacks built of logs—something like the old American frontier log cabins. The roofs were straw. The main street was unpaved, and dry and dusty under the hot sun. It was very different from a French or Italian village; the only point of similarity being the pigs and chickens.

The entire population turned out to watch us as we went by. They appeared strong and healthy and very friendly, but a bit poverty-stricken.

"I thought you told me," I remarked to Mr. Krimsky, "that your new communistic system was going to make everybody rich. I don't see much evidence of it here."

"Give us time," he replied. "In another ten years you won't know this place."

I drove on. Near the end of the street Mr. Krimsky made some inquiries, and we finally stopped in front of the house of a man called Chipkoff, who was to be our host and who was to be taught how to drive the tractor.

I could see right away that Comrade Chipkoff was a regular guy, and that he and I were going to get along. Of course he couldn't speak English, but he had an intelligent face and I liked his looks.

We followed him into the house. It had three rooms—instead of just one, as in most of the other houses of the village—and it was all scrubbed up clean, and very neat. There was a new wooden floor in the main room, and a big stove made out of bricks. There were good-looking copper cooking utensils hanging around, and in one corner I saw an American sewing machine. Comrade Chipkoff introduced us to his wife and two children. They were a fine-looking family.

Mrs. Chipkoff set out a meal for us—simple and plain, but very good—and afterward I gave the good comrade a driving lesson. Mr. Krimsky went along as interpreter, and we made splendid progress. My pupil had never before seen a tractor, but he had such a quick mind that he learned with great rapidity, and I am going to let him drive in the big plowing demonstration which I plan to put on tomorrow morning.

If one of their own people drives the tractor, I think it will make a better impression upon the inhabitants of the village. And it is the inhabitants—practically all of whom belong to the local branch of the cooperative society—who will have to vote on whether they want to buy the machine or not.

As I was saying, Comrade Chipkoff showed up very well. Unfortunately, however, the tractor did not, and we had a slight accident. As we were driving around a small pasture lot on the outskirts of the village, I was suddenly startled to see the motor burst into flames. Comrade Chipkoff, who was driving, at once stopped the machine. We leaped to the ground and began throwing handfuls of dirt onto the fire, and we managed to extinguish it before it did any damage.

Examination showed that the newly designed gasoline tank had been resting on the newly designed support bracket in such a way that the natural vibration of the motor had caused said bracket to wear a small hole in said tank. The gasoline had poured out, and had in some way caught fire, probably from the hot exhaust manifold.

Fortunately, there was very little fuel in the tank at the time, so the fire was small. And the only repair work needed was the temporary plugging of the leak with cotton and shellac. But you can understand that I was greatly annoyed at having to apologize to Mr. Krimsky, and to explain all over again that this was a new model and there were a few things that were not yet quite adjusted.

[*Note:* I would respectfully suggest that you ask the engineering department why in the name of heaven, after all these years of building tractors, they have no more sense than to design a new model with a gasoline tank placed in such a way that it cannot help wearing a hole in itself.]

One good thing about this accident was that it demonstrated Comrade Chipkoff's presence of mind and efficiency in emergency. I have every reason to believe that he will acquit himself nobly in our great plowing demonstration tomorrow.

It is now after supper. In a few minutes we are going down to a big village meeting at the communist clubhouse. An official from Moscow will be present to tell the people about the plans of the Soviet Government for agricultural improvement, and Mr. Krimsky will explain to them all about the tractor. After the meeting, we will have a good night's rest, and bright and early tomorrow morning we will show them what we can do.

Yours,
Alexander Botts.

THE NEW MODEL

ALEXANDER BOTTS
EUROPEAN REPRESENTATIVE FOR THE
EARTHWORM TRACTOR

Odessa, Ukrainia, U.S.S.R.
Wednesday, June 6, 1928.

Mr. Gilbert Henderson,
Earthworm Tractor Company,
Earthworm City, Illinois.

Dear Henderson:

It is with a feeling of deep despondency that I write this report. Our entire demonstration—mentally, morally, physically and mechanically—has gone completely haywire. It is hard for me to decide whether I am more disgusted with the absurd proceedings of the Soviet Government or with the pathetic performance of our boasted new-model thirty-horsepower Earthworm tractor. Both of them, to my way of thinking, are completely lousy.

The trouble began at the village meeting last night. Gadget and I, of course, could not understand any of the talk, but we could see that there was a very hot discussion going on. At the end of the meeting, Mr. Krimsky told us what it was all about. It appeared that the visiting Bolshevik from Moscow, with the support of a certain element in the town, had introduced, and finally carried, a resolution to expel our good friend Comrade Chipkoff from the local branch of the cooperative association. This was done on the ground that he was a *kulak*.

"And what," I asked, "is a *kulak*?"

"He is a man," explained Mr. Krimsky, "who violates the fundamental principles of communism by exploiting the labor of others for his own selfish gain."

"A sort of a grafter or profiteer?"

"Exactly. A *kulak* is a dishonest man."

"But Comrade Chipkoff seems to be such a good egg," I said. "I can't believe that he is really dishonest."

"I am sorry to say that he is. It was pretty definitely proved that he has been hiring laborers to help him with his farm work, by which he has made a selfish profit."

"You mean he didn't pay his hired help?"

"Oh, yes, he paid them very good wages. His crime was due to the fact that he made a profit for himself."

"But that isn't any crime at all back home," I said.

"Well, it is here," said Mr. Krimsky, "so poor old Chipkoff has been expelled from the association, and he is no longer eligible to drive the tractor. They have elected another man for this job."

"I suppose there is nothing we can do about it," I said, "but it certainly is a shame. Comrade Chipkoff has the makings of a swell tractor operator. What sort of a lad is our new candidate?"

"He is a *byedniak*."

"What kind of an animal is that?"

"It is not an animal. A *byedniak* is one of the poorer class of peasants. And the particular *byedniak* who has been chosen to drive the tractor happens to be Comrade Ivan Tschukovsky."

"Not that half-witted orangutan that stole the carburetor?"

"It was Comrade Tschukovsky that removed the carburetor," admitted Mr. Krimsky. "But it appears that he is a very good communist, and has a great deal of influence with the other *byedniaks*, and also with the *seredniaks*."

"Pardon me?"

"A *seredniak* is one of the middle class of peasants."

"You certainly have all these bozos ticketed," I said. "But this whole proceeding sounds awfully funny to me. I very much doubt if we want this Comrade Tschukovsky for an operator."

"He is just the man for us," said Mr. Krimsky. "He has been very active against the *kulaks*, and he has brought so many malefactors to justice that they have given him the name of Ivan the Terrible. He is very popular with the majority of the villagers—particularly, of course, the poorer elements. He has great influence. He can be of great assistance to us in making a sale."

"Then I suppose we shall have to use him," I said. "But I still have my doubts. He may have influence, and he may be a rip-snorting *kulak* bouncer, but that does not mean he would be so hot as a tractor driver."

"Didn't you tell me that this new model was so simple to drive that a mere child could handle it?"

"I guess you win," I said. "I believe I did say that. We will consider the matter settled. And now let's go back and get some sleep."

"All right," said Mr. Krimsky. "And that reminds me—we can't spend the night with Comrade Chipkoff after all."

"Why not?"

"He is now in disgrace, and it would be very unwise for us to associate with him. I have arranged for us to stay with Comrade Ivan Tschukovsky."

"O.K.," I said. "Let's go."

We got our suitcases from the Chipkoff house and took them over to our new residence. And here Gadget and I got the big shock of the evening. Ivan's house was even more terrible than he was. It was a one-room log shack with a dirt floor and a tremendous brick stove, the top of which was used as a bed by Ivan, his wife and four children. They assigned us a pile of straw in one corner. In another corner was a small pig—fortunately, penned in by some old planks—and there were about a dozen hens which roosted on the table and on two rough wooden benches. We tried to be good sports, and settled ourselves on the straw, without, of course, removing any of our clothes. But before long we were attacked by a small army of some sort of minute creeping fauna. So Gadget and I promptly moved outside. And soon afterward Mr. Krimsky followed. Luckily, it was a warm night and we managed to get a small amount of sleep.

At the first crack of dawn, we got hold of old Ivan the Terrible and started to give him a lesson in driving the tractor. And from then on, our troubles increased very rapidly. Although Mr. Krimsky, acting as interpreter, explained everything to him with the greatest care, the poor thick-witted baboon did not seem able to grasp even the first principles. After an hour's work he seemed to know even less than when he started. Accordingly, we adjourned for breakfast, and after a miserable meal served by Ivan's greasy wife, we discovered that all the villagers had assembled and it was time to put on the great plowing demonstration. They had chosen a field to the east of town, on the edge of the cliffs overlooking the River Bug.

I decided to start things off myself. I climbed into the driver's seat and had Comrade Ivan Tschukovsky sit beside me. I hooked onto the big gang plow and drove out to the field, followed by several hundred of the villagers. I then struck a back furrow from the side of the field nearest the village clear over to the edge of the bluff, leaving only a narrow headland to be plowed later.

As long as I drove the machine myself, everything went beautifully, and for a few brief minutes I had a feeling that all would be well. The soil was a wonderful, rich, black loam which turned over so easily that I was able to pull the entire six bottoms, set right down to a depth of fourteen inches. The motor roared, the machine rolled smoothly back and forth over the field, and I could see that the villagers were gazing at my performance with the deepest admiration and awe.

After four or five rounds, I stopped and consulted with Mr. Krimsky and Gadget, and Mr. Krimsky said it was now time to let old Ivan have a chance at the controls. I had him take the driver's seat and I sat beside him. We started off. We followed the last furrow which I had made across the field, and at first we got along fairly well. But when we reached the far end, I was startled to observe that Ivan made no effort either to stop the machine or to turn it around. The stupid brute merely sat perfectly still with his tremendous hands tightly grasping the steering wheel.

"It is time to turn!" I yelled.

Ivan did nothing.

"Turn it around!" I yelled.

Still Ivan did nothing. I grabbed the wheel myself, but Ivan was such a powerful creature, and he was holding it so rigidly, that I could not do a thing. And all this time we were rapidly approaching the edge of the bluff which overlooked the Bug River.

"You poor sap!" I yelled. "Turn that wheel!"

At last the huge gorilla seemed to get the idea. He gave one terrific heave with his massive arms. And the wheel, the steering post, and the entire precision-movement, super-delicate steering mechanism came out by the roots. Ivan twisted the fragments hither and thither in a vain effort to steer. But it was no use; everything was completely disconnected. And the tractor was almost at the edge of the bluff. I reached over and cut off the ignition. With my other hand, I jammed on the emergency brake, which I had readjusted so that it took hold all right. The machine stopped on the very brink of the bluff, with the front end of it hanging out in space.

For a moment, I thought we were safe, but I was mistaken. I suddenly felt that the edge of the bluff was beginning to crumble beneath the weight of the tractor. Apparently Ivan had enough sense to know what was going on. With a clumsy apelike bound, he jumped out of one side, while I leaped gracefully out the other. And the next instant my beautiful new-model thirty-horsepower Earthworm, with all its artistic red paint and everything, disappeared.

I stuck my head over the edge and looked down. I saw the great machine rolling and bounding across the sloping ground at the foot of the almost perpendicular cliff. Finally it came to rest on the level bottom land, a couple of hundred feet below me. And then, for the second time in two days, it burst into flames. This time there was no chance to throw on dirt. And there was a full tank of fifty gallons of gasoline. Obviously there was nothing to do but let it burn. The poor machine was such a complete wreck that I didn't even take the trouble to climb down the cliff to look at it.

The villagers all came rushing up in a high state of excitement, but I paid no attention to them. All at once I got mad. My disposition had not been improved by the uncomfortable night I had spent, and this disaster was more than I could stand. I walked right up to Mr. Krimsky and told him exactly what I thought of him and of the

Soviet Government. After a certain amount of more or less general derogatory remarks, which I will not repeat, I ended up as follows:

"This is all the fault of your silly communistic theories. You want to throw out all the good, intelligent, efficient farmers like Comrade Chipkoff, and you insist on turning over the important jobs to mental defectives like this Ivan the Terrible. I should think when you are getting up a new system of government you'd get up one that has some sense to it."

About this time Mr. Krimsky himself began to get a little sore. "You are all wrong," he said. "It was not Ivan's fault; he tried to turn the machine around. The trouble is all with your boasted super-delicate steering mechanism. 'One touch from a baby's hand and the whole machine turns around.' Indeed! One touch from anybody else's hand and it comes to pieces. I should think that when you people build a new model you would get out one that had some sense to it."

[*Note:* I will have to admit that there was a little justice in what Mr. Krimsky said. I would suggest that you tell the engineering department that there is such a thing as making a tractor a little too super-delicate. But, of course, I wouldn't admit anything like that to Mr. Krimsky.]

"I do not care to argue with you," I said in a very loud voice, while all the villagers gathered around. "I only want to tell you that your whole Bolshevik system of government here is rotten, and it would be better for the country if you had some sort of a Czar back again who would run the country properly."

"You had better be careful," snarled Mr. Krimsky. "There may be agents of the Gay-Pay-Oo in this crowd, and some of them may understand English."

"And what," I asked, "is the Gay-Pay-Oo?"

"It is the secret police who are charged with suppressing just such counterrevolutionary sentiments as you have expressed. It may interest you to know that they would have the power to send you to Siberia, or to the dreadful prison on Solovyetzky Island."

"I care not that," I replied, snapping my fingers with a magnificent gesture, "for your old Google-Goo-Gay, or whatever it is. I only hope they are here and can understand what I say. My wife and I are completely through with you and your so-called government. We are going back to Odessa at once, and from there we are sailing on the first boat to sunny Italy. Good-bye."

I took Gadget by the arm and we marched back to the village and down to the railroad station. Fortunately, there was a train for Odessa in just a few minutes, and we got aboard. I noticed that Mr.

Krimsky got on the same train, but he had sense enough to ride in another car. The trip to Odessa was uneventful, except for the fact that my angry passions began to subside.

As you know, I am naturally of a pleasant, friendly disposition, and I do not stay mad at anybody for very long. Consequently, by the time we reached Odessa I had regained my usual poise and had decided that, after all, there is no sense in nourishing grudges against people—particularly people like Mr. Krimsky, who is, at bottom, a fairly decent chap.

Apparently Mr. Krimsky had the same idea. Gadget and I met him on the station platform and we all shook hands most cordially and apologized for our lack of courtesy earlier in the afternoon. Mr. Krimsky suggested that we might still be able to do business together. I agreed. And sometime later in the week we are going to put on a demonstration with the old-model sixty-horsepower tractor. In a future report I will let you know how we come out.

As we started for the hotel, Mr. Krimsky said: "I have the greatest admiration for you tractor people and for the way you are developing a new model with so many novel and improved ideas. You are public benefactors. Keep up the good work. But, whatever you do, don't try to sell me your new model until you have it working a lot better than it is now."

"Well spoken," I said. "And my sentiments toward you are exactly the same."

"How so?"

"I have the greatest admiration," I said, "for you Bolsheviks and for the way you are developing a new system of government with so many novel and improved ideas. You are public benefactors. Keep up the good work. But, whatever you do, don't try to sell me your new ideas until you have them working a whole lot better than they are now."

"That also was well spoken," said Mr. Krimsky.

"Of course it was," I replied. "And before I wish you good evening I have one more message. I want to present you with the remains of that poor old tractor out there on the banks of the River Bug. I hope you will accept it, with the compliments of the Earthworm Tractor Company, as our contribution to National Junk Week."

And that is all at present from your hard-working salesman,

Alexander Botts.

THE PEACEMAKER

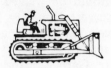

ALEXANDER BOTTS
SALES PROMOTION REPRESENTATIVE
EARTHWORM TRACTOR COMPANY

Hanging Garden Hotel, Babylon, Missouri.
Thursday evening, July 28, 1932.

Mr. Gilbert Henderson,
Sales Manager,
Earthworm Tractor Company,
Earthworm City, Illinois.

Dear Henderson:

I arrived here this afternoon, called at once on our local dealer, Mr. Ben Garber, and ran into such an unfortunate situation that I have decided to stick around several days, if necessary, to straighten it out. I know that ordinarily you don't want me to spend that much time on a small dealer. But this is a special case—as you will realize when I give you the melancholy facts as set forth by Mr. Garber.

"Last spring," he told me, "I had a swell prospect by the name of Peabody, and another by the name of Snodgrass—both of them wheat farmers who actually had plenty of money. I was just on the point of selling each one of these men an Earthworm tractor and an Earthworm combined harvester. And then the Earthworm Tractor Company butted in and gummed the whole deal."

"How?" I asked.

"By sending out an idiotic pamphlet called *Partnership Buying*. This pamphlet says that in many cases it is foolish for a farmer to buy a whole tractor all for himself—expecially if he doesn't have enough work to keep it busy all the time. It says the thing to do is to have a group of farmers buy one machine in partnership. And it also says that when a tractor is sold to grain growers of established credit, the usual down payment should be waived and no money at all demanded until after the harvest. Honestly, Mr. Botts, I never saw such a bunch of hogwash. Have you read this pamphlet?"

"Yes," I said, "I have read it."

"Well," continued Mr. Garber bitterly, "Mr. Peabody and Mr. Snodgrass—my two prospects—read it too. It was sent out to the whole mailing list. And right away they fell for the idea. I told them it would never work. I told them they could never agree on which one of them would use the machine when, or who would pay for how much of what repairs. But they wouldn't listen."

"So you sold them a machine in partnership?"

"I had to, or else lose the sale entirely. They combined with a third wheat grower—a widow woman called Hopkins—and bought one outfit consisting of a tractor and harvester. Terms: Nothing down, and the rest after the harvest—if I can get it, which I probably can't."

"Why can't you?" I asked.

"Because they are all fighting like cats and dogs. Everything has gone wrong. Two of the owners—Snodgrass and Mrs. Hopkins—have already used the machine for harrowing and cultivating. It is now in my shop here being tuned up for the harvest. The wheat will be ready to cut next week. If it isn't cut on time, part of it may be lost—it's apt to fall down, or dry out and shatter. Each one of the three tractor owners will need six days to cut his wheat. So each one demands the machine for all next week."

"Doesn't the partnership agreement say when each one is to have it?"

"Oh, yes. They adopted the plan recommended in that lovely pamphlet. It is all to be decided by majority vote. But there is no majority. Peabody claims he should get the machine now because the other two have already used it. Mrs. Hopkins talks about chivalry, and says she should be favored because she is a woman. And Snodgrass is a big, ill-natured brute who is just naturally stubborn and ornery. Each one of the three votes for himself, and says if he can't have the machine when he wants it, he won't pay one cent on it, and he'll sue the other two owners and me for damages."

"They're crazy," I said.

"Don't I know it?" said Mr. Garber.

"You could sue them," I said, "and make them pay. After all, they bought the tractor, didn't they?"

84

"Yes, but I can't afford a lawsuit. It would be too expensive—and bad for business. I can't afford to lose that money either. And I certainly can't afford to take the tractor back, now that it is secondhand. So there is only one solution. The Earthworm Tractor Company, by sending out that pamphlet, got me into this mess, and the company will have to get me out. It will have to take back this used machine and pay me the full list price for it."

"Holy Moses!" I said. "The company would never do that. Besides, it isn't necessary. All you have to do, Mr. Garber, is leave the whole thing to me. I will fix everything up."

"How?" asked Mr. Garber.

"By the use of diplomacy. Tomorrow morning I will go out and visit these three tractor owners. I will talk to them gently but firmly. By the use of remorseless logic I will show them that they are wrong. And by the use of tact and subtle suggestion, I will persuade them to get together in a reasonable way and work out a fair plan for the use of the tractor."

"What sort of a plan?" he asked.

"I will decide that as I go along. I will feel my way, and thus arrive at a perfect solution. They will then be completely satisfied. They will keep the machine and pay for it, and everything will be swell."

"It would be swell if you could do it. But you can't. I have already argued with these people till I am exhausted. And it does no good. They are all as stubborn as mules."

"Mr. Garber," I said, "for years my chief business with the Earthworm Tractor Company has been adjusting difficulties. I am an expert in the art of persuasion. I am a natural-born peacemaker. You just wait and see."

"All right," he said. "If you want to waste your time, it's O.K. with me."

He then told me how to find the three tractor owners. They all live on the same road to the north of here—Mr. Peabody nearest town, Mrs. Hopkins just beyond, and Mr. Snodgrass farthest out. I jotted down this information, and then wished Mr. Garber good afternoon and came over here to the hotel.

Tomorrow I will get busy on the diplomatic negotiations. Naturally, I can't expect to establish a permanent and lasting peace among three people who own one tractor. But I hope I can patch things up so they will get through the harvest and pay Mr. Garber. And, in the meantime, I would suggest that you suppress that pamphlet before it wrecks any more deals.

Incidentally, just who was the saphead that wrote this literary masterpiece? I wouldn't have supposed there was anyone in the

Earthworm Tractor Company so dumb as to think that any group of people anywhere could successfully cooperate in the ownership of a tractor.

Yours as ever,
Alexander Botts.

TELEGRAM

EARTHWORM CITY ILL
JULY 29 1932

ALEXANDER BOTTS
HANGING GARDEN HOTEL
BABYLON MO
YOUR JOB IS PROMOTION OF NEW SALES STOP SUGGEST THAT YOU DONT WASTE ANY MORE TIME ON MINOR QUARRELS BETWEEN DEALER AND TRACTOR OWNERS STOP THIS IS PRIMARILY THE DEALERS AFFAIR STOP PARTNERSHIP BUYING IS A PERFECTLY SOUND IDEA STOP I WROTE THAT PAMPHLET MYSELF STOP IF GARBER USED A GOOD IDEA ON THE WRONG PEOPLE THAT IS HIS RESPONSIBILITY NOT YOURS

GILBERT HENDERSON

ALEXANDER BOTTS
SALES PROMOTION REPRESENTATIVE
EARTHWORM TRACTOR COMPANY

Hanging Garden Hotel, Babylon, Missouri.
Friday, July 29, 1932.

Mr. Gilbert Henderson,
Sales Manager,
Earthworm Tractor Company,
Earthworm City, Illinois.

Dear Henderson:

Your telegram is here. And it gave me something of a jolt to learn that you wrote that pamphlet yourself. If I had known this, possibly I would not have criticized it so freely. But you will understand that I feel no malice against you personally. As a matter of fact, I was much pleased at the frank and honest way in which you admit that you are the author. It is a great comfort to me to know that I am working for a man who takes full responsibility for his mistakes, and never attempts to shift the blame onto anyone else.

I thoroughly agree with your idea that it is unwise to use up too much time on a small dealer like Mr. Garber. I will be on my way as soon as possible. However, I have got myself rather deeply involved in Mr. Garber's troubles, and it will be necessary for me to stay for another day, at least. I am sure that you will agree with me in this as soon as I have explained what I have done so far.

This morning—Friday—I rented a car at one of the local garages and drove out to visit the three partnership tractor owners. I called first on Mr. Snodgrass, who lives the farthest out. He turned out to be a very large, tough-looking baby—every bit as disagreeable as Mr. Garber had said. I found him just ready to start for town with a truckload of vegetables. When I announced that I wished to discuss the tractor situation, he told me, in a very vulgar manner, that he had no time to bother with a lousy city slicker. And, before I could explain that I was neither a city slicker nor infested with any sort of parasites, he drove off and left me.

At first I thought of chasing after him. But he seemed to be in such an unresponsive state of mind that I finally decided to let him go until some more auspicious time. Accordingly, I drove slowly down the road to the farm belonging to the Widow Hopkins. And here I met a very friendly reception.

Mrs. Hopkins is about thirty years of age, very good-looking, and most appealingly feminine. Since the death of her husband, about four years ago, she has been making a very brave fight to run the farm.

As soon as she learned that I was from the Earthworm Tractor Company, she smiled at me very prettily, and said that she knew I must be a wonderful mechanic. When I admitted that I was not so bad, she insisted that I must look at an electric paint gun which had broken down just as one of her hired men was starting to use it to spray whitewash on some of the farm buildings. I immediately took the whole thing to pieces, cleaned and adjusted the working parts, and in less than an hour had it working perfectly. Of course, it was a very simple repair job, but Mrs. Hopkins thought it was wonderful.

"You don't know how you thrill me, Mr. Botts," she said. "I am always just overcome with admiration for a man who is strong and masterful, and knows how to do things."

This appreciation gave me such a warm glow of satisfaction that I decided to operate the gun myself. So I relieved the hired man and worked all the rest of the morning, whitewashing a large henhouse, two pigpens and a corncrib. Mrs. Hopkins said it was the best job of whitewashing she had ever seen.

And the whole thing was a very clever move on my part. Mrs.

Hopkins not only invited me to lunch—serving up the most succulent viands—but she was so pleased with me that she was ready to discuss the tractor situation on a basis of complete friendliness and mutual confidence. In consequence, I was able to uncover certain very important facts which Mr. Garber's clumsy efforts had failed to reveal.

In talking with Mrs. Hopkins, I first checked up the facts which had been given me by Mr. Garber, and I found that they were substantially correct. Mrs. Hopkins, in spite of her affable manners, was just about as stubborn as Garber had said. She was willing to cooperate, but only in case she could cut her wheat first. She realized that the other two owners were also demanding first whack at the machine, and she admitted that, if the problem was to be solved, somebody would have to give in.

When I suggested the possibility that we might work on Mr. Snodgrass, she said that she was completely disgusted with the man, and would prefer not to have any dealings with him at all. As I had just had a sample of Mr. Snodgrass' boorishness, I was inclined to agree. Accordingly, we passed on to a discussion of Mr. Howard Peabody. And at once I ran into some brand-new information.

"How do you and Mr. Peabody get along?" I asked.

"In general," she replied, "very well indeed. In fact, I am really very fond of Howard. We have known each other a long time. He is, on the whole, a gentleman. He is refined. He is genteel. And he is well-mannered. But just at the moment I am a little provoked at him."

"About this tractor business?" I asked.

"It is partly that. You see, he came over here yesterday, and he offered to back down and let me have the tractor to do my harvesting first."

"What? He offered to let you have the tractor first?"

"Yes."

"Splendid!" I said. "That means it is all settled."

"I'm afraid not," she said.

"Why not?" I asked. "You and Peabody are a majority. If you vote together, you control the situation."

"But I'm not going to vote with Mr. Peabody. I told him I couldn't agree to his plan."

"Why not?"

"Because I was provoked at him."

"I don't understand," I said. "You mean you got sore because he offered to let you have the tractor?"

"It wasn't that. If he had just offered me the tractor and stopped there, it would have been all right. It was what he said afterwards that I didn't like."

"And just what did he say afterwards?"

"I don't know whether I ought to tell you."

"You'd better. I'm trying to help you. So I have to know the facts."

"Well," she said, "if you must know, Mr. Peabody asked me to marry him."

"What?" I said. "He asked you to marry him?"

"I don't see why you have to act so surprised," she said. "Am I so repulsive that nobody would want me?"

"My dear lady," I said, "you misunderstand me. I should think everybody would want you. Why, if I was not already happily married and the father of twins——"

"Really, Mr. Botts——"

"What I mean," I said, "is that I was surprised to learn that Mr. Peabody had so much sense. But I still don't understand why you should be provoked at him, as you say. If he wants to marry you, why shouldn't he ask you? It doesn't hurt you any. You don't have to accept him unless you want to."

"Oh, I didn't object to his proposing to me. As a matter of fact, I was flattered. I was delighted."

"Well, what is the matter?"

"I didn't like what he said beforehand."

"And what did he say beforehand?" I asked.

"I just told you. He said he would let me use the tractor first. The two things went together. If I would marry him, he would let me have the tractor. If I wouldn't marry him, he said I could just whistle for the tractor—those were his very words. It was most insulting."

"I don't see why," I said.

"Of course it was insulting," she said. "He put the whole thing on such a low plane. What he was doing was asking me to sell myself to him for a paltry piece of machinery."

"It is not so paltry," I said. "An Earthworm tractor is a real masterpiece of engineering. But I can see how you feel about it."

"I feel very much hurt," she said. "If he had really cared anything about me, he would have offered me the tractor without any humiliating conditions."

"Mrs. Hopkins," I said, "I understand your attitude perfectly. And I am very glad you told me all the facts in the case. I feel that I am now in a position to solve all your difficulties. I will go right over and see Mr. Peabody, and I am sure that I can persuade him to let you have the tractor without any reservations or conditions."

"That would be just wonderful," she said. "Do you really think you can do it?"

"Trust me," I said. "I will go at once."

"But aren't you going to finish the whitewashing?" she asked.

"I thought I had."

"Oh, no. There is still the horse barn."

"Very well," I said. "I will whitewash the horse barn."

"That is really very dear of you," she said. "And I wish I could watch you do it. But I have arranged to drive over into the next county to visit some relatives. And I want to get started right away. I'll be back early tomorrow morning—in case you have any news for me. You won't mind if I go off and leave you?"

"That will be quite all right," I said.

I helped her get the car started, and, after she had driven away, I put in several hours squirting whitewash about the horse barn. I will have to admit that this irked me a little. It seemed to me that the widow was imposing upon my good nature a little too much. But I did not want to do anything that would endanger the *entente cordiale* which had sprung up between us. So I worked bravely along, and did a good job. Toward the end of the afternoon I finished up and drove over to call on Mr. Howard Peabody.

I found him just finishing the chores. He was alone; the hired man, who usually looked after the farm, and the hired man's wife, who took care of the house, were both away on a visit. Mr. Peabody was such a timid-looking little guy that I could not understand Mrs. Hopkins' fondness for him. Mrs. Hopkins, you will remember, had told me that she was much more partial to men like me, who are strong, masterful and can do things. It just goes to show that you never can tell about a woman.

I started in on Mr. Peabody by introducing myself as a representative of the Earthworm Tractor Company, and also an old family friend of Mrs. Hopkins. At first he seemed a bit suspicious. So I spent about fifteen minutes ladling out the old applesauce—telling him what a privilege it was to meet him, and what a really swell guy he was. This had the desired effect of convincing him that I was a person of rare judgment, and a man to be trusted. I then got down to the business in hand.

"Mr. Peabody," I said, "I have come to tell you that Mrs. Hopkins is very fond of you. When you asked her to marry you, she was highly flattered. She was delighted. She would have fallen on your neck—except for one thing."

"And what was that?"

"She misunderstood your attitude. She thought you were proposing an ignoble commercial deal by which you would swap the tractor for her hand in marriage."

"Well," said Mr. Peabody, in a rather whining tone of voice, "that was the idea, in a way."

"But not in the way she understood it," I said. "She actually believed you were asking her to sell herself, in a most sordid manner, for a piece of cold machinery. And I am sure, Mr. Peabody, you never even thought of such a thing."

"Well, not in those exact words, anyway."

"You see," I said. "It is all a misunderstanding. And it can be fixed up very easily."

"How?"

"You and I will go to town right away. We'll get the tractor and harvester from Mr. Garber. We'll bring them out here. And tomorrow morning when Mrs. Hopkins gets back from a little trip she is making, we'll take them over and deliver them to her with no conditions attached. This will give her a concrete proof of your unselfish devotion. Then, after she has used the machinery for a few days, you can ask her any favor you want and she will grant it."

Mr. Peabody was doubtful. "I would hate to lose the tractor and the lady both," he said.

"Listen," I said. "Does it stand to reason that any mere woman, if you give her half a chance, could hold out very long against a man like you?"

Mr. Peabody smiled. "I guess you are right," he said. "We'll go after that tractor right away."

"Now you're talking," I said.

We both got into my car. We started for town. And, as we drove along, I reflected that I had handled this thing pretty well. I had every reason to suppose that events were rapidly moving toward a successful conclusion. It soon appeared, however, that I was wrong.

As we approached the outskirts of town, we observed, rolling along toward us, an Earthworm tractor pulling an Earthworm combined harvester. As we passed the tractor, we observed that it was driven by Mr. Snodgrass. A few rods farther on I stopped the car.

"There is something funny going on here," I said. "What does old Snodgrass think he is doing with that tractor?"

"How should I know?" said Mr. Peabody.

I looked back over my shoulder. The tractor and the harvester were rolling slowly but steadily along the road.

"We might go back and ask him," I said, "but he is a rather hard guy to talk to."

"He is," agreed Mr. Peabody.

"If we want to get the real dope on this," I continued, "it might be better to talk to Mr. Garber."

I started up the car and speeded on into town. We found Mr. Garber in his office.

"Is that the partnership tractor that Mr. Snodgrass is driving out of town?" I asked.

"It is," said Mr. Garber.

"What's the idea?" I asked. "Who told him he could have it?"

"I did."

"Why?"

"Well, it's like this: He came in here a little while ago. He had been peddling vegetables around town all day. He made me a proposition. He said that if I would turn the outfit over to him so that he could do his harvesting first, he would pay me spot cash for his one-third share, and he would take his chances arguing it out with the other two owners. So I let him have it."

"You had no right to do that," I said. "Didn't you know that the use of the tractor was to be decided by majority vote? And didn't you know that I was out working on these people and fixing up an agreement with them?"

"Yes, but I knew you wouldn't have any luck. And a real cash payment in days like these looks awful good. I couldn't afford to let it get away."

"You poor, simple-minded oaf," I said.

"What?" he asked.

"You poor, simple-minded oaf," I repeated. "I had this thing all fixed up. And now you have to go and spoil it all. But it may not be too late yet. . . . .Come on, Mr. Peabody. Let's get after that guy and take the machine away from him."

"I'm afraid we can't," said Mr. Peabody. "And we want to be awful careful. Snodgrass is a big guy and he's pretty rough. If we bother him too much, he might beat us up or something."

"Come on!" I said.

I dragged him down the stairs and into the car, and started after old Snodgrass. We caught up to him just beyond Mr. Peabody's front gate. I drove right past him, parked at the side of the road, got out, and waved my hand for him to stop. He stopped. I walked up beside the tractor.

"My good man," I said, "I will have to ask you to get off that tractor. Mrs. Hopkins and Mr. Peabody—a majority of the owners of this machine—have come to an agreement regarding its use. Mrs. Hopkins is to have it first. Mr. Peabody second. And you third.

Consequently, you will have to turn the machine over to me so that I can deliver it to Mrs. Hopkins. If you refuse, I warn you that we will have to use force."

During the course of this speech, Mr. Snodgrass occupied himself by glaring at me as ferociously as possible and interjecting various witless remarks that he had probably learned at the talking movies, such as, "Oh, yeah?" and, "Says who?" and, "You and what six other guys?" When I had finished, he merely opened the throttle and drove on. I followed along behind the tractor for a short distance, shouting out various remarks. But he paid no attention. Finally I rejoined Mr. Peabody, who had remained seated in my car.

He was inclined to be sarcastic. "So you are the hero who was going to take the tractor away from the tough guy," he said. "It seems to me you are pretty weak. If I had been talking to him, I would have made him get right off that seat and walk home."

"Well, why didn't you?" I said. "You were right here all the time."

"I didn't want to interfere with you," he said, "after all the big talking you had done about how you were going to handle things. And now you haven't accomplished anything at all."

"Oh, yes, I have," I said. "There are more ways than one of getting a man off a tractor. What did you think I was doing when I was walking along behind the machine there?"

"It looked to me," he said, "as if you were handing out a lot of words that didn't mean anything to a man that wasn't listening."

"I was doing more than that," I said. "I was opening up the little drain cock in the bottom of the gasoline tank."

"What was the idea of that?"

"By this time," I said, "that tank is empty. In another couple of minutes the small amount of gasoline in the vacuum tank will be used up. The machine will stop. Mr. Snodgrass will discover that he has no fuel. And he will have to go off somewhere looking for more. Then we'll take charge of the machine and drive it away. But first we'll have to have some gasoline, and there may not be enough in this car. Have you got any at your place?"

"Yes," said Mr. Peabody. "But we can't do anything like this. Suppose Snodgrass should come back and catch us? He might get violent."

"All right," I said, "let him."

I swung the car around, drove back to Mr. Peabody's place, entered the front gate and stopped in front of the barn.

"I don't like this at all," said Mr. Peabody.

"Where's that gasoline?" I asked. "In the barn?"

"No," he said. "My insurance won't let me keep it in there. It's in the root cellar."

He led me around beside the barn to a sort of hatchway. We went down a flight of brick steps. Mr. Peabody unlocked a large padlock, swung open a heavy, insulated door, like the kind they use on ice boxes, and snapped on an electric light. We stepped into a fairly good-sized underground brick vault. The place was evidently intended for storing root crops and other vegetables, but at this season of the year it was largely empty. There were several baskets of peaches, several piles of old newspapers and magazines, and a certain amount of miscellaneous junk. In one corner was a large drum of gasoline and a number of empty five-gallon oil cans. We filled up one of these cans.

"Now," I said, "we want to keep under cover until that guy gets out of the way. And we want to have some place where we can get a view of what's going on. How about the haymow?"

"All right," he said.

We carried the gasoline into the barn and set it in an empty stall. Then we climbed up a long, shaky ladder and floundered over the hay until we reached a small front window. From here we had a view of the road for quite a way in each direction. I was delighted to observe that the tractor and harvester were stalled about a quarter of a mile up the line.

"Look!" I said. "He seems to be walking around the machine. He is trying to find out what's the matter. Ah, ha! He's leaving. He's coming down the road this way. He'll walk right past here on his way to town."

"This is terrible!" said Mr. Peabody, in a weak little voice. "Maybe he's after us. Maybe he'll come right in here. I'm going to hide."

And then, believe it or not, the poor little shrimp began burrowing into the hay. In less than a minute he was completely covered up.

I remained at the window, cautiously peeking out. Mr. Snodgrass drew nearer. And, sure enough, when he reached the front gate he turned in.

"By the way," I said, speaking in a low tone of voice, "does this bum know where you keep your gasoline?"

A scared little whisper came up out of the hay. "Probably he does. He has been in here quite a few times."

"Did you lock up that cellar?" I asked.

"I'm afraid not. I was in too much of a hurry."

"Good Lord!" I said. "If he gets gasoline here, he'll start right

back to the tractor, and we won't have time to make a getaway. I'm
going down to lock that place up."

"You'd better not," whispered Mr. Peabody. "If he gets you, he
might kill you."

"Shut up!" I said.

I crawled across the hay, went down the long, shaky ladder as fast
as I could, hurried out of the barn and looked around.

There was no sign of Mr. Snodgrass. I rushed around the corner
of the barn, leaped down the brick stairs, slammed shut the big
door, pushed the hasp over the staple and snapped the big padlock
in place.

Then, as I turned around and mounted the steps, there occurred a
very peculiar phenomenon. I had a distinct feeling that I was hearing
things. It almost seemed as if lusty shouts, muffled by the thick
ice-box door, were issuing from the depths of the root cellar. I began
to wonder what had happened to Mr. Snodgrass, and, after a brief
examination of the premises failed to reveal his presence, it suddenly
occurred to me, as a remote possibility, that he might be inside the
cellar. If this were the case, it would be my duty to let him out. I
think I once heard somewhere that it is against the law to lock a man
up without a warrant or something.

But, as I thought the matter over, I decided that I had no real
reason for supposing that the man was in there at all. I had not seen
him enter. I had not looked inside when I shut the door. And the
faint sounds of shouting which I had thought I heard were probably
a mere hallucination. It is well known to scientists that even perfectly normal individuals, such as myself, may have slight temporary
derangements of the functioning of the auditory nerve which give
rise to such effects.

I decided that, on the whole, I had no responsibility in this matter
whatsoever.

I had a perfect right to lock that door. I had done so with the
consent of the owner. If Mr. Snodgrass had entered the cellar, it was
for the purpose of stealing gasoline. If he got caught, that was his
hard luck.

And it wouldn't do him any real harm, anyway. The place was
large; he would have plenty of air. The temperature within was
pleasantly cool as compared to the hot summer weather outside. He
had a good electric light and plenty of old newspapers and magazines
to read. If he got hungry, there were several bushels of peaches. What
more could he ask?

I walked around in front of the barn. From here the muffled

shouts were inaudible. I climbed up into the mow and finally succeeded in coaxing Mr. Peabody out of the hay.

"It's all right," I said. "The cellar is safely locked and Mr. Snodgrass has gone."

"Where? To town?"

"How should I know? He has gone somewhere to look for motor fuel. So it is up to us to get busy."

After much persuasion, I got Mr. Peabody down the ladder. We put the gasoline in the car and I drove up the road to the tractor. I primed the vacuum tank, closed the drain cock, poured the gasoline into the tank, and then drove the tractor and the harvester off the road, across one of Mr. Peabody's fields and into a dense clump of bushes, where it was effectively hidden.

All this time Mr. Peabody had been very fidgety. He appeared to be in a panic for fear Mr. Snodgrass might come back and beat him up. At first I thought of mentioning my vague suspicion that Mr. Snodgrass might possibly be locked up in the root cellar. But I decided not to. If he were really there, it would be, on the whole, better for our purposes if he remained there until after we had driven the tractor over to Mrs. Hopkins' in the morning. And I was afraid that if I mentioned the matter to Mr. Peabody he would insist on opening the door at once—on the theory that the big brute would be less dangerous at that time than after a whole night of captivity. It also seemed inadvisable to let Mr. Peabody spend the night at his farm. He might go into the root cellar after some of those peaches.

To guard against this possibility, I invited him to spend the night with me at the hotel in town.

My argument was that it would be unwise for him to stay at the farm alone. Mr. Snodgrass might show up at any moment, I said, and get violent. And I am happy to say that Mr. Peabody agreed with me.

So I brought him back to town with me. We had supper together. And since then, I have been writing this report in the lobby, while Mr. Peabody has been hiding up in my room.

So you see everything is going along fine. I have met with various difficulties, but I have overcome them all. And I expect to have everything finished up so that I can leave here on the noon train tomorrow—thus carrying out your desire that I do not spend too much time on these smaller dealers.

I will get this report on the night train, so that you will receive it in the morning.

Very sincerely,
Alexander Botts.

TELEGRAM

EARTHWORM CITY ILL
JULY 30, 1932

ALEXANDER BOTTS
HANGING GARDEN HOTEL
BABYLON MO
YOUR REPORT IS HERE AND I DISAPPROVE HIGHLY OF YOUR WHOLE
COURSE OF ACTION STOP IT IS BAD ENOUGH FOR YOU TO WASTE
YOUR TIME PLAYING THE PART OF CUPID BUT WHEN YOU LOCK UP
ONE OF OUR CUSTOMERS AND RUN OFF WITH HIS TRACTOR YOUR
CONDUCT IS HIGHLY DANGEROUS AND COMPLETELY UNWARRANT-
ED AND INEXCUSABLE STOP YOU ARE HEREBY ORDERED TO SEE
THAT SNODGRASS IS RELEASED AT ONCE AND YOU WILL THEN
LEAVE BABYLON BY THE EARLIEST POSSIBLE TRAIN

GILBERT HENDERSON

ALEXANDER BOTTS
SALES PROMOTION REPRESENTATIVE
EARTHWORM TRACTOR COMPANY

Hanging Garden Hotel,
Babylon, Missouri,
Saturday noon, July 30, 1932.

Mr. Gilbert Henderson,
Sales Manager,
Earthworm Tractor Company,
Earthworm City, Illinois.

Dear Henderson:

What a day this has been! Yesterday was fairly exciting, but today
has been positively frantic.

Early this morning I drove Mr. Peabody out to his farm. Everything was quiet and serene—except Mr. Peabody, who seemed a bit
nervous. I avoided the neighborhood of the root cellar, and steered
Mr. Peabody away from it. I stayed right with him while he fed the
stock and did the other chores. Then I dragged him over to where we
had left the tractor and harvester. I cranked up, we both climbed
aboard, and I drove out to the widow's farm.

When we arrived, I drew up beside the road, directly opposite the
house, and right at the edge of a ten-acre wheat field. As I stopped,
Mrs. Hopkins opened the door of the house and looked out. I cut off
the motor, and told Mr. Peabody to run over and speak his little
piece and ask the lady where she wanted us to put the machine.

So far everything had gone well, but just at this moment there arose a new and most annoying complication. As the roar of the motor died away, I heard a distant noise as of someone yelling. Looking back, I saw a man running toward us along the road from the direction of Mr. Peabody's farm. The man was a couple of hundred yards away, but he was approaching fast. He was waving his arms and shouting angrily. I recognized at once who it was. It was my old friend Mr. Snodgrass.

It became necessary for Captain Botts to think fast. And I did. It occurred to me almost immediately that Mr. Snodgrass might be a bit irate, and that he might so far forget himself as to try to take the tractor away from us. I decided, therefore, that it would be just as well to fix the machine so he could not get very far with it. I leaped nimbly to the ground. I opened the drain cock in the fuel tank, just as I had done yesterday. And the remains of our five gallons of gasoline went splashing down over the rear end of the tractor. As I climbed back into the seat, Mr. Snodgrass drew up alongside of us. Just as I had feared, his state of mind was not exactly genial. If he had not been so out of breath from running, I believe he would have climbed up and tried to throw us both off the seat. As it was, he merely addressed a few remarks to Mr. Peabody.

"I've got you now, you rat," he said. "So you thought you could lock me up and steal my tractor, did you? Well, I fooled you. I cut my way through that door with my pocket knife. And now I'm going to have my innings. You're going to state's prison for most of the rest of your life for robbery and kidnaping. And I'll take that tractor right now. Get off that seat!"

"Really, Mr. Snodgrass," I said, curling my lip in a scornful smile, "I must ask you to keep your shirt in its accustomed place. We know nothing about your being locked up. And Mr. Peabody has a perfect right to this tractor. He will tell you so himself. . . . . Speak up, Mr. Peabody, and tell this guy where he gets off at."

But Mr. Peabody did not speak up. Unfortunately for him, he was on the side of the tractor nearest Mr. Snodgrass—so close to the huge brute that he was completely cowed. He just sat there, all drawed up like a scared rabbit and unable to emit even the most feeble squeak.

"Come on, Mr. Peabody, pull yourself together," I said. "Be nonchalant. Blow some smoke in the big bum's face, and show him you're not afraid of him." I handed over a cigarette and a box of matches. Mr. Peabody accepted them mechanically, put the cigarette in his mouth, lit it, and threw the match back over his shoulder.

Well, it was just too bad. There was a sudden puff of flame behind us, and immediately the entire rear end of the tractor seemed to be on fire. Mr. Peabody leaped off one side of the machine, practically into the arms of Mr. Snodgrass, while I went bounding down the road and off into the wheat field. And this was not so good either. That wheat was dead ripe, and very dry. And I was no sooner in it than I found it was blazing and crackling furiously. Two or three vigorous jumps got me out of the fire, but it spread so rapidly that I had to keep right on running to save myself from being burned up.

After I once got started, it was impossible for me to go back to the road. I had to continue straight ahead. And the fire, driven along by a moderate breeze, kept right behind me. I went up a small ridge, down the other side and, finally, just as I was about to drop from exhaustion, I reached a back road which ran along the far side of the wheat field. Here the fire stopped, and there seemed little danger that it would spread in other directions. This particular ten-acre patch of wheat was gone, but the flames were held in on all sides by roads, and by woods and corn fields, which at this time were not dry enough to burn.

After resting myself for a few minutes, I started back. I attempted to circle around the still-smoldering wheat field. But I was so weary that my mind was a bit confused. While passing through a small patch of woods I must have lost my sense of direction. I staggered along through woods and corn fields for at least an hour, and finally reached a road which led me, not to the widow's farm, but directly into the little town of Babylon. In some ways this was rather fortunate, as it gave me a chance to go to the Hanging Garden Hotel, and get myself washed up.

When I entered the lobby, the desk clerk handed me your telegram. I opened it with eagerness. In my somewhat discouraged state of mind the rousing message of encouragement and confidence from my chief would have been a great help. You can imagine my disappointment when your communication turned out to be nothing but a good swift kick in the pants.

With greatly lowered vitality I wandered over to the office of our dealer, Mr. Garber. I hoped that he might have some news, and possibly a few words of good cheer. It turned out that he had some news, but absolutely nothing in the way of good cheer. Various reports about the fire had reached him from people who had come to town over the road which led past the widow's farm. And his nerves were very much on edge.

"So you are the guy," he said, "who called me a simple-minded oaf for letting Mr. Snodgrass take the tractor! And what do you do? You kidnap Mr. Snodgrass, who is one of my customers. You steal the tractor. And then you burn it up, along with a whole field of wheat belonging to Mrs. Hopkins, who is another of my customers."

"It was all an accident," I said.

"Accident or no accident," he said, "you and I are through with each other. You can just get out of this office, and out of town. And you can stay out. If you don't, I'll call in the sheriff and have you put in jail for arson and other misdemeanors and felonies."

"Very well," I said, "I'm on my way."

I withdrew in a dignified manner. And then I decided that I might as well go out and have a look at the remains of the tractor. By this time I was not as optimistic as I had once been as to the possibility of straightening out the affairs of the three tractor owners. But it seemed to me that it was still my duty to do anything that I could. I couldn't make things any worse, and there was a faint chance that I might be able to make them a little better.

I had a taxi man take me out to Mr. Peabody's farm. The owner was not there. I dismissed the taxi, climbed into the rented car—which I had left in Mr. Peabody's barn—and drove up the road. As I approached the Hopkins place, I decided to take no chances with Mr. Snodgrass. I would talk to him from the car, and I would keep the motor running so that I could make a quick getaway in case he got violent.

But when I arrived at the scene of the tragedy, there was nobody in sight but poor little Mr. Peabody. He was seated, the picture of dejection and despair, on the charred and blackened seat cushion of the tractor. His eyes were fixed on the remains of what had once been a pretty nice field of wheat.

I drove up beside him.

"Good morning," I said. "Is Mr. Snodgrass around anywhere?"

"No," said Mr. Peabody. "He has gone to town."

I stopped the motor. And then Mr. Peabody started in to tell me what he thought of me.

"A swell friend you turned out to be," he said. "You were going to fix everything up." He smiled bitterly. "Well, I guess you've fixed it. But if old Snodgrass thinks he can put over anything as raw as this, he'll find out he's mistaken. I'll sue him. I'll get the money back."

"What money?" I asked.

"That check he made me give him. He has probably cashed it by now. But he can't get by with it. It was highway robbery. And Mrs. Hopkins came out here, and she just stood around and never lifted a finger to help me. She'll be sorry she acted this way. I wouldn't marry her now if she came to me on bended knees."

"I don't understand," I said. "What happened?"

"I couldn't help myself," said Mr. Peabody. "Old Snodgrass claimed I started the fire."

"Well, you did, didn't you?" I said.

"You spread the gasoline all around. And you gave me the match. So it's really your fault. But Snodgrass blamed it all on me. He said I was the one who had ruined the tractor, and I would have to stand the loss. He made me buy out his share and Mrs. Hopkins' share. He took me by the neck and shook me all around. So I had to do what he told me. I wrote him a check for the full price of the tractor and the harvester."

"And what did he do with it?"

"He took it to town. He said he was going to cash it right away and pay Mr. Garber in full."

"What?" I said. "Mr. Garber is getting paid in full? Say, this is wonderful. This is marvelous."

"Yes. Just as marvelous as finding a dead cat in your soup. I suppose I ought to be giving three cheers and waving a flag. I pay the full price, and I get a burned-up wreck."

"Maybe it is not so bad," I said. "Let's look the old baby over."

I got out of the car and made a rapid inspection. The harvester was untouched. I looked over the tractor. The seat cushion and the paint at the rear end had been pretty well ruined. Aside from this there was no damage at all. It takes more than a small gasoline fire on the outside to do any real damage to a machine that is almost entirely steel and iron.

I drained several gallons of gasoline out of my car and put them in the tank. Then I cranked up the tractor motor. It ran fine.

"Mr. Peabody," I said, "there is nothing the matter with this machine. Fifty cents' worth of paint and a couple of dollars for a new seat cushion will make it just as good as new. You are a lucky man, Mr. Peabody."

"Well," he admitted, "I seem to be a lot better off than I thought I was."

"You are in fine shape," I said. "With a farm like yours you need a tractor and harvester all for yourself."

"I guess maybe that is right."

"Of course it is," I said. "So now you can just drive your machine on home. Thanks to me, you are sitting pretty."

"Thanks to you in a pig's eye," he said. "If I'm sitting pretty, it is due to pure bull luck. After all the monkeyshines you have been pulling around here, it is a wonder we both aren't in jail. I can't imagine why I was dumb enough to even let you come in my front gate. But you can be sure I never will again. Good-bye."

With these words he started up the machine, swung around and drove down the road toward his farm. As I stood watching him, I heard a cheery voice behind me. "Well, well! If it isn't Mr. Botts himself, the big paintgun expert!" I turned around. It was Mrs. Hopkins. "I came out to see what was going on," she said. "Is Mr. Peabody's tractor all fixed now? Will he have a big repair bill?"

"The machine was hardly hurt at all," I said. "The total repairs won't amount to more than two or three dollars."

"That's fine," she said. "So now everybody is happy."

"I am glad you are not sore at me, Mrs. Hopkins," I said. "And I can assure you that I am sorry your wheat got burned up."

"I am not worrying about the wheat," she said. "It was only ten acres. And I have a lot more. Besides, I have something else to think about that is much more important."

"You don't say?"

"Yes, Mr. Botts. And it's so important that I just can't keep it to myself. I'm going to be married."

"Are you sure?" I asked.

"Of course I'm sure."

"Well, that's fine," I said. "But, from what he told me, I sort of got the idea that Mr. Peabody had changed his mind."

"Mr. Peabody! That little shrimp! He has nothing to do with the case. I'm going to marry Mr. Snodgrass."

"What? The big gorilla?"

"Really, Mr. Botts. You do say the oddest things."

"Well," I said, "you change your mind so quick I can't keep up. Yesterday you said you didn't want to have anything to do with Mr. Snodgrass. You said you were completely disgusted with him."

"Of course I was disgusted with him—because he wouldn't pay any attention to me. Ever since he bought that farm and moved in two years ago, I have been just crazy about him. He is so big, so strong, so virile. He is a regular superman—the perfect answer to a poor widow's prayer. I kept trying to strike up a friendship with him, but he would never respond at all. And that is why I got disgusted with him. I didn't know then that he really wanted to be friendly, but that he was just too shy."

"He didn't seem very shy to me," I said.

"Oh, he's bold enough with men. But with women, Mr. Botts, he is just like a great, big, awkward boy. You know, he has been secretly in love with me all the time, but he was too timid to say so. He wanted to take my part in all these discussions about the tractor, but he was too bashful. So he finally got hold of the machine, and he was going to bring it out to me. Isn't it just too cute for words?"

"Yes," I said, "a very whimsical situation indeed."

"Even then, he wouldn't have dared tell me how he felt about it. So it is probably just as well that you and Mr. Peabody went crazy and stole the tractor and everything. Because when he saw my wheat field burning up, he was so sorry for me and so angry at Mr. Peabody that he forgot all his bashfulness. Oh, it was wonderful, Mr. Botts. I was so proud of the masterful way in which he handled the situation. He shook Mr. Peabody as a terrier shakes a rat. He made him pay for the machine. Then he was going to make him pay for the wheat. He was just like a raging lion. But when I said that we did not want to be too hard on Mr. Peabody, he deferred to my wishes as gently as a lamb. It just shows how much power I have over him. And it certainly gave me a thrill. And then he came in the house, and his bashfulness held off long enough for us to get engaged, and then he took the check and went to town in my car, and we're going to be married next week and—Look! Here he comes now."

I glanced down the road. A car was rapidly approaching.

"Well," I said, "I guess I'll be on my way. Good-bye and good luck to you."

As I climbed into my car, Mr. Snodgrass drove up, leaped out of the car and walked over to Mrs. Hopkins.

"It is all fixed up," he said. "I paid Garber for the old tractor and harvester, and I've bought a brand-new tractor and harvester for us. It will be delivered tomorrow." At this point he caught sight of me. "So you are the man," he said, "that helped Peabody lock me up and steal the tractor and burn up Mrs. Hopkins' wheat! I've a good mind to knock your block off."

He advanced toward me in a menacing manner, but Mrs. Hopkins held him back.

"Don't hurt poor little Mr. Botts," she said. "He means well. And most of the time he's harmless—in spite of the fact that he seems to be crazy."

"All right," said Snodgrass. "But he had better get away from here before I change my mind."

"I'm leaving right now," I said. I turned the car around and started for town.

And, as I drove along, I couldn't help but congratulate myself on the complete success of my activities. Think of it—a bitter fight settled, a very pretty romance started, and two complete tractor-harvester outfits sold where only one had been partially sold before. I tell you, Henderson, it just makes me feel good all over.

As ever,
Alexander Botts.

GOOD NEWS

EARTHWORM TRACTOR COMPANY
EARTHWORM CITY, ILLINOIS
Interoffice Communication

Date: Wednesday, September 5, 1934.
To: Gilbert Henderson, President.
From: Alexander Botts, Sales Manager.
Subject: Good news.

This is just a brief note to let you know that I am planning to be out of town for a while, and that I want you to look after my office work while I am away.

The cause of my sudden departure is a telegram just received from Mr. Sam Blatz, studio manager of Zadok Pictures, Inc., Hollywood, California. Mr. Blatz states that he is about to produce a motion picture called *The Tractor Man Comes Through*, with that well-known star, Buster Connolly, in the title role. The picture calls for twelve large tractors and twelve elevating graders. Mr. Blatz would like to use Earthworm machines. But they must be delivered in Hollywood within a week; otherwise he will have to employ equipment furnished by the Behemoth Tractor Company.

Naturally, I am getting after this business with all the energy I possess. It means not only a big sale but also a chance for us to get a truly stupendous amount of swell publicity. Imagine having our tractors and graders appearing in a motion picture which will be seen by millions of people all over the country, and throughout the world as well!

I am having shipped, this afternoon, twelve eighty-horsepower Earthworm tractors and twelve elevating graders on a special through-freight train which should reach California by next Monday. And, as this deal is too important to trust to our Los Angeles dealer, I am starting for the Coast tonight by plane.

You may rest assured that I am embarking on this venture with the greatest enthusiasm. After more than a month of dull office routine, I find myself with an irresistible yearning for action and excitement. And there ought to be plenty of both in Hollywood.

Don't forget to look after my job while I am gone. As it is only a little more than a month since I took your place as sales manager, on the occasion of your elevation to the presidency, you ought to remember enough about the sales work to get by all right.

As ever,

Alexander Botts.

P. S.: I wanted to tell you personally about this great opportunity. But when I called at your office a few minutes ago, your secretary informed me that, in spite of the fact that this is Wednesday, not Saturday, you had departed for an afternoon on the golf links. So I am forced to give you the glad news in this written communication, which you will probably read sometime tomorrow—provided you should happen to drift into the office.

A. Botts.

EARTHWORM TRACTOR COMPANY
EARTHWORM CITY, ILLINOIS
Office of Gilbert Henderson, President

Air Mail. Thursday, September 6, 1934.
Mr. Alexander Botts,
Care Zadok Pictures, Inc.,
Hollywood, California.

Dear Botts:

On my arrival at the office this morning, I found your communication of yesterday awaiting me. I wish you the best of luck in your attempts to make this important sale. And I will look after your work during your absence.

However, I wish to point out, for your guidance in the future, that your place, as sales manager, is here. Actual selling work in the field should be left to our dealers and salesmen. Furthermore, I wish to remind you that it is not the policy of this company to go to the heavy expense of shipping large orders way across the country until a sale has actually gone through. And, unless you have previously consulted me, I do not want you ever again to rush off this way on the assumption that I will handle your office work for you.

Please hurry back as soon as possible.

Very sincerely,
Gilbert Henderson.

HOLLYWOOD-PLAZA HOTEL
HOLLYWOOD, CALIFORNIA

Air Mail.

Saturday afternoon,
September 8, 1934.

Mr. Gilbert Henderson, President,
Earthworm Tractor Company,
Earthworm City, Illinois.

Dear Henderson:

Your letter is received. I want you to know that I appreciate your doubts as to the wisdom of my procedure in shipping the tractors and graders ahead of time and in coming out here myself. Also, I can understand your reluctance to take over the work of my office in addition to your own heavy duties as president of the Earthworm Tractor Company. But when I explain what I have already accomplished out here, and what I am planning to accomplish in the future, you will see that my course has been entirely justified, and you will be very glad to do your part by carrying on my work during my absence—even though it may interfere to some extent with your afternoons on the golf links.

I arrived at the Glendale Airport on Thursday morning, and at once took a taxi to the studio of Zadok Pictures, Inc., which is several miles southwest of Hollywood. My first reaction, quite naturally, was a tremendous thrill of excitement at finding myself suddenly set down right in the midst of the glamorous activities of the motion-picture business. The Zadok Studio is truly amazing—an enormous lot, half a mile square, covered with tremendous sound stages, elaborate outdoor sets, huge administrative buildings and other structures, and swarming with carpenters, electricians, various miscellaneous helpers, actors, and actresses—the latter being, in some ways, the most interesting. The whole place is possessed of a quality which I can only describe as enthralling.

Even the surroundings of the studio are full of interest. The adjoining boulevard is lined with handsome filling stations, gay and colorful signboards, and a lot of refreshment stands that are truly astounding—one of them, for instance, being in the form of an old mill, and another built to represent a gigantic ice-cream freezer. A short distance away is a huge alligator farm, where—for some reason which I have not as yet discovered—they are engaged in raising literally hundreds of these curious reptiles. At one side of the studio is a low hill with a complete oil field—scores of big derricks and dozens of storage tanks. And scattered all over the landscape are countless thriving real-estate developments with clusters of little plastered bungalows sprouting up like mushrooms.

When I called at the office of Mr. Sam Blatz, the studio manager, his secretary informed me he was so busy that he could not see me until the following afternoon. This caused a certain amount of delay. But, as it turned out, it was all for the best, because it gave me a chance to roam about the studio and pick up a whole lot of firsthand information about the motion-picture business.

And when I finally saw Mr. Blatz, yesterday afternoon, I was able to speak to him in his own language, and put over a sales talk that was a real wow. Even so, I had a hard time. Mr. Blatz had already seen the Behemoth tractor people, and they had offered him unusually generous terms. However, when I explained that our machines were vastly superior, that we would agree to terms just as generous as the Behemoth, and that we could make delivery early next week, his resistance broke down completely, and in less than ten minutes he closed the deal for twelve Earthworm tractors and twelve graders.

And this is not all. After thanking me most effusively for everything I had done for him, Mr. Blatz gave me a cordial invitation to remain at the studio as long as I desired. He pointed out that I could be a great help in handling the unloading of the tractors, in teaching the mechanics to operate them, and, later on, in acting as technical expert on tractors during the filming of the picture. He said that he would put a studio car at my disposal, and that I would be considered a guest of the company for as long a period as I cared to remain.

This hospitable offer I promptly accepted—not, as you might suppose, because of the selfish pleasure I would derive from hanging around this fascinating studio, but rather because of the very real service I can render the Earthworm Tractor Company by remaining on the job out here a little longer. How important this service is you will realize as soon as I describe the interesting project on which I am now engaged.

After thanking Mr. Blatz, and congratulating him for his good judgment in inviting me to remain at the studio, I asked him to give me a copy of the screenplay, *The Tractor Man Comes Through*. As soon as this was in my hands, I wished Mr. Blatz a very cordial good afternoon and hurried back to the hotel in my luxurious studio car. Last night I read the play, and as soon as I had finished it, I decided that it was all wrong. Not only was it weak in a dramatic sense but it did not have anywhere near enough tractor stuff in it. What it needed was a complete revision by a real tractor expert.

Accordingly, bright and early this morning, I set to work. And I am getting along so well that I expect to have an entirely new version all ready to present to Mr. Blatz on Monday morning. The changes I am making will improve the quality of the picture so much that Mr. Blatz is almost certain to adopt all of them. And the wealth of tractor stuff which I am introducing will provide publicity of incalculable value to the Earthworm Tractor Company. A brief resume of what I am doing will make this clear.

The original play is a rather uninspiring drama of love and hate in the swamps along the lower Mississippi River. The hero—played by Buster Connolly—is a more or less inconsequential young man in charge of a fleet of tractors which are being used in the construction of a levee. And the love interest is a girl who lives in the swamps. This is not a bad set-up, but the author has spoiled it by paying too much attention to the girl and not enough attention to the tractors.

I am changing this in two ways. In the first place, I am cutting out most of the silly love passages. And in the second place, I am improving the levee-building sequences by expanding them into an exhaustive pictorial study of tractor dirt-moving operations—including not only the work of the elevating graders but also a lot of activities with dump wagons, blade graders, sheep's-foot tampers, bulldozers, scarifiers, land levelers, fresnos, and a lot of miscellaneous scrapers, packers, rollers, winches, and other forms of equipment too numerous to mention.

In addition to this, I am building up the character of the hero. Instead of having him a mere second-rate straw boss on the levee, I am presenting him as a person of real consequence in the community. Besides his levee work, he is a road contractor, which gives me a chance to introduce a lot of scenes of tractors working on the roads. Also, he owns a large cotton plantation and a lumber camp, which provides an excuse for showing Earthworm tractors engaged in plowing, harrowing, cultivating and skidding logs. And, before I get through, I may even give the hero a trip up north, so we can run in some snowplow work.

Another improvement which I am making is in the method of killing off the villain. Instead of letting him drown in a very uninteresting way in the Mississippi River, I am going to have all twelve tractors run over him, one after the other. This ought to be a scene that will cause a real shudder of horror to sweep through the audience.

But my greatest and most sensational contribution is the grand climax. In the original play, when a big flood comes down the river and breaks through the levee, the hero rescues the girl from her house in the lowlands and carries her off on horseback to the safety of the hills. In my version, all this horseback foolishness is cut out, and the hero arrives in a tractor. He finds that the rescue is apparently impossible, because the girl is suffering from pneumonia or pellagra or something, and cannot be moved from her bed. In this desperate extremity, the hero hitches his tractor to the house, and drags the whole thing, with the girl in it, through miles of deadly swamps, swarming with alligators—which they can rent from the alligator farm down the road—and, after many bloodcurdling adventures, he finally reaches the safety of the hills. The hero's followers, with other tractors, haul away the barn, with the cows in it, and the various corncribs, hen houses and pigpens, with their respective contents. Not only is the girl rescued but all her property is saved. And it is just in the nick of time, because, right on the heels of this spectacular and astounding moving operation, comes the awe-inspiring influx of the swirling waters of the flood.

As you see, my improvements are going to be the making of this play, both as an artistic production and as a colossal advertisement for Earthworm tractors. So it is very fortunate that I came out here.

I must now get back to my literary labors. Good luck to you, and don't work too hard.

As ever,
Alexander Botts.

TELEGRAM
EARTHWORM CITY ILL SEP 10 1934

ALEXANDER BOTTS
HOLLYWOOD PLAZA HOTEL
HOLLYWOOD CALIF

DELIGHTED THAT YOU PUT OVER SALE BUT I AM WORRIED BY YOUR STATEMENT THAT YOU AGREED TO VERY GENEROUS TERMS STOP PLEASE WRITE ME FULL DETAILS AT ONCE AND ENCLOSE COPY OF SALES ORDER STOP I DO NOT FEEL THAT THE PUBLICITY VALUE OF THIS PICTURE WILL BE SUFFICIENT TO WARRANT YOUR WASTING ANY MORE TIME ON IT STOP THE IMPORTANT THING IS THE SALE OF THE TWELVE TRACTORS AND THE TWELVE GRADERS STOP THIS HAS NOW BEEN ACCOMPLISHED SO THERE IS NO REASON FOR YOUR

REMAINING IN CALIFORNIA STOP I AM TOO BUSY TO LOOK AFTER
YOUR JOB MUCH LONGER STOP YOU WILL RETURN TO EARTHWORM
CITY AS SOON AS POSSIBLE

> EARTHWORM TRACTOR COMPANY
> GILBERT HENDERSON PRESIDENT

HOLLYWOOD PLAZA HOTEL
HOLLYWOOD, CALIFORNIA

Air Mail.

Monday evening,
September 10, 1934.

Mr. Gilbert Henderson, President,
Earthworm Tractor Company,
Earthworm City, Illinois.

Dear Henderson:

Your telegram is here, and I am somewhat disappointed in it.

I believe you are making a mistake in feeling that the publicity this
picture is going to give us is only one of the minor advantages of the
deal which I have put through. I regret that you are placing undue
importance on the mere selling of the twelve tractors and the twelve
graders. Also, it is a bit unfortunate that you are in such a hurry to
know the exact nature of the somewhat generous terms which I
granted Mr. Blatz. And it is kind of too bad that you want me to send
you a copy of the sales order.

As a matter of fact, the publicity is not only the most important,
it is the only advantage we get out of this deal. The sale is of no
consequence at all, because the terms of my agreement with Mr.
Blatz provide that we lend him the tractors and graders free of
charge. Hence, there has been no sale, and I can't send you a copy of
the sales order because there is no sales order.

I fear that this news may be something of a shock to you, because
the wording of your telegram seems to indicate that you read my
former letter so carelessly that you jumped to the totally unwarranted conclusion that I had actually sold something out here. I
never said anything of the kind. If you will read over my letter, you
will see that I merely said I had closed a deal with Mr. Blatz. So it is
not my fault if there was any misunderstanding.

However, there is nothing to worry about, because my arrangement with Mr. Blatz is perfectly fair to everyone concerned, and the
terms are the best we could get, under the circumstances. Naturally,
I would have enjoyed selling all this stuff, but before I arrived, the
Behemoth Tractor Company had already offered to supply, abso-

lutely free of charge, twelve of their tractors and twelve of their elevating graders. And Mr. Blatz, although he preferred Earthworms, did not want them badly enough to actually pay any money for them. So there was only one thing to do. As a sale was clearly impossible, I abandoned all thought of making it, and concentrated my efforts on this wonderful opportunity for motion-picture publicity. And I have succeeded admirably. All I had to do, in addition to lending them a mere hundred thousand dollars' worth of tractors and graders, was to sign a simple agreement releasing the motion-picture company from liability in case there is any damage to this property while it is in their possession. And in return for this, we get a chance to put over at least a million dollars' worth of splendid publicity. So you see, the advantages are all on our side.

However, if we are going to exploit this magnificent opportunity to the fullest possible extent, it will be necessary for me to stay out here long enough to make sure that the picture is loaded with as much Earthworm-tractor propaganda as it can possibly hold. In a former letter I explained how I was revising the screenplay so that the picture will do right by our tractors. The revision was completed yesterday, and the next step is to submit it to Mr. Blatz. But I cannot do this right away, because the guy is out of town. He left unexpectedly last night by airplane for New York, where he is to confer with Colonel Zadok, the head of the company, and with various bankers who seem to have acquired, in some mysterious and insidious manner, a considerable influence in the business. Mr. Blatz expects to be back on Wednesday, and he left word that he hoped I would be able to attend a story conference which he will hold on that day for the purpose of discussing the tractor picture. Obviously, there is only one course for me to pursue. I will have to stick around here until Wednesday, at least.

In the meantime, I am finding plenty to occupy me. This morning, with the help of a large force of expert mechanics from the production department, I unloaded the tractors and graders, which had arrived on a nearby siding, and brought them over to the lot.

This afternoon I visited a number of people who are to be connected with the forthcoming tractor picture, and tried to sell them my ideas for revising the script. I wanted to get them on my side, so that they would back me up when I present my plans to Mr. Sam Blatz at the story conference on Wednesday. My efforts, however, were not very successful.

The first person I interviewed was Mr. Buster Connolly, the star of the picture. I found him a short distance outside the lot, looking at a large and elaborate bungalow which belongs to him and which was in

111

the process of being moved to the Zadok studio from another studio where he had previously worked. It appears that every motion-picture star that amounts to anything has to have a bungalow where he can loll around at such times as he is not actually working. When I arrived upon the scene, Mr. Connolly's bungalow was coming past the oil derricks on the shoulder of the hill at one side of the Zadok lot. It was being dragged along very slowly and painfully by means of an antique and clumsy arrangement of cables, pulleys and winches.

This gave me a wonderful opening. After explaining the changes I wanted to make in the forthcoming picture, I offered to bring up my tractors and put on a real demonstration. I told Mr. Connolly that I would move his bungalow down to the lot so fast that it would make his hair stand on end, and would also give him an idea of the sensational effect we would produce with the spectacular house-moving climax which I had decided to put into the picture. But Mr. Connolly was not impressed.

"I won't let you touch my bungalow," he said. "And, further-more, I don't like your machines. When Sam Blatz gets back I'm going to see him and have practically all the tractor scenes taken out of the picture."

"But, Mr. Connolly," I said, "the tractors will be the making of the picture. They'll be the most interesting thing in it."

"That's just the trouble," he retorted angrily. "The audience will be looking at the tractors all the time, and they won't pay any attention to my acting. Thus, the picture will be ruined."

"Oh, I see," I said. And, indeed, I began to see only too well what was on his mind. He knew the tractors would be splendid picture material. He was afraid they would steal the show from him. And he was so stubborn that I found it impossible to argue with him. Consequently, after a very disappointing interview, I left him and went around to see the director of the picture.

The director sprung an idea that was exactly the opposite of Mr. Connolly's, but just as bad from my point of view. He said he was in favor of cutting out practically all the scenes involving tractors, because tractors, in his opinion, are "slow-moving props," without any picture value whatever. I offered to disprove this assertion by giving him a demonstration. He refused. Then I tried to describe the thrilling effects which could be obtained by showing our Earth-worms plowing majestically across horrible swamps, through dense forests and over rugged mountains. But he would not listen. He had seen the tractors coming into the lot that morning. They moved slowly. Hence, they were slow-moving props, entirely devoid of interest. And nothing I could say had any effect. So, finally, I had to abandon my efforts, and leave him in the same state of besotted ignorance in which I had found him.

My next, and final, call was on the production manager, who has charge of the studio equipment. This guy promptly announced that he was going to advise Mr. Blatz to cut out all the tractor scenes, on the ground that they would necessitate very expensive sets or even more expensive trips to outside locations. And he was just as opinionated as Mr. Connolly and the director, so I soon gave up all thought of reasoning with him, and walked away in disgust.

But don't get the idea that I am discouraged. Mr. Sam Blatz is the boss around here. He has already shown his intelligence, and his appreciation of tractors, by arranging with me for the use of our machines. Consequently, I am able to contemplate the future with the greatest of confidence. When I see Mr. Blatz at the story conference on Wednesday, I will be prepared to present my ideas in such a clear, forceful and convincing manner that he is almost certain to follow my advice. Hence, the ignorant opposition of such unimportant underlings as the star, the director and the studio manager will count for nothing at all. And the picture will be produced in such a way that it will be not only a credit to Zadok Pictures, Inc., but also an invaluable piece of propaganda for the Earthworm Tractor Company.

Yours enthusiastically,
Alexander Botts.

TELEGRAM
EARTHWORM CITY ILL SEP 13 1934

ALEXANDER BOTTS
HOLLYWOOD PLAZA HOTEL
HOLLYWOOD CALIF

OUR ATTORNEY BELIEVES THAT YOUR LENDING TRACTORS TO MOTION PICTURE COMPANY IS VIOLATION OF NRA CODE ALTHOUGH AS USUAL HE IS NOT QUITE SURE STOP IN ANY EVENT IT IS ABSO-LUTELY CONTRARY TO OUR POLICY STOP YOU WILL NOTIFY MR BLATZ THAT HE MUST BUY THE TRACTORS AND GRADERS AND PAY FOR THEM STOP IF HE REFUSES YOU WILL REMOVE ALL THIS MA-CHINERY AND TURN IT OVER ON CONSIGNMENT TO OUR LOS ANGELES DEALER IN HOPES OF FUTURE SALE ELSEWHERE STOP YOU WILL RETURN TO EARTHWORM CITY AS SOON AS POSSIBLE AS WORK IN YOUR OFFICE HERE IS PILING UP

EARTHWORM TRACTOR COMPANY
GILBERT HENDERSON PRESIDENT

HOLLYWOOD RECEIVING HOSPITAL
HOLLYWOOD, CALIFORNIA

Air Mail.

Thursday evening,
September 13, 1934.

Mr. Gilbert Henderson, President,
Earthworm Tractor Company,
Earthworm City, Illinois.

Dear Henderson:

It is my painful duty to report to you that I have been suddenly overwhelmed by a series of crushing and incredible disasters. Your telegram has been forwarded to me here at my new address, but, in the present situation, it does not mean anything at all. I cannot do any of the things you want me to do. And I cannot even do any of the things I want to do myself. I cannot stay out here to help with the tractor picture, because there is not going to be any tractor picture. I cannot hurry back to Earthworm City, because I am laid up in the hospital with a broken ankle. And I cannot repossess the tractors and graders because there are no tractors and graders anymore. They have, in fact, ceased to exist as such. So, about the only thing I can do is sit up in bed and write you an account of the unbelievable combination of catastrophes which have defeated all my best-laid plans.

The first blow descended upon me early yesterday evening at the story conference held in Mr. Blatz's office at the studio. All the people concerned in the tractor picture were there, and each one was prepared to present his own ideas on the subject. But the wind was immediately taken out of our sails by Mr. Blatz himself, who had just arrived from New York full of a whole set of new and outlandish ideas.

Mr. Blatz told us that the financial powers had decided that what the company needs at the present time is something that will ring the cash register in a big way. And they had concluded that the best means of accomplishing this was to produce a picture which would cost more than any other picture heretofore produced in the entire history of the industry. The idea, if you can call it that, seems to be that, instead of making several ordinary pictures which would cost two or three hundred thousand dollars apiece and bring in perhaps a half a million apiece, they will concentrate all their efforts on one production which will cost over a million dollars, and will bring in—they hope—several millions at the box office.

In accordance with this plan, they are going to junk the tractor drama and three or four others that had been scheduled for early

114

production, and put everything they have into a stupendous, monumental, sensational, magnificent, and overpowering epic superspectacle based on Milton's *Paradise Lost.*

Mr. Blatz admitted, quite frankly, that, from a picture point of view, Mr. Milton's stuff is not so hot, but he was fairly goggle-eyed with enthusiasm over the commercial possibilities. He pointed out that this man Milton has been built up and advertised so long and so extensively by all the college professors and all the high-school teachers of English throughout the entire country that his name has become a household word, synonymous with culture and the higher things of life. This situation is just naturally made to order for the publicity department, which will rush about the country organizing John Milton Booster Clubs in every city, town, hamlet and crossroads. Endorsements will be sought, and doubtless received, from women's clubs, parent-teacher associations, literary societies, and all the rest of the innumerable organizations which are interested in improving the mind and raising the standard of good taste and artistic appreciation in America. Fathers, mothers, clergymen, schoolteachers, college professors and civic leaders generally will be so thoroughly sold on the high value of the picture that they will urge every man, woman and child throughout the length and breadth of the land to see it.

As director of the picture, they are hiring a world-renowned Russian theatrical producer. This bird knows nothing about motion pictures, and he cannot even speak English, so he will be completely useless around the studio. But the real work can be done by an American assistant director who really knows his business, and the name of the famous Russian will tend to pull in that large and influential group of Americans who believe that nothing can be truly worthwhile in an artistic way unless it comes out of Europe.

And this is not all. It is realized that there exists in America a considerable substratum of ignorant dumbbells who have a deep suspicion of anything they think is highbrow. To attract this element, they will use, in the cast, a whole group of stars who have a known appeal to the lower classes. Besides Buster Connolly, who has a great following among lovers of thrills and Western melodrama, there will be four popular comedians, three lady stars of the hot-mamma type, and various handsome juvenile men, to say nothing of acrobats, adagio dancers, circus performers, stunt men, and an enormous corps de ballet. The sets and the costumes will be the most elaborate ever seen—they have already ordered one thousand harps and one thousand pairs of wings, with real feathers, for the angels—and the dance ensembles will be lavish beyond description. In fact, there is only one place where they will economize—they won't have to pay anything to the original author.

As soon as Mr. Blatz had completed a description of his ambitious plans, the entire group at the conference—with one notable exception—gave voice to their admiration and approval. The only sour note was sounded by myself, in the form of a plaintive protest at the way they were letting the Earthworm Tractor Company down with nothing to show for all the expense we had incurred in bringing the tractors to California at Mr. Blatz's express request. But my objections were completely drowned out in the great flood of enthusiasm for Mr. John Milton.

And then, while I was still reeling from the effects of this first blow, there descended upon my unfortunate head a second disaster of even greater magnitude. The building was suddenly shaken by the shock of a distant explosion, and soon after we began to hear cries of "Fire!" We all rushed outside, and followed a crowd of excited studio employees to the western boundary of the lot. And here a truly appalling sight met our eyes.

One of the oil-storage tanks up among the derricks on the nearby hill had caught fire. Apparently this tank was only partly filled with oil; it must have contained a certain amount of air mixed with oil vapor in deadly proportions. At any rate, it had exploded, and spread the fire all over the hill. The flames were roaring up from dozens of derricks and tanks. And, as we watched, another tank blew up with a tremendous report, and a great river of burning oil started down the hill toward the studio of Zadok Pictures.

Much to our relief, the flow of this fiery river was arrested, high up on the hill, by a long, low bank of earth, which had presumably been thrown up as a protection for the studio in case of just such an emergency as this. But our relief was short-lived, for it soon appeared that this embankment was not high enough. A small quantity of the burning oil came over the top, and it was evident that, if a few more tanks let loose, the blazing fluid would come pouring down the hill and engulf the studio. Fire engines were already on the way from Culver City, Los Angeles, Hollywood, Beverly Hills and Santa Monica. But it was obvious that they would be of little use.

There was only one thing to do. I rushed over to the shed where my tractors and graders were stored. And, as I went, I called loudly for my mechanics to man the machines. Fortunately, several companies were on the lot, taking night scenes. So most of my mechanics were present. And they—gallant and intelligent fellows that they are—had already conceived the same idea which had come to me.

In less than five minutes I had men on every tractor and every grader. And in less than ten minutes, we came charging out through the big side gate of the lot, and advanced up the hill toward the fire.

By this time, the electrical department had mounted hundreds of enormous kleig lights at various vantage points. And these, in conjunction with the light from the fire, made the entire scene as bright as day.

Directly in front of us on the slope of the hill stood Buster Connolly's expensive but silly-looking bungalow. We promptly hooked onto it with three tractors and hauled it down into the lot. Then I started running the twelve tractors, each one pulling a grader, back and forth across the face of the hill so as to throw up a really effective barrier about halfway between the studio and the small dam which was temporarily holding the burning oil in check.

It began to look as if the studio might be saved. The tractors were roaring on their way, and the elevating graders were plowing up the earth and casting it onto the new embankment so fast that victory would be assured in fifteen or twenty minutes.

At this juncture, however, my own participation in the fight was abruptly terminated. As I was rushing to and fro, and hither and yon, shouting orders and encouragement to my trusty followers, I inadvertently tripped over a large plant of the variety known as prickly pear. This unfortunate accident not only filled me up with a lot of spines, in a most annoying way, but also caused me to sustain, as I landed on the hard ground, a broken ankle. It was the same ankle which I injured once before down in Mississippi. A number of husky lads promptly picked me up and carried me down to the highway. And before I knew exactly what was happening to me, I had been loaded into an ambulance and dragged away to this hospital, where the doctors proceeded to give me ether, so they could properly set the broken bones.

When I finally regained the full use of my mental faculties, several hours later, I insisted that the nurse call up the studio and find out how things were going. The news that she brought me was partly good but mostly bad. When the inevitable break in the upper embankment occurred, the lower one, so hastily constructed by our tractors and graders, had reached a height sufficient to stem the tide of the burning oil. So the entire Zadok Studio had been saved. But at the time of the break, our tractors and graders were on the upper side of the new earthwork. The brave mechanics had time to leap to safety over the barrier, but the twelve tractors and the twelve graders were all left behind, and were completely destroyed.

Thus ends the magnificent enterprise upon which I embarked, last week, with so much hope and enthusiasm. At the moment, I am feeling too wretched and miserable to make any definite plans for the future. But, probably, as soon as I am well enough, I shall come creeping piteously back to Earthworm City, hoping and praying that my job has not been taken away from me.

Yours, with deep sorrow,
Alexander Botts.

HOLLYWOOD RECEIVING HOSPITAL
HOLLYWOOD, CALIFORNIA

Air Mail
Friday afternoon,
September 14, 1934.

Mr. Gilbert Henderson, President,
Earthworm Tractor Company,
Earthworm City, Illinois.

Dear Henderson:

I have a little news for you. My ankle is getting along very well, and I am feeling quite comfortable.

This morning I got in touch with the local adjuster for the Illinois Eureka Fire Insurance Company, which, as you know, handles our business. The adjuster has inspected the remains of our tractors and graders, and is reporting them as a total loss. So, under the terms of our policy, we are to receive the full value, plus freight. This means that the fire wasn't such a bad idea after all; we get paid for these machines just the same as if we had actually sold them.

And here is more news. Mr. Sam Blatz called on me this morning to thank me for my part in saving the studio and thus making it possible for them to go ahead, without any delay, in the production of their great super-spectacle. When I asked if he was referring to the Paradise Lost picture, he replied that he was, except that their plans had been slightly changed and they were not going to use the great Milton epic after all. It appears they had hired some guy to read the book for them, so they could find out what it is all about. And they had also consulted with the Hays office. Most of the authorities had then agreed that it would be pretty difficult to get Paradise Lost past the censors and the various purity organizations. Apparently, one of the main characters in the book is Satan himself, and this puts entirely too much emphasis on sin. So they have decided to do John Bunyan's Pilgrim's Progress instead. This book—which apparently has nothing to do with Paul Bunyan, owner of the famous blue ox—contains a number of objectionable passages, but they can be eliminated without much trouble.

Mr. Blatz pointed out that the switch to the Bunyan opus was in reality only a minor change in their plans. The really essential features—such as the elaborate production and the publicity aimed at the culture groups—will go through just the same. The only real difference would be that, instead of forming Milton societies all over the country, the publicity department would bend its energies toward the formation of bigger and better Bunyan clubs.

"And in this new setup," Mr. Blatz explained, "we find we won't need Buster Connolly, so we are going to have him make the tractor picture after all—only there will be a lot of changes in that too."

"I suppose you're going to leave out all the tractors?" I asked suspiciously.

"I'm afraid we can't," said Mr. Blatz. "You see, the most spectacular part of the picture has been made already."

"I don't understand."

"It's like this, Mr. Botts. When that fire started, we had four separate companies working on the lot. And the entire production force was present, all ready to take advantage of this great opportunity. The electricians set up their lights, and the directors and the cameramen went into action. And the results are really extraordinary. Never before has a fire of this size been covered by so many expert cameramen with such a wealth of high-grade equipment. And never before have I seen such beautifully taken fire pictures. We have the whole thing—blazing oil derricks, exploding tanks, the moving of that bungalow from out of the very jaws of death, the building of the embankment, the escape of the tractor operators in front of the blazing river of oil, and the final destruction of the tractors and the graders. We even have a delightful bit of comedy relief—where some jackass tripped and did a beautiful high gruesome into a prickly pear. It is all so astounding, so magnificent, so colossal, that we are going to use it as the climax of our tractor picture. To do this, we shall have to shift the scene of our story from the Mississippi swamps to California, and have the hero rescue the girl and her house from an oil fire. We want to make this a real tractor picture, with lots of tractor stuff all through it, so we are hoping that you will be able to lend us twelve more tractors and twelve more graders to be used in the earlier sequences."

"Nothing would please me more!" I said. And then my warm enthusiasm was suddenly chilled by the icy fingers of a cold doubt. "I am afraid, however," I said sadly, "that it can't be done. Look at this."

I handed him your telegram. He read it and glanced at me inquiringly.

"We must face the facts," I said. "You will have to buy these tractors and graders, and pay real money for them, or else you'll have to use Behemoth machines."

"We can't use Behemoths," said Mr. Blatz, "because the most important part of the picture has already been made with Earthworms." He pondered the matter for some time. "Oh, well," he said at length. "It's only a hundred thousand dollars—a mere drop in the bucket as compared to what we ought to take in on this picture. Do you want me to sign an order or something for these things?"

"As a matter of form, you might as well," I said nonchalantly. "And you might make me out a check also."

So he did, and I am enclosing the order and the check herewith. Please ship the stuff at once. And I'm afraid you'll have to handle my office work a little longer, because the state of my ankle makes it necessary for me to leave tomorrow for several weeks' vacation, as the guest of Mr. Sam Blatz at his luxurious ranch in Hidden Valley up in Ventura County.

Yours respectfully,
Alexander Botts.

CONFIDENTIAL
STUFF

OFFICE OF ALEXANDER BOTTS
SALES MANAGER
EARTHWORM TRACTOR COMPANY
EARTHWORM CITY, ILLINOIS

Monday, November 20, 1939.

Mr. Gilbert Henderson,
President Earthworm Tractor Company,
Earthworm Tractor Company Branch Office,
San Francisco, California.

Dear Henderson:

I need your help. I have just visited Washington, D.C., in connection with the confidential matter we discussed the last time you were in Earthworm City. I had a long talk with that highly disagreeable, self-important stuffed shirt with the red face and the wart on the side of his nose, whom you will doubtless remember as unpleasantly as I do, and whom I will designate—because of the before-mentioned confidential nature of this matter—merely as General X.

Why they put this superannuated horse cavalryman in a position where he seems to have the final word on equipment for motorized outfits, I do not know. But there he is. And he gets worse all the time. He apparently thinks that the Behemoth Company makes just as good tractors as we do. He says he will consider nothing for the Army but what he calls "tested and tried" commercial models. And he refuses even to look at the new high-speed stuff which our experimental department is now developing.

But I am going to fool him. The old guy is leaving in a few days to spend the winter studying the various artillery outfits in Hawaii. So I am going to ship one of our new specials out there just as soon as it is ready—probably in about a month—and I will instruct our Honolulu representative to force a demonstration on him. If he once sees what we can do, even his obtuse mind cannot help but be impressed.

In the meantime, I want you to contact the guy and give him a sales talk in San Francisco. He will be at the St. Francis Hotel next week. And it is possible he may listen to you more readily than to me, because he is a great respector of rank, and he probably thinks the president of a company is more important and knows more than the sales manager.

I am sorry to be so vague regarding such details as the name of the general and the exact nature of the machine I am going to ship to Honolulu. But you will get the general idea, and I do not want to put too much confidential information in a letter which might fall into the hands of a third person. As you know, the War Department has warned us that we must take unusual precautions to protect our secret plans and designs from the horde of foreign spies which has recently invaded our country.

> Very sincerely,
> Alexander Botts.

TELEGRAM

> SAN FRANCISCO CALIF
> NOVEMBER 22 1939 5 P.M.

ALEXANDER BOTTS SALES MANAGER
EARTHWORM TRACTOR CO
EARTHWORM CITY ILL
THE SUGGESTIONS IN YOUR NOVEMBER TWENTY LETTER ARE NOTED AND I WILL TAKE UP ALL ANGLES WITH YOU ON MY RETURN TO EARTHWORM CITY IN ABOUT SIX WEEKS. IN THE MEANTIME FOR OBVIOUS REASONS I ASK THAT YOU KEEP ALL REFERENCE TO CONFIDENTIAL MATTERS OUT OF THE MAILS
> GILBERT HENDERSON
> PRESIDENT EARTHWORM TRACTOR CO

OFFICE OF ALEXANDER BOTTS
> Monday, December 18, 1939.

Mr. Gilbert Henderson,
San Francisco, California.
Dear Henderson:

Since receiving your somewhat brusque telegram, I have not written you at all for almost a month.

Merely keeping still, however, is not the only thing I have been doing. While following your advice—excellent as far as it goes—and observing the well-known military principle of keeping important information away from possible enemies, I have been actively turning my attention to a second, equally well-known principle which you have apparently never even heard of. This second principle requires that we must not, while shutting off the light from others, plunge ourselves into the Stygian darkness of our own smoke screen. In other words, we must have some safe method of transmitting secret information among ourselves.

Having come to the above conclusion soon after receiving your telegram, I promptly appealed to the War Department, and was referred to the Bridgeport Protectotype Corporation, of Bridgeport, Connecticut, from whom I have purchased six of their latest, improved, multiple-cam cipher machines.

These devices are the last word in scientific cryptography. To encipher a message, you pound out the words on a keyboard like a typewriter, and the letters come through completely scrambled up and neatly arranged in groups of five. To decipher, you merely reverse the process. The makers of these machines explain that the basic principle involved in their operation depends on a sequence of alphabetical displacements of varying degree, mechanically produced through the agency of an almost infinite number of minute indentations in the periphery of a series of interchangeable precision-built enciphering cams which are supplied in identical sets for all machines in a group, and are serially numbered, so that a different cam may be used for each message—all of which is supposed to be very simple, but if you can't understand it, don't worry, because I have arranged a setup that is efficient and completely foolproof.

One of the machines has been installed here at the home office, and the others have been sent, with full directions, to our five principal branches. A wire from the San Francisco manager reports that his machine has been placed in charge of a trustworthy employee, and that she has become, after a week of intensive practice, a thoroughly competent operator.

I will therefore bring these remarks to a close, and write out a secret message which will be enciphered by our newly established Department of Cryptography, and enclosed herewith. As soon as you have had the message run through the machine out there, you will be in possession of a bit of confidential news so interesting and important that I am sure you will be both surprised and pleased.

Awaiting your congratulations, I remain,

Your active and resourceful salesman,
Alexander Botts.

ENCLOSURE

EARTHWORM TRACTOR COMPANY
EARTHWORM CITY, ILLINOIS
DEPARTMENT OF CRYPTOGRAPHY

MESSAGE NO. 1, CAM NO. 77.

DEAR HENDERSON:

OFUTH QSWED MLJKU CVFGR ERDSZ QPGHC GJOLA SKDJV GUTYW
RTFGV IOJKN BHGRT WESDX ZSASQ KOMHJ DKHFZ ZFJIP NHFES
ZBHIY DFRTF CCBHI MWTSQ ZSEXS KUIRF LXPDF HTYEF XHJBD
SPHJE CBVHT FGRTC DFERS HJUIN MJKIO GHTYR ALGHT PFPFJ
VHRYF GSTEZ CJTHD KKGIY VHRTE AEAIO HGYTE XFQTW ADSEK
FGRPB MNKJY CGRDT FSRQW DVFGT NMJKI XCSDW QWASZ NMJKU
HPAAL VBGHE DFRTC HTYGB VFGRT DJIEB PDHVN MZVCN DGAKH
YEURO BGTRE ZGUOP NNFHR GHVIQ FURGE DFTOB CGYKM NGDEW
ALGHB EICMY NFUWJ CFYHL HNGFW QSDEL HUGWS MQDFL LPFSA
CBTPO BFGEW SRWSZ XCVPD LJKHJ VBMNS DQYSK XSCEJ RHXOO
BNGLS CVGIQ ZXSKN MWGPD FHTBC MWUFD SHTOI YUREJ VBAMP
XAZMN ZXSQW JKMPO FGRTC DVEFS HJBUG FKQHG BDFET IYJZX
BRTFG CVMPL GFQSW QGFIB VHGTE CHGYR NSJGE DLJUX KHJRG
FGDEQ XCHOU SCCHU DFTJN MKORD XSQYH BHJTT DFYIK MHGRD
CICHR FVHIO NGREW SUJBS VHTYR NMKOD FIVBQ STDGE BNHIN
BHTYS VHKIK GHEWQ FQJPB CVFGT NMHYQ XCDFO PLKFW CGRUN
BFTED SHUIC NGYER FYYDU NGRWK ZXSFX BVGHT MNJUI MKWYF
SEXCK JJGHY NGREO POLKI SDWEA GFTDR HRIGY YGTES VJUON
MGUIM GHRYD DFERF GHTVA SJGUE BVGHT MJKUI VBKJY MBHER
DSGTU NGHBU DVEFS VBGHT NMJKU UYHGB ERDFC WESDX QWASZ
RTFGC MJKUI PHOLM MHUSJ ERDOD CBFGU HGUSM GNRKS VBGDK
BVGHY MHAGE VGFTD NHJYR HSLBC BBAXZ UYIHJ RXXXX

VERY SINCERELY YOURS,
ALEXANDER BOTTS.

TELEGRAM

SAN FRANCISCO
DEC 20 1939

ALEXANDER BOTTS
EARTHWORM CITY
YOUR SCRAMBLED MESSAGE RECEIVED AM PRETTY DOUBTFUL
ABOUT THIS BUT WILL WITHHOLD FURTHER COMMENT UNTIL I GET
IT DECIPHERED

GILBERT HENDERSON

TELEGRAM

EARTHWORM CITY
DEC 27 1939

GILBERT HENDERSON
SAN FRANCISCO
JUST BACK FROM CHRISTMAS HOLIDAY AND FIND NO NEWS FROM
YOU SINCE YOUR WIRE OF A WEEK AGO PLEASE ADVISE WHETHER
ACTION HAS BEEN TAKEN ON MY IMPORTANT CIPHER MESSAGE OF
DECEMBER EIGHTEEN

ALEXANDER BOTTS

EARTHWORM TRACTOR COMPANY,
BRANCH OFFICE
SAN FRANCISCO

Thursday, December 28, 1939.

Mr. Alexander Botts,
Earthworm City, Illinois.

Dear Botts:

Your telegram is here, and I am glad to inform you that your
cipher message is perfectly safe, and will be attended to next week.
As this somewhat lengthy delay is a natural result of imperfections
inherent in your cipher system, I am glad that it has occurred so early
in the game. It will show you the disadvantage of rushing so
heedlessly into an experiment which, to my mind, is distinctly
impractical.

The difficulty in the present instance arose because your message
arrived just after Miss Priscilla Pratt, our cipher operator, had left for
a two weeks' vacation in Pasadena. The local manager and I did not
want to break in another operator, especially when all available
employees were busy with other tasks.

Besides, it would have been unfair to Miss Pratt to ask her to come
all the way back to San Francisco just to decipher one message. She
had postponed her vacation from last summer, and had especially
arranged to have it just at this time, because she is to appear in the
Pasadena Tournament of Roses, riding on a float entered by the
Santa Clara County Prune Growers' Association. She told us that she
is to wear a robe of dark purple, and represent the Queen of the
Prunes. And she is so thrilled by the idea that we could not think of
disappointing her.

Obviously, there was only one thing for me to do. I locked your message in the office safe, and I will have it deciphered next week when the young lady returns.

Hoping this delay will cause you no inconvenience,

Most sincerely,
Gilbert Henderson.

On Board Westbound Air
Liner NC 13997,

Saturday, December 30, 1939.

Mr. Gilbert Henderson,
San Francisco.

Dear Henderson:

It is my painful duty to inform you that your failure to cooperate in my carefully worked-out cryptographic plan has plunged the Earthworm Tractor Company into a crisis more appalling than anything I have previously encountered in my entire twenty years in the business. I am now racing westward by plane in a desperate attempt to undo some of the mischief which has resulted from your indifference and inaction. And I have decided to explain the entire situation to you in the hope that you may be able—even at this late hour—to give me a little help. I should have preferred to send this information in a cryptographic telegram before I left Earthworm City. But, as long as you will apparently be unable to decipher any messages until the return of your little friend, the Queen of the Prunes, I shall have to hand you the bad news in plain English—hoping and praying that the secret matters I am about to discuss may not be pried open by the evil eyes of foreign agents.

To begin with, I will reveal the information which you so unfortunately failed to get out of my cipher message of December 18. On that day I shipped from Earthworm City, en route to Honolulu, the first of our secret, new, experimental, high-speed, sixteen-ton, heavy-artillery tractors—a truly magnificent machine, powered by a 500 horsepower air-cooled radial airplane motor, protected by seven-eighths-inch, heat-treated, nickel-steel armor plate, equipped with heavy-duty hydraulic bulldozer for emergency road repairing, and accompanied by a 155-millimeter long-rifle cannon mounted on special Earthworm high-speed carriage—the entire outfit being intended to provide the egregious General X with a sensational demonstration of what we can do when we start moving heavy artillery at hitherto unheard-of velocities.

To prevent news of this shipment from leaking out, I loaded the tractor and the gun, secretly and under cover of night, into an end-door automobile boxcar—M.K.T. 337991. After sealing the car, I cleverly contrived to have the shipment billed as two ordinary commercial tractors consigned to our San Francisco branch. I mailed the bill of lading, in the ordinary routine manner, to our office out there; thus completely throwing off the track all snoopers who might be looking for military materiel. And I then requested you, in cipher, to see that the tractor and gun were secretly transferred to a ship and sent on to Honolulu, where I had cryptographically notified our local representative to receive them.

The above precautions—inspired by a letter from the War Department requesting that we exercise great care in protecting military secrets—were admirably conceived and efficiently executed from my end. Their success, however, depended on a certain minimum amount of cooperation from your end.

You may imagine my consternation, therefore, when I received your astonishing letter in this morning's mail and learned for the first time that you had not made so much as a feeble attempt to get even as far as halfway to first base in this affair.

My alarm was increased by a second letter in the morning mail, in which the War Department advised increased precautions because of recently discovered plots by alien espionage agents who have been attempting to steal secret military devices, smuggle them over the Mexican border, and finally ship them across the ocean to certain foreign totalitarian states.

But the final straw was a routine report, also in the morning mail, from the shipping department of our San Francisco branch. This report revealed the hideous fact that M.K.T. Boxcar 337991, instead of going through to San Francisco, had been diverted at Ogden, by request of our San Francisco office, and rerouted to a new destination bearing the strange name of "The Oscar Mroczkowicz Ranch, Oviedo, California."

When I had read this report and had learned, by consulting the map, that Oviedo is in Southern California, right on the Mexican border, I was, to put it mildly, aghast.

At once a flood of ominous questions began welling up in my mind. Who, I asked myself, was this mysterious Mr. Oscar Mroczkowicz, who had apparently acquired a ranch at such a suspiciously strategic point on the border? Was he one of these insidious foreign spies? Had he in some devious manner discovered the true nature of the secret shipment in M.K.T. Boxcar 337991? Had he, himself, inveigled Miss Priscilla Pratt into appearing as the Queen of the Prunes at Pasadena—thus blocking the decipherment of my message? Had he insinuated himself into the confidence of our sales force on the Pacific Coast, pretending that he wanted to buy a couple of tractors for his ranch? And had he then insidiously argued you or somebody else out there into rerouting this particular boxcar? Unfortunately, I did not know.

But one thing was painfully clear and plain. This Mr. Oscar Mroczkowicz was now, or soon would be, in a position where he could, with the greatest ease, smuggle our carefully guarded, secret-model, heavy-artillery tractor across the border, move it by circuitous trails across uninhabited deserts and through lonely mountain passes to some obscure port, and then ship it on an inconspicuous freighter to the shores of a treacherous and malevolent foreign power. In short, one of the most vital secrets of our national defense was in deadly peril. Something had to be done.

At once I sprang to action. Grabbing the telephone, I put in one long-distance call after another; running up an impressive toll bill but accomplishing very little else. Repeated calls to various railroad offices and freight depots all the way from Ogden to Oviedo finally revealed that M.K.T. Boxcar 337991 would probably reach Oviedo tomorrow afternoon. But when I asked that delivery on the car be stopped, I received the idiotic reply that this could not be done unless I produced the bill of lading—which was manifestly impossible over the telephone, even if I had had the bill of lading, which I did not. I explained this to them, over and over, but they paid no attention.

Having failed with the railroad officials, I considered appealing to the police. But this would have revealed our secrets to too many people. So then I tried to call our San Francisco office, and I tried to call you at your hotel, but everybody was away—fiddling like Nero, I suppose, at various pre-New Year's weekend orgies, while I, like Rome, was burning up with futile anger back in Earthworm City.

Finally, I abandoned the telephone in disgust and headed for the airport. I am now halfway to Los Angeles. And when I land there tomorrow morning, I will proceed as fast as possible to Oviedo, where I will take such measures as seem appropriate in view of whatever the situation may turn out to be.

In the meantime, if you have the bill of lading at San Francisco, you may be able to stop delivery on this fateful shipment before it is too late. If not, you will have to gather a force of resolute, trustworthy men, supply them with arms, and fly down to the border. And if I can find some way—legal or illegal, peaceful or violent—to hold things up until you get into action, we may yet thwart our adversaries.

The future is ominously uncertain. But I can assure you of one thing—if that tractor is taken out of this country, it will be over my dead body.

Yours with grim determination,
Alexander Botts.

P.S.: I have just landed at L.A., and will mail this at once.

Joe's Diner, 17 Main Street,
Greasewood Valley,
California,
January 1, 1940. 5 p.m.

Mr. Gilbert Henderson,
San Francisco.

Dear Henderson:

This has been a terrible day. I am so slowed down by mental and physical fatigue, and at the same time so speeded up by emotional excitement, that it is doubtful whether I can write a coherent letter.

But I need your help. So, fortified by five cups of coffee and a large order of hamburg and onions supplied by the excellent chef of Joe's Diner here, I will attempt to give you an account of what has been going on. As I cannot trust you to decipher anything, I shall have to use plain English. Besides, I left the cipher machine back in Earthworm City.

It was a little after sunset last night when I finally arrived at the little village of Oviedo. As the train approached the station I observed, through the car window, a locomotive pulling a single boxcar along a sort of spur or side track which seemed to lead out across the desert. In the dim twilight I was just able to read, on the side of the car, the inscription, "M.K.T. 337991."

With a single mighty spring I shot from my seat, without even stopping to pick up my traveling bag, and landed halfway down the aisle, headed for the car door. A moment later I had leaped from the still-moving train and started running as hard as I could along the side track in pursuit of the boxcar. It was moving too fast for me, however, and in spite of all my efforts it gradually disappeared in the gathering darkness ahead.

Doggedly I followed. After a couple of miles I came to a ten-foot barbed-wire fence, with a closed gate across the track. On the gate was a sign, "Oscar Mroczkowicz Ranch." Inside was a tough-looking guard with an automatic pistol. He told me there was no admittance here for anybody, and pointed to a sign on the fence which read, "Danger. 2100 Volts. Keep Off." But he absolutely refused to give me any further information.

I therefore wished him a pleasant good evening, walked back to town, stole a shovel that somebody had left outside the freight station, and circled around through the desert to a remote section of the fence, where I started digging a passage in the sand under the bottom wire. This job took most of the night, but I finally managed to crawl through. Half an hour later I found the railroad track, evidently a private spur, and followed it till I reached the outskirts of a group of ranch buildings. All was quiet except for a single guard, who was walking a fairly long beat, taking in all of the somewhat scattered buildings.

By this time there was a faint glow in the east—the approaching dawn of the year 1940. But, unlike some other people, I had no time for a New Year's celebration. Waiting until the guard was at the far end of his beat, I crept forward and soon discovered M.K.T. Boxcar 337991 standing at the very end of the track beside a small machinery shed. The end door was open. Cautiously I climbed in, and found myself beside the armored bulk of our mighty sixteen-ton artillery tractor. Then I heard voices. My heart began knocking like a motor with loose connecting rods. Peering out, I saw approaching, through the semidarkness, a dozen or more shadowy forms.

"Yes, sir," said a voice, "I filled up the fuel tank last night, and hitched on the gun. She's all ready to go."

"O.K.," said another voice. "Some of you men bring a few of those timbers over here and lay up a ramp, so we can unload."

By this time the moving shadows—in all probability as ruthless a gang of cutthroats as could be found anywhere—were so close that escape was impossible. There was nothing for me to do but conceal my presence as long as I could. Silently I opened the steel door of the tractor and climbed into the cab. Silently I closed the door and fastened the catches. Then I peered anxiously out through the narrow slits at the front—at the rear—at the sides. I could see nothing.

Nervously I shifted myself around. One of my feet touched the starting button. There was an ear-shattering roar. The five hundred horses in the great motor had come to life.

And at the same moment, in a sudden flash of inspiration, I

realized that I was all set to go places. Not only could I bring about my own escape but I could also rescue the tractor.

For the first time this year, I smiled a smile of pure joy and happiness. I set the gears. I opened the throttle. I slammed in the clutch. With a leap like a charging elephant, the huge tractor debouched from the end of the car, dropped four or five feet, and hit the ground with a shock that practically knocked me cold. But the sturdy machine was unharmed. And a few seconds later, when I came to, I found that I was rolling merrily along across the desert. A glance through the slit in the rear of the cab showed me that the big cannon was dutifully following behind.

I shifted into high, speeded the tractor up to about forty miles per hour, turned on the headlights, and began looking for the railroad track, so that I could follow it back to civilization and the protection of the law. But before I found the railroad I came to a deep and, at the moment, completely dry irrigation ditch, with a lot of jagged boulders along the edge.

I stopped. Glancing through the slit in the rear of the cab, I noticed signs of intense activity around the ranch buildings several miles to the rear. A number of automobiles seemed to be setting out in my direction. Then I saw a red flash. A few seconds later there was a bloodcurdling howl, and a violent explosion several hundred yards away from the tractor. It didn't take me long to figure that one out. Those miscreants at the ranch had thought of everything; they had apparently stolen a piece of field artillery somewhere, and they were going into action in a big way.

For a moment I thought of shooting back at them with my own cannon, which was twice as big as theirs. But I had no ammunition. So I decided I had better move along and put as much distance as possible between myself and the enemy artillery. But I did not see how I could get through all those big rocks and across the ditch.

Then I thought of the heavy-duty hydraulic bulldozer on the front of the tractor. At once I lowered the sturdy blade and pushed several cubic yards of desert sand up over and in between the jagged boulders. Then I began skillfully shuttling back and forth, pushing up load after load of sand, building a road across the boulders and partially filling in the ditch. A rotary bulldozer would have thrown the dirt farther and faster. But the plain one did well enough. And after about ten minutes' work I drove across the ditch with the greatest ease.

A short distance beyond, I crashed through a section of the electric fence, setting off an interesting little shower of sparks, but escaping without any damage to myself or the tractor.

In the meantime, the criminals at the ranch had been dropping shells all around me. But they failed to get any direct hits, and the fragments rattled harmlessly off the armor. Even so, the firing was distinctly annoying, so I resumed my speed of forty miles per hour, and before long I was out of range.

It was now broad daylight, and I could see that I had completely lost my way. The railroad and the town of Oviedo were nowhere to be seen. Instead, there loomed up directly ahead of me a rugged and desolate range of high mountains. Too late, I realized that I had come in the wrong direction. But it was now impossible to turn back.

Someday I hope to give you a full account of how I drove that tractor and that gun up the slopes of that awe-inspiring range, winding my way through steep canyons, crashing over crags and ledges, creeping along the edges of dizzy cliffs, and clawing my way up forty-five-degree slopes. Someday I will give you the whole story. But right now I have neither the time nor the energy. Suffice it to say that I finally crossed the ridge. And a short time later, having almost exhausted my fuel supply, I concealed the tractor in a desolate, narrow canyon, placing it so that I could use the bulldozer to roll big rocks down on any of Mr. Mroczkowicz's mugs who might try to follow me.

Then I walked down to this little town of Greasewood Valley. After allaying the suspicions of the natives by telling them I was a lone prospector looking for gold in these here hills, I bought myself some refreshment and started writing this letter. As soon as I have mailed it, I will return to mount guard over my precious machinery.

What I want you to do is organize a relief expedition. You must provide gasoline and oil, and a gang of strong men to carry it up into the mountains. These men should be heavily armed. You must send a boxcar to some lonely point on the railroad. And you must provide a guide who can lay out a route which will enable us to reach the railroad and load the machinery without publicity.

Of course, I could do all these things much more efficiently myself, but I do not dare leave the tractor for more than an hour or two at a time. I will, however, sneak into the town of Greasewood Valley once a day. You can contact me there at Joe's Diner, 17 Main Street. Please hurry. If the criminals from across the mountains get here first, you may find nothing to rescue but the dead body of one who perished fighting for his country.

Your somewhat scared, but ever determined sales manager,

Alexander Botts.

Mroczkowicz Ranch,
Oviedo, California.
January 4, 1940.

Mr. Alexander Botts,
Care Joe's Diner,
17 Main Street,
Greasewood Valley, California.

Dear Botts:
Your two letters have been forwarded to me here. I highly disapprove of this continuous discussion of confidential matters in plainly written letters. However, you seem to be so completely misinformed about almost everything that I feel compelled to give you the real facts before you engage in any more outlandish exploits. And as long as your cipher scheme has proved so impractical, I will have to use straight English.

It may interest you to know, in the first place, that your plan to ship the new artillery tractor to Honolulu was based on an entirely erroneous assumption. Your friend General X—as you might have known if you had taken the trouble to investigate—changed his plans. Instead of going to Honolulu last month, he came here to Oviedo, where the United States Army has recently purchased a large tract of land known as the Mroczkowicz Ranch, and established thereon a secret and supposedly well-guarded proving ground for mechanized equipment. Mr. Mroczkowicz, the former owner, has nothing more to do with the place. Furthermore, he is not a foreign spy but an honorable, patriotic American citizen who, several years ago, was one of the famous Fighting Irish on the Notre Dame football team.

A week or so ago General X asked me to send to Oviedo a couple of our commercial machines for demonstration purposes. Owing to the inefficient working of your pet cipher scheme, I supposed that M.K.T. Boxcar 337991 contained the machines described in the bill of lading, so it was perfectly natural for me to reroute the car.

Last Saturday I came down here myself to be present at the demonstration. When the car arrived on New Year's Eve, and we discovered that we had one of the new experimental models, the general—nowhere near as dumb as you think—was so interested, and so impatient to see it perform, that he arranged for a demonstration as early as possible the next morning. Thus it came about that he and I were both members of that shadowy group of "cutthroats" which you so dimly discerned in the pale dawn of New Year's Day.

As you have never been lacking in imagination, you can appreciate our surprise and bewilderment when the tractor and the gun apparently unloaded themselves, bursting out of the car, landing on the ground with a terrifying crash, and then rolling off across the desert. As we did not know you were driving, and as your course was perilously close to the international boundary, we had a bad spy scare ourselves. That is why we used everything we had, including an old French seventy-five, in a vain attempt to stop you.

The manner in which you eluded our pursuit prompts me to say a few words about your handling of the tractor. In the past I have had but little opportunity to see you in action, and my knowledge of your driving ability has been largely derived from your own letters, which sometimes, I must admit, have impressed me as being more like fairy tales than factual narratives. Your most recent letter, however, seems, if anything, to understate the facts. So I must apologize for my past skepticism, and offer you my present congratulations. Your performance on Monday was, without exception, the finest piece of rough cross-country tractor driving that I have ever seen.

What you thought was a dry irrigation ditch lined with jagged boulders was really an experimental antitank trench bordered by pointed concrete blocks. This setup was supposed to present an absolutely impassable barrier to all forms of mechanized equipment. So the speed with which you smothered it with sand and then rolled across had the general practically speechless with astonishment.

But later on, as the general, peering through a telescope, followed your course over that appalling mountain range, he regained his voice and pretty near wore himself out complaining that he had found exactly the machine he needed, and here it was, as he supposed, escaping across the border on its way to the laboratories of some foreign power where its secrets could be stolen.

During the succeeding three days, the general's state of mind was rendered even worse by the failure of all pursuing parties to find any trace of the fugitive tractor. And it was not until this morning, when I showed him your letter, that he calmed down sufficiently to tell me that after seeing our tractor in action, he has decided to recommend that the Army place a large order. In view of the general's influence, I consider that this pretty much puts the deal in the bag.

In a few minutes, the general and I are starting by plane for Washington to arrange final details. This means that I cannot take charge of any rescue party. However, we are sending a platoon of cavalry to Greasewood Valley with all necessary supplies. And I will entrust this letter to the platoon leader.

In conclusion, I wish to thank you for staging your remarkable demonstration where I could see it.

Yours with gratitude and admiration,
Gilbert Henderson.

P.S.: I still don't like your cipher machines.

THE COCKROACH CAVALRY

OFFICE OF ALEXANDER BOTTS,
SALES MANAGER
EARTHWORM TRACTOR COMPANY
EARTHWORM CITY, ILLINOIS

Thursday, May 1, 1941

Mr. Gilbert Henderson,
President, Earthworm
Tractor Company,
Earthworm Branch Office,
Washington, D.C.

Dear Henderson:

This is to let you know that I have decided to resign my position as sales manager of the Earthworm Tractor Company and join the Army. My reasons are as follows:

I have just heard that the Army has canceled their contract for five hundred of our recently developed "fighting cockroaches" or one-man midget tanks—and this at the very moment when we are getting into actual production. As you, in spite of all your efforts at Washington, have been unable to prevent this disaster, I feel that it is up to me to do something about it.

Instead, however, of attacking this and other related problems in my present capacity as a representative of the company, I have decided that I can accomplish more by getting a commission and working inside the Army—which is where most of our difficulties seem to originate.

Another reason for my action is that I am getting sick of my job as sales manager. Ever since the national-defense program began to create a demand for more tractors than we can produce, I have had to spend all my time persuading customers not to buy tractors—a job which would drive any good salesman crazy.

In view of the above considerations, I am today forwarding to the War Department my application for a commission as a tractor expert in the Specialist Reserve of the United States Army. As I am probably the leading tractor expert in the country, I should think the rank of colonel would be about right. I want you to use any influence you may have with the brass hats down there to see that this application goes through at once.

Yours patriotically,
Alexander Botts.

EARTHWORM BRANCH OFFICE
WASHINGTON, D.C.

Wednesday, May 7, 1941.

Dear Botts:

Your letter of resignation was a surprise. After thinking it over, however, I am inclined to believe that your decision to join the Army is a wise one.

In the past, the principal flaw in your otherwise sterling character has been an unfortunate tendency toward insubordination and lack of respect for authority. For this reason, I feel that a period of service under the strict discipline of the Army will do you a lot of good.

As we shall want you back after the emergency, I am granting you a leave of absence rather than accepting your resignation. And it is my earnest hope that when you return you will have seen the error of your ways, and that you will agree with my feeling that efficiency in any organization can be achieved only when all orders are obeyed cheerfully and promptly, with no monkey business or back talk.

I am happy to inform you that I have taken up your case with a number of my friends in the War Department, with the result that you have been commissioned a captain in the Specialist Reserve assigned to the mechanized cavalry. You will receive orders to report for duty in a few days.

Wishing you the greatest possible success in your new career,

Cordially yours,
Gilbert Henderson

THE COCKROACH CAVALRY

To: Mr. Gilbert Henderson, Washington, D.C.
From: Captain Alexander Botts, Fort Clemens, Missouri
Date: Monday, May 12, 1941
Subject: A Hideous Mistake Has Been Made

This is to inform you, Henderson, that your well-meant efforts to start me on my Army career have resulted in getting me launched completely upside down, backward and in the wrong direction. When my commission and orders arrived last week, I was naturally disappointed to find that I was only a captain, and that, instead of receiving an important post in Washington, I had been assigned to a regiment stationed in Missouri. But that was not the worst. It was not until this morning, when I arrived to report for duty here at Fort Clemens, that I became aware of the horrible fate that was in store for me.

As I entered the camp gate—attired in my new uniform and riding in a taxi which I had hired at the nearby railroad station—I began craning my neck in an attempt to see what sort of tanks and other mechanical equipment this regiment employed. At once a cold chill came over me. A feeling of ominous foreboding gripped my vitals. There were no tanks. There was no mechanical equipment. Instead, my horrified gaze rested upon rows and rows of horses, tied to picket lines. In every direction they cluttered the landscape—horses, horses, horses, horses—swishing flies with their silly tails, gnawing at bunches of hay, or just gazing about in a vacant manner.

We stopped in front of the tent of the regimental commander, Colonel H. H. McKenzie-Morton. I entered, introduced myself, and presented my orders. The colonel, an elderly gentleman, perhaps sixty years old, was unusually stiff and military. Right away I knew I didn't like the guy. And I have reason to suspect that he felt somewhat the same about me.

"Listen, colonel," I said, "I thought I was coming to a tank outfit. What is the meaning of all these horses I see outside?"

"This is a cavalry regiment," said the colonel, with a touch of austere pride. "Thank the Lord, we have not yet been forced to adopt this modern craze for vile inanimate machinery."

"In that case," I said, "the sooner I get out of here the better."

"What do you mean?"

"When you gaze on me," I explained, "you are gazing on a man who is probably the greatest authority on tractors and crawler equipment the world has ever known. Up until last week I was the sales manager of the great Earthworm Tractor Company. My commission is supposed to be in the mechanized force. But apparently some half-wit at the War Department has ignorantly assigned me here. So there is only one thing to do, colonel. I want you to put through an order in a hurry sending me back where I belong."

"Do I understand," asked the colonel, "that you are presuming to issue orders to me, your superior officer?"

"Don't be silly, colonel," I said affably, "I am a businessman. You won't get anywhere trying to pull this hard-boiled military stuff on me. All I'm trying to do is to correct a foolish mistake."

Unfortunately my attempt to smooth matters down only seemed to goad the colonel into a deplorable exhibition of military unreasonableness.

"Captain Botts," he said, "you are now in the Army. You have been ordered to duty with my regiment. You will obey this order."

As he spoke, Colonel McKenzie-Morton kept glaring at me so fiercely that I almost laughed in his face.

"Come on, colonel," I said. "Be yourself. Be reasonable. You may not have a great deal of sense, but you must have enough to realize that there is no point whatever in having me hang around this dump with all these silly horses. If you won't give me permission to go, I'll just have to leave without permission."

At this the colonel rose to his feet. "Captain Botts," he said, speaking quietly but with suppressed passion, "no subordinate can come into my post of command and speak to me as you have spoken. Ordinarily I should be only too glad to dispense with the services of an officer who is nothing but a mechanic. But in your case I feel that I have a certain duty to perform. Quite obviously, you have not the slightest conception of the meaning of military discipline. For your own good, therefore, and for the good of the Service, I must take it upon myself to knock a little sense into you. Your request for a transfer is hereby refused, and you will remain in this organization until such time as you get over your insubordinate attitude and give evidence that you are fit to perform the duties of an officer in the United States Army."

About this time it gradually began to come over me that Colonel McKenzie-Morton meant business, and that very likely the big bum had the necessary authority to carry out his idiotic ideas.

"I will have an orderly show you to your tent," said the colonel. "You will remain there to await further orders. And let there be no mistake. When I say that you will remain there, that is exactly what I mean. If there is any attempt on your part to leave this camp without my permission, you will be placed under immediate arrest. Have I made myself clear?"

"Yes, sir," I said.

That terminated our little conference, and I have been spending

139

the rest of the morning sitting here in my tent writing this letter. Now that you understand the situation, you will realize, I hope, that the Army system of discipline—far from improving me, as you apparently hoped—has merely made it possible for this colonel to practically kidnap me, and thus sabotage all the good I might have done toward improving the mechanization of the Army.

The next move is therefore up to you. You must rush around to the War Department at once, see all your influential friends, and insist that I be rescued from this wretched livery-stable outfit at once.

Yours,
Alexander Botts.

TELEGRAM

NEW YORK, N.Y.
MAY 14, 1941.

TO CAPTAIN ALEXANDER BOTTS.
FORT CLEMENS, MO.
YOUR LETTER FORWARDED TO ME HERE. I WILL TAKE UP YOUR CASE WITH WAR DEPARTMENT WHEN I RETURN TO WASHINGTON IN ABOUT TWO WEEKS. IN THE MEANTIME, I AM SURE YOUR EXPERIENCE WITH REAL ARMY DISCIPLINE WILL DO YOU A LOT OF GOOD.

GILBERT HENDERSON.

Fort Clemens, Missouri,
Thursday, May 15, 1941.

Dear Henderson:

Your callous indifference to my fate does not bother me as much as might be supposed. As a matter of fact, I am now getting along so well here that I want to stay a little longer. This does not mean that I am weakly submitting myself to the absurd Army system of discipline. Quite the contrary. What I am doing is giving the system a much-needed cleaning up and delousing—commencing with old Colonel McKenzie-Morton as Louse No. 1.

The opportunity for opening my campaign came on the afternoon of the day I arrived, when the colonel summoned me to his tent and spoke about as follows: "Captain Botts, your ignorance of horses and military matters makes it impossible for me to assign you to any duty with this regiment in keeping with your rank. I have therefore decided to give you a pick-and-shovel job. Unfortunately, as you are an officer, I do not feel justified in requiring you to swing a pick personally—much as I should like to. So I am putting you in charge of a small detail of enlisted men—most of them unruly characters who are being given extra fatigue duty as punishment for insubordination. They are to dig a ditch for a water main. My adjutant will take you out at once and explain the nature of the operation. You will start work tomorrow morning. Tomorrow afternoon I shall inspect what you have been doing. And I shall expect to find that you have made satisfactory progress. That is all."

When the adjutant showed me the ditch-digging project, I saw at once that it was a real honey. A half mile of four-inch water main had to be buried four feet deep. And only twelve men with picks and shovels had been assigned for the entire job.

The adjutant—a good egg—gave me some helpful information. "I think the colonel is trying to ride you," he said. "These men he is giving you are a mean bunch. They are all mechanics who enlisted in the cavalry on the understanding that they would be placed in mechanized units. When, through some mistake, they were sent here, they became sullen and rebellious. So you'll have to be plenty tough if you expect to get anything out of them."

"It seems to be a custom in this Army," I said, "to put square pistons in round cylinders. But thanks for the tip. I think I can handle these birds."

I promptly went to the camp telephone exchange and called our St. Louis Earthworm Tractor dealer. Appealing to his sense of patriotism, I asked for help. And I am happy to say he rallied around at once—not, like some people, after about two weeks.

The next morning, when I marched my little pick-and-shovel brigade out to the diggings, I had a pleasant surprise in store for them. Our St. Louis dealer, after traveling all night, had arrived with a fleet of large trucks, loaded down with no less than three ditch-digging machines, several small tractors with bulldozers, and a lot of miscellaneous equipment. As soon as the eyes of my mechanics lit on all this beautiful machinery, their bitterness vanished like a bug sucked into a tractor radiator. With lusty goodwill they unloaded the equipment, and in almost no time the dirt began to fly.

By noon the ditch was completed. By 3 p.m. the pipe was laid in the bottom, and the ditch had been backfilled. After we had thanked the dealer, he disappeared with his machinery. I then gathered my crew in the shade and served them with refreshments from a passing ice-cream wagon.

About this time Colonel McKenzie-Morton came trotting up on a handsome steed. When he saw that the entire detail, instead of being hard at work, was lolling about on the greensward lapping up ice-cream cones, he practically went off his nut.

"Captain Botts," he yelled, glaring down from his high horse, "I gave you a definite order to perform a certain definite task. And what do I find? You permit your men to loaf about as if they had nothing to do. What do you think this is, a Sunday-school picnic? Have you any explanation as to why you have deliberately disobeyed my orders?"

While this harangue was going on, I had called my men to attention—a procedure which, according to my vague memories of 1918, seemed the proper thing under the circumstances. I advanced to a point directly beside the colonel's horse, saluted as snappily as I could, and glared up at the old guy. I then got off a little speech whose effect I was able to heighten by using that obsolescent third-person form of discourse occasionally affected by old-fashioned and superannuated military men. "Sir," I said, "as long as the colonel has seen fit to reprimand Captain Botts in the presence of his men, Captain Botts requests the privilege of answering this reprimand at once and in the presence of these same men."

"If you've got anything to say for yourself, you'd better say it quick, without all this beating around the bush."

"The colonel's charges reveal that he does not know what he is talking about," I said. "Therefore, Captain Botts demands a trial by court-martial, at which he will be prepared to prove that he has carried out the colonel's orders *in toto*——"

"Don't be a damn fool," said the colonel.

"And at which Captain Botts will also be prepared to prove that the colonel has used profane language unbecoming an officer and a gentleman——"

"All right," snarled the colonel, "you'll get your court-martial."

"Easy now, colonel," I said, relapsing into ordinary English. "The only orders I got were to dig a ditch, lay a water main, and fill up the ditch again. Okay—the job is done."

"Are you trying to tell me that with only twelve men working less than a day, you have buried a half mile of pipe four feet deep? It's impossible!"

"That's what you think," I said. "And, in the horse-and-buggy age in which you exist, it would be. But to a modern mechanic like me, it is as simple"—I snapped my fingers—"as that."

I then took the old colonel over to the scene of our labors and

142

showed him the freshly turned earth. I explained how I had very sensibly borrowed the necessary equipment, and exactly how the job had been accomplished. He was convinced—but far from licked.

"Captain Botts," he said, "you seem to be a very bright young man, but you are not quite bright enough. I'm going to let you off this time, but you will soon find that in the Army this smart-aleck attitude will get you into very serious trouble. That is all." He turned his horse and trotted back to camp. The rest of us followed on foot.

That was day before yesterday. Since then, the colonel has been using me and my twelve-man detail on various odd jobs cleaning up around the camp. I have told my men if they will play ball with me now, I will do everything I can to get them into a mechanized outfit later on. They are therefore working for me very dutifully.

I have thus completed the first part of my Army-improvement campaign. The colonel has been shown that my up-to-date system of intelligent leadership plus machinery works much better on a ditch-digging job than his antiquated system of bull-headed discipline and horse-and-buggy technique. Although he is still sore, he has undoubtedly lost much of his previous feeling of infallibility. And he is therefore ripe for the next phase—in which I plan to demonstrate how mechanical cavalry, intelligently led, can skin the pants off of his quaint medieval horse outfit.

In preparation for this event, I have wired the factory to ship me—at one of the nearby towns—a half dozen of our recently perfected small cockroach tanks. These machines I will keep in hiding until next week, when there is to be a war game—or sham battle—between this cavalry outfit and an infantry regiment from Fort Leonard Wood. Then, as soon as McKinzie-Morton gets into trouble—as he is sure to do with all these fool horses to cope with—I will offer the services of my tanks. As the colonel will want to win the battle, and as he must have at least a faint substratum of common sense in his otherwise heavily hossified intellect, he will have to accept. I will then put over a real mechanized attack which will win the battle.

In gratitude, the colonel will be constrained to listen to my request for a transfer, and to put in a good word for our tanks with the War Department, thus making it easier for me to get our contract reinstated. If everything goes as I expect, it will be unnecessary for you to take up my case with the big shots at Washington. I have a feeling that I am going to work everything out by my own efforts.

Yours,
Alexander Botts.

143

TELEGRAM

NEW YORK, MONDAY, MAY 19, 1941.

TO CAPTAIN ALEXANDER BOTTS,

FT. CLEMENS, MO.

AS YOU ARE NOW ON LEAVE OF ABSENCE FROM THE EARTHWORM COMPANY, YOUR ACTION IN ORDERING SHIPMENT OF THOSE SIX TANKS IS ENTIRELY UNWARRANTED—ESPECIALLY AS YOU HAVE NO AUTHORITY TO ACCEPT THEM ON BEHALF OF THE ARMY. YOU WILL SHIP THEM BACK AT ONCE. I WOULD FURTHER SUGGEST THAT YOU ABANDON YOUR FUTILE EFFORTS TO IMPROVE THE ARMY AND CONDUCT YOURSELF IN SUCH A WAY THAT THE ARMY MAY HAVE A CHANCE TO IMPROVE YOU.

GILBERT HENDERSON.

To: Mr. Gilbert Henderson, Earthworm Branch Office, Graybar Building, New York City.

From: Captain Alexander Botts, Fort Clemens, Missouri.

Date: Wednesday, May 21, 1941.

Subject: Trouble with the Army System of Discipline.

I beg to report that the Army system of discipline is still doing me no good. As a matter of fact, it has now got me under arrest and confined to quarters, so I am utterly unable to ship back those tanks as you request. Furthermore, I am facing court-martial charges which the colonel may be able, this time, to make stick.

I must therefore renew my request that you get down to Washington in a hurry, pull all the wires in sight, and try to get me out of this mess. And, in order that you may appreciate the seriousness of the situation, I will give you a brief and snappy account of what has occurred.

Night before last, Colonel McKenzie-Morton called in all of the officers of the regiment and explained the two-day sham battle which was to start the following morning. It seemed that an infantry regiment, supported by several batteries of field artillery, was to advance from the south up the narrow Ozark valley in which our camp is located, and try to capture a small town ten miles behind us. Our job was to prevent this—not by shooting, of course, but by outmaneuvering the enemy. The issue would be decided by umpires—Army officers with white hatbands—who were supposed to swarm all over the field and decide who had got there first with the most fire power.

"Our mission is defensive," said the colonel, "but a real cavalryman"—here he swelled out his chest—"thinks only of attack. Our defense will therefore be dynamic. Holding the lines in the valley here with half our force, we shall send the other half through the mountains on our right to fall upon the enemy's flank and annihilate him. And I wish to point out," he continued, fixing his gaze directly on me, "that for work such as this the horse is still supreme. As both our flanks rest on mountainous country devoid of good roads, we have no use whatever for mechanical innovations such as portees."

Note: Portees are motor trucks used for transporting cavalry horses when they have to get someplace in a hurry. Modern cavalry, of course, fights on foot. But a good cavalryman is so dependent on the companionship of his horse that he always has to take him along, even when he has to drag him in a truck to a battle where he won't be any use after he gets there. This procedure is obviously so cumbersome that I could well understand Colonel McKenzie-Morton's doubts on the matter.

When the colonel had concluded his remarks, I arose and attempted to make a little speech. "Colonel," I said, "I am just as skeptical of portee cavalry as you are. But that does not mean all motorized equipment is no good. If you want to put on a real flank movement tomorrow, the ideal equipment is the Earthworm Tractor Company's cockroach cavalry——"

"Captain Botts," interrupted the colonel severely, "no one has asked for any comments from you on this or any other matter."

"All right," I said to myself. "If you won't listen to me, I will have to show you."

Next morning, after the bulk of the regiment moved out, I marched five of my twelve mechanics to the freight station where our six little one-man cockroach tanks had arrived several days previously. The boys at the factory had done a remarkably thorough job on the equipment, each tank being supplied with a machine gun, plenty of blank ammunition, lights, winch, cable, tools, and everything else that could be desired. When my men saw these mechanical masterpieces, their enthusiasm knew no bounds. And after a brief period of instruction they were raring to go. We climbed aboard, and started forth on a flanking movement which, for sheer speed and scope, was designed to make the horse cavalry look like a bunch of paleological snails.

The horses had started around our right flank, so I chose the left. And, on account of my superior speed, I decided to move in a very wide arc, sweeping so far out beyond the enemy's right flank that the possibility of meeting hostile patrols was practically eliminated.

The hardest part was getting over the first ridge. We followed trails so narrow that no tank bigger than our three-foot-wide midgets could have gotten through. We crossed mountain swamps which would have mired down any man or horse. And at one place we had to use the winches and cables to pull the machines up over an almost vertical thirty-foot cliff. By this time I began to realize that Colonel McKenzie-Morton had probably been very wise in not attempting this particular terrain with his horses. Even with our splendid little mechanical cockroaches the going was very slow indeed. By sunset we had covered, according to a map I had mooched from the adjutant, only ten miles. But we were over the ridge, and had reached a good gravel road in the valley beyond.

From here on it was easier. Speeding along country roads at thirty to forty miles an hour, we zigzagged our way—east, then south, then west, and finally north—a sweep of over two hundred miles which brought us directly behind the center of the enemy's lines. This, I hoped, would be the one place they would not be expecting us.

And I am happy to report that I was right. Our first contact with the enemy came shortly after dawn, when we rounded a blind curve in the road and found ourselves directly behind a battery of field artillery. Swinging into line, we almost scared the cannoneers to death with a mighty burst of blank ammunition from our machine guns. At once an umpire popped up and demanded an explanation. I opened the shutter of the turret. I explained that I had just annihilated the battery. He seemed puzzled. He said he had not been informed that the opposing forces had any tanks. I assured him that we did. And, as I had the machines right there to prove it, he finally admitted that his information must have been faulty, and ruled that the battery was out of action.

Encouraged by this success, I led my fighting cockroaches down the road for another mile, where we had the rare privilege of shooting up a squad of military police, but got no credit for it because there was no umpire around. After that we did not bother with enemy forces unless we saw the white hatband of an umpire nearby. We roared up one road and down another. We caught one whole infantry company in a field, and an umpire ruled that half of them were out of action. After a couple of hours, we got another battery of field artillery.

Later in the morning we grabbed a messenger on a motorcycle and read the messages he was carrying. From these we learned that two batteries, consisting of eight seventy-five-millimeter field pieces, had been withdrawn from the lines and concealed at various crossroads throughout the area as a defense against our little roving fleet of tanks. I realized that if we got in range of one of these seventy-fives, the umpires would at once rule us out of action. So I decided that it might be wise for us to get out of there and head for home.

On the way back, however, I resolved to attempt a final exploit which, if successful, would be far more brilliant than any of our previous successes. What I planned was nothing less than the capture of the commander-in-chief of the enemy.

We had heard that this gentleman, an infantry colonel, had his headquarters in a camp behind the left flank of his regiment. As the terrain between us and this camp was by this time presumably infested with seventy-fives, we decided on another grand sweep.

We drove thirty miles south until we were well out of the battle area, then straight west into a group of mountains, then north, and finally east so as to take the camp on the opposite side from where they would probably be looking for us.

This maneuver took longer than we expected. We got lost several times. But about two o'clock in the afternoon we finally emerged from the wooded mountains, and saw the camp directly ahead of us. Roaring down the dusty road at forty miles per hour, we shot full speed into the camp gate, discharging bursts of blank machine-gun fire as we went. In front of me I saw a tent with two flags in front of it. Straight for that tent I headed. At the last minute I skidded to a stop with the front end of my tank just inside the door. Peering into the gloom of the interior I saw an officer with what looked like silver eagles on his shoulders. Beside him was a man with the white hatband of an umpire. I flung open the shutter of the turret.

For a moment I considered the possibility of getting off a real historic wisecrack, something like "Surrender in the name of the Earthworm Tractor Company and the Cockroach Cavalry!" but somehow this seemed a little fantastic. So I merely said, "Sir, you are my prisoner."

It was my moment of triumph. As I clambered out of the tank, I said to myself, "If only that suspicious and skeptical old Colonel McKenzie-Morton could see me now!"

This wish, I regret to say, was granted with startling suddenness.

"Captain Botts," said Colonel McKenzie-Morton—for it was indeed he—"what is the meaning of this outrageous conduct?"

I gazed at him with speechless astonishment. Slowly I began to realize what had happened. While lost in the mountains, we had traveled farther than I had supposed. We had turned the flanks of both armies. We were once more behind our own lines. And I had just captured my own commanding officer.

But he would not stay captured. With a burst of military language which almost blew the sides out of the tent, he informed me that I was the one who was a prisoner. I was under arrest. "Last week," he said, "you made a smart-aleck request for a court-martial. All right, this time you are going to have it. And now you can get out of here, and take your filthy machinery with you. And don't try to give me any back talk."

So now, Henderson, you can see how the Army system of discipline—which you have so fatuously affected to admire—has permitted this equimaniac colonel to halt all my efforts toward modernizing the Army. This halt, however, will be only temporary—provided you do your part. You must hurry to Washington. You must explain the situation to the highest authorities in the War Department. You must persuade them to order the court-martial charges dropped, to transfer me out of this livery-stable outfit, and to put me in the Ordnance Corps, where I can be of real service in the defense of my country. Do not fail me. I am counting on you.

Yours hopefully,
Alexander Botts.

P.S. Next Morning. May 22, 1941.

This is to report that Colonel McKenzie-Morton came in about an hour ago to announce that my punishment would be even worse than he had previously intended.

"Captain Botts," he said, "I have just received from the umpires a complete account of your activities yesterday and the day before. It appears that you accomplished a very remarkable flanking maneuver, going completely around the enemy, and causing a degree of confusion behind their lines which was an important factor in this regiment's successful defense of its position. All this, however, in no way excuses your gross insubordination in acting without any authority from me. I have decided, therefore, that I cannot let you off with a mere trial by a military court."

"But listen, colonel——"

"I have decided," he continued, "that your complete lack of any sense of military discipline will make it impossible for you ever to become a successful cavalry officer. I am, therefore, throwing you out of this magnificent arm of the service and—at the request of a couple of Ordnance officers who have been acting as observers at the maneuvers—I am demoting you to the Ordnance Corps. You are, therefore, released from arrest. You will report at once to the two Ordnance officers whom I mentioned, and you will be prepared to leave with them this afternoon. Good-bye."

The two Ordnance officers turned out to be splendid fellows. They had been so impressed by the performance of the cockroach tanks that they are going to recommend the reinstatement of our contract. And they rank so high that their recommendation is certain to be followed. They have arranged to transfer my twelve mechanics into a mechanized outfit. And they are going to appoint me as chief inspector at the factory in Earthworm City during the production of the tanks.

In view of all this, I am happy to inform you that I will not need your influence at the War Department after all. And I also wish to inform you that I have seen the error of my ways and come around to your way of thinking on the subject of discipline. I am now prepared to admit that obedience is necessary for the proper conduct of any enterprise. And whenever I have occasion, in my future career as inspector at the factory, to issue any orders to you, Henderson, I shall expect them to be obeyed promptly and cheerfully, without any back talk or monkey business.

Yours,
Alexander Botts.

BOTTS IS BACK ...
WITH ALL PAPERS
IN ORDER

Care of Daniel Denman,
Earthworm Tractor Dealer,
Seattle, Washington.
Thursday, August 22, 1946.

Mr. Gilbert Henderson, President,
Earthworm Tractor Company,
Earthworm City, Illinois.

Dear Henderson:

It gives me great pleasure to announce that I am no longer Major Alexander Botts. I am back from the Pacific, the proud possessor of a splendid collection of war souvenirs. I am out of the Army, with my discharge and all other necessary documents in perfect order. I am full of ideas and energy.

The only thing I seem to lack right now is money. But that does not worry me, because I am resuming, as of today, my former identity as Mr. Alexander Botts, sales manager of the Earthworm Tractor Company. And you will be delighted to know that I have already started correcting some of the more serious mistakes that you people back home have been making while I have been off winning the war.

This morning I called on one of our oldest and most valued customers out here, Mr. Henry Stevenson, and at once uncovered a truly shocking state of affairs. Mr. Stevenson is now engaged in a big logging operation which is of tremendous importance in the housing program. His prewar Earthworm tractors are practically worn out. And he has had ten of our 100 h.p. Earthworms on order for almost a year—with no results whatever.

"If I don't get delivery on those machines by the end of this month," said Mr. Stevenson, pounding on the desk, "I'll cancel the whole order and buy myself a fleet of those new Blue Ox tractors."

"What?" I said. "You aren't actually considering any such hopeless monstrosity as the Blue Ox."

"I know your Earthworms are better," admitted Mr. Stevenson, "but I can't get delivery on them. These Blue Oxen seem to be available. So I'm going to grab them. What else can I do?"

"I'll tell you what you can do, Mr. Stevenson," I said. "You can hand over all your troubles to Alexander Botts. I am sorry you have been treated so badly during my absence. But, now that I am back, things are going to change. You can trust me, Mr. Stevenson. I will see that you get your ten tractors by the end of the month."

"You really mean that, Mr. Botts?"

"It is a promise," I said.

I then wished Mr. Stevenson a cheery good-bye and called on our new Seattle dealer, Mr. Daniel Denman.

After introducing myself, I pounded on the desk even more vigorously than Mr. Stevenson had done, and told the man exactly what was the matter with him and what he ought to do to correct it.

"I am astonished," I said, "at the neglect you have shown in handling this important order from Mr. Stevenson. You will get in touch with the factory right now and demand that those ten tractors be shipped at once by fast freight."

I regret to say that Mr. Denman merely yawned in my face. I yelled at him some more. Then I discovered that he did not know who I am; he had been connected with our organization such a short time that, incredible though it may seem, he had never even heard the name "Alexander Botts." Besides which, the poor muttonhead quite obviously thinks he knows as much about the tractor business as I do. He not only refused to take orders; he would not even listen to suggestions. Apparently he has not yet learned that the war is over and it is once more fashionable to be polite. And that, Henderson, is why it becomes necessary for me to appeal to you.

First, I want you to ship those ten tractors to Mr. Stevenson at once. Second, I want you to instruct Mr. Denman that from now on he is to take orders from me . . . and without any back talk or monkey business. Third, you will tell the cashier at Earthworm City that I am once more on the payroll and that he is to honor my expense accounts without any of the unnecessary quibbling which, I regret to say, has occasionally characterized his handling of such matters in the past.

Incidentally, you might ask him to wire me a couple of thousand dollars in advance expense money to relieve the financial stringency which I mentioned at the beginning of this letter.

In case you are still as inquisitive as you used to be about my private affairs, it might be well for me to explain that my present lack of ready cash is perfectly natural under the circumstances. I received my discharge early this year in the Philippines. For several months I remained overseas getting together and preparing for shipment the splendid collection of souvenirs to which I have previously referred. I landed in the United States about a month ago, since which time I have been awaiting the arrival of my souvenirs and enjoying a holiday with my wife and children here on the Pacific Coast. All this I have kept confidential, because I felt that I needed a vacation, and I knew that if you learned I was out of the Army, you would immediately start pestering me to come back to work.

Now, however, my vacation is over. I am once more on the job. And as my activities grow in importance, the expenses will naturally expand.

As soon as I get things straightened out here in Seattle, I plan to take off in a private plane on a grand tour of the United States for the purpose of stirring up all our dealers and modernizing their methods. In the course of two or three months I shall probably land at Earthworm City with a report on what I have done to the dealers and with suggestions for the reorganization and improvement of the factory and the home office.

Don't forget to have the cashier wire me the two thousand dollars.

Cordially yours,
Alexander Botts,
Sales manager, Earthworm Tractor Company.

P.S. To be on the safe side, make it three thousand.

EARTHWORM TRACTOR COMPANY
EARTHWORM CITY, ILLINOIS
OFFICE OF THE PRESIDENT

Saturday, August 24, 1946.

Mr. Alexander Botts,
Care of Daniel Denman,
Earthworm Tractor Dealer,
Seattle, Washington.

Dear Botts:

Your letter is here, and I want you to know that the Earthworm Tractor Company is standing solidly behind its promise to take back

152

all former employees who have been absent in the armed services. We are ready to do this regardless of added expense and inconvenience, and even though the returned veteran may have been away so long that his ability to carry on his former job has become considerably impaired.

To the end that matters may be handled with fairness to all, we have established in our Personnel Department a special Veterans' Division, staffed with experienced psychiatrists and other experts who devote their entire time to assisting former soldiers, such as yourself, in the difficult problems of readjustment to civilian life.

Such being the case, I must ask that you come to Earthworm City at once for a refresher course in the principles of salesmanship, and for general consultation, reorientation and re-education. In the meantime, I must insist that you refrain from interfering in the affairs of our Sales Department.

Mr. Stevenson's tractors cannot be shipped for several months. Strikes and shortages have limited our production, and he will have to take his turn with our other customers. As I am not yet ready to put you on the payroll as sales manager, I cannot give you any authority over Mr. Denman. I most certainly cannot grant you the sort of unlimited expense account that you seem to desire. And your plans for a grand tour in a private airplane are completely out of the question. I can sympathize with your feeling in this matter—I wish I had a private plane myself—but the Earthworm Tractor Company simply cannot afford to finance such luxuries.

Instead of the three thousand dollars requested, I am enclosing a check for one hundred dollars for advance expense money. This should be ample to bring you here to Earthworm City, where I hope to have the pleasure of seeing you in the immediate future.

> Very sincerely yours,
> Gilbert Henderson.

> Care of Daniel Denman,
> Earthworm Tractor Dealer,
> Seattle, Washington.
> Tuesday, August 27, 1946.

Dear Henderson:

Your letter came yesterday. I am sorry that I cannot agree with your quaint idea that I ought to come in to the factory to put on a vaudeville act with your trained psychiatrists and to submit myself to some vague course in reorientation and readjustment—whatever that means. The truth of the matter is that you, Henderson, ought to snap out of your swivel-chair lethargy and get out here in the great open spaces where you could learn a few of the facts of life about the tractor business in relation to the cash customers.

When your letter arrived, I must admit that I was considerably annoyed at your unenlightened attitude in refusing to ship the tractors, confirm my authority over Mr. Denman and supply me with adequate funds.

I spent most of yesterday evening composing a series of blistering telegrams which I had planned to send you every hour on the hour all day today. However, at nine o'clock this morning, before I got around to sending the first one, I received a piece of good news, which has made this whole telegraphic project unnecessary. The news dealt with an event which will make it possible for me to handle everything out here without any assistance from you or the home office. Mr. Stevenson is going to get his ten Earthworm tractors tomorrow, plus a lot of extra equipment. He has already kicked out the salesman for the Blue Ox tractor. In the meantime, I have Mr. Denman practically eating out of my hand. And I have plenty of money for all my immediate needs.

This happy situation has been brought about entirely because of the unusual collection of war souvenirs which I mentioned in my letter of last Thursday. As some of these souvenirs are now involved in a business transaction to which the Earthworm Tractor Company is a party, it seems reasonable that you, as president of the company, should be informed of the facts. This makes it necessary for me to trace the history of the great Botts collection.

As you probably know, almost all American soldiers are enthusiastic collectors of souvenirs. When they come home from overseas, they are apt to drag along Japanese swords, rifles, helmets and all manner of useless junk such as battle flags, uniforms, grass skirts, native carvings, and so forth and so on.

During my career in the Army I became interested in collecting souvenirs myself. Anything that I do at all I like to do well. So it is natural that I should have gone far beyond the sort of piker activities which characterize the average soldier.

One of the big problems of souvenir hunting in the Army overseas has been the difficulty of bringing the stuff home. On many Pacific islands, for instance, the entire terrain would be literally covered with trucks, jeeps, tanks, airplanes, tractors and similar materiel. On the beaches there would often be stranded landing craft and sometimes even larger vessels.

The average soldier was, of course, licked by the transportation problem. But not Alexander Botts. After my discharge from the Army in the Philippines, I got together with a small group of discharged Army and Navy officers and organized the Alexander Botts Salvage and Souvenir Cooperative, Inc. In the course of about two months, we were able to salvage two LST's from the beaches of an island called Yuk. After hiring crews to operate our craft, we spent another two months accumulating and loading our cargoes. We started for home about six weeks ago, loaded with probably the finest assortment of war relics ever assembled by any group of private collectors.

As I was in a hurry, I came ahead by plane. And all through my vacation with my family, I have been anxiously awaiting the arrival of the two LST's.

I did not say very much about all this in my first letter, because I was not sure when the stuff would arrive. But I am now delighted to report that the first LST came sailing into Puget Sound yesterday morning, and has now run its bow up on a beach which I had previously rented in a secluded cove on the Olympic Peninsula. This beach is cheaper than a pier at a regular port. It is also more private—which is a definite advantage for any project like this which might cause trouble with the authorities.

In addition to a large collection of the usual type of souvenirs, I have ten 100 h.p. Earthworm tractors, complete with bulldozers, winches and other miscellaneous equipment, all of which we had been able to pick up in surprisingly good condition.

These well-equipped tractors, as I have previously indicated, will be in Mr. Stevenson's hands by tomorrow. And I have already worked out the business and financial details so as to produce the greatest amount of good for the greatest number of people. First, acting as sales manager of the Alexander Botts Salvage and Souvenir Cooperative, Inc., I have made out a bill of sale transferring the machines to the Earthworm Tractor Company. Then, as sales manager of Earthworm, I have made out a bill of sale transferring the stuff to our dealer, Mr. Denman. Finally, I have had Mr. Denman make out a bill of sale passing everything along to Mr. Stevenson.

I quoted Mr. Stevenson a flat price of one hundred thousand dollars, or ten thousand dollars for each of the ten big tractors. Mr. Stevenson, after inspecting the stuff, eagerly closed the deal. Being a bona-fide big operator, he passed over his check for the full amount at once.

Following my basic principles of letting anybody who does business with me make a good profit, I am permitting Mr. Denman to hold out the standard 20 percent commission. With this twenty thousand dollars' worth of pure gravy all set for him to lap up, it is no wonder that he is—as I previously remarked—practically eating out of my hand.

After deducting Mr. Denman's commission, there remains eighty thousand dollars, on which I am allowing the Earthworm Tractor Company a 10 percent profit, or eight thousand dollars, which I feel is ample, considering how little work the company has done on this deal. This eight thousand dollars, incidentally, I am retaining out here as expense money. This is a little more than the three thousand I asked for, but I can probably find a use for it.

The remaining seventy-two thousand dollars goes into the treasury of the Alexander Botts Salvage and Souvenir Cooperative, Inc., thus providing ample funds to pay off the crews of our LST's, and also providing handsome cash dividends for myself and my business associates, in addition to a liberal distribution of miscellaneous souvenirs.

In view of my sensational success in this deal, you will naturally want me to keep right on as sales manager, without wasting any time in futile visits to the factory. In this I heartily agree with you. It is also probable that you will be tempted to start boasting to everybody about how good I am. Ordinarily, this would be all right. But in this particular case, I have a very distinct feeling that silence might be the better policy.

Do not get me wrong. I have done nothing dishonest. My salvage operations were carried out with the knowledge and consent of the authorities concerned. I even have documents which tend to prove this. These documents, however, are not at the moment available. So I should much prefer, for the time being, that my activities remain hidden from the prying eyes of overzealous officials. As soon as I have any more definite information I will let you know.

Cordially yours,
Alexander Botts,
Sales Manager, Earthworm Tractor Company.

TELEGRAM
EARTHWORM TRACTOR AGENCY,
WASHINGTON, D.C.,
AUGUST 30, 1946.

TO: ALEXANDER BOTTS,
CARE EARTHWORM TRACTOR AGENCY,
SEATTLE, WASHINGTON.
YOUR LETTER HAS BEEN FORWARDED TO ME HERE IN WASHINGTON
WHERE I AM MAKING A BRIEF BUSINESS VISIT. YOUR SALE OF

SALVAGED ARMY EQUIPMENT SEEMS TO ME OF SUCH DUBIOUS LEGALITY THAT I FEEL IT SHOULD BE CHECKED AT ONCE BEFORE WE BECOME INVOLVED ANY MORE DEEPLY. ACCORDINGLY I HAVE CONSULTED ARMY AND NAVY AUTHORITIES. THEY SAY ARMY AND NAVY EQUIPMENT SALVAGED ON THE BATTLEFIELD IS STILL DEF-. INITELY GOVERNMENT PROPERTY REGARDLESS OF ANY DOCUMENTS YOU MAY HAVE WHICH "TEND TO PROVE" THAT YOUR SALVAGE OPERATIONS WERE DONE WITH THE KNOWLEDGE AND CONSENT OF THE AUTHORITIES CONCERNED. OBVIOUSLY, NOBODY IN THE SOUTH PACIFIC WOULD HAVE THE AUTHORITY TO PRESENT YOU WITH A LOT OF GOVERNMENT PROPERTY AS A FREE GIFT. THIS MEANS THAT THE TRACTORS NEVER BELONGED TO YOU, AND WHEN YOU SOLD THEM YOU COMMITTED A SERIOUS CRIME. OFFICIALS HERE ARE WIRING WEST COAST OFFICIALS TO INVESTIGATE AND TAKE WHATEVER STEPS MAY BE NECESSARY. PLEASE ADVISE ME ON FUTURE DEVELOPMENTS, INCLUDING WHAT FURTHER ACTION YOU ARE TAKING.

> GILBERT HENDERSON,
> PRESIDENT, EARTHWORM TRACTOR COMPANY.

> Seattle, Washington,
> Saturday, August 31, 1946.

Dear Henderson:

I am writing this after a long and painful session with the Federal cops.

Honestly, Henderson, I can't understand why you act the way you do. When I courageously save you from your own folly and correct all your mistakes by refusing to desert my post, by skillfully talking this hitherto reluctant dealer into active cooperation, and by supplying the necessary tractors and putting through a deal by which we preserve the good will of our customer and set up a nice profit for both the company and our dealer—when I do all this, all you can think of is to go tattletaling to the Federal Government with such an ignorant and distorted version of the facts that you throw everything once more into confusion and fill the jails of our fair land with innocent persons.

It was yesterday morning that the Federal cops, egged on by your ill-advised chatter, descended upon us.

One group seized the ten tractors at the logging camp—thus throwing another monkey wrench into the already sadly impaired housing program. They also arrested Mr. Henry Stevenson on the absurd pretext that he was a receiver of goods stolen by the Earthworm Tractor Company. He was soon released on bail, but the incident must have dampened—at least temporarily—the enthusiasm for our organization which I had been working so hard to build up in his mind.

A second group of cops came swarming into the Earthworm Tractor Agency, arrested Mr. Denman and held him several hours until he could arrange bail. Apparently they were also after me. Fortunately, however, I had received your telegram a few minutes before the raid. As the officers came in the front door, I was already on my way out the back window.

I hurried to the cove, where I found that the second LST had just come in with the rest of the souvenirs, including several jeeps, peeps, trucks and a couple of C-47 transport planes. There was also a trunk full of documents, which I had been anxiously awaiting, and which I was fortunately able to take along when my pursuers caught up with me and dragged me back for questioning to the office of one of the assistant Federal attorneys here in Seattle.

The documents included all the different kinds of papers that are now required when you ship anything into this country from overseas. As I am always most meticulous in such matters, I had provided everything I knew was necessary, everything I thought was necessary, and everything I feared might be necessary. The trunk was jammed with an impressive array of affidavits, invoices, receipts, manifests, declarations, clearances, de-clearances, permits, releases, licenses, navicerts, bills of lading, bills of sale and dozens of other documents from the United States Bureau of Customs, Immigration Service, Bureau of Internal Revenue, Public Health Service, the Departments of Labor, State and Commerce, the War Shipping Administration and various other commissions, boards, services, bureaus, divisions, administrations and offices.

Ordinarily, this would have been enough for anybody. But the assistant district attorney before whom I had been hailed was hopelessly prejudiced.

"There seems to be nothing wrong," he admitted grudgingly, "with the documents covering the actual shipment and landing of these goods. But that does not alter the fact that you are guilty of selling stolen property."

"It is not stolen," I said. I handed him a formal document, signed and sealed on the island of Yuk, by which His Gracious Majesty, the King of the Island, in consideration of the payment of one million dollars in lawful Yuk seashell money, transferred ownership of all former Army and Navy equipment on the island to the Alexander Botts Salvage and Souvenir Cooperative, Inc. "There you are," I said. "I bought the stuff perfectly honestly. You have no case against me at all."

Unfortunately, the man was still so dominated by the suspicions which you, Henderson, had so unwisely disseminated that he could no longer think straight.

"This is even more serious than I supposed," he said ominously.

"How so?" I asked him.

"Our government," he explained, "is naturally solicitous for the welfare of the inhabitants of islands which have been taken over by our forces in the course of the war. To the end that the simple-minded natives may be protected against exploitation by unscrupulous traders, an agency known as the Federal Office of Insular Economics has been set up, with powers to regulate commerce and trade, and to impose severe penalties against persons such as yourself who are guilty of swindling the natives by schemes such as purchasing valuable equipment for so-called money consisting of almost worthless seashells."

"I know all about this Federal Office of Insular Economics," I said. "There was a *Fooie* representative on the island of Yuk while I was there. We used to play gin rummy together. And—following the system, which I learned in the Army, of protecting myself at all times with adequate official papers—I procured a copy, on official *Fooie* stationery, of this man's report on my operations."

I handed over the document—which told the whole story. For many generations—according to the report—the natives of Yuk had used for money a special kind of seashell which occurs naturally only on an island many hundreds of miles away. During the war years there were no traders to bring in fresh supplies of these shells. The natives, in their frail canoes, had no way to get them. The amount of shell money gradually dwindled because of breakage and other factors. And a severe monetary depression resulted.

Then the Alexander Botts Salvage and Souvenir Cooperative, Inc., arrived. We sized up the situation and made a deal with the king. As soon as we had repaired one of the C-47 planes, we made a number of trips to a distant shell island and brought back several tons of seashell money—enough to equal one million dollars at the official rate of exchange set up by the king, myself and the *Fooie* representative.

With all this money in the treasury, the king was able to establish a truly progressive regime patterned after our own Federal Administration in Washington. He promoted himself to the office of president, and then began pouring out money for social security, unemployment compensation, public works, subsidies to coconut farmers, public housing, education, hospitalization and hundreds of other worthy projects. All this spending so primed the pump of business activity that before I left the island they were enjoying a real boom. For some reason the cost of living began to go up, but the *Fooie* representative was able to handle this problem very successfully by persuading the president to set up a price-control board, which began cracking down so vigorously on chiselers and black marketeers that all complaints against the government were silenced—at least for a while. The official conclusion of the *Fooie* representative was that my timely action in expanding the money supply had saved the economic life of the entire island.

This should have satisfied the assistant Federal attorney. But it did not.

"This report," he admitted, "seems to clear you in the matter of cheating the natives. But it does not change the fact that the stuff is United States Government property, which the natives had no right to sell to you, and which you have no right to sell to Mr. Stevenson."

"Wrong again," I said.

Reaching into my precious pile of documents, I dragged out a certified copy of an official Army order, with a number of supporting affidavits, showing that when the United States forces had turned over the island of Yuk to the Australians, all Army supplies and materiel—including the two stranded LST's, the tractors, the airplanes and other equipment—were likewise turned over to the Australians. I also produced a formal treaty by which, in return for work done by the natives, the Australian commander, upon quitting the island, definitely transferred ownership in everything he was leaving behind to His Gracious Majesty, the King of the Island of Yuk.

This made the man angrier than ever. "When that stuff was transferred to the Australian government," he said, "the transaction must have been under Lend-Lease. This means that the United States government still has official title to the property. And you are guilty of selling stolen goods—just as I said in the beginning."

"Look," I said. "If I am guilty of selling stolen goods, so is His Majesty the King of Yuk. And what is more important, so is the Australian government. If you arrest me for this, are you also going to arrest the Prime Minister of Australia and the Australian General Staff?"

"Don't be silly. You know I can't do that."

"All right then. I have the papers to prove that I bought these tractors in perfectly good faith. Do you actually think you can get any jury over here to convict me on nothing more substantial than your unsupported claim that the goods were stolen, long ago and far away, by the Australian government?"

This question seemed to be the last straw as far as the assistant United States attorney was concerned. Enmeshed in the net of paper work which I had woven about him, all he could do was sound off with helpless rage.

"Mr. Botts," he yelled, "I am thoroughly convinced that you are a crook! This time you have covered your tracks very successfully with this blizzard of documents! But I give you fair warning, if I ever catch you with your paper work down, I will prosecute you to the fullest extent of the law!"

"Not a chance," I said. "My years in the Army have taught me that in dealing with the government it is always wise to remember that old Latin motto: 'Papyrus correctus, omnis correctus'—which means that if the paper work is okay, everything is okay."

"That will be enough out of you," said the attorney. He called in a couple of muggs with badges on their vests. "The case against Stevenson, Denman and Botts is being dropped," he snarled. "The seized machinery is to be released. As for this character here"—he pointed at me—"you will eject him from this office at once. And I hope I never see him again."

I was promptly grabbed by the collar, hustled outside and deposited on the sidewalk along with my trunkful of papers. Later in the day I had a conference with Stevenson and Denman. I am pleased to report that both of them are now feeling fine. So everything is okay. And from now on, things are really going to happen.

The two LST's are proceeding by way of the Panama Canal to St. Louis, where I plan to sell them to our local dealer to be used in delivering tractors along the Mississippi River.

One of the C-47 transport planes is being flown to Earthworm City to be turned over to you, Henderson, absolutely free of charge and with my compliments. This ought to take care of that pathetic lament in your letter of several days ago: "I wish I had a private plane myself—but the Earthworm Tractor Company simply cannot afford to finance such luxuries."

I will soon take off in the other plane on my grand tour of inspection. My eight thousand dollars will probably last me until you have time to put me on the payroll and set up a regular expense account for me. After all, my expenses will be quite moderate. The plane has been acquired without cost to the Earthworm Company, so future charges will be limited to gasoline, oil, maintenance, airport fees, hotel bills and salaries for pilot, copilot and hostess.

Yours enthusiastically,
Alexander Botts.

BOTTS GETS
A NEW JOB

Care of Earthworm Tractor Agency,
Atlanta, Georgia,
Thursday, February 6, 1947.

Mr. Gilbert Henderson, President,
Earthworm Tractor Company,
Earthworm City, Illinois.

Dear Henderson:

I hereby tender my resignation as sales manager of the Earthworm Tractor Company. My reasons are various and cumulative.

Since my discharge from the Army, and since I resumed my former job as sales manager of the company, I have, as you know, been traveling about the country in a salvaged Army plane, visiting our dealers and investigating conditions. Everywhere I have gone, I have heard nothing but complaints—no tractors, no service, no parts, no satisfaction, no cooperation. I have sent you countless letters of protest. I have demanded action. You have replied with weak excuses. You have whined about strikes, shortages and the difficulties of reconversion. From time to time you have urged me to abandon this highly necessary inspection trip; and you have even refused to put me on the payroll and give me an expense account until I should come in to the factory to be personally installed as sales manager.

So far I have paid my own expenses out of the proceeds of various secondhand-tractor deals. But my money has been running low. The whole situation has been getting so unbearable as to be practically intolerable. And today came the final straw in the form of a letter from Mr. Chester Hamilton, of Kansas City.

You will remember that when I was in Kansas City a short time ago I wrote you about Chester, who is not only the son of one of our most important customers—Mr. George Hamilton—but also one of the finest young men I know. He is a perfect gentleman, a college graduate and a war veteran. He wanted a position through the winter in the bookkeeping department of the Earthworm Tractor Company, so that he could gain some practical experience which would prepare him to handle the accounting and bookkeeping on a large roadbuilding job which his father is starting next summer.

Two weeks ago I sent the young man to you with a letter of introduction. Today, in a letter just received from him, I learn that instead of taking him around to the bookkeeping department and fixing him up with a job, you merely referred him to our general employment office. Apparently this office has been completely reorganized and is now being run by as arrogant a group of crackpots as could be found anywhere outside of Washington, D.C.

Instead of giving Chester the job he wanted, they put him through a "battery of aptitude tests"—whatever that may be. Then they blandly told him he was not fitted to be a bookkeeper. In spite of the fact that there must be dozens of jobs in the bookkeeping department which could be competently filled by anyone with enough brains to graduate from college, they turned him down. So he went back to Kansas City.

The young man is too polite to write me what must be his real opinion. But I am not too polite, Henderson, to write you that I think this is an utterly outrageous way to treat the son of an important customer. It is, as I said before, the last straw. Coming on top of everything else, it is the final grain of salt that causes the solution to reach a point of supersaturation, so that the camel is precipitated to the bottom of the test tube.

In other words, I am through. I have ended my inspection trip. I have sold my plane. I am quitting. I am resigning. But this does not mean you have heard the last of me. I have my plans. I am going to do some undercover investigating. And I will write you as soon as I have anything further to report.

> Yours,
> Alexander Botts,
> Former sales manager,
> Earthworm Tractor Company.

EARTHWORM TRACTOR COMPANY
EARTHWORM CITY, ILLINOIS
OFFICE OF THE PRESIDENT
Saturday, February 8, 1947.

Mr. Alexander Botts,
Care of Earthworm Tractor Agency,
Atlanta, Georgia.
Dear Botts:

You cannot resign. You have not even been hired yet. But we want to hire you. We need your energy and initiative to carry our sales department through this difficult reconversion period. If you will only follow my repeated requests and come in to the factory, I will put you on the payroll at once. Now that you have got rid of your extravagantly expensive private plane, there should be no difficulty about your expense account. I can promise you my full cooperation in solving the problems mentioned in your letter.

Our factory manager tells me that the production of new tractors is gradually rising. The head of our Parts Department assures me that everything possible is being done to cooperate to the fullest extent with everyone concerned, and he further reports that splendid progress has already been made in the implementation of an accelerated program for the more efficient processing of parts orders.

Although I have had no direct word, I am sure your friend Chester Hamilton has received fair treatment. The new director of our Employment Office reports gratifying progress in applying scientific techniques in the analysis of basic individual aptitudes, to the end that they may be integrated to the specific requirements of the various spheres of activity comprised in the totality of our organizational structure.

I am leaving tomorrow for a two weeks' stay in Washington, D.C. I shall be glad to see you there, or, later on, here at the factory.

Most sincerely,
Gilbert Henderson,
President, Earthworm Tractor Company

Earthworm City, Illinois,
Friday, February 14, 1947.

Mr. Gilbert Henderson,
Earthworm Tractor Agency,
Washington, D.C.
Dear Henderson:

Your letter—which arrived just before I left Atlanta—is a splendid example of what I was talking about when I said that the situation has been getting so unbearable as to be practically intolerable. The basic trouble, Henderson, seems to be that you are trying to run this business entirely from the top down.

When I protest about the Parts Department, all you do is consult the slick-talking yes man whom you have mistakenly placed in charge of same. He apparently claims that he is performing miracles with his implementation and processing and finalizing, and he puts out this information in such a jet-propelled fog of high-octane language that he completely conceals the fact that he is falling down on the only thing that matters—shipping the parts.

When I ask about the Employment Office, you let yourself become involved in a verbal gas attack dealing with the totality of our organizational structure—and you never find out what is actually happening. This is why I have been forced to take drastic action.

Last week, as you know, I resigned as sales manager. This resignation, of course, is purely temporary; I shall want the job back again just as soon as I complete my present project. In the meantime, I do not want anyone—not even you, Henderson—to know what I am doing. I am not even going to mail this letter to you until the need for secrecy has passed.

It was the day before yesterday that I arrived in Earthworm City in a state of complete incognito. I spent the night at my home on Earthworm Heights. I cautioned my wife and children to keep my arrival a dark secret. Yesterday morning I approached the factory— advancing cautiously behind the cover of a luxuriant beard which I grew in the South Pacific, shaved off on my return, and then grew again because I feel that it gives me such an air of distinction. Instead of going through the front gate, I sidled around the corner and entered the door marked Employment Office. My plan was simple. What I wanted were the true facts about the company's two outstanding sore spots—the Employment Office and the Parts Department. I had therefore decided to enter the Employment Office as an ordinary mug and apply for a job in the Parts Department. By going through the mill, I hoped to get a worm's-eye view of both places.

Note: So far I have progressed no farther than the Employment Office. And what I have found is so much worse than anything I had even dreamed could be possible that I will give you a full account of my almost unbelievable discoveries, so that you will have all the information necessary to act upon my recommendation that the entire personnel of the Employment Office be fired at once for the good of the company.

The first person I met when I entered the door of the Employment Office was the receptionist, who is so courteous and good-looking that you might possibly keep her when you clean out the rest of the gang.

"Good morning," I said. "I want to apply for a job as a sweeper, cleaning out the Parts Department."

Note: I had decided that a job with a broom would be ideal for my purposes. It would provide an opportunity to travel around all over the Parts Department. The work would be light. And it would leave my mind free to observe what was happening, and to meditate thereon.

The receptionist handed me a five-page questionnaire printed in quintuplicate with carbon between the sheets.

"Thank you very much," I said, "but this will not be necessary. All I want is a job with a broom, cleaning out the Parts Department."

"I am sorry," she said, smiling pleasantly, "but the basic questionnaire must be filled out by all applicants for employment."

So I spent a couple of hours filling out little blank spaces with labels such as: Date, Last Name, First Name, Middle Name, Maiden Name, Age, and so on through page after page, giving information on previous employment, social-security status, education, citizenship, and ending up with a request for character and business references, birth certificate, naturalization certificate, Army discharge, if any, and I forget what else.

Since I have been in the Army, filling out idiotic questionnaires is an old story. In the present case, for the purpose of concealing my real identity, I had already chosen a nom de plume. To go with it, I now worked out a complete life history, expressly designed to ward off embarrassing questions and requests for documents. I described myself as Mr. Abner Hopkins, age fifty, born in a wild section of the Ozarks where they had never heard of birth certificates. I further claimed I was unmarried, had no children, and had lived all my life as a sort of hermit farmer in the same remote region. As I had never been employed and had no near neighbors, I could not present any references from anybody or any papers of any kind.

This somewhat flabbergasted the young lady at the desk. But I am a good talker, and I soon convinced her that I simply did not have any documents, and that it was therefore useless for her to demand them. I then asked to be given a broom and shown to the Parts Department. But it was not that easy. I was taken into an inner room with a lot of other applicants. Another smart young lady handed me a book full of little pictures. The title of the book was Mechanical Aptitude Test—Form 37XG.

"Listen, lady," I said. "I don't need to bother with this kid's picture book. All I want is a job cleaning out the Parts Department."

"All applicants for employment are required to take this test," she said.

So I went through the whole book. I looked at all the little pictures of gear wheels and pulleys and little men lifting weights, and I counted hundreds of cubes in pictures. It seemed to me I was getting most of the answers right, but I could not be sure. When I had finished, it was lunchtime.

After a good meal in the factory cafeteria, we were all herded into another room, and handed a paper labeled Basic Vocabulary Test—Form G746.

There were twenty-five words. After each word there were four different meanings. You were supposed to mark the one that came the nearest. The first line read as follows: "Viscous, (a) wicked, (b) sticky, (c) transparent, (d) lively." With my long experience with tractor-cylinder oils, I naturally knew that sticky came the nearest to being right. The rest of the words were familiar for one reason or another. I thought I was doing okay, and I thought I would soon be through this nonsense. But at this point they pulled a dirty one.

They brought in another lady teacher, and she ran the papers through a large electric marking machine. This is one of the most appalling devices I have ever seen. Apparently a guy could work for hours on an examination, and then this thing would flunk him in a tenth of a second—which is just what happened to me. The head teacher, after looking over the papers, announced that class was dismissed—all except Mr. Hopkins. I then heard her whisper to the other teacher: "Give this man the extra hard one, Form XX300."

"Hey," I said, speaking up, "all I want is a job cleaning out the Parts Department."

"I am sorry," she said, "but we must ask you to take this extra test." The other girl brought in Form XX300, which had several hundred words of a type which I can only describe as real stinkers.

Normally, I ought to be able to pass any reasonable vocabulary test. After all, I am a master of the English language, with an ability to express myself far beyond the average. This Form XX300, however, was definitely out of this world.

Just to make it more bewildering, there were a few perfectly ordinary words like horse and cow which would not give anybody any trouble. Then there were double-talk words, which mean something according to the dictionary, but signify nothing when used by businessmen like yourself in such expressions as "the implementation of an accelerated program for the more efficient processing and finalizing of parts orders." Such words, of course, gave me no trouble.

The test was also loaded down with polysyllabic monstrosities such as chimopelagic, atroceruleous, autochthonous, syzygy and dichotomy.

These Greek and Latin derivatives, however, were not the worst. Somebody, with fiendish ingenuity, had run in a lot of good old Anglo-Saxon words like lither, mome, slub, inkle—so short and so simple that everybody ought to understand all of them, except that practically nobody ever heard of any of them. So I presumably flunked this test, although I don't know for sure as yet. By the time I finished, it was five o'clock, the office was closing and they told me to come back the next day.

I spent the evening meditating on such questions as why a sweeper in the Parts Department should be expected to distinguish between a syzygy and a dichotomy. And would it help him in his work if he knew what happened when a lither mome starts to slub an inkle? As the answers eluded me, I finally went to bed.

Bright and early this morning I was back at the Employment Office—where the procedure at once sank to a new low. Probably you won't believe it, Henderson, but they started me in on a lot of nursery-school games. The teacher brought out a lot of wooden building blocks and had me build a sort of cubistic edifice. To make it worse, the blocks were lopsided, wiggly and defective. The idea was to fit them together as fast as possible.

I had a little bad luck at this point. While bending over the work with intense concentration, I got the end of my beard built into the block structure. A moment later, when I pulled my head back, everything was jerked apart. This caused considerable delay. I was slow in finishing. And the teacher announced that I was very low in structural visualization.

"What," I asked, "is structural visualization?"

"It is much the same as spatial perception," she said.

"Haven't you got a broom test?" I asked. "What I want is a job cleaning out the Parts Department."

By way of reply they gave me a lot of little steel pegs about the size of phonograph needles and had me pick them up with my fingers and fit them, three at a time, in little holes in a board. Then they handed me a pair of tweezers and had me put a lot of other pegs in a lot of other holes in another board. A number of young women applicants for employment took these tests at the same time I did. I noticed that most of them seemed to be doing the job much faster and more skillfully than I was.

At once I began to suspect that these girls were friends of the examiners, and had received unusually easy-to-handle pegs, while I had been stuck with pegs so slippery that nobody could do anything with them. The harder I tried the more elusive they became. Maybe they were magnetized—how do I know? Pretty soon I was chasing them all over the table—getting madder and madder all the time. Then I found myself pursuing them along the floor. The harder I worked the less I accomplished. Finally, just as the bell rang to show that the time was up, I knocked over the table. So I was marked zero on both finger dexterity and tweezer dexterity.

After this I had to check long columns of figures, and I got so mixed up that the teacher said my accounting aptitude was so low as to be practically nonexistent. Next they gave me something called an Occupational Interest and Preference Test, with a lot of questions like whether I would rather spend the evening at a symphony concert, a prize fight, reading a book at home or attending a party.

I can't remember all the other idiocies. There was a Word Association Test which indicated I was either an extrovert or an introvert—I am not sure which. There were psychiatric questions where they wanted to know about headaches, dreams and whether I thought I was usually treated fairly. By this time I had a feeling everybody was treating me unfairly, and I so stated in no uncertain terms—which was probably the wrong answer. And there was also some sort of an Unintelligence Test with questions like, "If the third letter before the fifth letter after M in the alphabet is also the fifth letter after the third letter before m, answer no, but if it is some other letter answer yes."

By the time I had plowed through this, it was lunchtime.

After lunch they photographed me, took my fingerprints and gave me a long physical examination—in which I seemed to do all right. When I got back to the schoolroom where I had taken the mental examinations, I announced, for the hundredth time, "All I want is a job cleaning out the Parts Department."

As usual, however, this did no good. It merely annoyed the lady teachers. And they sent me off—apparently in disgrace—to the office of the principal, a man called Blake.

As soon as I got inside his office, I repeated, for the one hundred and first time, "All I want is a job cleaning out the Parts Department." He started a long discussion to the effect that the tests I had been taking indicated I might be better suited for some other job. So I told him the tests were silly. I pointed out that I knew what I wanted, and he did not. I said I would take a sweeping job or nothing. I further stated, quite frankly, that I intended to write a letter to the president of the company, informing him exactly how the Employment Office was wasting the time, energy and money of both the company and the applicants for employment. The man replied with a lot of arguments to which I naturally paid no attention. After a half hour of completely futile conversation, he threw me out and told me to appear once more at eight in the morning. So I came back home here, where I have been spending most of the evening writing this report.

By this time, Henderson, I sincerely hope I have been able to give you some slight idea of the astonishing way in which the process of hiring a man like myself to sweep out the Parts Department—or a man like young Chester Hamilton to work in the Bookkeeping Department—has been loused up to a point where the luckless applicant is harried for days at a time by being subjected to an incredible series of tests and examinations devised by this group of pseudo-scientists who in some unaccountable manner have insinuated themselves into our previously efficient Earthworm Tractor organization.

Tomorrow I will make a last attempt to get into the Parts Department through the Employment Office. If this effort fails, I will get into the Parts Department some other way. And as soon as I am in possession of all the facts, I will send you a complete report. We can then reorganize the Parts Department and the Employment Office. After this, we can give Chester Hamilton a job in the Bookkeeping Department. And, finally, I will be very glad to grant your request that I resume my old job as sales manager.

Most sincerely,
Alexander Botts.

EARTHWORM TRACTOR COMPANY
INTEROFFICE COMMUNICATION

Date: 4 p.m., February 14, 1947
From: George Blake,
           Director of Employment Office,
           Earthworm City, Illinois
To: Gilbert Henderson, President,
           Earthworm Branch Office,
           Washington, D.C.
Via: Teletype

This is to ask your advice on a very unusual problem.

Yesterday morning a rough-looking character with a heavy beard, giving his name as Abner Hopkins, appeared at the Employment Office and applied for a job cleaning out the Parts Department. Mr. Hopkins could give no references and he had no documentary evidence about himself—a lack which he explained by saying he had spent his entire life in hermitlike seclusion somewhere in the Ozark Mountains.

Mr. Hopkins was given the routine Mechanical Aptitude Test, and passed it reasonably well. In the short vocabulary test, he got all twenty-five words right—which is so unusual that the examiners gave him the most advanced test in their files. This is composed of words so difficult that the average person is not able even to get started on it. To the astonishment of all, the uncouth Mr. Hopkins plowed through this verbal obstacle race like a bulldozer through soft mud. Toward the end he naturally missed a good many words, which had been purposely inserted because they are unknown to over 99 percent of the adult population. But he ended up with a score considerably higher than anyone who has ever taken this test during the entire existence of our Employment Office.

Following this, the examining staff really went to town on this character. Naturally, they did not want him to waste his talents as a mere sweeper. They gave him a complete battery of tests, a report of which is now on my desk. Some of the more important findings are as follows:

Vocabulary: very high
Personality: extremely extrovert
Habitus: moderately pyknic
Creative imagination: very high
Mechanical comprehension: good
Accounting aptitude: very low (practically nonexistent)
Structural visualization: low
Finger dexterity: very low
Tweezer dexterity: very low

After studying the report on Mr. Hopkins, I had him come to my office for a personal interview. Unfortunately, he seemed pretty well worn down after two days of tests and examinations. He was in such an irritable frame of mind that it was difficult to carry on a rational conversation with him. I therefore sent him home with the request that he return tomorrow morning. In the meantime I want to get all the information about him I can.

The tests, plus the personal interview, indicate a highly unusual and contradictory personality. Superficially, Mr. Hopkins has many emotional difficulties. He showed great impatience over his inability to handle the little pegs in the finger and tweezer dexterity tests. He announced that he was going to complain to you, Henderson, that our methods are a mere waste of time. He apparently resents being ordered around. With his almost complete lack of accounting ability he would undoubtedly be the type that is always in trouble with an expense account.

Fundamentally, however, he is emotionally mature and well-adjusted—self-reliant, aggressive, optimistic and sociable. Furthermore, he has an unusual power of sticking tenaciously to a single idea. All examiners, including myself, noted the subject's tendency, during the entire testing period, to revert over and over to his basic purpose, expressed in the constantly repeated assertion: "All I want is a job cleaning out the Parts Department."

In analyzing this case, I could not believe that Mr. Hopkins had spent all his life in the remote fastnesses of the Ozarks. And it was completely absurd to think of giving him a job with a broom, cleaning out the Parts Department. The extrovert personality, the low structural visualization and the high creative imagination all indicated that the man ought to make an unusually successful salesman. The astonishing vocabulary indicated a mentality similar to that found in high executives. In other words, the man had aptitudes which would admirably qualify him to be sales manager of the company—or even president or chairman of the board.

By the time I had reached this conclusion, I received a special report from our Fingerprint Division, stating that the fingerprints of Mr. Abner Hopkins are identical with a set of prints taken before the war of Mr. Alexander Botts, who was at that time our sales manager. There is thus no doubt that Mr. Hopkins and Mr. Botts are one and the same.

This naturally throws me into a quandary. I am hoping you can help me out. What is Mr. Botts' present status—if any—with this company? Why is Mr. Botts applying for a humble job under an assumed name? And how do you want me to handle this case?

Most sincerely,
George Blake.

EARTHWORM TRACTOR COMPANY
INTEROFFICE COMMUNICATION

Date: 5 p.m., February 14, 1947
From: Gilbert Henderson, President,
      Earthworm Branch Office,
      Washington, D.C.
To: George Blake,
      Director of Employment Office,
      Earthworm City, Illinois.
Via: Teletype

Mr. Botts is still on a leave of absence which was granted him when he entered the armed services. Following his discharge from the Army, he was told that he would be taken back as sales manager as soon as he complied with certain conditions—including a visit to the factory and the disposal of a private airplane. As he has now apparently complied with these conditions, his reinstatement would seem to be in order.

In a recent letter, Mr. Botts bitterly criticized various departments of our company—especially the Employment Office—and threatened to do some "undercover investigating." This undoubtedly explains his present bizarre conduct.

My advice would be that you explain to Mr. Botts the results of your aptitude tests, then offer him the job of sales manager, and see what he says.

Don't worry about any complaints which Mr. Botts may send me. Your estimate of Mr. Botts' aptitudes and personality is so astonishingly accurate that I am more than ever convinced of your usefulness to this company. In two days you have found out almost as much about him as I have discovered in years of close association.

Incidentally, Mr. Botts may withdraw his criticisms of you when he hears your opinion of him—which, on the whole, seems to be most flattering, and the sort of thing most people like to listen to. After all, almost any fortuneteller is a success with his clients as long as he tells them what they want to hear.

Most sincerely,
Gilbert Henderson.

Earthworm City, Illinois,
Saturday evening,
February 15, 1947.

Mr. Gilbert Henderson,
Earthworm Branch Office,
Washington, D.C.
Dear Henderson:

This is an urgent appeal to you to pay absolutely no attention whatsoever to anything I said in the letter which I wrote to you last night, which I did not intend to send you until later, but which got mixed in with some family letters and was erroneously put in the mail this morning. Since I wrote this previous letter, the situation has entirely changed. I arrived at the Employment Office this morning a little late, and ran into young Chester Hamilton coming out of Mr. George Blake's private office. At once he shook hands with the greatest enthusiasm.

"Good morning, Mr. Botts," he exclaimed. "How can I ever thank you for everything you have done for me?"

"I was not aware," I said, "that I had done anything for you that deserved any thanks. I sent you to Mr. Henderson, who sent you to Mr. Blake, who refused to give you a job in the Bookkeeping Department. So you returned to Kansas City——"

"Yes, Mr. Botts. But now I am back again, and Mr. Blake has given me exactly the job I wanted——"

"In the Bookkeeping Department?"

"Oh, no, Mr. Botts. That's the last thing in the world I would want."

"In your letter to me," I said, "you told me very distinctly that you came here and asked for a job in the Bookkeeping Department."

"That is right."

"I don't get it."

"It is like this, Mr. Botts. I asked for a job in the Bookkeeping Department, so I could get some experience. I thought my father needed me as a bookkeeper. But after I had taken a lot of tests, Mr. Blake told me I had no accounting aptitude at all. But he claimed I was exactly fitted for an opening in the Experimental Department. So he offered me the job—which is exactly what I wanted—but I didn't think it was right to take it."

"So what did you do?"

"I went back to Kansas City, and I told my father what Mr. Blake had said, and my father was delighted."

"He was?"

"Yes, he said I had always been so poor at figures that he was pretty much appalled at the thought of having me handle his books, but he was going to give me the job because he thought I had set my heart on it. On the other hand, I knew I was hopeless at figures. But I was going to take the job because I thought father had set his heart on having me do it."

"Well," I said, "you and your father are two of the politest people I ever met. In this case you were too polite."

"Yes, but we found it out before it was too late. So father has hired a real bookkeeper. He feels fine. I have come back here. Mr. Blake has just given me the job in the Experimental Department that I am really fitted for and that I really want. Naturally, I feel wonderful. And that is why I am so grateful to you."

"Oh," I said.

"If it had not been for you, I might never have met Mr. Henderson and been referred to Mr. Blake. And if it had not been for Mr. Blake and his aptitude tests, I might have taken the wrong job and been a square peg in a round hole all my life. So I thank you, Mr. Botts, from the bottom of my heart."

"You're entirely welcome," I said.

He shook hands again and breezed out of the room, leaving me slightly befuddled. A moment later, the receptionist announced that Mr. Blake was ready to see Mr. Abner Hopkins. As I entered Mr. Blake's office I pulled my scattered wits together and greeted the man with a certain new respect.

"Mr. Blake," I said, "I want to be completely fair with you. Yesterday I was somewhat critical of your methods. But this morning, after talking to Mr. Chester Hamilton, I am ready to admit that in some cases it is barely possible that some of your tests may have a certain limited value."

"It is very kind of you to say so," said Mr. Blake. "Please sit down."

I did so. "Yesterday," I said, "when you discussed my own tests I had a feeling that you were talking nonsense, so I paid no attention. This morning, however, if you care to repeat yourself, I shall be glad to listen."

"Very good," said Mr. Blake.

He then gave me a complete explanation of his testing methods—which I will not repeat because it would be too technical for you. The main points, however, are easy to understand. It seems that very early in the testing process the examiners recognized that I was far too gifted to waste on a mere job with a broom. That is why they gave me a complete battery of tests—which proved conclusively that I am ideal material for a high executive position. In the vocabulary test—which all experts agree is far more important than a mere layman such as yourself, Henderson, would suspect—I had a higher score, according to Mr. Blake, than anyone he had ever tested. In the course of further discussion I learned that these tests had been given, as an experiment, to most of the higher Earthworm Tractor executives, including yourself, Henderson. Thus although Mr. Blake did not say so directly, it became obvious that my superior score made me better fitted for each and every high position in the company than any of the present incumbents—including, of course, yourself.

I had a definite feeling that Mr. Blake would have been glad to certify me for any of these higher jobs, but he felt it would be wiser to pick out some position which he supposed was open. Consequently, he offered me the job of sales manager.

"Mr. Blake," I said, "permit me to congratulate you. You have perhaps made a few minor errors. The ratings you have given me in certain unimportant fields such as accounting and finger dexterity are probably too low. Furthermore, someone has misinformed you concerning the vacancy which you think exists in the position of sales manager. I have reason to know that Mr. Botts' resignation is merely temporary. However, in your handling of the case of young Chester Hamilton, and even more in your recognition of my own high qualifications, you have proved that your testing methods are completely sound. I am happy to accept the position of sales manager, and, in so doing, I am going to make an announcement which will literally stun you with astonishment."

"Really?" said Mr. Blake.

"Yes," I said. "The name Abner Hopkins is merely an alias which I assumed for the purpose of making an undercover investigation of the Employment Office and the Parts Department. As my investigation of the Employment Office is now completed, there is no longer any need for me to conceal my true identity."

I rose from my chair, expanded my chest and threw back my shoulders. "When you gaze on me," I said, "you are gazing on none other than Alexander Botts, sales manager of the Earthworm Tractor Company."

Mr. Blake, to do him justice, managed to conceal his surprise fairly well. I asked him to keep the big news confidential and to certify me as a sweeper in the Parts Department, so that I could go through with my investigation. He agreed.

So I will conclude this letter on a note of complete satisfaction with my achievements. I have successfully settled young Chester Hamilton's affairs. I have proved that the Employment Office is doing a splendid job, so you can now start raising salaries rather than firing everybody. I, myself, am now back on the payroll as sales manager. And as I consider this position more important than the presidency of the company, you need not worry about me taking your job away from you—even though it has been scientifically proved that I am better fitted for it than you are.

When next you hear from me, I will be cleaning out the Parts Department in a big way.

Yours enthusiastically,
Alexander Botts.

BOTTS DISCOVERS URANIUM

Palace Hotel,
Denver, Colorado,
Monday, April 3, 1950.

Mr. Gilbert Henderson, President
Earthworm Tractor Company
Earthworm City, Illinois
Dear Henderson:

The comptroller of our company has disallowed the following items on my last week's expense account:

1 Geiger counter	$ 352.50
1 chemistry set	298.00
1 camping outfit	246.90
1 secondhand station wagon	1050.00
Miscellaneous and working capital ..	552.60
	$2500.00

I know you have given the comptroller the job of auditing the expense accounts of all company executives. With some it may work. With me it does not. Most of the time I am out in the field in close touch with the customers. I know what I am doing and what I ought to spend far better than any dried-up little adding-machine expert at the home office. Kindly instruct this character to pass my last week's expense account in full and wire me the entire amount at once. Also, tell him to pass without question all future expense accounts that are signed by

Alexander Botts,
Sales Manager,
Earthworm Tractor Company.

TELEGRAM

EARTHWORM CITY, ILLINOIS

APRIL 5, 1950

ALEXANDER BOTTS
PALACE HOTEL
DENVER COLORADO
WHY DO YOU NEED ALL THAT STUFF?

HENDERSON

Palace Hotel,
Denver, Colorado,
Wednesday, April 5, 1950.

Dear Henderson:

I need all that stuff—and I need it in a hurry—to help out one of our oldest and most valued customers, Mr. George Bixby, of the Bixby Construction Company, of this city. Last Friday morning I made a routine call on George. I found him seated in his office, conferring with a man whom he introduced as Prof. Henry Van Zandt. "The professor," George explained, "has almost persuaded me to cancel about half of an order which I recently placed with your local dealer for $200,000 worth of Earthworm equipment." At once I gave Professor Van Zandt a keen and appraising glance. He was tall and thin, and he had a small black mustache. I decided I was not going to like him.

Note: In the first place, his profession is against him. After all, if he were perfectly sane and normal, why would he want to be a professor? In the second place, he had been advising one of our customers not to buy Earthworm tractors. This definitely makes him a public menace. Clearly it was my duty to do everything I could to defeat his nefarious schemes. I went into action at once.

"Just who do you think you are?" I demanded. "What gives you the idea that you can come in here and louse up an important tractor sale? What have you got against the Earthworm Tractor Company?"

The professor replied with an air of assumed politeness, which did not fool me any. "I am a professor of mining engineering," he said. "I am not trying to louse up any sale. I have nothing against your excellent company——"

"Then what is your game?"

The professor's manner became even more smooth. He said, "I have recently purchased all rights in an old abandoned mine at a place called Tungsten Ridge. It is about a hundred miles from here—up in the mountains. The mine was opened years ago in a vein of wolframite——"

178

"A vein of what?"

"Wolframite. It is an ore of tungsten. Unfortunately, the vein was not rich enough. The project was abandoned. Recently, however, I have discovered—mixed with the low-grade wolframite—enormous quantities of pitchblende. This is a very rich ore of uranium, which is now in tremendous demand by the United States Atomic Energy Commission."

"Very interesting," I interrupted, "but what I want to know is why George Bixby is cutting in half his order for Earthworm equipment."

"I have suggested," said the professor, "that Mr. Bixby go into partnership with me in my uranium mine. To do this he will need $200,000—the amount he had planned to spend on Earthworm equipment to use on a road-building job in the southern part of the state."

I turned to George.

"What!" I said. "You are actually going to give up that road-building job, George?"

"I am considering it," he said. "Then, instead of $200,000 worth of Earthworm road-building machinery I would buy only $100,000 worth, which I would use to open up the approaches to the mine. The other $100,000 I would turn over to Professor Van Zandt to purchase drills and other hard-rock mining equipment."

"Why don't you take on both projects?" I said.

George shook his head. "No," he said, "I don't have the resources to swing both of them. It's got to be one or the other."

"Have you seen this mine yet?" I asked.

"Not yet. Professor Van Zandt plans to take me up in a week or so. But his reports are so complete I may go ahead without waiting for a personal visit."

"George," I said, "you are one of the best earth-moving contractors in the business. You are ready to start work on a wonderful road-building contract. You have placed a large order for Earthworm machinery—which is the finest in the world. You are all set to go. And then you start going crazy in your old age. Instead of relying on your own knowledge and skill, you begin listening to fantastic tales about a mine you have never even seen. You put your trust in a mere college professor. Don't you know that college professors are all theory, with no practical knowledge? Don't you realize that a man who would try to ruin an Earthworm sale is obviously a crook? Can't you see that you are acting like an idiot?"

George jumped from his chair. He started yelling in my face: "That will be enough out of you, Mr. Botts! Professor Van Zandt is a recognized authority on mining. He is a gentleman and a scholar. He was introduced to me by the president of the bank. I invited him in here to confer with me. And no mere tractor peddler like you is going to insult him in my presence. Furthermore, you are not going to tell me—right here in my own office—that I am acting like an idiot."

"I was just trying to help you," I said.

George calmed down a little—but not enough. "Before you came in," he said, "I was still in doubt about this proposition. But your insulting remarks have convinced me that I will be far happier, and far better off, dealing with a gentleman like Professor Van Zandt rather than with a vulgar and blatant salesman like you."

He sat down again at his desk, picked up the telephone, called our Denver dealer and spoke as follows: "I have just been having such an unsatisfactory talk with Mr. Alexander Botts that I have decided to cancel approximately half of my recent Earthworm order."

"I could hear the dealer pleading and protesting at the other end of the wire—but to no avail. George read off a list of the items to be canceled, and slammed down the telephone. Then he signed a letter which was lying on his desk.

"This letter," he explained, "informs the road commissioners that I am taking advantage of the escape clause and canceling the big road-building contract we were discussing. I dictated this letter several days ago. But I had not decided to send it off until just now."

He pressed a buzzer on his desk. A secretary came in. He gave her the letter.

"See that this gets in the mail this afternoon," he instructed.

Then he turned to me. "As we have nothing more to discuss," he said, "I know you will pardon me, Mr. Botts, if I resume my conversation with Professor Van Zandt. Good afternoon."

Too late I remembered that old George—in spite of our long and cordial friendship—has always had a tendency to blow up and yell at me whenever he thought I was trying to push him around. As I am a good judge of human nature, I realized I could accomplish nothing by descending to his level and yelling back. I therefore withdrew in a dignified manner.

But I was not licked. I was still convinced in my own mind of one basic fact: Anyone who persuades one of our customers not to buy Earthworm tractors is, *ipso facto*, a crook. This meant that the uranium project was undoubtedly fraudulent. And it was my duty to investigate the mine so that I could prove to Mr. Bixby that my suspicions were well founded.

As I knew nothing at all about uranium, I had to do a bit of preliminary research—which I undertook with my usual energy and enthusiasm. I discovered an excellent local establishment called The Miner's Supply Company. Here I purchased, for thirty cents, an authoritative booklet called *Prospecting for Uranium*, published by the United States Atomic Energy Commission and the United States Geological Survey. I spent the rest of the morning and half of the afternoon poring over this volume. By 3 p.m. I had covered the entire sixty-four pages, and I knew all that any miner or prospector needs to know about uranium—including such related subjects as geology, mineralogy and chemical analysis. I had also become a competent atomic scientist, well versed in nuclear physics.

As you, Henderson, are no doubt densely ignorant of all these matters, I will not confuse you with a lot of scientific terms which you might have considerable difficulty in understanding. I will merely state that in testing mineral deposits for uranium, it is necessary to have an instrument known as a Geiger counter, and sufficient equipment to make the type of chemical analysis which we scientists refer to as a bead test.

Unfortunately, The Miner's Supply Company had no Geiger counters and no adequate chemistry sets on hand. So they have ordered this material for me from Chicago. It should arrive in a few days. As I would not want to take any chances on poor equipment I have decided to get the best of everything. The Geiger counter is a superb portable model in a genuine leather case, with three sets of earphones as well as a dial indicator. Furthermore, it is thoroughly tropicalized—that is, protected against heat, humidity and termites. The chemistry set includes an unusually fine battery-operated portable ultraviolet lamp. It also includes small samples of uranium ore such as pitchblende, carnotite and pyrochloremicrolite.

As I may have to spend several days investigating the mine, I have ordered an adequate camping outfit, including sleeping bag, tent, gasoline stove, provisions, fishing tackle, hunting rifle, etc. The station wagon is obviously necessary to transport everything. It is very cheap at $1050. Miscellaneous items and a reserve for future expenses bring the total to an even $2500.

This is a very modest sum when you consider it is being used to save an order for $100,000 worth of Earthworm equipment. Please wire me the entire amount at once. As I have not established credit with The Miner's Supply Company, they will not let me have the equipment until I pay for it. And I must pick it up promptly so I can prove that Van Zandt is a crook before George Bixby gives him the money to buy the deep-rock mining equipment. Do not fail me.

Alexander Botts.

EARTHWORM TRACTOR COMPANY
EARTHWORM CITY, ILLINOIS
OFFICE OF THE PRESIDENT

Friday, April 7, 1950.

Dear Botts:

I do not believe that you can become an atomic scientist by skimming through a thirty-cent government booklet. And the purchase of a fancy Geiger counter and an elaborate chemistry set cannot qualify you to dispute the findings of a reputable professor of mining engineering. If you follow your present course, I am afraid you will succeed only in further antagonizing Mr. Bixby.

I am, therefore, compelled to deny your request for $2500. I suggest that you cancel your extravagant order for the Geiger counter and all the other unnecessary equipment, and that you cease your unfortunate attempts to interfere in the private business affairs of Mr. George Bixby.

Most sincerely,
Gilbert Henderson.

Palace Hotel,
Denver, Colorado,
Tuesday, April 11, 1950.

Dear Henderson:

Your letter is here. But it does not mean anything, because I have already demonstrated—to my own satisfaction at least—that I am a competent atomic scientist. I have made some startling discoveries. And I am ready not only to dispute Professor Van Zandt's findings but also to prove conclusively that he is a liar or an ignoramus or both.

Yesterday morning the Geiger counter and the chemistry set arrived. All of the other equipment was ready. As no money had come from you, I was forced to appeal to our local dealer. Unfortunately, he was definitely hostile. He blamed me for the loss of half the Bixby order. And he was so reluctant to help me that I had to give him a demand note, signed "Earthworm Tractor Company, by Alexander Botts, Sales Manager." I had to promise him that you would pay him back within a few days. And I had to do a lot of persuading. But I finally got an advance of $2500. I then called at The Miner's Supply Company, and picked up the Geiger counter, the chemistry set, and the camping outfit. I loaded them into the station wagon. I paid all bills. And I headed for the mountains.

About noon I arrived at Tungsten Ridge. I had no trouble in finding the mine. Disregarding a "No Trespassing" sign, which bore the name Henry Van Zandt, I entered a tunnel or gallery which had been cut about fifty feet into the solid rock. Here and there I noticed large chunks of a black mineral that looked a little like anthracite coal. Judging from its appearance it might have been wolframite—or it might have been pitchblende. The best way to find out was to get busy with the trusty Geiger counter.

I returned to the station wagon and lifted out the delicate instrument. I adjusted the earphones. I watched the second hand of my wristwatch. And I took the "background count"—the number of little clicks which register the cosmic rays and the normal faint radioactivity which is present throughout the universe. There were twenty-eight clicks per minute.

I reentered the tunnel. I explored it from end to end. I placed the counter against the walls, the roof and the floor. I set it down beside hundreds of separate pieces of black ore. There was no increase in the background count. This indicated a total lack of the strong radioactivity which is always associated with uranium. Just as I had suspected, the mine was a dud.

To make doubly sure, I pounded up a few samples of ore. I opened up my chemical set. I dipped the little wire loop in the bottle of lithium fluoride. I heated it over the flame of the alcohol lamp. I touched it to the rock sample. I heated it again. Then, in the darkness of the tunnel, I exposed the little molten bead to the mysterious, invisible rays of the ultraviolet lamp. If there had been any uranium present—even so small an amount as .05% uranium oxide—the bead should have shown a bright yellowish-green fluorescence. But—as I had anticipated—there was no reaction whatever. By this second test I had proved once more that the mine contained no uranium.

I started for home. And I felt that I had done a good job. Most people would have considered it enough for one day. But not Alexander Botts. On the drive back to Denver I kept trying out the Geiger counter, here, there and everywhere. As a result, I made a truly sensational discovery.

Shortly after dark, I stopped at a filling station. While the gas tank was being filled, I sat in the front seat of the station wagon experimenting with the Geiger counter. There was no noticeable reaction—just the usual average of twenty-eight clicks per minute.

Then a big truck came along. The road was rough. The truck was heavy. As it drew near, I could feel the ground trembling. Finally the truck turned into the filling station. The driver slammed on the brakes and stopped with such a jolt that the ground shook like a miniature earthquake. The windows in the little filling station rattled. Several cans of oil and an old alarm clock fell off a shelf near the filling station door. And the proprietor began yelling to the truck driver to be careful. But the most sensational response came from the Geiger counter. As soon as the earth began to shake, the earphones began popping away like a whole battery of miniature machine guns. For a moment I was baffled. Then, because of my scientific knowledge, the amazing answer burst upon me.

The little filling station—located on the level gravelly floor of a small mountain valley—was obviously perched right on top of an incredibly rich bed of uranium ore. This ore had been undisturbed for so long that the radioactivity had died down. When it was shaken up, the effect was similar to shaking a coal fire in a grate. Only, instead of a shower of sparks and ordinary flame, the result in this case was a great burst of radioactivity. My heart began to beat wildly, but I was careful to control all outward signs of emotion. To keep my great discovery secret, I promptly put the Geiger counter back in its case.

After the truck had left, I got out my flashlight. I helped the proprietor recover the alarm clock and several of the oil cans which had rolled under my car. While I did this, I was able to make a surreptitious but thorough examination of the terrain. Unfortunately, the driveway was covered with gravel which had evidently been hauled in from a distance. But my trained scientific eye finally spotted one small black pebble the size of a walnut. I slipped this into my pocket. After leaving the filling station I stopped a half mile down the road and set up the chemistry set. I ran a bead test on a small fragment of the pebble. And I got a beautiful yellow-green fluorescence. Here, indeed, was uranium.

I hurried back to the filling station. I worked on the proprietor for over an hour. I had with me $500 in cash left over from what the dealer had advanced me. And I finally persuaded the proprietor to sell me, for this sum of money, an option to purchase the entire filling-station property, including mineral rights, for $5000. With this paper duly signed I climbed happily back into the station wagon and returned to Denver. I have been writing this report at the hotel.

Now that you know what I have been doing, Henderson, you will have to agree with me that the future is bright. Within the next few days Professor Van Zandt plans to take George Bixby up to the mine. Although I am not invited, I will follow along. When they arrive I will make a sudden and dramatic appearance with my trusty Geiger counter and my beautiful chemistry set.

This will no doubt enrage the professor, but before he can do

184

anything I will put on my devastatingly convincing demonstration—proving that all my accusations are true. The professor will then slink away—hanging his head in shame—and I will lead George Bixby to the genuine uranium deposits at the filling station. I will explain to him how these deposits are in level gravel beds so that they can be worked by Earthworm tractors, scrapers and shovels. I will sell him the option on the property, and complete my triumph by persuading him to reinstate the canceled half of his Earthworm order.

At the moment, my only difficulty is my lack of $2500 to pay off our dealer. I had promised that I would have it before this and he is becoming very impatient and very nasty about it. Please wire the $2500—which is a small price to pay for the reinstatement of George Bixby's big order. With things going so well, how can I miss?

Alexander Botts.

TELEGRAM

EARTHWORM CITY, ILL.
APRIL 13, 1950

ALEXANDER BOTTS
PALACE HOTEL
DENVER, COLORADO
THERE ARE PLENTY OF WAYS YOU CAN MISS. CONSIDERING YOUR SCANTY KNOWLEDGE, I CAN PLACE NO FAITH IN YOUR ALLEGED SCIENTIFIC TESTS. KINDLY LAY OFF BIXBY. LEAVE THE POOR MAN ALONE. FURTHER INTERFERENCE IN HIS AFFAIRS IS SURE TO DO MORE HARM THAN GOOD.

GILBERT HENDERSON

Palace Hotel
Denver, Colorado,
Thursday, April 13, 1950.

Dear Henderson:

I regret to report that things have not been going so well. This morning Professor Van Zandt and George Bixby drove up to Tungsten Ridge. I followed along, unobserved. When they reached the mine, I made my dramatic appearance with a carefully prepared speech.

"Mr. Bixby," I said, "even though you have spurned me in the past, I am still your friend. I have come all the way up into these mountains for the sole purpose of saving you from the nefarious machinations of this false friend—Professor Van Zandt. At vast expense, I have purchased, and brought with me, a reliable Geiger counter and the most up-to-date chemical set that money can buy. All I ask is that you let me repeat a few scientific tests which I made a few days ago—tests which will prove conclusively that there is not a single atom of uranium in this entire mine."

I had expected that the professor would start getting hostile, and that George Bixby, remembering our past friendship, would spring to my defense. However, it was George who started ordering me off the property. And it was Van Zandt—the big crook—who crossed me up by putting on a false air of cordiality and politeness.

Turning to George he said, "As long as Mr. Botts has come all the way up here with his Geiger counter, I think we should take advantage of his kind offer. It is true that I have brought my own Geiger counter, but I do not want you to rely entirely on my equipment or on my word. I should much prefer that you have a fair test by some impartial person like Mr. Botts."

"Botts is not impartial," George growled, "and he doesn't want to make a fair test. He just wants to show you up as a boob so he can sell me more of his lousy Earthworm machinery."

"I think," said the professor quietly, "that we ought to consider Mr. Botts innocent until he is proved guilty. Come on—let's see what he has to offer." He promptly picked up my Geiger counter and obligingly carried it—along with his own—into the mine tunnel. I was so surprised at this great show of politeness that I followed along without quite knowing what I was doing, and helped adjust the three sets of earphones on my counter so we could all listen. I then made the mistake of speaking up a little too soon.

"You see," I said triumphantly, "there is no reaction at all—which proves there is no uranium here."

The professor looked at me innocently and said, "Is this the way you made your test a few days ago?"

"It is," I said.

"Then no wonder you got no results."

"Why not?"

"You haven't turned on the switch."

"That's right," I said. "You hurried me in here so fast that I forgot."

"And I suppose you also forgot when you were up here a few days ago?"

"Certainly not! Of course I turned on the switch; at least, I think I did."

"We all make mistakes," said the professor in a kindly tone.

"That was no mistake!" said George. "This guy is just trying to break up this mining deal for his own selfish advantage."

186

"Why don't you turn on the switch now?" the professor asked.

I did so, and as soon as the tubes had warmed up, the earphones began sounding off at such a terrific rate that it was impossible to count the separate clicks. I was astonished. I moved the Geiger counter here and there. The uproar kept on as loud as ever. The whole mine sounded as hot as the Bikini Lagoon.

It occurred to me that the counter might have gone haywire. I took it outside the mine. At once the count went down to the normal average background of twenty-eight per minute. I brought the counter back into the mine. Again the noise was terrific. We tried out the professor's Geiger counter, and got the same results.

I was badly shaken. But I was not yet licked. I said, "Apparently there is a certain amount of radioactivity around here, after all. But it may not be uranium. It might be thorium, or something else."

The professor suggested I run a bead test. I did. And I got a beautiful greenish-yellow fluorescence.

"I can't understand it," I said. "Why didn't I get any reaction the other day?"

Again the professor spoke up in his oily voice, "This rock is partly a tungsten ore called wolframite and partly a uranium ore called pitchblende. The two minerals look something alike. When you made your bead test the other day you probably got hold of a piece of wolframite."

"Maybe so," I said. "I will have to admit that there really is some uranium here. But it is deep down in hard rock—very difficult to get out." I turned to George Bixby. "If you really want to go into the uranium business," I said, "I will lead you to a deposit down in the valley. It is right on the surface. It can be scooped up with the greatest of ease by Earthworm tractors and scrapers or Earthworm shovels. If you take one look at this valley deposit, you will forget all about the hard-rock mining equipment that Professor Van Zandt wants you to buy. And you will invest all of that $200,000 in Earthworm equipment."

Unfortunately, this very fair proposition did not interest George Bixby. And once more it was Professor Van Zandt who persuaded him to listen to reason. On the way back to Denver we all stopped at the little filling station. Bravely, I brought out the Geiger counter. This time I made sure it was turned on. We adjusted the earphones. We listened. All we got was the normal average of twenty-eight clicks per minute. We got the same result from the professor's instrument.

I explained about my previous test—how a big truck had come in—shaking the ground, rattling the windows, jolting the oil cans and the alarm clock off the shelf, and disturbing the soil to a point where it became violently radioactive. I also explained how I had found a black pebble that showed uranium in the bead test.

We waited while several trucks went by. Finally one came rolling into the filling station—shaking the earth even more than on the previous occasion. But there was no reaction from either Geiger counter. I searched the entire locality. But I could not find another black pebble.

Finally Professor Van Zandt came up with another of his plausible-sounding explanations.

"Shaking the ground," he said, "does not promote radioactivity. It is possible, however, that the alarm clock you mentioned had a luminous dial of the kind that contains a minute quantity of radium. As this clock rolled under your car it may well have sent out rays strong enough to register in your Geiger counter. Regarding that black pebble, it may have been picked up when you loaded your equipment at the mine, and it may have fallen out of the station wagon when you drove in here."

At this, George Bixby began sounding off in a very abusive manner. "Mr. Botts," he said, "I don't believe a word of anything you have told us this afternoon. I think you are a liar. I think you have dreamed up all of this tall tale because you thought you could bust up my partnership with Professor Van Zandt and get me to reorder that $100,000 worth of Earthworm equipment that I had conceled. Fortunately, I can see through your low-down schemes. And I don't want to have anything more to do with you or with your company. I am going right back to Denver. Tomorrow morning I am going to cancel the balance of my Earthworm order. And I don't want you to show up again anywhere around my place of business. Good-bye!"

He grabbed Professor Van Zandt by the arm and ushered him back to his car. They drove away. As I could think of nothing else to do, I got into my station wagon and returned here to Denver—where I have been writing this report at the hotel.

At the moment, I am forced to admit that things do not look too favorable. What is worse, I cannot seem to think of any way to improve the situation. This momentary discouragement, however, may be due to the fact that I have had a hard day. I am tired. I will, therefore, go to bed. During the night I will let my subconscious mind work on my problems. And I have every confidence that in the morning I will have some new plan of action. Yours wearily but hopefully,

Alexander Botts.

TELEGRAM

EARTHWORM CITY, ILLINOIS
APRIL 15, 1950

ALEXANDER BOTTS
PALACE HOTEL
DENVER, COLORADO
YOUR LETTER HERE, ALSO WIRE FROM OUR DENVER DEALER
CHARGING YOU WITH FULL RESPONSIBILITY FOR TOTAL LOSS OF
BIXBY'S BUSINESS. DEALER DEMANDS IMMEDIATE PAYMENT OF
THAT $2500. AS YOU SIGNED THE NOTE IN THE NAME OF THE EARTH-
WORM COMPANY, IT IS POSSIBLE WE MAY HAVE TO PAY THE FULL
AMOUNT AND COLLECT IT IN INSTALLMENTS FROM YOUR FUTURE
SALARY. KINDLY RETURN TO THE HOME OFFICE AT ONCE SO THESE
MATTERS MAY BE STRAIGHTENED OUT.

GILBERT HENDERSON, PRES.
EARTHWORM TRACTOR CO.

Palace Hotel,
Denver, Colorado,
Monday, April 17, 1950.

Dear Henderson:

Your telegram arrived last Saturday. But, like so many of your
former messages, it does not mean anything because the situation
here has once more completely changed.

When I wrote you last Thursday night, I was so tired and so low in
my mind that I had actually begun to doubt my ability as an atomic
scientist. I had absorbed so much of your pessimism that I had even
begun to feel I might have made some serious blunders.

On Friday morning, however, I awoke rested and refreshed. And
out of the depths of my subconscious mind there emerged an idea so
obvious that it is amazing I had not thought of it before. In a burst of
inspiration, it occurred to me that in the past I have almost always
been right and everybody else has been wrong. It was reasonable to
assume, therefore, that in my present scientific activities, I have also
been completely right. This meant that when I first tested the mine
last Monday, my findings were absolutely accurate—there definitely
was no uranium there. And when I tested it three days later on
Thursday there really was a lot of uranium present.

How could this have been possible? The answer was obvious.
Sometime between Monday and Thursday, some crook must have
moved in a lot of pitchblende and mixed it with the loose wolfram-

ite. The identity of the crook was easy to guess. And I decided that if I could find out where he got the pitchblende, and how he handled the job, I would have definite proof of his guilt.

I rushed down to The Miner's Supply Company. I said, "Last Monday I bought from you—among other things—a small sample of pitchblende. Do you, by any chance, sell this stuff in larger quantities?"

"We do, if we have any," said the proprietor, "but a few days ago our whole supply was stolen."

"Aha!" I said. "Tell me more."

The proprietor explained: "We had a ton of pitchblende in hundred-pound sacks in an open shed behind the building here. We were saving it for the Atomic Energy Commission; they wanted it for experimental work. But sometime between five o'clock last Monday and eight o'clock Tuesday morning it was stolen."

"Who do you think stole it?"

"We don't know. A number of people had previously come in and asked if we had pitchblende for sale. We told them we had a ton, but it was already promised. Maybe one of these people took it."

"Did one of them go by the name of Professor Henry Van Zandt?"

"Not that I remember. Some of them were people I did not know. And I did not take down their names."

"Was one of them a tall thin guy with a little black mustache?"

"Yes, I think I remember somebody like that."

"That is the man!" I said. "He absolutely had to have that pitchblende so he could salt the mine before he took George Bixby up there. He was desperate. When he couldn't buy any, he just rented or borrowed a truck, helped himself and headed for the hills. That was Monday—the day I first visited the mine. When I stopped at that little filling station on the way back, he stopped at the same filling station on the way up. No wonder my Gieger counter went crazy—with a whole truckload of uranium ore driving in right beside me. And that little black pebble that I picked up was a hunk of pitch-blende that must have fallen out of his truck."

"I don't understand what you are talking about," said the proprietor.

"You don't have to," I said. "Come with me and I will show you the man who stole your pitchblende."

We drove first to the police station. I gave the cops a complete description of Professor Van Zandt, and told them the whole story. They asked me to look through their files, and before long I turned up a leaflet with Van Zandt's picture and the information that he was wanted in various parts of the country for a number of big swindles. In all of them, according to the leaflet, he had "used his scientific knowledge and his remarkable powers of persuasion to get himself accepted as a genuine scientist by businessmen, bank presidents, and prominent citizens generally." Armed with this leaflet we got a warrant. The proprietor of the supply house and a couple of cops and I drove to Mr. Bixby's office. We arrived just as Bixby and Van Zandt were discussing the final arrangements by which Bixby would turn over $100,000 to Van Zandt—ostensibly for the purchase of mining equipment.

The bogus professor was promptly grabbed by the cops. The proprietor of the supply house identified him as one of the men who had tried to buy pitchblende. We confronted him with the leaflet. And I denounced him for his attempt to swindle George Bixby.

When he saw that we had the goods on him, Van Zandt confessed everything. He admitted that he had rented a truck, stolen the pitchblende, and salted the mine just as I had suspected. His whole purpose had been to get away with George Bixby's $100,000.

After the cops had taken the crook to jail, and after the proprietor of The Miner's Supply Company had departed, old George shook my hand with gratitude—and also with sadness. "If only I had listened to your advice sooner," he said, "I would be a lot better off."

"Everything is all right," I said. "All you have to do is reorder that $200,000 worth of Earthworm equipment."

"But I have canceled the road-building job. How could I have made such a mistake?"

"That reminds me," I said, "of a rather embarrassing mistake I made myself. You remember that letter you signed when I was in your office a while back?"

"The letter canceling the contract?"

"Yes," I said. "You handed it to your secretary. She put it in the outgoing mail basket in the outer office. I knew you were very anxious to have it mailed. I wanted to be helpful. So, to make sure it got to the post office as quickly as possible, I unobtrusively picked it up as I went out. I intended to mail it——"

"But you didn't?"

"I'm sorry," I said. "I put it in my pocket and forgot. Here it is." I slapped it on his desk.

George picked it up and said, in a voice trembling with emotion, "May I always do business with people who make constructive mistakes like you!"

That was three days ago. I have delayed writing you so I could give you the complete story.

This morning, our Denver dealer mailed Mr. Bixby's renewed $200,000 order to the factory. And this afternoon the cops handed me a $5000 reward which had been offered for the apprehension of Professor Van Zandt. I have already transferred $2500 of this to our dealer to repay him for the money he advanced for the purchase of the Geiger counter, and for my other expenses, including the $500 filling station option which we have decided not to use.

The remaining $2500 would, under normal conditions, be turned over to the Earthworm Company. It is money which came in as a result of work which I am paid to do as a company executive. However, in this particular case, the comptroller, by disallowing my expenses, has definitely dissociated the company from my recent financial operations. So I will keep the second $2500 as a sinking fund for such future expenses as are apt to be turned down by our comptroller, but may prove necessary if I am to carry on effectively as your highly successful Sales Manager,

Alexander Botts

BOTTS RUNS
FOR HIS LIFE

EARTHWORM TRACTOR COMPANY
EARTHWORM CITY, ILLINOIS
OFFICE OF THE PRESIDENT

Wednesday, January 10, 1951.

Mr. Alexander Botts
Sales Manager Earthworm Tractor Company
Waldorf Astoria Hotel
New York, N.Y.

Dear Botts:

While you are traveling around calling on the trade I hope you will have time to contact one of our old customers, Mr. James Jorgensen, who is now engaged in a big logging project in the Green Mountains near Middlebury, Vermont. He has purchased a sawmill and lumber yard and is cleaning up several million feet of timber which blew down in a severe wind storm last November. He is using fifteen of our Earthworm tractors, and for the past month has been having continuous mechanical difficulties.

Several service mechanics, sent up last week by our Albany dealer, were unable to remedy the trouble. And Mr. Jorgensen became so enraged that he orderec them off the job and at the same time announced that he was going to transfer all his business to the newly reorganized Superba Tractor Company.

Following the departure of the service mechanics, one of our district representatives called on Mr. Jorgensen and attempted to smooth him down by pointing out that the Superba tractor is one of the worst-built machines in the field. Unfortunately, Mr. Jorgensen did not believe this fact. And, after a bitter argument, he ejected our representative bodily from his sawmill and threw him down an icy slope with such violence that he was painfully bruised and lacerated.

We have considered complaining to the police, and also filing a civil suit for damages. Since we do not like to take legal action against a customer, it occurs to me that you might be able to call on Mr. Jorgensen and work out some solution—provided you are not afraid to tackle such a violent customer.

Most sincerely,
Gilbert Henderson,
President Earthworm Tractor Co.

Waldorf Astoria Hotel,
New York, N.Y.
Saturday evening, January 13, 1951.

Dear Henderson:

You don't have to worry about my being afraid to tackle a violent customer like Mr. Jorgensen. I have already gone into action. Immediately after receiving your letter last night, I took the 10:30 p.m. train from Grand Central, and arrived early this morning right in the lion's den, so to speak, at Middlebury, Vermont. At once I began making inquiries. I learned that Mr. Jorgensen is regarded as a rough character, but completely honest and a good businessman. If I could approach him in exactly the right manner, I was sure that our meeting would mark the beginning of a truly beautiful friendship, and that I would have no trouble at all in convincing him of the folly of replacing his splendid Earthworms with any such mechanical atrocities as are perpetrated by the Superba Tractor Company.

To make the best possible first impression, I felt I should know something about Mr. Jorgensen's present mental attitude. I therefore decided to interview a man called Harold Quincy, who is a representative of the Superba company, and who, I was told, had been spending the last two days with Mr. Jorgensen. It was reported that Mr. Quincy was leaving on the 12:22 p.m. train for New York. As I was unable to contact him beforehand, I resolved to travel back to New York with him. I took a taxi to the railroad station, where the taxi driver pointed him out.

He was strutting up and down, swinging a briefcase marked in big gold letters: "Harold Quincy. Superba Tractor Company." He wore a Tyrolean hat with a shaving-brush ornament, a checked overcoat and yellow gloves.

At once I sized him up as a typical low-grade salesman—smart aleck, conceited, and not too bright. He was, in short, just the opposite of the typical high-grade salesman—well bred, modest and intelligent—which is so well represented by myself. I knew this man would be as putty in my hands.

When the train pulled in I let him get on board first. He entered the smoking lounge. At the last moment I boarded the day coach, where I remained until the conductor had punched my ticket. Then I walked forward to the lounge, where I found my quarry. He had removed his overcoat and hat, revealing a rather loud suit and an even louder necktie. Timidly I sat down beside him.

"Do you mind if I sit here?" I asked in a mournful tone of voice.

"It's a free country," he said.

I pointed to his briefcase. "Are you Mr. Harold Quincy?" I asked.

"That's right."

"And you're a tractor salesman?"

"You said it, big boy. I'm the best tractor salesman in the country."

This palpable falsehood—uttered, ironically enough, in the very presence of the man who really is the best tractor salesman in the country—gave me exactly the opening I needed. As long as Mr. Quincy was wandering so far from the truth, I felt that a few minor inaccuracies on my part would be entirely justified.

"My name is Ebenezer Boggs," I said.

"Pleased to meet you, Mr. Boggs," he said heartily.

"I'm a salesman, myself," I continued. "I've been up in Montreal, trying to sell candy bars for a firm in New York. But I didn't make a single sale. Maybe you could help me, Mr. Quincy, by telling me the secret of your success."

At this flattering approach, the man's chest swelled with pride. "Always glad to help a fellow salesman," he said. "What seems to be your main trouble?"

"I don't know," I said hopelessly. "I call on a candy-store proprietor. I give him what I think is a wonderful sales talk. But he always says he's perfectly satisfied with the candy bars he's already handling. So I never get anywhere. Maybe you could tell me what to do. There must be times when you have to sell one of your tractors to a man who is completely satisfied with some other kind."

Mr. Quincy smiled with smug satisfaction. "As a matter of fact," he said, "I am right now engaged in selling a whole fleet of Superba tractors to a man who has always used machines called Earthworms, and who, until I met him, was completely satisfied with them."

"It looks like a tough proposition," I said. "It would take a better sales talk than anything I ever heard."

"That's exactly the point, Mr. Boggs. You second-rate salesmen try to do everything with a sales talk. Me—I go beyond that. I am

195

constructive. I manipulate the various factors in the situation so as to create an atmosphere that will be favorable to my plans."

"I don't understand," I said.

"Of course you don't. You're just a small-time operator. In this deal I started to tell you about, I found myself up against a stubborn old bird called Jorgensen. He runs a sawmill near Middlebury, Vermont. He had been using Earthworm machinery so long he wouldn't consider anything else. When I first met him, about a month ago, he was in such a rut, mentally, that he wouldn't let me even start a sales talk. I could see that I had no chance, at the time, to create in his mind a desire for Superba tractors. So I changed my tactics. I decided to make the old fool dissatisfied with his Earthworm tractors."

"Wouldn't that be pretty hard to do?"

"Not for a practical man like me. I stopped wasting my time on mere sales talks. I went out in the woods. I looked over his tractors. And especially I looked over his tractor operators."

"What was the idea of that?"

Here Mr. Quincy got very confidential. "In any tractor sale, Mr. Boggs, the important thing is not the tractor. It's the human element. If you want to be a successful salesman, always concentrate on the people—not on the product."

"Mr. Quincy," I said, "I think maybe you've got something there."

"Of course I have. And this basic principle has been of vital importance in the deal I am promoting in Middlebury. About noon of the second day I found a young man named Oswald who was highly dissatisfied with his job as a tractor operator. So right away I started working on him. I got him talking about himself."

"How did you do that?"

"Get him talking about himself? It's easy if you know how. All you got to do is flatter the guy, ask him just enough questions to draw him out, and then listen while he sounds off."

"I never thought of that," I said. "What did this man Oswald tell you?"

"It was the usual line of a typical sorehead. He said he was the finest mechanic in the state of Vermont. Old Jorgensen should have put him in charge of all the repair and maintenance work of all the tractors. He should have doubled his salary. But he didn't appreciate him. So I sympathized with the poor sap and led him on, and pretty soon he began telling me about his girl."

"This Oswald had a girl?"

"Yes. They wanted to get married. They had picked out a little dream of a house in Middlebury that was for sale for only fifteen thousand dollars. But, as long as he was being exploited by this old tightwad Jorgensen, he couldn't even scrape together enough money for a down payment. By this time the setup was so simple that even you, Mr. Boggs, could guess how I handled it."

"I wouldn't have the slightest idea," I said.

"Well," said Mr. Quincy, "I made this man Oswald a proposition. 'Oswald,' I said, 'you don't have to worry anymore about what these boobs and nitwits think about you. I'm going to make you an offer. I am planning to open a Superba tractor dealership right here in Middlebury. I'll have a big service and repair shop. I'll need a first-class man in charge. So I'll give you the job, at $7,500 a year. And, as an extra bonus, if you'll sign a five-year contract with me, I'll buy that $15,000 house and give it to you and your wife as a wedding present.' "

"That certainly was a generous offer," I said. "Pretty near sensational."

"That's what young Oswald thought," he said. "I could hardly keep him quiet long enough to explain the conditions."

"Oh," I said, "there was a catch to this offer?"

"Of course there was. I explained it to Oswald like this: 'Before I establish the dealership in Middlebury,' I said, 'I've got to make at least one big sale around here. The only big prospect is Jorgensen. I'm trying to get him to turn in his fifteen old Earthworms, and buy fifteen new Superbas. So far, he has refused to do this because he claims he's completely satisfied with the Earthworms. So, Oswald, you've got to make old Jim dissatisfied with his Earthworms.' "

"How could he do that?" I asked.

"As I explained it to Oswald, the answer is obvious. 'You are a regular employee around here,' I said. 'You have access to the fuel and the oil and the tools and supplies. You can go in and out of the repair shop and the equipment shed anytime you want. Nobody spies on you. Nobody would object if you stuck around to work on your tractor after hours.' "

"Wait a minute," I said. "You weren't suggesting, were you, that you wanted this man to sort of sabotage those Earthworm tractors?"

"I wasn't suggesting anything, Mr. Boggs. All I did was set forth the facts. And I went on to explain that if the Earthworms accidentally started to have all kinds of mechanical breakdowns, it would be possible that old Jim might decide to switch to some other make of tractor. Does that sound logical to you?"

"It certainly does."

"It also sounded logical to Oswald. I had sized him up right. He has just enough low cunning so that he caught on to what I wanted. And he could figure out exactly how to do his dirty work so nobody would suspect anything."

"Just what did he do?"

"I don't know. And I don't want to know. All I care about is the way things are working out. It is now a month since I had that little talk with Oswald. And all through this month those Earthworm tractors have been breaking down and getting so little work done that Jorgensen is about frantic. I have been spending the past two days with him, and when I left, he asked me to bring up a Superba tractor. He said if I could prove in a competitive demonstration that my machine is better than the Earthworm he would trade me all his Earthworms for half what he paid for them and buy a whole fleet of Superbas."

"Say, that's wonderful," I said. "I suppose you're going to ship a tractor to Middlebury right away?"

"I have already ordered it. It should be there early next week. I will be busy with some important conferences in New York for several days, but I go back to Middlebury and put on a demonstration for Jorgensen next Friday. I can probably finish the demonstration in the morning. And in the afternoon the old boy will sign up to turn in his Earthworms and buy fifteen of my machines."

"If the Earthworms are in such bad shape," I said, "I shouldn't think you would want to take them in on trade."

"Don't worry about that. Young Oswald has pulled off nothing but minor breakdowns. Fundamentally they're as good as ever. As soon as I get hold of them they'll start running fine, and I can resell them at a handsome profit."

"And you're really going to give Oswald a house and a job?"

"Certainly not. Whatever gave you that idea?"

"That's what you told me you were going to do."

"Oh, no. That's not what I told you. That's just what I told Oswald. But you are forgetting that this man is a crook. If I gave him a house or paid him a big salary for what he did to those Earthworm tractors I would be rewarding a dishonest act. You wouldn't want me to do anything as immoral as that, would you?"

"No, I suppose not," I said. "But won't Oswald make a big row when he finds out you've let him down?"

"He can't prove anything against me, and the more he hollers the more he'll be telling everybody how crooked he is. Not only would he lose the job he's got but he'd have a tough time getting a job anywhere else. There won't be any trouble from young Oswald. I'll put the sale through like the high-powered salesman that I am."

"Mr. Quincy," I said, "you don't know how educational your talk has been. I feel that it is going to help me a lot in my own business. I thank you."

"Mr. Boggs," he said, "it has been a pleasure." He reached into his briefcase and handed me a lot of Superba advertising literature and a large lapel button labeled "Superba Tractors."

From here on, our talk drifted about through various subjects. Mr. Quincy explained to me exactly why business ethics are so much higher in America than in other parts of the world. I came back with a few of my best Swedish jokes. And when we finally parted at Grand Central Station I thanked him again. I then came to the hotel where I have been writing this report.

I have given you this very full account of my activities so that you may realize how well I am handling the problem you have assigned me. Even though I went all the way to Vermont and came back without seeing Mr. Jorgensen, I have accomplished far more than if I had barged in after the manner of our district representative and, like him, succeeded only in getting myself thrown out.

As things now stand, the difficult case of Mr. James Jorgensen is, for all practical purposes, in the bag. Such being the case, I will spend next Monday, Tuesday and Wednesday taking care of several urgent matters here in New York. I will return to Middlebury on the Wednesday night train—arriving on Thursday, one day ahead of Mr. Harold Quincy. I will then prove to Mr. Jorgensen that Quincy and Oswald have been playing him for a sucker. As soon as he understands what has been going on, he will throw Mr. Quincy out on his ear, and fire young Oswald. From then on, his Earthworms will run perfectly. And harmony and justice will prevail.

Yours, with keen satisfaction for a job well done,

Alexander Botts,

Sales Manager Earthworm Tractor Co.

EARTHWORM TRACTOR COMPANY
EARTHWORM CITY, ILLINOIS
OFFICE OF THE PRESIDENT

Monday, January 15, 1951.

Mr. Alexander Botts
Waldorf Astoria Hotel
New York, N.Y.

Dear Botts:

Your letter is here. I am very much disturbed over your plans. In your final paragraph you say that on Thursday you will arrive in

Middlebury and "prove to Mr. Jorgensen that Quincy and Oswald have been playing him for a sucker." At first sight this may seem like a plausible method of approach. Unfortunately, however, you have nowhere in your letter given the slightest indication that you are in a position to prove anything to Mr. Jorgensen. Please remember that Jorgensen has been having trouble with the Earthworm company. From the very moment you meet him, he will be violently prejudiced against you. On the other hand, his relations with the Superba company have, as far as we know, been completely friendly. Jorgensen will therefore be definitely prejudiced in favor of Mr. Quincy.

To deal with this adverse situation, I fail to see that you can present anything in the way of facts or figures or concrete evidence. All you have is an incredibly fantastic story involving the most serious accusations against a trusted employee and against a rival tractor salesman. These accusations will undoubtedly be denied by Mr. Harold Quincy and this man Oswald. As you have nothing to offer in rebuttal except your own unsupported word, you cannot hope to get anywhere. If you approach Mr. Jorgensen in the manner indicated you will succeed only in getting yourself thrown out in exactly the same way as our district representative was thrown out.

I would suggest, therefore, that you refrain from accusations which you cannot back up. And when you meet Mr. Jorgensen, I feel that you should:

1. Keep the conversation on a high plane.
2. Prove to him the superiority of Earthworm tractors by giving him a straightforward, scientific discussion of the obviously superior qualities found in our product.

> Most sincerely,
> Gilbert Henderson.

> Porter Hospital
> Middlebury, Vermont
> Friday, January 19, 1951

Dear Henderson:
Your letter arrived before I left New York. And I regret to inform you that it has been impossible for me to follow your advice. How could I keep the conversation on a high plane with all the low and slimy skulduggery that has been going on? And how could I convince Mr. Jorgensen of the superiority of Earthworm tractors by a mere scientific discussion, when Mr. Jorgensen's Earthworm tractors were breaking down all over the landscape? Merely to ask these questions

is to answer them; your suggestions were absolutely and obviously impractical.

However, you may perhaps derive a little wry satisfaction in learning that at least one of your predictions has come true. Owing to a slight miscarriage in my plans, Mr. Jorgensen became violently enraged under circumstances which caused him to throw me out even more violently than he threw out our district representative, and to send me skidding down the same icy slope with such force that I have been in the hospital ever since.

Fortunately, it is a good hospital. My injuries are not critical. I expect to be out tomorrow. And I am pleased to report that I am not in any way discouraged. To the end that you may understand how much better I have handled this situation than would have been the case if I had followed your advice, and in order that you may realize how I would have achieved a complete success unmarred by any hospital interlude if it had not been for the unforeseen presence of a fire escape outside the window, I will now give you a full account of my activities since I arrived in Middlebury yesterday morning.

After a good breakfast at the Middlebury Inn, I hired a taxi and drove to Mr. Jorgensen's sawmill at the foot of the mountain. I did not, however, introduce myself as a representative of the Earthworm company. The plan which I had evolved was much more subtle. I had decided that I would pretend I represented the Superba Tractor Company. I would persuade Oswald, the mechanic, to tell me all about his sabotage operations. He would suppose the conversation was confidential. But all the time Mr. Jorgensen would be listening around the corner of a building or from some other vantage point. Thus Oswald would be convicted out of his own mouth, the fat would be in the fire, the Superba company would be in the doghouse, and the Earthworm would be on top of the heap.

This plan, of course, was not complete. I had not yet worked out any technique for enticing Mr. Jorgensen into a concealed position and keeping him quiet while I attempted to trick young Oswald into giving himself away. These questions, however, were unimportant. I had created a grand master plan. And I could follow my usual custom of leaving the minor details completely fluid so they could be altered according to changing conditions.

Upon arriving at the sawmill I told the taxi driver to wait. I put on the "Superba Tractor" button Mr. Quincy had given me. I picked up my briefcase, in which I had a lot of the Superba advertising folders, and I accosted a couple of men who were piling boards. I asked them where I could find Mr. Jorgensen. They said he was in his office on the second floor of a long wooden storage building beside the mill. I entered the building. I tiptoed up a flight of stairs, along a hallway, and around a corner to an open door. I peered into the room beyond. Mr. Jorgensen, a man of powerful build, was seated with his back to me. He was working with some papers at his desk. The setup seemed favorable. So I quietly withdrew.

I returned to the men who were piling boards. I asked them where I could find a mechanic named Oswald. They said he was behind the sawmill, moving some logs with his tractor. I went around and found him. I told him he was to report to Mr. Jorgensen's office. He said he would be there in five minutes. I went back, climbed the stairs and waited in the upper hall around the corner from the door of Mr. Jorgensen's office. He said he would be there in five minutes. I went back, climbed the stairs and waited in the upper hall around the corner from the door of Mr. Jorgensen's office. Here, according to my plan, I would intercept the treacherous mechanic and trick him into a discussion which would reveal all of his nefarious activities to Mr. Jorgensen—provided, of course, that Mr. Jorgensen remained quietly in his office, listening to what went on.

Unfortunately, however, Mr. Jorgensen turned out to be the kind of man who likes to spring to action at the slightest excuse. I had hardly taken my position when I inadvertently shifted my weight onto a loose floor board. The board squeaked.

There was a yawp from the office. "Who's that out there?"

I decided I had better try to smooth down the old guy. I walked around the corner and into the office. "Are you Mr. Jorgensen?" I asked.

"I am."

"I represent the Superba Tractor Company," I said glibly. "Mr. Harold Quincy sent me up to make a thorough study of your job here so that we can give you the best possible demonstration when our tractor arrives. It has been nice meeting you. And now, if you will excuse me, I will be on my way." I started out.

"Wait a minute," said Mr. Jorgensen. "Mr. Quincy gave me a Superba catalogue, and there's something about the drawing of the power take-off that I don't quite understand. I want you to explain it to me."

"I will do my best," I said modestly.

Mr. Jorgensen continued: "My bookkeeper has the catalogue in his office at the other end of the building. I'll call him and ask him to bring it over."

He flipped a switch on a metal box on his desk. The box bore a name plate: "Signal Corps—U.S. Army—interphone Amplifier BC-605-D."

"This," he explained, "is surplus Army equipment that I picked up a while back. It's a great convenience—even though you have to wait for the tubes to warm up."

"Very interesting," I said. "How does it work?"

"There's a mike and a speaker in a little box over in the bookkeeper's office," he said. "It's connected to this thing here by a pair of wires. When I want to call the bookkeeper I throw this other little switch to the position labeled 'Talk.' When I want to hear what he has to say, I change it to the position labeled 'Listen.' Do you hear that faint humming?"

"Yes."

"That means the tubes are warmed up." He moved the switch to "Talk" and began yelling, "Hey, there, George! Are you there, George?" Then he flipped the switch to "Listen," and waited. Nothing happened. "I guess George is out somewhere," he said. "I'll have to go and get that catalogue myself." He rose and started down the hall.

The situation was getting out of hand. Oswald, the mechanic, was due to arrive at any moment. I began to think fast. How could I keep this energetic Mr. Jorgensen quiet and in one place long enough so he could hear the conversation I was hoping to stage with Oswald? I kept on thinking—faster and faster. And gradually, in the back of my mind, I began to get a sort of vague hunch. Possibly that Army interphone contraption might fit into my plans.

I followed Mr. Jorgensen down the hall for several hundred feet to the far end of the building. He opened a door marked "Bookkeeper," walked into the room, and started pawing through a pile of pamphlets and catalogues on a desk.

I stood in the hall outside and sized up the situation. On the desk was a metal box—obviously the other end of the interphone system. The room had one window. As we were on the second floor, I did not think this window would provide a practical means of exit. There was one door. I examined it closely. I saw that it was of stout construction. And then I noticed something that caused all my half-formed ideas and hunches to crystallize suddenly into a complete and beautiful plan of action. The door was equipped with a heavy hasp. On the jamb there was a heavy staple. And hanging on the staple was a heavy open padlock. "Eureka!" I said. "This is it!"

"What's that?" asked Mr. Jorgensen.

By way of reply I slammed the door, removed the padlock, shoved the hasp over the staple and replaced the padlock.

The old boy was safely locked in. I was safely outside. I raced back to Mr. Jorgensen's office. Oswald had not yet arrived. I made a quick test. With the little toggle switch pushed up to the position marked "Listen," I could hear everything that went on in the bookkeeper's office. There was a great pounding, and the sound of Mr. Jorgensen's voice yelling, "Open this door, you fool!"

I threw the switch to the position marked "Talk." I could no longer hear anything from the bookkeeper's office. But Mr. Jorgensen could hear everything that went on at my end of the line. Or, at least, that is what I hoped.

I settled myself quietly in the chair behind the desk. A moment later Oswald, the mechanic, came in.

"Oswald," I said, "Mr. Jorgensen has stepped out for a few minutes, so this is a good chance for us to have a serious confidential talk. I represent the Superba Tractor Company. Mr. Harold Quincy sent me here to find out why you are falling down so badly on the job which you agreed to handle for him."

Oswald looked startled. Then he asked suspiciously, "What job?"

"You can speak frankly," I said. "I know the whole story. Mr. Quincy says he hired you to sabotage Mr. Jorgensen's Earthworm tractors so thoroughly that the old guy will become completely disgusted with them and will buy a fleet of Superba tractors. Mr. Quincy says you promised to do this. But so far, he says you have accomplished practically nothing. What's the matter with you?"

Young Oswald looked uncomfortable. He went to the door and glanced up and down the hall. "I was afraid somebody might be listening," he said.

"You can see we are alone," I said. "Come on—speak up."

"I don't like to discuss this thing with strangers," he said.

"But I'm not a stranger. I'm Mr. Quincy's confidential adviser. Unless you can give me some reasonable assurance that you will go through with this thing, the deal is off. You won't get the $15,000 house, and you won't get the $7,500 job."

"But I'm doing the best I can," Oswald whined. "I got to go slow and cover my tracks, or I would spoil the whole thing."

"Have you done anything so far?"

"Sure I have."

"It can't be much. I notice your own tractor seems to be running all right."

"Of course it is. If I louse up my own machine I would get fired. And that would spoil everything."

"Have you wrecked any of the other machines?"

"I'm not supposed to wreck them. Mr. Quincy plans to take them in on trade, so he doesn't want any serious damage. He just wants a lot of minor breakdowns."

"And you claim you've actually accomplished something along that line?"

"Sure I have."

"What, for instance?"

"Well, for one thing, I've been working on the radiators. I sneak around at night. I drive a nail into the radiator core and plug the hole with chewing gum. The next day, when the tractor is way off in the woods, the chewing gum works loose and all the water runs out. They lose a lot of time bringing in the machine or sending a man out to solder it. And they always think, just because they first noticed it in the woods, that the damage must have been done out there. So they never suspect me. They figure the hole must have been punched by a branch of a tree or something, and they decide the Earthworm radiators must be poor quality. And that's not all."

"You have other tricks?"

"I'll say. I stole all the solder out of the repair shop and replaced it with some trick solder out of a toy chemistry set that a friend of mine bought for me down in New York. This trick solder melts in boiling water. When they use it to repair a leaky radiator, it lasts only till the engine gets well heated up. And the mechanics around here are so dumb they never notice the difference. They have nothing but trouble and more trouble. But one of my best ideas is putting potatoes in the cooling system."

"Potatoes in the cooling system?"

"Sure. I've fixed up ten or twelve Earthworms that way. I do it at night when nobody is around. I take off the water manifold and I wedge several raw potatoes into the manifold or into the water jacket around the cylinders."

"What's that for?"

"The potatoes cut off part of the circulation in the cooling system. The engine heats up. The radiator starts to boil. So the operator shuts down. He looks in the radiator. He takes off the radiator cap. He looks inside. There is plenty of water. So he checks the fan. He checks the water pump. He checks everything. He calls the chief mechanic. And by that time the potatoes have all boiled away, and the cooling system is full of a kind of potato soup that is so thin that it looks practically the same as water. So they finally get the machine running again. But a lot of time has been wasted. And they never find out what was the matter."

"Oswald," I said, "permit me to congratulate you. You have given a very convincing account of your activities. I am sure you will be suitably rewarded. And now I think you had better be getting back to your tractor before Mr. Jorgensen arrives. Good-bye."

Oswald departed. As soon as he was out of earshot, I flipped the switch on the interphone amplifier and listened intently for any audible reaction that might come from Mr. Jorgensen over in the bookkeeper's office. There was none. The silence was complete.

This was disturbing. If the violent-tempered Mr. Jorgensen were still trapped in the bookkeeper's office, he most certainly would be yelling his head off. The ominous silence indicated that he must have escaped. If he had escaped before he had a chance to hear my conversation with Oswald, he would undoubtedly want to beat me up for having locked the door on him. On the other hand, if he had escaped after hearing the conversation, he would probably want to beat me up for conspiring against him. In any case, he would be after me—and with blood in his eye.

I decided I had better get out of there before he caught me. I ran down the stairs and out the door. But I was a little late. Just as I emerged into the open air, Mr. Jorgensen came charging around the corner of the building with all the fury of an enraged rhinoceros. I ran in the opposite direction. I circled around the building.

At the far end I caught a brief glimpse of a fire escape with an open window at the top. Then I knew how Mr. Jorgensen had escaped so easily from the second-floor room.

I kept on running. Three times I circled that building—with Mr. Jorgensen in hot pursuit. At the beginning of the fourth lap he caught up to me and gave me a shove which sent me down what must have been the same icy slope which had been previously traveled by our unfortunate district representative. Mr. Jorgensen did not continue the pursuit.

I was eventually rescued by the taxi driver and brought here to the hospital, where I have been treated for a sprained ankle, a sprained wrist, and various cuts, bruises and contusions.

That was yesterday. This morning Mr. Jorgensen arrived at the hospital. He had learned my true identity from various papers in the briefcase I had accidentally left behind when I departed so hurriedly from his office. He had learned of my plans and of the duplicity of Mr. Quincy from a carbon copy of the letter I sent you last week, Henderson. Any lingering doubts were removed by the conversation between Oswald and me. He had heard the whole thing. And he told me somewhat regretfully that Oswald had taken alarm and disappeared before he had a chance to fire him in his usual forcible manner. He stated further that he was through forever with the Superba Tractor Company, and he said he would stick with Earthworm the rest of his life.

"Has Mr. Quincy shown up yet?" I asked.

"Yes, indeed," he said pleasantly. "Mr. Quincy arrived this morning and promptly departed down that same icy slope." He glanced out the window and continued, "Just as I expected. The ambulance has arrived and they're bringing him in now. So the only thing that worries me is the unnecessarily rough treatment I handed out to you, Mr. Botts, before I realized that you were helping me so much. Can you ever forgive me?"

"Not only do I forgive you, Mr. Jorgensen," I said, "but I have a feeling that this is the beginning of a beautiful friendship."

Most sincerely,
Alexander Botts.

DEAR HENDERSON: I QUIT! (SIGNED) ALEXANDER BOTTS

EARTHWORM TRACTOR COMPANY
INTERDEPARTMENTAL
COMMUNICATION

To: Gilbert Henderson
        President Earthworm Tractor Company
        Earthworm Branch Office
        Washington, D.C.
From: Alexander Botts,
        Sales Manager
        Earthworm Tractor Company
        Warsaw Hotel
        Warsaw, Maine
Date: Tuesday, August 9, 1955.

Dear Henderson:

You will be happy to know that I have worked out some necessary improvements on the instructions contained in your letter to me at Earthworm City last week. You said you had heard that a man named George Buttrick, president of the Buttrick Mining Corporation of Winnipeg, was planning to buy—for use at one of his important mining properties in Northern Canada—a million dollars' worth of excavating equipment from the Jumbo Wheel Tractor Company. And you ordered me to go to Winnipeg at once and persuade Mr. Buttrick to switch his order to the Earthworm Company.

Now, switching a million-dollar order is not as easy as it sounds in your letter. Before embarking on any such important project, I decided to find out all I could about Mr. Buttrick. I consulted our

208

files and found that this man—although he is a big operator in both Canada and the United States—has only recently entered the mining field. The only information I could dig up concerned a recent deal at one of his mining properties at a place called Warsaw, Maine. The local manager of this property recently placed a small order for Earthworm equipment. A few days later Mr. Buttrick arrived in Warsaw, engaged in a violent argument with our Maine dealer, and canceled the order. There were no details.

At once I decided that it would be useless for me to see Mr. Buttrick until I had learned exactly what had happened in Warsaw, Maine. Consequently, instead of obeying your order and going direct to Winnipeg, I first came here to Warsaw. And it is a very good thing I did so. In less than one day I have learned a number of vital facts about Mr. Buttrick and his operations. And I have already started to stir things up in such a sensational manner that I am sure to achieve some real results.

I arrived in town this morning, called at the small downtown office of the Buttrick Mining Corporation and introduced myself to the local manager, a young man named Jim Williams. He looked intelligent. Also he looked worried. He was puffing nervously on a cigarette. I got down to business at once. "I am here," I said, "to reinstate that order for Earthworm equipment."

"There is nothing I would like better, Mr. Botts. What this job needs is Earthworm equipment. But I can't convince Mr. Buttrick, the head of the business. So the whole situation is hopeless."

"Nonsense," I said. "Nothing is ever hopeless—especially the present situation now that Alexander Botts has entered the picture. When it comes to overcoming sales resistance and convincing people to buy Earthworms, I am probably the world's greatest expert. All you have to do, Jim, is explain everything to me and I will solve your difficulties. In the first place, I want to know exactly what sort of a mine you are operating here."

"We're not operating anything as yet, Mr. Botts. We're just getting ready. Last spring Mr. Buttrick bought an extensive deposit of pegmatite a few miles north of town here."

"Pegmatite?"

"It's a kind of mixed ore—containing minerals like quartz, mica and feldspar. This particular deposit is unusually rich in beryllium, which is a rare metal used in alloys."

"Have these pegmatite deposits ever been worked before?"

"No, Mr. Botts. Mr. Buttrick plans to open them up. He hired me about a month ago and sent me up here to take charge."

"You are a mining engineer?"

"Yes. I'm a graduate of the Colorado School of Mines. And I've also had some experience in road construction. But this is the most important job I ever had. Or at least that's what I thought at first. Now, I wish I had never heard of this place."

"Go on," I said. "What seems to be the trouble?"

Jim lit another cigarette from the butt he had been smoking. I noticed that his ash tray was pretty well filled with butts. "This pegmatite is a weathered surface deposit in a rather densely wooded area. We plan to dig it up with power shovels and haul it out over six miles of poor dirt road. Before this road can be used for hauling it will need a good coat of gravel—about twenty thousand yards."

"So graveling your road is the first job you have to do?"

"Yes, Mr. Botts. And I want to get started right away so as to finish before winter and have everything ready to begin mining operations in a big way in the spring. I've located a plentiful supply of gravel in the bed of a small stream known as the Gravel River. It's so far out in the wilderness that nobody has ever developed it, but it's close to our road and it's just what I want. I was planning to buy an Earthworm shovel and an Earthworm tractor with bulldozer to dig the gravel out of the river, and an Earthworm motorgrader to maintain the road. Next year I would use the same equipment for our mining operations."

"How about trucks?"

"I can hire them locally. But the whole thing is off now."

"What happened?"

"Well, after I had called up your Earthworm dealer down at Portland and ordered what I needed, Mr. Buttrick—the head of the company—arrived on a whirlwind visit and raised a big uproar because he thought your prices were too high."

"Where did he get that idea?"

"He talked to some people at the Jumbo Wheel Tractor Company, and found that Jumbo prices are lower than Earthworm. Also, they offered him a special discount. So he demanded that the Earthworm dealer give him a forty percent discount. He said that would just about put your prices in line with Jumbo."

"He's crazy," I said. "Doesn't he know that the Earthworm Company is completely fair to all customers? Doesn't he realize that we treat everybody alike, and that nobody gets a discount?"

"That's what your dealer told him, Mr. Botts. But he wouldn't believe it."

"Besides," I said, "those Jumbo machines are so wretchedly built that they fall apart almost before they get started. The upkeep is terrific. They would be extravagantly expensive even if the company

210

gave them away free. So—if you want to save money you should buy honest Earthworm quality at an honest Earthworm price. Don't you realize that?"

"Yes, Mr. Botts. But I can't convince Mr. Buttrick."

"What's the matter with him?"

"Unfortunately," said Jim, "Mr. Buttrick is not a mining man. He is not a construction man. He is a sort of financial manipulator who is so impressed with his own importance that you can't tell him anything. I tried to reason with him. But he just canceled the Earthworm contract."

"And told you to buy Jumbo equipment?"

"That's what he wanted to do, Mr. Botts, but the Jumbo company had notified us they cannot deliver any of their equipment here for at least three months."

"That," I said, "is good."

"Yes—because I couldn't use that Jumbo stuff anyway. It's all mounted on wheels, and this job of taking gravel out of the river will need Earthworm tracks. But that is not the worst of it."

"No?"

"Mr. Buttrick's final order was to let out this road-graveling job to some local contractor. He told me to ask for bids and as soon as I had heard from everybody that might be interested to award the contract to the low bidder."

"What's the matter with that?"

"This is a backwoods region, Mr. Botts. There are very few contractors nearby, and all the good ones already have as much work as they can handle. I've driven all over this region. I've telephoned contractors all over the State of Maine. And so far I have just one bid—from a man who owns a gravel pit thirty miles away across the mountains. If he brings the gravel that far, he says he will have to charge us five dollars a yard. That means $100,000 for 20,000 cubic yards spread over six miles of road."

"That's outrageous," I said.

"Of course it's outrageous, but it's the only bid I can get."

"Couldn't you persuade this man to use the gravel out of the river?"

"No. All his equipment is mounted on wheels. It would be no good in the river. And he's not interested in buying any track-laying equipment. So you can see where that leaves me, Mr. Botts."

"If you ask me," I said, "it leaves you in a very strong position. All you have to do is tell Mr. Buttrick that he doesn't know what he's talking about."

"I wouldn't dare tell him that, Mr. Botts."

"Why not? Tell him if you follow his orders this gravel will cost him a hundred thousand dollars. If he handles it your way, he can do it for less than half that amount. It's very simple."

"It may sound simple, Mr. Botts, but you don't know Mr. Buttrick. He's stubborn. He's pig-headed. You can't tell him anything."

"Yes—that's what you said before."

"Furthermore, Mr. Buttrick has too much to think about. He's trying to run at least half a dozen other projects that are bigger than this. He doesn't really have time to put his mind on anything. So he just makes a snap decision, and issues an order, and wants it carried out without any back talk. When I tried to argue with him he told me he was not interested in what I thought about this job. He had no time to listen to my objections. Either I could obey his orders or I could consider myself fired."

"Apparently he talks pretty tough."

"He means it, too, Mr. Botts. He has fired other men for talking back to him. And he would just as soon fire me. So I wouldn't dare talk back to him the way you want me to."

"Jim," I said, "let me get this straight. You seem to be telling me that you don't dare tell your boss certain facts that he ought to know for his own good. If you did, he would fire you."

"That's right, Mr. Botts."

"On the other hand, if you fail to tell him these facts, you would be failing to protect his interests. You would be falling down on your job. And you would richly deserve to be fired."

"I'm afraid that's right too. But there's nothing I can do about it."

"There's plenty you can do about it," I said.

"What?"

"If I were in your position, Jim, I wouldn't hesitate a minute. I would tell this guy the truth. And, before he had a chance to fire me, I would quit."

"But I can't do that, Mr. Botts."

"Why not?"

"I need this job. I have a wife to support. I have three children in school. Last month I bought a home here, and it's mortgaged up to the limit. With all these commitments, I can't afford to lose my job."

"Jim," I said, "I am about to give you some fatherly advice. When you say you can't afford to lose your job, you are putting the whole thing backward. Under the present circumstances, you can't afford to keep your job."

"What do you mean?"

"Anyone who is so afraid of losing his job that he doesn't dare tell his boss things that the boss ought to know is no longer a free man.

He is a slave to his own fears. He is a mere 'yes' man who is accomplishing nothing either for himself or for his employer—a weakling who will soon be fired anyway for pure inefficiency."

"It's easy for you to talk this way, Mr. Botts. But you don't have a boss like mine. You don't know what I'm up against."

"Jim," I said, "that is where you are completely wrong. I have a boss by the name of Gilbert Henderson who is every bit as unreasonable as your boss. Henderson sends me so many foolish orders that I find myself constantly talking back to him and telling him where he is wrong. And that is not all."

"No?"

"I not only talk; I act. In other words, I don't believe in the literal-obedience type of discipline which is so popular in certain military circles—I believe rather in that higher form of discipline whereby a subordinate obeys not necessarily the order which his superior has actually given, but rather the order which that superior would have given if he had known what he was talking about."

"And you actually get by with this system?"

"Of course I do. Only last week Henderson sent me a letter ordering me to Winnipeg to persuade Mr. Buttrick to buy Earthworm equipment. I immediately decided Henderson was all wrong and that I ought to come here first to find out what was behind Mr. Buttrick's aversion to Earthworms."

"And Mr. Henderson let you change your plans?"

"Ha, ha! He didn't have a chance. I just came."

"But won't he fire you for disobeying his orders?"

"He might. He has fired me before—but never permanently. I'm such a valuable man—largely because I stand up for what I know is right—that he can't afford to lose me. And even if he did fire me permanently, I'm such a good salesman that I could easily get another job. So I don't have to worry at all."

"That must be wonderful, Mr. Botts. I only wish I had the nerve to speak up and talk back and act independent the way you do. But I have so many obligations—my wife, my children, that mortgage——"

"Listen, Jim. If you really want to take care of those obligations you had better act like a man, not like a mouse. You are a good engineer. You have ideas. Why don't you stand up and fight? If you do, you may suffer a temporary setback, but in the end, you'll be way ahead. There are plenty of good jobs in the country for men that really deserve them. Of course, if you take things lying down, if you let your boss walk all over you, you don't deserve a good job, and you won't have one very long. But you're not that kind of a coward."

"Well, I hope not, Mr. Botts."

"As an engineer you want to do this gravel job right, don't you?"

"I sure do."

"And you're getting a little fed up with Mr. Buttrick?"

"That's right."

"It would give you a lot of satisfaction to call him up on the long-distance telephone and tell him exactly where he gets off?"

"It certainly would, Mr. Botts."

I picked up the telephone and called long distance. "Kindly put in a person-to-person call," I said, "for Mr. George Buttrick, of the Buttrick Mining Corporation, Winnipeg, Canada." After a few minutes the operator reported that Mr. Buttrick had left on his private plane for the wilderness of Northern Canada and would not return for several days. "As soon as he gets back, have him call up," I said.

When I relayed this news to Jim Williams he looked a bit relieved. "Perhaps it's just as well," he said. "As long as I can't get hold of Mr. Buttrick, I suppose I might as well go ahead and carry out his orders."

"You will do no such thing," I said. "This is your big chance to stand up and assert your rights. If you weaken at this point you'll probably never amount to anything all your life. So I'm going to stay right here with you until you get in touch with your boss and tell him what is what."

So now, Henderson, you can see how fortunate it was that I disregarded your orders and came here to Warsaw before proceeding to Winnipeg. You can also understand why I have to stay here for the next few days. Jim Williams is a splendid fellow, but he is naturally in something of a quandary. He knows he ought to stand up like a man and talk back to his boss. But it is a hard thing for him to do.

However, I am going to stand by for as long as may be necessary to insure that he puts on a real fight.

Yours proudly,
Alexander Botts.

TELEGRAM

WASHINGTON, D.C.
AUGUST 11, 1955

ALEXANDER BOTTS
WARSAW HOTEL
WARSAW, MAINE
STOP NEEDLING WILLIAMS TO FIGHT HIS BOSS. YOU SHOULD REAL-
IZE YOU CANNOT SELL TRACTORS BY STIRRING UP TROUBLE INSIDE

I QUIT!

THE ORGANIZATION OF AN IMPORTANT PROSPECTIVE CUSTOMER.
YOU WILL LEAVE AT ONCE FOR WINNIPEG AS ORIGINALLY DIRECT-
ED. YOU CAN EITHER OBEY MY ORDERS OR QUIT YOUR JOB. THIS
TIME I MEAN IT.

GILBERT HENDERSON

TELEGRAM

WARSAW, MAINE
AUGUST 11, 1955

GILBERT HENDERSON
EARTHWORM BRANCH OFFICE
WASHINGTON, D.C.
ALL RIGHT, I QUIT. LETTER FOLLOWS.

ALEXANDER BOTTS

Warsaw Hotel
Warsaw, Maine
Wednesday, August 17, 1955

Dear Henderson:

I have been so busy since our exchange of telegrams last week that
only today have I found time to write you a full account of what has
been going on. By a rare stroke of good fortune your telegram of
August 11 was taken over the telephone by Jim Williams, who
happened to be visiting me in my hotel room. When he read your
threat that I could either obey your orders or quit my job, he jumped
to the conclusion that you had effectively called my bluff and that I
would immediately back down and do as I was told. This, of course,
gave me a wonderful opportunity to assert my independence, and to
provide exactly the kind of example that Jim needed to inspire a
similar stand on his part.

I promptly requested Jim to call back the telegraph office and I let
him repeat to the operator my simple but dignified reply, "All right,
I quit." I could see that Jim was considerably impressed, so I
followed up my advantage by delivering one of the finest orations
ever heard on the subject of freedom, liberty, independence, and the
right of every citizen to talk back to his boss.

And I am happy to tell you that my efforts were crowned with
complete success. Even before I had finished my oration the long-
distance operator reported that Mr. Buttrick had arrived back in
Winnipeg. She put him on the line. And, while I stood by to lend

approval and encouragement, Jim Williams really laid down the law. He said, "I am not obeying your orders, Mr. Buttrick. I am not accepting the low bid on the gravel contract. I am going to buy some Earthworm equipment so we can do this gravel job ourselves and do it right. If you will give me five minutes I can explain to you exactly why I think I am doing the right thing."

Mr. Buttrick, however, was not willing to grant the five minutes. I could hear a confused buzz of angry words coming through the receiver. Evidently Mr. Buttrick was protesting violently.

It took Jim quite a while to get a word in edgewise. But when he did, I was really proud of him. "Mr. Buttrick," he said, "you are going to let me do this job right or I won't do it at all." There was another torrent of angry words from Mr. Buttrick. Finally, Jim put down the phone and turned to me. "I'm fired," he said. "Mr. Buttrick is sending a new man to take charge. He will arrive next Tuesday night—with orders to accept the low bid on the gravel job."

"Congratulations!" I said, shaking Jim cordially by the hand. "This is indeed good news."

But Jim was beginning to have doubts. He said, "It doesn't sound to me like good news for a man to lose his job."

"Of course it is," I said. "You and I have both lost our jobs. And we are both to be congratulated. We are now free men. We are no longer subject to stupid orders from ignorant superiors."

"That part is all right," said Jim. "But what am I going to do now? How can I support my family? How can I take care of the payments on the mortgage?"

"That's easy. You're going to get another job."

"But where? How?"

"You don't have to worry any more than I do," I said. "For a good engineer like you there are hundreds of opportunities—just as there are hundreds of opportunities for a good salesman and contact man like me. And we don't even have to look around. There is one very fine opportunity staring us right in the face."

"What do you mean?"

"I mean that you and I are going into the gravel business. By the time Mr. Buttrick's new man arrives next Tuesday, we're going to be all organized. We'll put in a bid lower than that outrageous five-dollars-a-yard proposition. The new superintendent will have to give us the contract. And we'll be all set to make a big profit."

"But I have no money to put into a business."

"We'll do it on credit," I said. "And now let us stop moaning about the doubts and the difficulties. Let us get down to business.

Have you found out who owns the gravel in this Gravel River that you were talking about?"

"Yes, Mr. Botts."

"Have you acquired the right to dig it out?"

"No, Mr. Botts, I haven't."

"All right," I said. "Let's go."

We spent the next few days in a mad whirl of activity. We made so many inquiries, we called on so many people, we argued and negotiated on so many different matters that it would take too long to give you all the details. The important points are as follows:

Jim and I will handle this thing as a partnership to be known as Botts and Williams.

The gravel deposits in the Gravel River are owned by Mrs. Fanny Twitchell, a wealthy and eccentric old lady who has a large and expensive summer home in the midst of the wilderness on the river bank. Before going to see Mrs. Twitchell, I instructed Jim to let me do all the talking. As I am an unusually good judge of human beings in general, and old ladies in particular, I was able to handle the negotiations in a truly masterful manner. I sensed at once that Mrs. Twitchell likes to prattle along about her own personal problems. I therefore gave her every opportunity. And I listened sympathetically for several hours while she talked incessantly about her troubles and difficulties. In this way I succeeded in so ingratiating myself with the old girl that I was able to arrange the terms for removing the gravel on an unusually favorable basis for Botts and Williams.

I have been in touch by telephone with our Maine dealer at Portland, and I have arranged to buy an Earthworm shovel, an Earthworm tractor with bulldozer, and an Earthworm motorgrader. This equipment is secondhand, but in splendid condition. The price is $40,000, but this is of minor importance because the dealer thinks that I am still working for the Earthworm company and that the Earthworm company is underwriting the deal. He is therefore giving me very favorable terms—nothing down and the balance whenever I feel like paying it.

A contractor in Portland who owns a fleet of dump trucks has agreed to haul and spread the gravel for a dollar a yard.

All of the above preliminary arrangements led up to the big important contract we have just signed with Mr. Buttrick's new superintendent. This gentleman arrived last night and I immediately submitted a bid to supply and spread 20,000 yards of gravel on his road at $1.25 a yard—making a total of $25,000. As the best previous bid had been $5.00 a yard, or a total of $100,000, he was naturally impressed. And this gave me a splendid opportunity to put on a terrific sales talk to the general effect that this sensational saving is due entirely to the efficiency and excellence of the Earthworm machinery which we are planning to use.

He promptly accepted our bid—which assures a handsome profit to the firm of Botts and Williams. He will make a full report tomorrow to Mr. Buttrick—informing him, I hope, that he is saving $75,000 on this deal because the work will be handled by Earthworm equipment. This news will naturally bring Mr. Buttrick to his senses. He will abandon his hostile attitude. And in the future he will give all his business to the Earthworm company. In view of this happy outcome, I have a feeling that you will soon be prepared to admit that you have been wrong and I have been right in this affair. And you will doubtless want me to resume my position as sales manager. At the moment, I am not sure whether I would care to accept your offer, but at least it will receive my earnest consideration.

In the meantime, if our Portland dealer makes any inquiries about my purchase of equipment from him, I would suggest that you assure him the Earthworm company stands behind the deal one hundred percent. Otherwise, he might try to repossess the machinery—which would have a disastrous effect upon my very important operations.

With cordial greetings from the new firm of Botts and Williams, I remain,

Yours very sincerely,
Alexander Botts.

TELEGRAM

WASHINGTON, D.C.
AUGUST 19, 1955

ALEXANDER BOTTS
WARSAW HOTEL
WARSAW, MAINE
OUR ENGINEERING DEPARTMENT ESTIMATES IT WILL COST AT LEAST THIRTY CENTS PER YARD TO DIG GRAVEL OUT OF STREAM AND LOAD IT IN TRUCKS. YOU SAY YOU WILL PAY $1.00 PER YARD FOR HAULING AND SPREADING. AS YOU HAVE BID IN THIS CONTRACT AT $1.25 YOU WILL BE LOSING 5¢ ON EVERY YARD DELIVERED PLUS WHATEVER YOU HAVE TO PAY FOR THE GRAVEL. THE EARTHWORM COMPANY CAN ASSUME NO RESPONSIBILITY FOR ANY

I QUIT!

SUCH ABSURD ENTERPRISE. I AM ADVISING OUR PORTLAND DEAL-
ER OF THESE FACTS AND SUGGESTING HE REPOSSESS THE MACHINE-
RY AT ONCE. UNDER THE CIRCUMSTANCES I OUGHT TO ACCEPT
YOUR RESIGNATION. BUT, FOR OLD TIMES SAKE, I AM WILLING TO
GIVE YOU ONE MORE CHANCE. IF YOU CAN WIND UP THE UN-
FORTUNATE AFFAIRS OF THE BOTTS-WILLIAMS PARTNERSHIP, IF
YOU CAN STRAIGHTEN OUT THE MESS YOU HAVE CREATED IN THE
BUTTRICK COMPANY IN SUCH A WAY AS TO REGAIN THE GOOD WILL
OF MR. BUTTRICK, AND IF YOU WILL PROMISE TO OBEY ORDERS IN
THE FUTURE, YOU MAY HAVE YOUR JOB BACK.

GILBERT HENDERSON

Warsaw Hotel
Warsaw, Maine
Friday, August 19, 1955

Dear Henderson:

Your unnecessarily long telegram—with its excessively high cost
to the Earthworm company—is here. But it no longer means anything. Your knowledge of the facts is so incomplete, and the situation has changed so radically that you not only never did but even
more obviously do not now know what you were or are talking
about.

Possibly this is partly my own fault. In my haste to give you the
broad outlines of the picture here I did not spell out all of the minute
details. When I told you that I had made unusually favorable terms
with Mrs. Fanny Twitchell, I assumed you would take my word for
it. But you have apparently jumped to the totally erroneous conclusion that I am paying for this gravel.

Such is not the case. Instead of rushing in and offering Mrs.
Twitchell the customary five or ten cents a yard for her gravel, I
followed my usual system of starting a conference by letting the
other party do most of the talking. This not only pleases the other
party but often brings out information of considerable value.

As I think I told you, I listened for several hours while Mrs.
Twitchell told me all her troubles. And this exhibition of sympathy
and courtesy on my part paid off. I learned that one of the lady's
greatest difficulties has been the tendency of the Gravel River to
overflow its banks every few years and cause thousands of dollars'
damage to her property. She told me that a couple of years ago a
contractor from Portland had offered, for fifty thousand dollars, to

remove the flood danger by deepening the channel of the river. She had turned down this offer—not because of the expense, which apparently means nothing to her—but because the contractor was going to dump the gravel from the river bed along the bank in such a way as to ruin the beauty of the grounds.

At once I offered to do the job for fifty thousand. And I agreed to haul the gravel away at no extra charge. This generous offer was promptly and gratefully accepted by Mrs. Twitchell—which means that the financial picture is most favorable. The firm of Botts and Williams will receive $50,000 for digging the gravel out of the river and $25,000 for delivering it on the road, making a total of $75,000. Out of this we will pay $20,000 for trucking, and another $40,000 for the Earthworm equipment. Running expenses will probably use up $5,000—making a total outlay of $65,000. Thus we will finish the contract with a cash profit of $10,000 plus $40,000 worth of machinery all paid for.

Or perhaps I should say we would have finished with the above results if I had remained a member of the firm of Botts and Williams. Actually, I have just made arrangements to sell my share of the business to our Portland dealer who came up here yesterday to see what was going on, and who was so impressed by the money-making possibilities under our contract that he offered to buy me out for $10,000 cash. This sum of course is much less than my share is actually worth, but I am accepting it because I always like to see the other fellow make a profit, and because I have other plans.

Day before yesterday the new manager for the Buttrick Mining Company sent a report to his boss, informing him—just as I had hoped he would—that the reduction in the gravel cost from $100,000 to $25,000 is due entirely to economies resulting from the use of Earthworm equipment. Apparently this has caused the impulsive Mr. Buttrick to completely revise his opinion of Jim Williams. He has just sent an urgent telegram stating he now realizes Jim was right all the time. And he has offered him a much better job on one of his other properties. Fortunately, however, Jim has now learned what it means to be free and independent. He has politely turned down the offer and plans to continue in the gravel business.

As for me, I am also feeling delightfully free and independent. I have decided that Mr. Buttrick has now been sufficiently softened up so that it is time for me to go to Winnipeg and work on him personally. I have been seriously considering your offer to take back my job as sales manager. However, if I am on the payroll you will expect me to obey orders. And, in my efforts to sell Mr. Buttrick the idea of buying large quantities of Earthworm equipment, I am planning a sales campaign so sensational and so colossal that I cannot afford to have my efforts hampered by foolish instructions from the home office.

I can easily finance myself with the $10,000 received from our Portland dealer. This money, of course, would have belonged to the Earthworm company if the company had seen fit to underwrite this gravel deal. Under the circumstances, however, I feel that it belongs to me. This afternoon I am starting for Winnipeg, a completely free agent, amply supplied with funds and filled with happiness, hope and enthusiasm. Yours with cordial best wishes,

Alexander Botts.

BOTTS AND
THE BIGGEST DEAL
OF ALL

EARTHWORM TRACTOR COMPANY
INTERDEPARTMENTAL COMMUNICATION

To: Gilbert Henderson, President
        Earthworm Tractor Company
        Earthworm City, Illinois
From: Alexander Botts, Former Sales Manager
        Earthworm Tractor Co.
        Winnipeg Hotel
        Winnipeg, Canada
Date: Monday, April 23, 1956

Dear Henderson:

It has occurred to me that in my somewhat hasty letter of resignation last week, I may have failed to explain the exact reasons for my drastic action. If this neglect has caused you any worry or distress, I am sorry. And I hasten to assure you that I am not mad at you or at the Earthworm Tractor Company. My only reason for quitting is to give me greater freedom of action, to permit me to operate without being hampered by foolish orders and senseless restrictions from the home office, and thus to enable me to do a far better job in promoting the company's interests.

After I complete my operations here in Winnipeg, you will be so impressed by my success that you will undoubtedly want me to resume my position as sales manager. And it is possible, if I am sufficiently urged, that I might accept. Thus it would be much better if you did not hire anyone to take my place. I would not want you to be embarrassed by having to fire a new sales manager almost immediately after hiring him.

As I am now a free man, no longer subject to your orders, I do not need to tell you anything I am doing. However, in view of our long friendship, and because you are undoubtedly interested, I will give you a brief report of my recent activities.

You will doubtless remember that about two weeks ago you received news that Mr. George Buttrick, of the Buttrick Mining Company, Winnipeg, Canada, was planning to buy a million dollars' worth of excavating equipment from the Jumbo Wheel Tractor Company. You promptly directed me to rush up here to Winnipeg and help our dealer get the order shifted to Earthworm. You will also remember that instead of obeying your hasty directive I first visited one of Mr. Buttrick's mining properties in the state of Maine. And it is well I did so. I picked up a lot of information about Mr. Buttrick's background. And I made $10,000 on a gravel contract—of which I still have $6,000 available after setting aside a reserve for taxes.

Thus, when I finally reached Winnipeg this morning, I arrived amply supplied with both information and funds. I promptly called on our Winnipeg dealer. And I found him sunk in despair.

"That million-dollar Buttrick order," he said, "is blowed up, gone with the wind, down the drain and lost in the deep blue sea! The biggest order I ever worked on—and now it is sunk without a trace."

"Come, come," I said. "It can't be that bad."

"It is, Mr. Botts. This man is the toughest customer I ever ran into. In the first place, he's a really big operator—has made millions in stock-market speculation and financial manipulation. Apparently he avoids taxes by capital-gains setups. And he owns enormous mining properties both in Canada and the United States. But that's not the worst."

"Go on," I said.

"Mr. Buttrick is not really a mining man at all. He has no practical knowledge or experience of mining operations. But he has been so successful in financial matters that he thinks he knows everything. He's obstinate, opinionated, conceited, arrogant——"

"They told me all that in Maine," I said. "What I want to know is the latest developments on this million-dollar tractor deal. Just why does Mr. Buttrick need so much equipment?"

"He has recently acquired some big mineral deposits in British Columbia at a place which he has named Buttrick Canyon."

"What kinds of minerals?"

"Various rare metals used in defense industry. I forget what they are called, but that is not important. What matters is that Mr. Buttrick is in a hurry to build an airstrip, so he can fly in supplies and equipment. Later there will be an enormous open-pit mine, and a big mill to concentrate the ore."

"The concentrate will be brought out by plane?"

"Yes."

"Just where is this Buttrick Canyon?" I said. "Can he build a road in to it?"

"He claims the country is too rough." The dealer turned to a wall map and put his finger on a dot in Northern British Columbia between the Alaska Highway and the Pacific Coast. "That's the place," he said. "Completely surrounded by mountains and canyons and jagged rocks."

"No roads anywhere near?"

"Just a few mountain trails—almost impassable. The only inhabitants are a few Indians and trappers. There's a rumor that the government is planning a radar station somewhere in the region. But there are no towns, no settlements. The mineral deposits were found by a lone prospector. Mr. Buttrick bought him out and then sent in a party of mining engineers. They have just made their report, and it is so favorable that Mr. Buttrick has decided to go ahead in a really big way."

"In country as rough as that," I said, "it's going to be pretty hard to build an adequate airfield—maybe even harder than building a road."

"That's what I told Mr. Buttrick, but he is too stubborn and opinionated to listen to me. He says there is a flat area several miles square right next to the canyon. All he has to do—or so he claims—is to clear off the trees, and he'll have a first-class landing field."

"All right," I said, "if that's what he wants, we'll sell him a fleet of our Earthworm tractors, bulldozers and whatever else he needs. He can ship them by railroad to Dawson Creek, run them up the Alaska Highway about as far as the Toad River, and then drive them overland the last hundred miles or so to Buttrick Canyon."

"By strange coincidence, Mr. Botts, that's exactly what I told him myself."

"Good for you," I said.

"I even presented him with a detailed order for Earthworm equipment I thought he would need—just over a million dollars' worth."

"What did he say?"

"He told me I was crazy. He said no tractors could possibly get through those mountains."

"Of course, they can," I said. "I've never been to Buttrick Canyon, but I know in general what that region is like. I was up there in 1942 when we were building the Alaska Highway. And I know we can get through."

"That's what I tried to tell him, Mr. Botts, but he said he wouldn't dream of wasting any of his money on any such off chance—especially since the Jumbo Wheel Tractor Company has offered to do the whole job entirely at their own expense."

"Listen," I said, "those miserably built Jumbo wheel tractors could never get in there in the first place. They're no good in rough country. They could never get through the mountains."

"They don't have to get through the mountains, Mr. Botts. The Jumbo people are planning to fly their equipment in."

"If there is no airfield, how are they going to land? On a lake? On a river? Or will they use helicopters?"

"There are no lakes or rivers nearby, and I understand they can't hire enough helicopters. So they're going to take their tractors and other machines apart, drop them by parachute in small packages, and then reassemble them on the ground."

"That's going to cost a lot of money," I said. "Just why are the Jumbo people doing it at their own expense?"

"They're so crazy to get this Buttrick order that they have made all kinds of concessions. They even offered a 25 percent discount. But that wasn't enough to satisfy Buttrick. He demanded a free demonstration. If Jumbo will build an airstrip at Buttrick Canyon and get it finished ahead of anybody else, he says he will give them the million-dollar order and pay for the airstrip besides."

"Did he make the same offer to you?"

"Yes. He even gave me a set of specifications for the airstrip he wants—300 feet wide and a mile long. The trees and the fluff and duff have to be cleared off and the hardpan has to be leveled. If pavement is necessary, he'll put that in himself later."

"Very generous of him," I said. "What did you tell him?"

"I told him I simply could not afford, as a dealer, to go to any such expense on the mere chance that I might get his order."

"So the deal is off?"

"Yes. I understand several other tractor companies have turned him down too. The Jumbo dealer is the only one who is going ahead. Apparently the president of the Jumbo company is financing him— which is more than the Earthworm president will do for me."

"You have taken this up with Mr. Henderson?"

"Yes. After my interview with Mr. Buttrick I sent a wire to Mr. Henderson asking if he would finance this proposition. He turned me down flat."

"He would," I said.

"However," said the dealer, "you are the sales manager of the company. You have influence with Mr. Henderson. Maybe you could persuade him to help out."

"Not a chance," I said. "In the first place, I am no longer sales manager. In the second place, I have no influence with Mr. Henderson. And, in the third place, nobody in the world could ever persuade Mr. Henderson to take any such sporting chance as this."

The dealer looked at me in amazement. "You mean to tell me that you are no longer sales manager of the Earthworm Tractor Company?"

"That's right. I resigned last week."

"Then what are you doing here? Why are we discussing company affairs?"

"I am now in business for myself," I said. "I am an expert adviser on tractor problems, a counselor on sales promotion and a business consultant. I shall be delighted to take over your entire campaign for this million-dollar order."

"You can have it, Mr. Botts. I have given up. I know when I am licked."

"I shall have to ask a small commission," I said. "Now that I am no longer on the Earthworm payroll, I have to earn my own way. If I am unsuccessful, you will owe me nothing; I will even pay my own expenses. If I land this million-dollar order, you will owe me a commission of one percent. That will be ten thousand dollars."

"If you actually land this order, Mr. Botts, I will be happy to pay you a whole lot more than that."

"No," I said magnanimously, "I am not an avaricious man. All I want is the thrill of putting across an exciting deal plus enough money to cover expenses and provide sufficient funds for the next venture."

The dealer looked at me with admiration. "For anyone so generous and unselfish, Mr. Botts, you are incredibly self-confident—almost conceited. Here I have completely given up hope on this deal, but you talk as if you are certain you can put it across. What are you planning to do? Just how are you going to go about this thing?"

"Frankly, I don't know," I said. "All I can do is use the same methods I have employed in the past. I will turn this matter over and over in my mind. I will let it soak into my subconscious. I will examine all aspects of the situation. And in time I'm sure to come up with a solution."

"It sounds pretty hopeless."

"Not at all," I said. "In the course of our conversation, I have fitted together certain disjointed facts you have given me. I have related these to certain other facts I have learned in my long experience in the tractor business. And already a vague pattern has begun to emerge—the first faint glimmer of what may turn out to be the dawn of a brilliant idea. And now I would like a copy of that million-dollar order and a copy of Mr. Buttrick's airstrip specifications."

"Here you are." He handed them over.

"Thank you," I said.

My next move was a visit to the office of the Buttrick Mining Company. Here I learned that Mr. Buttrick is in Labrador, so I would have to wait until his return on Monday, May seventh.

After learning this disappointing news, I called at the establishment of the Winnipeg dealer of the Jumbo Wheel Tractor Company. Instead of going in the front door, I circled around to the rear and discovered a group of mechanics taking apart a big Jumbo wheel tractor. In a casual way I engaged one of the mechanics in conversation, and was told that this was one of a large fleet of tractors and scrapers which was to be flown piecemeal and dropped by parachute at Buttrick Canyon.

The mechanic said it was a rush job. But part of the equipment had not yet arrived from the factory. And there had been a delay in arranging for cargo planes. So the big airlift could not possibly get started until about May tenth. This was indeed good news. While Mr. Buttrick was in Labrador, I would have two weeks to prepare my sales campaign. And after his return I would have three whole days to work on him before the Jumbo people got started.

I returned to the hotel to meditate on the situation. For a few minutes I considered calling you, Henderson, by long-distance telephone and asking you to instruct our Service Department to disassemble, fly to Buttrick Canyon and drop by parachute sufficient equipment to build an airstrip ahead of the Jumbo company. If you really got busy on this I knew you could do it, but I refrained from calling you, first, because I know you dislike emergency long-distance telephone calls, and second, because I realize you are too timid and too conservative to spend the large amount of money this operation would require.

Besides, I had by this time dreamed up another more promising idea. I had remembered that an old friend of mine, Colonel Angus MacNab, of the Canadian Army Engineers, lives here in Winnipeg. In the old days Angus and I were associated on the Alaska Highway, the Canol Pipe Line and other military and construction projects. More recently he has worked on airport and other construction jobs for the Aircraft Warning Service. But, wherever he is, he always seems to be in charge of a lot of heavy equipment. And he and I have often helped each other out. On various occasions I have lent him a few extra Earthworm tractors. At other times he has returned the favor. And once—believe it or not—he used one of his large helicopters to pull one of my tractors out of a mudhole. It occurred to me that good old Angus might be a real help in the present emergency.

I called on him. I explained the entire situation. And together we evolved a plan of action which is almost certain to land that million-dollar order for the Earthworm company.

This plan is so simple and yet so beautiful that I would like nothing better, Henderson, than to explain the whole thing in this letter. However, the methods we are going to use involve one of the most closely guarded secrets in the entire Canadian Army. This means that I must maintain complete silence. And you, Henderson, must control your curiosity for the next two or three weeks—at the end of which time I hope to send you a sensational report of complete success.

In the meantime, I wish to remind you of your good fortune in having a sales manager who has the foresight to resign temporarily from his position. It is possible that my operations here may involve the expenditure of several thousand dollars. And, as long as I am unable to tell you exactly what I am doing, I doubt very much if these expenses would be O.K.ed by the company comptroller or by you, Henderson. Consequently, if I were still sales manager I would be in serious financial difficulties. Having resigned, however, I can get by very easily. I will make up the deficit by accepting from our dealer the $10,000 commission which I have previously mentioned, and which I naturally could not accept if I were still sales manager.

With this happy thought I will close.

Most sincerely,
Alexander Botts

EARTHWORM TRACTOR COMPANY
EARTHWORM CITY, ILLINOIS
OFFICE OF THE PRESIDENT

Wednesday, April 25, 1956

Dear Botts:

Your letter is here. And, for once, I agree with much that you have to say. Neither the company comptroller nor I would even consider passing an expense account from you or anybody else when it involved the outlay of thousands of dollars for activities claimed to be so secret that they could not even be described.

You are also right in assuming I would never authorize the expenditure of large sums of money to fly a lot of equipment into the wilds of Canada on the mere chance that we might thereby make a sale.

Your glib talk about military secrecy does not sound to me like a legitimate attempt to keep valuable information from an enemy power. It seems more like something you dreamed up to hide embarrassing facts. I can well believe that your friend, Colonel Angus MacNab, may have succeeded in pulling a tractor out of a mudhole with a helicopter. But it would take more than Colonel MacNab and a whole fleet of helicopters—if that is what you have in mind—to fly in enough equipment to build an airstrip a mile long in any reasonable length of time. Also, it would cost more money than the six thousand you say you have on hand plus the ten thousand you expect to receive from our dealer. However, it's your misfortune and none of my own.

In closing I feel it is my duty to tell you that we cannot hold the position of sales manager open for an indeterminate length of time, as you seem to expect. We are therefore accepting your resignation.

Most sincerely,
Gilbert Henderson, President,
Earthworm Tractor Company

Winnipeg Hotel
Winnipeg, Canada,
Monday, May 7, 1956

Dear Henderson:

Your letter arrived in Winnipeg over a week ago, but I have been too busy to answer it until this evening. Now, however, I have plenty of time. My activities in the matter of Mr. Buttrick's million-dollar order have progressed to the point where I am on the very brink of complete success.

In the two weeks since my previous letter, I have been working hard with good old Angus MacNab. He has cooperated 100 percent. And yesterday we completed all of the preliminary work for one of the most stupendous sales operations of my entire career.

This morning Mr. Buttrick got back from Labrador. This afternoon I called on him. And I am happy to report that I was able to hand him a sales talk so sensational and so effective that I will now quote it in full, so that you, Henderson, and the boys at the office may have an authentic example of how a real salesman handles a big deal. Realizing that Mr. Buttrick is a self-important stuffed shirt who is too impatient to listen to a logical and reasonable presentation, I decided to make my remarks so apparently outrageous that he would be tricked into listening and answering back. In order to make my entrance as dramatic and interesting as possible, I ignored the usual formalities. Pushing past the receptionist, I burst into Mr. Buttrick's private office completely unannounced. And I started talking at once.

I said, "You want an airstrip at Buttrick Canyon. You are in a hurry. All right, if you will give me the job, I will have the whole thing completed, according to your own specifications, in exactly three days. Think of it—only three days!"

This approach, I am happy to report, was successful. Mr. Buttrick's interest—and also his anger—was immediately aroused. He sat up straight. He glared at me. He pounded his fist on the desk. Then he started yelling, "You're crazy! You don't know what you're talking about! Who are you anyway? Who let you in?"

"Calm yourself," I said suavely. "I am not crazy. I know what I am talking about. My name is Alexander Botts. Nobody let me in, I just came. Formerly, I was sales manager of the Earthworm Tractor Company. At present I represent the local Earthworm dealer. He tells me you offered to buy approximately a million dollars' worth of Earthworm equipment, according to this sales order, provided we could construct an airstrip according to these specifications, ahead of anybody else." I laid the order and the specifications on his desk. "Is that correct?" I asked.

"I made the offer. But you people turned it down two weeks ago. In the meantime the Jumbo dealer is going ahead. He plans to start flying his equipment to Buttrick Canyon next Thursday. That means he can finish the airstrip this fall."

"You can forget about having to wait till fall," I said. "All you have to do is give us the word, and we can have the whole job finished by next Thursday—three days from now—before the Jumbo people even get started."

By this time Mr. Buttrick had calmed down somewhat. But he was still interested enough to argue. "As I told you before," he said, "you are crazy."

"Not at all," I said. "With old-fashioned methods it would take weeks or months to complete this job. But we are using some very special construction techniques which have been developed by the

230

Earthworm Tractor Company in cooperation with the Canadian Army."

"And just what are these techniques?"

"I am sorry, Mr. Buttrick, I cannot tell you."

"Why not?"

"It's a military secret."

"But the whole thing is impossible. You can't build that airstrip in three days."

"Mr. Buttrick," I said, "has it never occurred to you that we live in an age of miracles?"

"Maybe so, but——"

"And do you not realize that many of these miracles—like the atom bomb—have been developed in secret?"

"You mean you have a fleet of secret machines of some kind that you can transport to a remote section of British Columbia and build an airstrip—all in three days?"

"The details are top secret, Mr. Buttrick. I cannot divulge any of our actual methods. However, I can suggest certain ideas which may possibly make it easier for you to believe my seemingly incredible claims. Have you ever stopped to think that an airfield is one of the first things needed by an invading army when it lands on a foreign shore?"

Mr. Buttrick looked puzzled. "I suppose so," he said.

"And how have such airfields been built in the past?"

"Mostly by bulldozers, I suppose."

"Correct. Tractors, bulldozers, scrapers—all kinds of heavy machinery have been needed. And it has been necessary to land this equipment—often with great difficulty and considerable delay—through pounding surf, on rocky shores and often many miles from the terrain suitable for a landing field."

"Probably that's true."

"Of course it's true," I said. "And, if you think it over, you will readily understand that any progressive military establishment like the Canadian Army would try to develop better and faster methods."

"Such as what?"

"Use your imagination," I said. "Earth-moving machinery does not have to be heavy. It does not have to crawl slowly along the ground. Have you never heard of rockets? Or jet propulsion?"

"Yes, Mr. Botts."

"If you want to clear away a forest, Mr. Buttrick, you don't necessarily have to chop down the trees with old-fashioned axes.

You don't even have to use chain saws or push the trees out of the way with bulldozers. After all, there are such things as shaped charges and other types of modern explosives. And it is even conceivable that we might use an atomic flame thrower."

"And you mean to tell me, Mr. Botts, that you actually have on hand machines and devices such as you have been describing?"

"Certainly not, Mr. Buttrick. The methods we use are entirely different—and completely secret. I have mentioned these other things merely to broaden your outlook and to indicate to you that the field of military engineering is not limited by the conventional techniques of former years."

"Listen, Mr. Botts," he said. "I am a busy man. I have no time to listen to all this fantastic chatter. It just happens that I am going to fly in my private plane to Buttrick Canyon next Thursday. Naturally I am not planning to land. I merely want to look the place over from the air and watch the parachute operation that the Jumbo Wheel Tractor Company is planning for that day."

"By next Thursday I will have your airstrip all finished," I said. "I would suggest therefore that you notify the Jumbo people so that they may be spared the expense of this useless expedition."

"Ha!" said Mr. Buttrick. "I will do exactly that. It will be amusing to hear what they say." He put in a call, and then spoke into the telephone, "There is a character here who claims he will build an airstrip at Buttrick Canyon within the next three days. . . .He wants to save you the expense of flying your equipment up there only to find you are too late. . . .No, I don't believe it any more than you do. . . .All right, if you want to go ahead, it's O.K. with me." He hung up.

"Apparently," I said, "the Jumbo people are going to fly up there anyway."

"Yes. They think this whole thing is a cheap trick on your part to scare them into abandoning the job, so you can go up later and have the field to yourself. So, from now on, it is action, not words, that will count. My offer is still open, Mr. Botts. If you have the airstrip finished by the time I get to Buttrick Canyon next Thursday, I will pay all reasonable costs of construction. And the million-dollar order will be yours—even though you refuse to match the discount offered by Jumbo. So now, Mr. Botts, I would suggest that you turn off your foolish-sounding stream of talk and get out of here so I can attend to more important matters."

At this point I decided that I had put across my ideas so successfully that further conversation would be useless. Accordingly, I took my leave and returned to the hotel, where I have been writing this report. By the end of the week I hope to inform you that the big order is definitely in the bag for the Earthworm Tractor Company. And at that time I will be most happy to return to my regular job as sales manager of the company. I only hope you have followed my advice and refrained from hiring a new sales manager, so that you will be spared the embarrassment of getting rid of him on such short notice.

> With all best wishes.
> Most sincerely,
> Alexander Botts

TELEGRAM
EARTHWORM CITY, ILLINOIS
MAY 9, 1956

ALEXANDER BOTTS
WINNIPEG HOTEL
WINNIPEG, CANADA
WE HAVE NOT YET HIRED NEW SALES MANAGER. IF YOU ACTUALLY PUT ACROSS THIS MILLION DOLLAR DEAL, YOUR OLD JOB WILL BE WAITING FOR YOU. HOWEVER, YOUR CLAIMS DO NOT MAKE SENSE. THE EARTHWORM COMPANY HAS NEVER COOPERATED WITH THE CANADIAN ARMY IN DEVELOPING ANY SUCH SECRET MACHINERY AS YOU INDICATE. IT IS THE UNANIMOUS OPINION OF OUR ENGINEERING DEPARTMENT THAT THERE IS NO EQUIPMENT IN EXISTENCE WHICH COULD BE MOVED INTO AN UNINHABITED WILDERNESS AND BUILD A MILE-LONG AIRSTRIP—ALL IN THREE DAYS. IT IS ONLY FAIR TO TELL YOU I AM HIGHLY SKEPTICAL.

> GILBERT HENDERSON

> Winnipeg Hotel
> Winnipeg, Canada,
> Saturday, May 12, 1956

Dear Henderson:

No wonder you are skeptical. You have read my reports so carelessly that you have missed a number of important points. And you have jumped to a lot of unwarranted conclusions. If you will read over my remarks, you will see that I never said the Earthworm Tractor Company had cooperated with the Canadian Army in developing secret machinery. I merely said that the company (represented by myself, even though I have been on temporary leave) was cooperating with the Canadian Army on construction methods. And this is perfectly true. Colonel Angus MacNab and I have been cooperating on secret methods, not machinery.

Furthermore, I never said I would construct a mile-long airstrip in three days. I merely said I would have it finished in three days—which is entirely different.

Your lack of understanding, Henderson, is of course partly due to the fact that I was compelled, for reasons of military secrecy, to withhold a few of the more important facts. Now, however, my friend Angus has informed me that the situation has changed sufficiently so that I may reveal what has heretofore been top secret. I will therefore explain exactly what I have been doing, and I will do so as nearly as possible in words of one syllable, so that even you, Henderson, may be able to understand what has been going on. I want you to notice that if you had read my previous reports a little more carefully, you could have guessed at a great many of the conclusions which I was unable to explain fully.

In my first letter I reported that our dealer had casually mentioned a rumor about a radar station near Buttrick Canyon. I also told you that Colonel Angus MacNab, who had formerly been in charge of Earthworm tractors and other heavy equipment on such projects as the Alaska Highway, has recently been doing some sort of work in the Aircraft Warning Service. Putting all these facts together, I decided—before I even talked to Angus—that he was probably in charge of building radar stations—including the one near Buttrick Canyon. If so, he might have some heavy equipment in the neighborhood.

I lost no time, therefore, in calling on Angus. And I was delighted to find that the situation was even better than I had hoped. Not only was Angus in charge of setting up radar stations, he had actually been working for over a month on the station near Buttrick Canyon. It seems the job is semi-secret. It is apparently impossible to conceal a radar station completely, but the government prefers to keep these installations as inconspicuous as possible. Rumors get around, but the general public knows very little about what is going on.

Angus told me that he had spent the preceding month with a fleet of twenty-four Earthworm tractors and auxiliary equipment in building a tractor trail—as narrow and as inconspicuous as possible—from the Alaska Highway to the site of the radar station. All of this equipment was still on hand only ten miles from Buttrick Canyon.

This was one of those lucky breaks which you, Henderson, like to refer to as "purely accidental" or "mere luck." However, I would like to point out that this kind of luck occurs only to people like me who go after it. Our Winnipeg dealer had heard the rumor about the radar station. He had worked with Colonel MacNab in the past on various construction projects and knew of his recent connection

234

with the Aircraft Warning Service. But he never did anything about it. I gave you all the facts, Henderson, two weeks ago. And you never did anything. You never even thought of doing anything. But I am a man of action. And I am proud to report that I have finished up this project as brilliantly and efficiently as I started it.

It was not easy. First I had to convince Angus—by a great flood of inspirational oratory—that Mr. Buttrick's mining operations are of such vital importance to defense industry in both the United States and Canada that it was his patriotic duty to use his big fleet of tractors to build the airstrip at Buttrick Canyon.

Then I had to persuade him to do the job right away, without waiting for permission from his superior—a rather unreasonable general who was taking a trip somewhere in the South Pacific.

"You can do the job first," I said, "and ask permission afterward. You don't have to tell him about this yourself. And you can keep the news from leaking out and reaching him indirectly by declaring the whole operation top secret—which will be entirely in accordance with established military tradition."

"How so?"

"Military secrecy," I said, "is sometimes used to conceal vital facts from the enemy. But it is employed even more often to hide embarrassing facts from superior officers, from investigating committees and even from the general public."

Angus hesitated. But finally he agreed to go ahead—keeping the whole operation secret. So you were completely right, Henderson, when you suggested in your recent letter that my talk about military secrecy was something I dreamed up to protect Angus and myself.

Building the airstrip was fairly easy. Angus sent out advance orders by radio, and we both arrived on the scene the following day, after a rush trip by plane and jeep. With all that machinery available, the construction work was pure routine. We scraped off the scrubby growth of spruce, jack pine and aspen, including the fluff and duff around the roots. Then we smoothed up the hardpan so that we had a reasonably good landing field of the kind called for in Mr. Buttrick's specifications.

The whole job was finished in about ten days. When I got back to Winnipeg, however, I had the problem of persuading Mr. Buttrick, who had just returned from Labrador, to reinstate the offer which our dealer had turned down. Mr. Buttrick was already much impressed by the Jumbo offer to sell him what they claim is a million dollars' worth of machinery for only $750,000. My only chance to argue him into spending a full million for Earthworm was to promise him a hurry-up job on his airstrip. But I could not tell him the airstrip was already finished. Even you, Henderson, will admit that I could not successfully bargain with a tough customer by offering him something he already had. Furthermore, I could not tell him how the job was done; that was a military secret.

That is why I had to give him the highly imaginative sales talk which I quoted in my previous letter. Fortunately, I was able to get him to renew his offer. And this afternoon, when he returned from a hasty inspection trip to Buttrick Canyon, I think he actually believed I had done the whole job in three days. Anyway, he signed the million-dollar order. He paid the airstrip construction costs—which I am turning over to Angus. And he notified the unfortunate Jumbo people that they were out in the cold. If he finds out later that we did the job ahead of time, it will do no harm.

Just before I started to write this report, my friend Angus telephoned that his commanding officer had returned in such an unexpectedly affable mood that he had taken a big chance and told him the entire story of our little project in British Columbia. The general promptly gave his ex-post-facto approval, so the job is no longer top secret and I am free to tell you all about it.

Our dealer has enthusiastically paid me the ten thousand dollars' commission, so I am accepting your offer and returning to my old job as sales manager—this time with a very satisfactory little nest egg to use in case I should decide at some future time that I can best further the interests of the company by re-resigning.

Cordially yours,
Alexander Botts

BOTTS TURNS
TRAITOR

EARTHWORM TRACTOR COMPANY
EARTHWORM CITY, ILLINOIS
OFFICE OF GILBERT HENDERSON, PRESIDENT

Monday, September 9, 1957

Mr. Alexander Botts
Sales Manager, Earthworm Tractor Co.
Hotel Fairfield
Pittsburgh, Pennsylvania

Dear Botts:

Our dealer in Mine City, Pennsylvania, reports that he is in trouble and needs help. For some time he has been working on a contractor by the name of George Crampion, who specializes in moving buildings of all kinds. Our dealer was trying to sell this man one of our big X-20 Earthworm tractors. He had reached the point where he thought the sale was practically in the bag when his prospect suddenly informed him that the whole deal was off.

It seems that a man bearing the fancy name of Vincent Van Verdingham had arrived in town, had announced that he was a salesman for the Goliath Tractor Company and had then handed out a sales talk as fancy as his name. He told Mr. Crampion that our crawler-type Earthworm X-20 does not have sufficient traction to move large buildings. It does not grip the ground the way it should. When it attempts to haul a heavy load, the tracks merely spin and dig a hole in the ground. The Goliath tractor, on the other hand, is equipped with a new type of giant-size rubber pneumatic tires,

237

approximately eight feet in diameter and with completely new and revolutionary treads.

To the casual observer these treads look like any others. But, according to Mr. Vincent Van Verdingham, they are provided with thousands of microscopic vacuum suction cups. These cups, although they are invisible to the naked eye, have the power to grip the ground, or any other surface on which they travel, with a tenacity similar to the suction cups on the tentacles of an octopus. In consequence, the Goliath tractor never slips; it never skids; and it can pull up to four times as big a load as any Earthworm or other tractor of similar weight. At least this is the line that Mr. Van Verdingham was putting out.

Mr. Crampion was so impressed that he held up his order for an Earthworm and demanded a competitive demonstration.

The Goliath man promptly brought in one of his tractors. He rented a small warehouse filled with about a hundred tons of Portland cement. And he announced that he would jack up this building, place it on skids and haul it to any place Mr. Crampion desires. He plans to have the heavy cement in the building and to use skids instead of wheels or rollers, so as to make the job more difficult and thus demonstrate the superiority of his machine. He has challenged our dealer to hook onto this load either before or after his own demonstration.

Our dealer has accepted the challenge. He thinks an X-20 Earthworm tractor can move the warehouse. He does not think the Goliath tractor can handle it, but he is not sure. He does not know much about the Goliath. He never heard of these special suction-grip tires. And he wants us to give him all the information we may have.

I would suggest that you go to Mine City at once. You have been out in the field more than I have. You have had many opportunities to observe the Goliath tractor in action. So I feel you are the ideal man to advise our dealer as to what he should do.

Most sincerely,
Gilbert Henderson

MINE CITY HOTEL
MINE CITY, PENNSYLVANIA

Wednesday evening, September 11, 1957

Dear Henderson:

Thanks for your letter. In sending me to deal with the machinations of the upstart Goliath Tractor Company, you have indeed selected the best man in the entire tractor industry. I know all about the wretched Goliath Company. As I may have reported to you on previous occasions, this outfit was organized several years ago by a group of unscrupulous promoters who know nothing about tractors, but who are possessed of considerable low cunning in putting across shady financial deals. They have managed to acquire, by fair means or foul, a large quantity of surplus engines, gears and other parts— some of them from our own government and some from foreign countries. Much of the material has been rejected as defective. Nevertheless, the Goliath Company has managed to throw it together so as to produce several thousand so-called tractors which they are now attempting to unload on the unsuspecting public.

In order to put over their nefarious program, they have hired as salesmen a motley crew of former carnival barkers, confidence men and swindlers of all kinds, who go about the country employing the technique of the big lie by repeating their outrageous claims so loudly and so insistently that a certain number of naive souls have been tricked into putting their names on the dotted line.

I had never before heard this sales talk about the microscopic vacuum cups in the treads of tires. Apparently it is merely the latest example of the sort of pseudoscientific hogwash which Goliath salesmen spread around. Nevertheless, Mr. George Crampion has been sufficiently impressed to hold up his order for an Earthworm. And he might even be so credulous as to switch his order to Goliath. Such things have happened in the past. They may well happen in the future.

But not in this case. I have arrived on the scene, and I have already started preparations for a campaign which is sure to end in complete victory for the Earthworm.

I reached Mine City about seven this evening. After registering at the hotel and eating dinner, I telephoned our dealer, whom I have never met. I was told that he was out of town, but would be back early tomorrow morning in plenty of time to prepare for the big house-moving demonstration which is scheduled for three o'clock in the afternoon. As I had never before been in Mine City, I decided to take a walk and look over the town.

It is well that I did so. At the south end of Main Street I discovered the Earthworm Tractor Sales and Service Agency. The front office was dark, but there was a light in the repair shop. The door was ajar. I entered and found a rather peculiar-looking character trying to start the engine of an X-20 Earthworm tractor. He was tall and thin. He had red hair and a freckled face.

"My name," I said, "is Alexander Botts. I am the sales manager of

239

the Earthworm Tractor Company. And I have arrived in town to help you people in the big house-moving demonstration tomorrow."

The man was a little startled at my sudden appearance, but he soon calmed down and introduced himself. He told me that he worked for our dealer and that most people addressed him as "Red."

"You seem to be having some trouble with that tractor," I said. "Is this by any chance the machine you are going to use in the big demonstration tomorrow?"

"That's right," said Red. "I want to drive it out tonight to the scene of the demonstration, so everything will be ready to start testing it out first thing in the morning. But I can't seem to start the engine."

"Let me take a look at it," I said. I made a few adjustments, and after several false starts I discovered the basis of the difficulty. "Red," I said, "I take it you have never driven this latest-model X-20?"

"I never have. This is the first of the new models that we have received. It arrived yesterday on a flatcar, and one of the other men unloaded it and drove it in here."

"Then you have not heard of the new locking device on the fuel line?"

"I don't know what you're talking about," said Red.

"Take a look at that small brass gadget just behind the fuel pump." He looked. "That," I continued, "is a fuel cutoff valve. It is operated by a cylinder lock, and it is used to prevent unauthorized persons from operating the tractor."

"Like the ignition lock on a car?"

"Exactly. Diesel engines such as this have no ignition systems; hence it is manifestly impossible to equip them with ignition locks. But the Earthworm Tractor Company, always alert to serve the best interests of its customers, has developed this ingenious little lock, which answers the same purpose. Obviously the man who drove the machine in here must have closed the valve and walked off with the key, thus making it impossible for anyone else to start the machine."

"Maybe," said Red, "I could uncouple the whole fuel line and install another one. But that would take a long time—even if I had another fuel line, which I haven't."

"Calm yourself," I said soothingly. "Alexander Botts is here to help you, and when he undertakes to help anyone, he always comes through."

"But what can we do?"

"As sales manager of the Earthworm Tractor Company, I have

been supplied with a master key which fits all of these new locks. And I always carry it with me."

Pulling the key from my pocket, I inserted it in the lock and gave a quick twist. I then told Red to let her go, and a moment later the big engine started up. Red drove the machine outdoors. I closed and locked the repair shop, and Red thanked me profusely. "If it had not been for you, Mr. Botts," he said, "I never would have got started at all."

"Don't give it a second thought," I said. "I'm always happy to be of service."

As Red drove off into the night, I walked back to the hotel, where I have been writing this report. As it is now midnight, I will bring this letter to a close, take it across the street to the post office and then retire to bed, suffused by that warm glow of satisfaction which always comes from the performance of a good deed.

Cordially,
Alexander Botts

MINE CITY HOTEL,
MINE CITY, PENNSYLVANIA

Thursday evening, September 12, 1957

Dear Henderson:

After I wrote you last night, events have been moving very rapidly. As a result of certain unfortunate circumstances completely outside my control, our dealer here suddenly became so hysterical that he accused me of stupidly ruining all of his chances to make a sale to Mr. Crampion. He told me he would never have any dealings with me in the future. And he said he was going to write you a letter denouncing me in the strongest possible terms and demanding that I be fired from my job.

As he was planning to mail his letter this morning, and as I will not be able to mail this letter of mine until late this evening, it is highly probable that you will hear from him before you hear from me. And, having known you for a long time, Henderson, I can predict exactly what your reaction will be when you get the bad news. You will become excited and unreasonable. You will jump to a number of false conclusions. You will promptly dictate an angry letter to me, accusing me of sins I did not commit and denouncing me for disasters for which I am in no way to blame. You will end your letter on one of your typical pseudoconstructive notes by demanding that I get busy and attempt to clean up the mess I have created. And you will suggest that in the future I use a little more intelligence.

In reply to the above remarks, as expressed in the letter which you have already written or will soon write, but which I have not yet received, I will now give you a reasonable account of exactly what has been going on, so that you may understand how unfair you have been.

This morning, after an early breakfast, I telephoned our local dealer. I opened the conversation with an enthusiastic account of my activities of the previous evening. I explained how I had unlocked the tractor and helped the redheaded mechanic drive it away. Then I waited hopefully for a word of thanks and appreciation.

What I got was an outburst of abuse and profanity so violent and so incoherent that I had considerable difficulty in understanding anything.

"That redheaded mechanic," he said, "used to work for me, but he does not work for me anymore. Last week I found out he had been stealing tools and supplies from my repair shop. So I fired him and called in the cops. But before they arrived, this lowdown heel told me he was going to get even with me by tipping off the Goliath Tractor people about my prospective sale to Mr. Crampion. Then he got on his motorcycle and disappeared. And probably he did notify the Goliath people. Anyway, it was the next day that Mr. Van Verdingham arrived in town with his outlandish sales talk."

"Have the cops asked this Van Verdingham if he knows anything about your redheaded mechanic?"

"Of course they have asked him, but he just acts innocent and says he knows nothing about it. Then you come along"—and at this point our poor dealer once more went into a temper tantrum—"then you come along and put on as fatheaded an exhibition of pure idiocy as I have ever heard of. You make friends with a robber. You unlock one of my tractors and help the crook to steal it. You even lock the barn door after the horse is stolen. Then you wait until the next morning and call me up to boast about how helpful you have been."

"Well," I said, "I am sincerely sorry for what has happened, but it will do us no good to brood over past misfortunes. We must be constructive. We must seize the initiative and get that tractor back."

"Oh, yeah? And just how do you propose to get it back?"

"A big tractor," I said, "is too conspicuous to hide. If we notify the police, they ought to be able to locate it, and then it will be a simple matter to recover it."

"That's what you think. But you are wrong again. The criminal

242

has already told us where the tractor is. The police have verified this. But that doesn't help us at all."

"What do you mean?"

"That redheaded skunk left a letter behind. I found it on a bench in the repair shop. He said he was taking the tractor to get even with me for reporting him to the police. He claimed he was going to fix it so I couldn't use the machine in the demonstration this afternoon—and very likely I couldn't ever use it again. He said he was drowning it under nine hundred feet of water."

"What did he mean by that?"

"He was talking about an old coal mine about half a mile from town. Since it was abandoned, fifty years ago, the main shaft, which is about nine hundred feet deep, has filled up with water. As soon as I got the letter I drove out there. And sure enough, the fence, which had been built around it to keep people from falling in, had been broken down and there were fresh tracks of an Earthworm X-20 tractor leading right over the edge and into the shaft. So that is the end of that tractor as far as the demonstration this afternoon is concerned. And it is probably the end of it for good."

"Maybe," I said, "you could fish for it with a big hook on the end of a chain."

"A fat chance we'd have fishing for anything nine hundred feet down."

"Maybe you could get a deep-sea diver."

"I don't know whether divers go down that deep. But that is more your problem than mine, Mr. Botts. As long as you were an accomplice in stealing this tractor, I hold you personally responsible. And I also hold the Earthworm Tractor Company responsible. So you are going to ship me a brand-new X-20 Earthworm tractor, and then you can have what is left of the one that is in the mine—if you can get it out."

"It seems to me you are asking a good deal," I said.

"Either I get a new tractor free of charge, or I'll sue you and the company for the full value. And I'll have you prosecuted as an accessory to the crime. At that, I'm letting you off easy. I ought to have you put in jail right away, and I ought to sue you for damages to my business because I have lost the tractor that I need for my demonstration this afternoon."

"You must have other tractors available."

"Sure. I can use one of the older models—which is too bad because Mr. Crampion is interested primarily in our brand-new X-20. That's what I promised to demonstrate. And the only X-20 in my whole territory is the one that you dumped into the mine."

"I didn't dump it into the mine. How could I know that guy was a crook? I was just trying to be helpful. And I still want to be helpful. So I will be on hand at the demonstration this afternoon."

"You certainly will not."

"But don't you want me to help you?"

At this point our excitable dealer once more blew up and started yelling: "You have helped entirely too much already. You're nothing but a meddling jackass. I absolutely forbid you to come anywhere near this demonstration. I don't even want you anywhere in my territory. I'm going to write a letter right now to the president of your company. I'm going to tell him exactly what kind of an idiot you are. And I'm going to demand that he fire you from your job. Good-bye."

There was a click in the receiver. And that was the end of a conversation which I can only describe as unsatisfactory. After a few moments' meditation I decided that our dealer was in such a negative mood that it would be useless, for the time being, to try to reason with him. I decided, however, that, even if he spurned my assistance, I could help him out to some extent. In his rage and frustration he had tended to magnify some of his difficulties. Just because there were no X-20 Earthworm tractors available in his territory, he had jumped to the conclusion that it would be impossible to obtain one for his demonstration. I knew better.

I called our Pittsburgh dealer, whose territory adjoins that of our Mine City dealer. I asked him if he had an X-20 on hand.

"Yes," he said.

"Would you put it on a trailer and rush it down here to Mine City right away?"

"Certainly. It's now nine o'clock. I'll have it there by eleven."

"Will you send along a good operator? We want to use it in a house-moving demonstration."

"O.K."

Having taken care of this small matter, I spent the next three hours in deep thought, going over the various problems confronting me. I considered at least a hundred different plans for fishing the tractor out of the mine—and rejected them all as impractical. I considered various procedures for soothing and mollifying our irate Mine City dealer into a state of mind where I could reason with him about his absurd demand that we supply him with a new tractor free of charge. Unfortunately I was unable to think of anything along this line that seemed in any way promising.

I then thought over the strange case of Mr. Vincent Van Verdingham, the Goliath salesman, and his outlandish sales talk about the microscopic vacuum cups in the tires. Apparently he was acting on the well-known theory that the bigger the lie the more chance it has of being believed. I knew, of course, that the Goliath could not beat the Earthworm in a fair contest. But I was afraid that he might be able to manipulate the demonstration in such a way as to make it possible for him to explain away the obvious shortcomings of his wretched Goliath tractor, and to outwit our own somewhat emotional and dull-witted dealer.

I decided therefore that my presence at the demonstration was vital. It was up to me to help out our dealer. It is true that he had refused my help, but this presented no difficulties. I would attend the demonstration incognito. Our dealer had talked to me on the telephone, but he had never met me. The other people at the demonstration had never met me either. All I needed to do was to introduce myself under a pseudonym, or *nom de guerre*, and no one would recognize my true identity.

Having reached this conclusion, I banished all worries from my mind and ate a hearty luncheon. I then called the local newspaper and suggested they send reporters and photographers to the demonstration. A bit later I walked out there, and found myself in a field that had apparently been used for previous demonstrations; the ground was scarred with the tracks of various earth-moving machines.

In the middle of the field was a long, sturdy wooden building about the width of a garage. It was mounted on heavy crossties and skids, and for added support, thick chocks filled the spaces between the ties at the center of the building. It had a tin roof, with a stovepipe sticking out the top. Hitched to one end was a big clumsy Goliath tractor. On the front of this tractor was a bulldozer blade, and the wheels were equipped with enormous rubber tires—which may or may not have had microscopic vacuum cups. Nearby stood one of our beautiful new X-20 crawler tractors. And between the two machines men were standing around engaged in conversation. As I approached, they stopped talking and looked at me inquiringly. I thereupon advanced and introduced myself in a dignified and scholarly manner.

"Gentlemen," I said, "I am Doctor Horatio Robinson, of the Pennsylvania Tractor and Diesel Engine Research Institute. We are conducting a scientific investigation of various makes and models of tractors and other heavy-machinery units, with a view to ascertaining performance factors not only relative to the work actually accomplished in the field but also relative to the achievement quotient of each machine in comparison to others in the same or in different classes. The results, after being coordinated and evaluated, will be published in a pamphlet which will be of great help to prospective purchasers in assessing the conflicting claims of rival manufacturers."

Note: If you read the above speech carefully, Henderson, it may occur to you that I was using a little innocent deception. The reason should be obvious. Just as a detective is justified in using deception in investigating a crime, so I was justified in using deception in investigating a situation quite obviously involving fraud and chicanery.

For several seconds after my impressive introduction, the group looked at me in awed silence. Then one of the men stepped forward. "Pleased to meet you, doc," he said. "You had me guessing for a moment, but now I think I get you. You want to watch this demonstration, find out which of these two tractors is the best, and then write it up so Joe Doaks can learn the facts."

"That is correct," I said.

"All right; my name is Vincent Van Verdingham. I represent the Goliath Tractor Company. Stick around and you'll see my machine show up that Earthworm for the pathetic crawling junk pile that it really is."

"Thank you," I said.

The other members of the group introduced themselves—our local Earthworm dealer, the Earthworm operator from Pittsburgh, the mayor of Mine City, the local chief of police, various newspapermen, photographers, idle spectators and finally Mr. George Crampion, the man for whom the demonstration was being held.

The operator of the Goliath tractor climbed into the driver's seat. But, as often happens with cheap and carelessly thrown-together machinery, the engine refused to start. And, while the operator was making one futile adjustment after another, Mr. Crampion drew me to one side and started a very interesting conversation.

"Doctor Robinson," he said, "I'm very glad that you are here. There are certain things about this demonstration that puzzle me. And I would very much like to get the opinion of a scientist, such as yourself, who is not only an expert on tractors but is also completely impartial."

"I shall be most happy," I said, "to give you all possible assistance. After all, that is the purpose of the Pennsylvania Tractor and Diesel Engine Research Institute. What seems to be bothering you?"

"I don't quite trust one of these tractor salesmen."

"You mean you can't quite believe Mr. Van Verdingham's sales talk about the microscopic suction cups?"

"It isn't that, Doctor Robinson. Even though his sales talk may sound a little fantastic, the man himself seems very straightforward. He took me inside the door of this small storage building and showed me that it is almost completely filled with Portland cement. I estimated that there must be at least three thousand bags. The Goliath man, however, was honest enough to tell me that there are only about two thousand bags. Even so, that would make about ninety-four tons, which is a very respectable load for one tractor to pull over bare ground on skids."

"And the Goliath man expects you to believe his tractor can pull that big a load?"

"He doesn't expect me to believe anything, Doctor Robinson. That's what I like about him. He just asked me to watch his demonstration and draw my own conclusions. It's the Earthworm man that I'm suspicious of. He has been making some very weird statements."

"Such as?"

"This morning he asked to have the demonstration postponed. He said his only X-20 Earthworm had been stolen, and it would take several days to get another. But while he was talking, a brand-new X-20 arrived on a trailer from Pittsburgh. So then he agreed to go ahead as planned. But he still sticks to his weird story about the first X-20 being stolen."

"Just what does he say?"

"He says he fired a redheaded mechanic for stealing tools and supplies. And the redheaded mechanic, to get even, stole the tractor and dumped it down a nine-hundred-foot mine shaft which is full of water. Furthermore, the Earthworm dealer actually accuses the sales manager of the Earthworm Company of helping the thief steal the tractor. This seems to me almost incredible. How could a man as stupid as that ever become sales manager of a large corporation?"

"It does seem a bit odd," I said.

"And that's not all. The Earthworm dealer claims the redheaded crook and the Goliath salesman have been working together. He has no real evidence, so it looks to me as if he is just trying to blacken the reputation of a competitor. But he won't get anywhere with me that way. Unless he can bring in some real evidence, I won't have anything to do with him."

As Mr. Crampion paused for breath, I cut in with a few soothing words. "Possibly," I said, "we can look into this matter later on. Right now I think we should pay attention to the demonstration and find out whether Mr. Van Verdingham can prove his claims regarding the Goliath tractor."

You will note, Henderson, that I made a very clever reply to the accusation that the Earthworm dealer had made various claims which he has not yet proved. In pointing out that the Goliath salesman had also made various claims which he has not yet proved, I was preparing the way for a truly blistering attack just as soon as the Goliath failed in the demonstration. Unfortunately for me, however, the demonstration provided not only one but two of the most incredible surprises I have ever known in my entire career in the tractor business.

The engine of the Goliath finally started up, roaring and spitting, missing fire and pouring out great clouds of black smoke in the way that badly designed and wretchedly constructed engines usually do. For a moment I smiled in smug satisfaction at this demonstration of inferiority.

But my smile did not last. The Goliath operator let in the clutch and, to my utter astonishment, the machine moved off across the field, pulling the cement-storage building with the greatest of ease. After a few hundred feet on level ground, it pulled its load up a fairly steep slope, made a wide sweeping turn and started back. The tractor roared and clanked. Clouds of black smoke continued to pour from the exhaust. A tiny wisp of vapor came from the stovepipe on the storage building. And most of the spectators burst into wild cheers. When the Goliath had brought its load back to the starting point, it was unhitched.

The Earthworm was then hitched on and I was subjected to another disagreeable surprise. The Earthworm operator started the engine. It ran smoothly, with only the faintest suggestion of smoke from the exhaust. But when the operator let in the clutch, the tractor did not go anywhere at all. The tracks turned round and round—but the building did not move. Just as Mr. Van Verdingham had predicted, the grousers merely dug a hole in the ground. Two or three times the operator threw out his clutch and let it in very gently in the hope that he might get some traction but it was useless. All he did was dig the hole deeper. He finally gave up. And I began to regret that I had invited the reporters and photographers.

Mr. Crampion then spoke up. "That settles it," he said. "The Earthworm loses on both counts. Mr. Van Verdingham has proved that the Goliath can outpull the Earthworm. And the Earthworm dealer has offered no proof of his scandalous charges."

For a moment I was completely consternated. I was horrendisized. Clearly it was up to me to do something. And, as I could not think of anything else, I started talking. At first I talked merely to gain time.

"Mr. Crampion," I said, "your conclusions are amply justified when considered in relation to the facts we have before us. However, as a scientist, I feel it is my duty to point out that there may be other, less obvious facts which we have not yet discovered. In other words, there may be more to this demonstration than meets the eye."

"What more do you want? The Goliath pulled this heavy load across the field and up the hill. The Earthworm could not even start the same load on level ground."

Up to this time I had been talking merely to gain time. But Mr. Crampion's final sentence suggested the faint beginnings of a new idea. And from here on my talk became an exercise in thinking out loud. I led Mr. Crampion a short distance from the others.

"Listen," I said, "did you say that the Earthworm could not even start what you referred to as the same load?"

"Exactly."

"Are you sure it really was the same load?"

"Certainly. How could it be anything else?"

"I don't know exactly," I said. "But I do know that an Earthworm can outpull a Goliath anywhere, anytime. When a Goliath seems to outpull an Earthworm, there must be something crooked about it."

"Such as what?"

By this time I was gradually beginning to formulate a more or less definite idea. "Possibly," I said, "there may be something about that building that makes it easier to move at one time than at another. There is something queer about it."

"I don't see anything queer."

"I do," I said. "There is a stovepipe coming out the roof. And during the demonstration I noticed a very faint wisp of smoke."

"Probably they have a stove in there."

"They don't need a stove in a cement-storage building. And even if they had one, they would not need a fire on a warm day like this."

"If it's not a stove, what is it then?"

"Can you think of anything else," I said, "that sends out smoke?"

"Well, that Goliath tractor poured out plenty. And I think the Earthworm produced a little."

By this time my ideas were really getting somewhere. "Exactly," I said. "And this leads us directly to the matter of the stolen tractor. Apparently the redheaded mechanic told the dealer that he stole the machine and dumped it in the mine merely to get revenge. But this does not sound reasonable. Why should he go to the trouble of starting up the machine and driving it all the way to the mine when he could have sabotaged it much more easily by setting it on fire or blowing it up? I think he stole the machine because he wanted to use it. I don't think it is in the mine at all. I think the thief merely drove the tractor to the edge of the mine and then backed up very carefully in the same tracks. He was planting evidence."

"But why?"

"It's an old trick," I said. "It's called throwing the pursuit off the scent. If the cops are convinced the tractor is at the bottom of the mine, they won't look for it elsewhere around town."

"You really think it's hidden somewhere around here?"

"Maybe we can find out," I said.

"I approached Mr. Van Verdingham. "Some of your competitors," I said, "claim that the Goliath bulldozer blade is very weak. I rather doubt this, but I would like to see a test. Would you just as soon have your operator drive the tractor around to the rear of this building and see if you can push it with the bulldozer blade?"

"Certainly."

"And may I ride along?"

"Of course. But wait just a minute." Mr. Van Verdingham opened the door of the cement-storage building. He stepped inside. A few seconds later he came out. He motioned to me to go ahead. I climbed up onto the wide seat beside the operator.

The operator drove the Goliath around to the rear of the building, eased the blade against the main sill and opened up the engine. At once the tractor and the building began to move forward.

This was what I had been waiting for. Reaching over so quickly that the operator could not stop me, I cut out the engine. The Goliath stopped with a jolt. But the house kept moving on—slowly and steadily! From inside came a beautiful rhythmic roar which I recognized as the sound of an X-20 Earthworm tractor. Up to this time, of course, this noise had been drowned out by the outlandish racket made by the Goliath.

From then on, things happened fast. Mr. Van Verdingham dashed out in front of the building and flagged it down. I asked the chief of police to arrest him. Various bystanders swarmed into the building and removed enough of the cement to reveal the stolen X-20 Earthworm. It was in an open space at the center of the pile, where it had been lowered through a hole cut through the floor and the center crossties, so that its tracks rested on the ground. It was securely fastened to the floor timbers, so that whenever it was driven forward it dragged the building with it. The exhaust was connected to the stovepipe. A wooden framework kept the piled-up cement from falling on the tractor. And a small peephole next to a window permitted the operator to see where he was going.

The operator—to the astonishment of everyone but me—turned out to be the redheaded mechanic. He has been lodged in jail along with Mr. Vincent Van Verdingham. Mr. Crampion has bought the Earthworm. Our dealer is very happy, but he is still in such a bewildered state of mind that I do not wish to confuse him further.

I am therefore planning to leave town in the morning and come back at some future time to reveal my true identity.

Cordially yours,
Alexander Botts.

ALEXANDER BOTTS, SECURITY AGENT

EARTHWORM TRACTOR COMPANY
EARTHWORM CITY, ILLINOIS
OFFICE OF GILBERT HENDERSON, PRESIDENT

Tuesday, December 9, 1958

Mr. Alexander Botts
Sales Manager, Earthworm Tractor Co.
Earthworm Tractor Proving Grounds
Coquina Beach, Florida
Dear Botts:

This letter is to demand an explanation for your highly unpatriotic failure to cooperate in the educational program which we have set up in an effort to do our part in overcoming the alarming superiority of the Russians in science and engineering.

About a year ago our board of directors, appalled by the Russian success with the first Sputnik, investigated the situation in our own company. An exhaustive survey by one of the country's leading psychological institutes revealed that many of our top executives, although highly competent as businessmen, were woefully ignorant of the engineering and mechanical features of our products. To remedy this shocking condition we set up our first annual two-week Engineering School for Company Executives at our Earthworm Proving Grounds, Coquina Beach, Florida. A selected group of our vice-presidents and department heads, including yourself, were assigned to this school. All of these men attended the school and profited immeasurably thereby—except you. You completely disregarded this assignment—claiming you were occupied with more important matters.

This year I directed you to attend the second annual Engineering School starting yesterday at the same place. Apparently you are not taking this year's school any more seriously than last year's. One of our engineers, who was at the school yesterday and who flew back to Earthworm City last night, reports that you attended the first hour of instruction, but spent most of your time yawning and reading a newspaper. At the end of the first hour you disappeared from the classroom. Later you were seen with another idler sunning yourself on the beach.

You are hereby directed to attend future classes and pay attention. How do you expect to get ahead of the Russians if you take no interest in education?

Yours,
Gilbert Henderson

Earthworm Proving Grounds
Coquina Beach, Florida
Wednesday, December 10, 1958

Dear Henderson:

Your letter arrived by airmail this afternoon. You have got me wrong. I have always taken an intense interest in education. I did not absent myself from the school down here because of any lack of interest in learning. On the contrary, by leaving I was able to find greater educational opportunities elsewhere. To the end that you may better understand what I am talking about, I will give you a brief account of exactly what has been going on at this so-called Engineering School.

The opening session on Monday was conducted by a long-winded pedagogue who gave us a dismal preview of what we were supposed to endure for the next two weeks. There would be, he said, an exhaustive discussion of lubricants, with special attention to chemical composition, viscosity, flash points and flame points. We would hear about such additives as rust inhibitors, corrosion inhibitors, antioxidants and detergents. There would be demonstrations of thickness gauges, micrometers, sclerometers, and dynamometers. We would learn the basic characteristics of steel, cast iron, malleable iron, bronze and other materials as influenced by various forms of heat treatment and by such components as carbon, nickel, molybdenum, titanium, manganese, chromium and even tin. And there would be much more.

As the man droned on, it came over me that most of the information to be handed out in this school would be stuff I did not need to know and did not want to know. For an engineer it would be hot stuff. For me it would be a waste of time.

At the end of the first hour I turned to an Army major who had been yawning and drowsing in the next seat. "Just what are you doing here?" I asked.

"Military orders," he said.

"Do you think you are going to learn anything worthwhile?"

"No."

"Me neither," I said.

By common consent we adjourned to our rooms at the hotel, put on swimming trunks and repaired to the beach. As we relaxed in the sunshine and contemplated the blue waters of the Gulf of Mexico, I gave the major a brief explanation of my advanced ideas on education.

"We cannot outdo the Russians," I said, "merely by imitating them. From what I hear, the Russians have copied the former German system wherein everything was controlled by the higher authorities and run from the top down, with the accent on discipline, obedience and conformity. In Germany this system produced a nation of highly trained technicians who were perfectly happy to take orders from a man like Hitler. No wonder Germany lost in the end to nations with more liberal ideas."

"How right you are," said the major.

"The Russians," I continued, "now seem to be worse than the Germans ever were. They are producing an entire nation of skilled automatons conditioned to obey a Stalin or a Khrushchev or anybody else who happens to be on top. To get ahead of such people we must do exactly the opposite of what they are doing. We must resist the present attempt of the Earthworm Company to ram down our throats a lot of erudite nonsense which we do not want. And we must assert our rights as free men controlling our own intellectual development."

"I could not agree with you more," said the major. "Already, by listening to you for five minutes, I have learned more than during an entire hour of this alleged school."

"Thank you," I said. "Just what are your duties around here?"

"I am assigned to the United States Army Coquina Proving Ground, which is adjacent to the Earthworm Proving Ground, and is largely used to test out Army equipment made by your Earthworm Company. Are you familiar with what we are doing?"

"No," I said. "This special stuff is made in shops separate from our regular factory. I have never had a chance to look it over."

"If you are interested, Mr. Botts, I will arrange to take you over tomorrow and show you the last word in radio-controlled tractors. I will even let you operate one of them."

"Splendid," I said.

The major departed to make arrangements for my visit, and I spent the rest of the day on the beach.

The next morning—yesterday—the major conducted me to the Army Proving Ground, an area of several square miles surrounded by a high barbed-wire fence. The major had been unable to procure the necessary papers for me in advance. I was therefore subjected to a long and stupid examination. I filled out endless questionnaires. I exhibited my birth certificate. I was fingerprinted and photographed. Finally they gave me a pass and a badge.

The major explained this nonsense by telling me that they had a new security officer who had just been attending some sort of security school, where he had learned all the most cumbersome methods for protecting military secrets.

We entered the gate, and the major took me to a parking area where he pointed out an XX77 Earthworm tractor outfitted in a truly remarkable manner. It was covered with armor and equipped with a bulldozer blade on the front, and a set of gang plows on the rear. There was a turret with a window, and a machine gun and a number of metal rods which looked like radio or TV antennas.

"Is this the new radio-controlled tractor?" I asked.

"Yes, Mr. Botts. This is the latest model with all the most up-to-date improvements. The machine is designed so that it can travel, without any operator, through areas contaminated by atomic fallout. It can scrape the fallout to one side or plow it under so as to open a safe path for troops to march through. It can also be used for reconnaissance, for hauling artillery and supplies, and even for combat. The control unit is over there."

We entered a booth filled with electronic equipment. There were a lot of levers, knobs and buttons, and a screen which the major explained was designed to carry a picture picked up by a TV camera mounted behind bulletproof glass in the turret of the tractor.

The major and I took turns operating the controls, which are effective up to a distance of ten miles. It was not only a lot of fun but also highly educational. We drove the tractor hither and thither about the parking area, sounding a big siren and yelling at military pedestrians through a mike in the booth and a speaker on the tractor. We could hear the reactions of the pedestrians through a mike on the tractor and a speaker in the booth.

We drove to a test area and plowed up a lot of earth with the bulldozer and the plows. We stopped in at a target range and tried out our amazingly accurate machine gun. Then we drove several miles to the far side of the reservation, where a half dozen workmen on a loading platform were boxing for export another of the radio-TV tractors. The box bore a stenciled address showing it was to be shipped via Tampa to an Army base in Panama. There was a smaller box, also consigned to Panama, which the major told me contained a control unit similar to the one we were using.

"Does each tractor have to have its own individual control unit?" I asked.

"No," said the major. "Any control unit can be tuned to control any tractor."

"Then couldn't the enemy tune in on one of our tractors and steal it from us?"

"No, because nobody except the United States Army has any of these tractors or any of these control units, and the mechanism is top secret. Hundreds of soldiers and civilians have learned how to operate these machines, but the working parts are sealed and are accessible only to our most highly trusted technicians."

The major then showed me how to tune in on the other tractor. I twirled the necessary controls, and at once the picture on our screen blacked out. Since the tractor was inside the box we could see nothing, but we could hear the voices of the workmen and the pounding of their hammers.

"This is too good to miss," I said. I touched the button and sounded a mighty blast on the faraway siren. I could imagine the terrified workmen scattering in all directions. The major and I had a good laugh. Then I spoke reassuringly over the sound system.

"Excuse it, please," I said. "Just testing."

Switching the controls to the first tractor, we brought it back to the parking ground next to the control unit.

"That's enough for today," said the major. "But I hope you can come back tomorrow. A civilian expert from Schenectady is arriving to give a demonstration of this equipment to a group of officers from the Pentagon. You might be interested."

"Indeed I would," I said. "I am always eager to improve my mind by taking advantage of real educational opportunities."

At this point the chief security officer arrived, conferred privately with the major and then conducted both of us to the main gate. After we were outside, the major smiled with quiet amusement.

"Ever since that guy went to security school," he said, "he has been taking his responsibilities very seriously. He has just received word of a suspected Communist plot to steal one of our radio-controlled tractors and a control unit and ship them to Russia. The whole thing sounds pretty fantastic to me, but he is so alarmed that he has revoked your security clearance. You can't come back tomorrow."

"He's barking up the wrong tree," I said. "I'm not working for the Communists."

"I know it," said the major, "and you know it, but he doesn't know it. So he won't let you inside the fence anymore. And there is nothing we can do about it."

We spent the rest of the day—yesterday—and all of today on the beach, where I did a lot of meditating. Your letter arrived late this afternoon. I have been spending the evening writing this letter and doing a lot more meditating. And I am more than ever convinced that getting ahead of the Russians requires more than the dull routine of the classroom. The victims of the Earthworm Engineering School are merely having their minds cluttered with a lot of useless facts and figures which most of them will never need. Even worse is the plight of the security officer, who knows nothing about his job except routine and conventional methods. While the poor man is throwing out such honest citizens as myself, barring the front gate, and fooling around with birth certificates, badges and passes, he cannot possibly have time to find out what the enemy is actually doing.

Fortunately, Alexander Botts is on hand—unhampered by doctrinaire teachings—the one person who has what it takes to protect our radio-controlled tractors from enemy agents. Tomorrow I will start a thorough investigation of the situation, avoiding the front gate and concentrating on the rear areas. I will try various methods for crawling under, breaking through or climbing over the barbed-wire fence. I will feel out the weaknesses of our position. I will apprehend all enemy agents that may be lurking in the vicinity. At the close of the investigation I will make a complete report to the authorities, so they may set up adequate security measures.

Yours,
Alexander Botts

EARTHWORM CITY, ILLINOIS
DECEMBER 12, 1958

ALEXANDER BOTTS
EARTHWORM PROVING GROUND
COQUINA BEACH, FLORIDA
YOU ARE DIRECTED TO RETURN AT ONCE TO OUR ENGINEERING SCHOOL AND ATTEND REGULARLY UNTIL END OF COURSE. GET-

TING AHEAD OF RUSSIANS REQUIRES SOLID SCIENTIFIC TRAINING, NOT LOLLING AROUND ON THE BEACH, ENGAGING IN CHILDISH PLAY WITH RADIO-CONTROLLED MACHINERY AND GIVING WAY TO SPY HYSTERIA. ANY ATTEMPT ON YOUR PART TO ENGAGE IN AMATEUR CLOAK-AND-DAGGER PROJECTS DESIGNED TO TRAP IMAGINARY FOREIGN AGENTS CAN ONLY RESULT IN SERIOUS TROUBLE.
GILBERT HENDERSON

Coquina Beach, Florida
Friday, December 12, 1958
Dear Henderson:

Your telegram did not arrive until this evening—too late for me to heed your warning that my spy-hunting activities might get me into serious trouble. As I am always ready, Henderson, to give you full credit when you are right in your predictions, I will now explain how—through my earnest attempts to protect the security of our great country—I managed to get myself in the middle of a conflict between the forces of good and the forces of evil, and how I was shot at by both sides and even placed under arrest by those who should have been helping me.

Yesterday morning, Thursday, I sallied forth with a small but sturdy toy shovel. I started to walk around the great Coquina Army Proving Ground, carefully inspecting the barbed-wire fence. About two miles from the main gate, where the major and I had entered, I found another gate. To test the effectiveness of the guards, I applied for admission and was politely informed that no one could enter without a pass.

"What kind of a pass?" I asked.

"They issue them at the security office at the main gate," said the guard.

"Would it be possible," I asked, "for a Communist spy to forge one of these passes?"

"Maybe—but it wouldn't work. Every time a pass is presented we telephone the security office to find out if it's genuine."

At this point a large platform truck drove up with a driver and a helper. The driver produced a pass which was handed over to the sergeant of the guard. I heard him make a telephone check, and the truck was permitted to enter.

I resumed my tour of inspection and soon found myself in an area of dense junglelike vegetation. It extended for some distance on both sides of the fence, which ran through the middle of a cleared strip several yards wide. Lurking in the concealment of the bushes, I noticed a guard marching along the inside of the fence.

The situation was familiar. As a boy in Smedleytown, Iowa, I had supplemented my routine school education by carrying on various original research projects. One of these involved the cop who patrolled the local ball park; by conducting a scientific time study of his movements I learned exactly when certain sections of the fence were unprotected, and I was thus able to see many ball games without paying admission.

Years later this part of my education once more came in handy. I timed the guard at the Proving Ground. He was absent for twenty minutes in one direction, two minutes in the other. I waited until he started one of his twenty-minute tours, and then I began digging a hole under the fence. Ten minutes later—just as the hole was big enough to crawl through—I heard, from a highway behind me, the roar of a truck, followed by a loud squeaking of brakes and then silence. As I was on a scouting expedition, I decided to investigate. I concealed the hole under the fence with a couple of branches. I made my way to the vicinity of the highway and peered out through the bushes.

And what I saw, Henderson, was something you will find it hard to believe. The truck which I had previously seen at the gate, and which was now loaded with the two export cases consigned to Panama, had been stopped by two vicious characters with revolvers. Even as I looked, they climbed into the cab and forced the driver to turn off into a narrow, little-used road through the underbrush. I followed cautiously.

After about a mile the truck stopped on the bank of a lonely inlet. The two highjackers got out and tied the truck driver and his helper to a couple of trees.

"Where's that shrimp boat?" one of the crooks asked.

"I can see it coming," said the other, "about a mile down the inlet."

Right then I decided to get out of there. But I moved too fast. I slipped and fell down with a great crash of breaking twigs and branches. This was a mistake on my part, because it alarmed the criminals. They yelled for me to halt. When I did not, they started shooting at me. This was a mistake on their part, because they not only missed me but stimulated me into a truly remarkable burst of speed. In what must have been considerably less than four minutes I covered something over a mile and arrived at the gate which I previously mentioned.

As soon as I could catch my breath I began shouting, "Quick! The Communists have stolen the tractor! They've been shooting at me. Didn't you hear them?"

"I heard shots," said the guard, "but they don't mean nothing. There's target ranges all around here."

"But the Communists have stolen the tractor," I repeated. "You've got to send out a patrol! You've got to catch them before they get away!"

The guard acted annoyed. "Are you the same boob that was here a little while ago talking about Communist spies forging passes?"

"Yes."

"And now you're talking about Communist spies stealing tractors?"

"Yes."

"Listen, buddy," said the guard, "my job is to watch this gate—not chase spies. The trouble with you is you read too many comic books. You're beginning to see things. You better run along or I'll lock you up."

I walked away. I thought of looking up my friend, the major, but I did not know where to find him. I thought of hurrying to the main gate and appealing to the security officer. But I was sure that his theoretical, classroom mentality would react even more slowly than the guard at the gate.

There seemed only one thing to do. I ran as fast as I could to the place where I had dug under the fence. Without waiting to check on the guard, I crawled through. This was another mistake on my part. Just as I was darting into the bushes on the inner side of the fence the guard came in sight and yelled for me to halt. When I kept running, he fired a couple of shots. Fortunately he missed. But I knew he would raise an alarm. There would be an attempt to track me down. I had to act fast.

I managed to sneak through the brush unnoticed. I made my way to the parking ground, where I found the tractor and the control unit right where the major and I had left them on Tuesday. A dozen officers were standing around. I felt sure none of them would believe my fantastic spy story. It would be necessary, therefore, to use a subtle and indirect approach. I spoke to one of them, "You are the group from the Pentagon, I presume?"

"Yes," he said; "we are waiting for Mr. Patterson of Schenectady, who is to give us a demonstration."

"You need wait no longer," I said. "I am Mr. Patterson."

In the twinkling of an eye my resourceful mind had decided on a course of action. The officers gathered around as I climbed into the

260

control unit. In my wild dash through the shrubbery I had become somewhat disheveled, and at first they were a bit suspicious; but apparently they decided that a scientist from Schenectady is apt to be slightly eccentric. And before long they were watching and listening with deep respect as I put on what may well go down in history as the outstanding tractor demonstration of all time.

"Gentlemen," I said, "to illustrate the versatility of our radio-controlled tractor, I have evolved a dramatic situation to show you how one of these machines may be used in counterespionage activities. For the purposes of this demonstration we are going to assume that a radio-controlled tractor and a control unit were boxed for export, loaded onto a truck and started this morning for Tampa, from which port they were to be shipped to an Army base in Panama. But the local security officer has been so busy with his questionnaires and fingerprints that he has neglected to provide adequate guards. The truck has been highjacked by Communist agents and has been driven to a lonely inlet a few miles from here. The enemy agents are planning to load the tractor and control unit into a shrimp boat which will take them to some secret rendezvous in Cuba, Mexico or elsewhere, to be transshipped to the Soviet Union. Do you follow me?"

"It's a pretty fantastic story," said one of the officers, "but it's all right if you don't expect us to believe it."

"That's a good point," I said. "We are going to assume that one of us has seen the highjacking and followed the truck to the inlet where the shrimp boat is expected to arrive at any moment. The highjackers are armed. Our man has no weapons. What should he do?"

"He should notify the authorities."

"Unfortunately," I said, "his story—as one of you has pointed out—is too fantastic. We must assume, therefore, that nobody would believe him. What should he do then?"

None of the officers seemed to have a good answer for this one.

"Very good," I said, "I will tell you. I will also show you. All our man has to do is burrow under the fence, come to the Proving Ground and enter this control booth, as I have just done. Next, he warms up the tubes—like this."

I spun the knobs until the picture on the screen reproduced the view from the turret of the nearby tractor.

I continued, "Now that we know the controls are working properly, we shift this pointer so as to tune in on that tractor several miles away on the bank of the lonely inlet. Have I made myself clear?"

"There must be something wrong," said one of the officers. "There isn't any picture on the screen anymore."

"Exactly," I said. "That tractor down there at the inlet is inside a packing case. Naturally we can't see anything, but maybe we can hear something."

I cut in the sound system, and right away we could hear a faraway voice yelling, "All right—swing that boom over here and we'll hook onto the first box."

"Aha!" I said. "We are just in time. I am now going to rescue that tractor right out from under the noses of the conspirators."

I started spinning knobs, pressing buttons and throwing switches—using all the skill I had acquired a couple of days before. I started up the engine in that distant tractor. I drove the machine with a tremendous crash out the end of the packing case. The screen came alive with a view from the turret, and the picture gave a mighty heave as the tractor rolled off the end of the truck and dropped to the ground.

Turning proudly to my audience I said, "You have just seen one of the advantages of remote control. If one of us had been on the seat of that machine when it dropped off the end of the truck, he would have suffered a bone-shattering jolt. As it is, we have not felt the slightest jar. And now I want you to watch closely and listen carefully as I take charge of the situation down there on the bank of the inlet."

Once more I began my expert manipulation of the controls. I spun the turret and pointed the television camera hither and thither, so that we all had a splendid view of the entire scene. The shrimp boat had tied up at a primitive landing pier. It looked like any other shrimp boat, except that it had an oversized mast, with a boom big enough to handle heavy loads. A half dozen evil-looking characters— obviously the crew of the boat—were standing on the deck. The two highjackers were on the bank. The truck driver and his helper were still tied to trees.

I began shouting commands, "All right, you two on the bank there! Untie your prisoners!"

Their only reply was to pull out their revolvers and start shooting at the tractor. I then swung the machine gun into action. Taking advantage of all the delicate refinements of the beautifully designed controls, I plowed up the mud near their feet. Then I deftly shot off their hats.

This completely cowed them. As they untied their prisoners, I resumed my lecture to the assembled group from the Pentagon. "What you have just seen," I said, "is a further illustration of the advantages of remote control. You can shoot it out with a couple of gunmen without the slightest danger of getting hit yourself."

A quick glance at my audience revealed that they were speechless with astonishment and admiration. I turned back to the sound system and resumed my operations at the distant inlet.

"Ahoy, there!" I shouted. "I want you men on the deck to come ashore. And don't try to escape by going below. If you do, I'll shoot holes all along the water line and sink the boat."

The men meekly came ashore—at which I will have to admit I was a little disappointed. It is not often that I have a chance to sink a shrimp boat with a machine gun. It would have been lots of fun. But I reminded myself that such frivolous amusements have no proper place in serious counterespionage activities. I returned sternly to the business at hand.

I lined up the two highjackers and the six crewmen on the road leading back to the proving ground. I swung the tractor in behind them. I directed the two released prisoners to take charge once more of their truck. I then started a triumphant parade. The highjackers and the crew marched ahead. The tractor rolled along behind them. And the truck brought up the rear. To keep the criminals in a properly cooperative frame of mind I sent an occasional burst of machine-gun fire into the ground beside them—first on one side and then the other.

When we reached the gate, I made so much noise working the siren and yelling through the sound system that the entire guard turned out. The truck driver and his helper told their story to the officer of the day, and he ordered the crooks locked up.

As I turned off the controls, a detail of Military Police arrived, accompanied by the security officer, my friend the major, and a little man who turned out to be the scientist from Schenectady. I was immediately placed under arrest. But after I had explained everything and after the major had come to my defense, I was turned loose and thanked for blocking a dangerous Communist conspiracy. And—what pleases me even more—I had a chance to give a final bit of advice to the officers from the Pentagon.

"If you want to beat the Russians," I said, "you have to rise above the dull routine of the classroom. You have to think and act for yourselves. Such being the case, I recommend that you now adjourn for an afternoon of relaxation and meditation on the beach."

They went—after shaking hands and congratulating your unusually well-educated sales manager,

Alexander Botts.

ALEXANDER BOTTS, JAILBIRD

EARTHWORM TRACTOR COMPANY
EARTHWORM CITY, ILLINOIS
OFFICE OF GILBERT HENDERSON, PRESIDENT

Friday, September 23, 1960

Mr. Alexander Botts
Earthworm Sales Manager
Hotel Pennsylvania
Philadelphia, Pennsylvania

Dear Botts:

Our Trenton, New Jersey, dealer writes me that the Jones Construction Company has a contract to fill up a large ravine in preparation for a housing development at North Harwood, New Jersey. The material for the fill is to come from a clay deposit near the ravine.

Our dealer had hopes of selling a lot of Earthworm equipment for this job but has recently run into stiff competition from the Gyro-Excavator Company of Indianapolis. This is a new company with a new product about which we know very little.

Kindly get in touch with our Trenton dealer and help him persuade the Jones Company to buy Earthworms. Also, I want you to find out all you can about this new Gyro-Excavator.

Most sincerely,
Gilbert Henderson

Hotel Pennsylvania, Philadelphia
Monday evening, September 26, 1960

Dear Henderson:

Your letter arrived here in Philadelphia this morning. Instead of contacting our dealer in Trenton, I decided I would first investigate the situation on the job at North Harwood. I drove out there, and I am happy to report that not only have I had a most interesting time but I have ended the day with $5,000 more than when I started.

At the housing project, which is next to a small airport, I found a house trailer fixed up as an office with a sign: Jones Construction Company. After knocking at the door, I was admitted by a watchman who told me that Mr. Jones, the head of the company, has his headquarters in New York City and has not yet come to North Harwood. The superintendent on the job is a Mr. Albert Potts, who was out of town, but is expected back tomorrow.

As I was starting back toward my car, a light plane landed on the nearby airport and taxied up to a small hangar. Painted on the side of the plane were the words: *Gyro-Excavator Company, Indianapolis, Indiana.* A man alighted and walked toward me. He carried a raincoat and a handsome briefcase with gold lettering: *George W. Quackenbush, Gyro-Excavator Company.* As the man drew near, he said, "Are you Mr. Potts?"

Note: At this point, Henderson, I did some very fast thinking. It sounded to me as if the man had asked for "Mr. Potts." However, I could not be absolutely sure. It was just possible that he had asked for "Mr. Botts." Naturally I did not want to be so dishonest as to claim I was "Mr. Potts," when in reality I was "Mr. Botts." But, if he was making an honest mistake in thinking I was "Mr. Potts," when I was actually "Mr. Botts," it would be equally honest for me to think he was asking for "Mr. Botts" when he was actually asking for "Mr. Potts." Furthermore, it occurred to me that if he thought I was "Mr. Potts," the local superintendent for the Jones Construction Company, instead of "Mr. Botts," the sales manager of the Earthworm Tractor Company, it was just possible that he might divulge a certain amount of interesting information. Accordingly I stepped forward and shook him warmly by the hand.

"Yes," I said, "I am Mr. Botts."

Note: You will observe, Henderson, that I was telling the exact truth, even though I did pronounce the word "Botts" so rapidly that he quite obviously thought I said "Potts."

"My name," said the man, "is George W. Quackenbush. I represent the Gyro-Excavator Company. Probably you were not expecting me."

"Well, no," I said, sort of feeling my way. "I guess I was not."

"You were, of course, expecting my colleague, Chet Morgan. Unfortunately he is in the hospital with a slipped disc or something. He is unable to travel."

"Well, well," I said. "Poor old Chet. It is too bad."

"It is, indeed, Mr. Potts. But I have come in his place. Chet said that when he was here two weeks ago he promised to return and take up certain important and confidential matters with you."

"And just what are these important and confidential matters?"

"Ah, Mr. Potts, I can see that you are a very cautious man. You know perfectly well what I am talking about. But, in view of the delicate nature of the subject under discussion, you are perfectly right in refusing to commit yourself any more than you have to. You are right in expecting me to take the lead, and I will. Let us first of all look over the machine."

"What machine?" I asked.

"The Gyro-Excavator. Chet told me that two weeks ago he arranged to ship one out here. Last week you wired him that it had arrived and was stored in your machinery shed. As there is only one machinery shed around here, that must be where it is."

He walked over to a recently constructed wooden building and swung open a big door. I followed him inside and found myself gazing at one of the most outlandish pieces of machinery I have ever seen. It was as complicated as an old-fashioned combine harvester, or a newspaper-printing press—only more so. The machine was mounted on eight wheels with enormous tires. Jutting out from the front were some rooters and scoops, apparently designed to dig up earth and deliver it to an endless chain equipped with buckets, which in turn passed it through a series of rotating steel claws and beaters to a conveyor belt that would ultimately dump the earth into trucks.

"Let's start this thing up," I said, "and see how it works."

"Unfortunately, Mr. Potts, our mechanic has reported a slight difficulty with one of the gear assemblies. It is nothing serious, but it will take a couple of days to get the new parts. In the meantime I will be glad to explain anything you do not fully understand. I presume Chet Morgan described for you our revolutionary earth-conditioning feature, and how it will be of tremendous importance on this particular job?"

"He may have described it. But I would like to hear you go over it again."

"The seemingly useless complications of this machine have a definite purpose, Mr. Potts. And this purpose is something we keep strictly confidential. We never put it in writing. We never put it in our advertising or in our literature. We talk about it only to good customers like you and only by word of mouth."

"Go on," I said.

"The Gyro-Excavator is carefully designed to agitate, beat, whirl and fluff up the earth—thus modifying its physical structure so as to produce a remarkable increase in volume."

"Like increasing the volume of cream by whipping it?"

"Exactly. Chet Morgan tells me the clay you will be handling here has a type of crumb structure which responds unusually well to our soil-conditioning process. When our beaters and agitators get through with one yard of that clay, you will find it has been fluffed up to a volume of two yards."

"In other words," I said, "for every yard of earth we dig up we get two yards of fill. We can do the job quicker. We can do the job cheaper."

"Which will be wonderful for the Jones Construction Company, and even more wonderful for you personally, Mr. Potts. I understand Mr. Jones has put you in complete charge of this project. You choose the equipment. You boss the job. And you get a handsome bonus for every day and every dollar you save in completing the work."

"This seems like a very fine proposition," I said. "But I want to make sure of everything. Most contracts provide that an earth fill must be tamped in some way."

"Very true, Mr. Potts. This particular contract—as you know— calls for the use of sheep's-foot rollers——"

"Which would compact the clay almost back to its original volume?"

"That would be true only if you used the ordinary type of sheep's-foot rollers. But you will remember that we are going to sell you six of our special rollers with spring-mounted feet so designed that they recede into openings in the surface of the roller and thus avoid any harmful over-compaction."

"Even so," I said, "isn't there some danger that over a period of years this expanded clay might gradually slump back to its original volume?"

Mr. Quackenbush said, "There has been no time for us to test this out."

"There might be a lot of trouble," I said. "Suppose the people who buy property in this development find the whole area is collapsing—streets, lawns, trees and houses sinking down, down——"

"That would be sort of too bad, wouldn't it?" Quackenbush said. "But no such misfortune could possibly occur for several years. By that time the Gyro-Excavator Company would have been paid for its equipment. The Jones Construction Company would have been paid for the fill. You would have received your bonus. The real-estate-development company would have unloaded its houses and lots. All of us would have taken handsome profits and moved out of the picture. And if, in years to come, the fill should actually collapse, it would be a purely natural disaster like an earthquake, a flood or a tornado. The unfortunate homeowners would have to follow the usual procedure of getting relief from the Federal Government."

"You are very reassuring," I said.

"And now," said Mr. Quackenbush, "I suggest we finalize our agreement." He drew some papers from his briefcase. "I have here," he said, "the purchase order for the equipment you agreed to buy from Chet Morgan—two Gyro-Excavators, six special self-propelled, sheep's-foot rollers and an assortment of miscellaneous equipment, attachments and supplies—everything you will need except the trucks, which I understand you already have on hand."

I made a show of reading the order with meticulous care. "This looks all right to me," I said.

"Very good," said Mr. Quackenbush. "That brings us to another delicate and confidential matter. The Gyro-Excavator Company realizes, Mr. Potts, that you have done a lot of conscientious work in investigating our machinery. You have exerted yourself far beyond the call of duty. We offer you our heartfelt thanks. But we also feel we should express our gratitude in a more definite manner."

"That's very kind of you."

"Not at all, Mr. Potts. I have here a small honorarium to compensate you, at least partially, for your professional services." He put down his raincoat and pulled from his ample briefcase a rather large cloth bag.

"It looks to me," I said, "like something more than a *small* honorarium."

"I hope it is adequate. As a matter of fact, Chet Morgan told me that he had discussed this whole matter with you and that you had agreed to accept $5,000—provided it came in used bills of five-, ten- and twenty-dollar denominations without any consecutive numbering."

"I will stand by the agreement," I said. "Did Chet explain why I wanted old bills without consecutive numbers?"

"As I understand it, Mr. Potts, you both felt it would be more discreet to keep this confidential. In some ways, of course, it would be more straightforward to put through a check. But a check is a matter of record, and it might become known to the wrong people."

"What wrong people?" I asked.

"Well, you know and I know that this deal is completely ethical. But there are people who are so morbidly suspicious that they see evil in everything. Such people have coined a series of unfortunate expressions like payola, kickback, slush fund and others even worse."

"Yes," I said sadly, "I have heard these expressions. I deplore them as much as you do. But they exist, so I agree with you that we must preserve our privacy. If you'll hand over the money, I will be happy to count it."

I reached for the bag, but Mr. Quackenbush held onto it. He said, "The agreement was that you were to sign first and get the money afterward."

"Certainly." I signed the order in duplicate, "Jones Construction Company, per A. Potts." I took one copy. Mr. Quackenbush put the other in his briefcase. He handed over the money, and I counted it. The total was exactly $5,000.

"It is a pleasure," I said, "to do business with people as honest as you are."

We walked over to the small airport. Mr. Quackenbush opened the door of his plane and shoved his briefcase under the seat.

"Wait a minute," I said. "Didn't you have a raincoat?"

"Thanks for reminding me. I must have left it in that shed." He started to walk back.

I stayed with the plane. And it suddenly occurred to me that it might be a good thing to get back that signed order. I waited until Mr. Quackenbush disappeared into the machinery shed. I jerked the briefcase out of the plane, hid it in the hangar and got back to the plane before Mr. Quackenbush emerged from the shed.

This time he had his raincoat. He climbed into his plane. He took off. I retrieved the briefcase. And I drove the company car back to Philadelphia.

After depositing the $5,000 in the hotel safe and examining the sales literature, order blanks and other material I found in the briefcase, I ate a good dinner and returned to my room, where I have been spending the rest of the evening writing this report.

I think you will agree, Henderson, that I have pulled off a very brilliant maneuver in painlessly extracting $5,000 from our competitors. It is true that I had to sign on behalf of the Jones Construction Company a large order, but I borrowed Mr. Quackenbush's briefcase, so I no longer have to worry about that. The only remaining problem is to put over an order for Earthworms to replace the Gyro-Excavator order.

At the moment I cannot think of any way to do this. So I will consign the entire matter to my subconscious mind. And when I awake tomorrow morning, I am sure to have an answer to what is now a somewhat baffling question.

Yours with hope and good cheer,

Alexander Botts
Sales Manager,
Earthworm Tractor Company

EARTHWORM TRACTOR COMPANY
EARTHWORM CITY, ILLINOIS
Office of Gilbert Henderson, President
Wednesday, September 28, 1960

Dear Botts:

Your letter is here. At various times in the past you have conducted yourself in a manner so erratic and unorthodox as to cause me grave concern. But your recent activities, as related in your letter, are little short of appalling. You impersonate the construction superintendent of a firm to which we had hoped to sell a large order of Earthworm equipment. You give your approval to a completely fraudulent scheme for cheating a real-estate company by charging them for two yards of earth when they will actually be receiving only one. You sign a false name to a sales order. You brazenly accept $5,000 under completely false pretenses. And you make a feeble attempt to justify all this with a line of double talk so transparent that it would not fool a mentally retarded five-year-old.

I am hereby ordering you to do everything you can to clean up this mess as fast as possible. You must notify Mr. Jones of the Jones Construction Company of exactly what has been going on. You will do everything you can to persuade Mr. Jones to buy Earthworm equipment. You will get rid of that tainted $5,000. Any failure on your part to clean up this mess will almost certainly result in irreparable damage to the high reputation of the Earthworm Tractor Company. And it may very likely land you in jail.

Yours,
Gilbert Henderson

Hotel Pennsylvania
Philadelphia, Pennsylvania
Friday, September 30, 1960

Dear Henderson:

I have just returned to Philadelphia and find your letter awaiting me. By a strange coincidence, I had started following at least part of your advice as long ago as last Tuesday—three days before the receipt of your letter. Unfortunately the course of action which you recommended and which I had independently decided upon did not keep me out of jail. On the contrary, it had the effect of landing me in jail with surprising promptness and keeping me there for three days.

I am not blaming you for this, but I do blame you for accusing me, in effect, of moral turpitude. Consider the facts. I found myself confronted by a thoroughly evil conspiracy. If I seemed to take part in this conspiracy, it was only—as I wrote you last Monday—because I was forced to fight fire with fire. I was merely trying to ascertain all the facts, so I could expose the whole filthy plot and bring the slimy perpetrators to justice. I will admit that my plans have not worked out exactly as I had intended. But when I tell you of all the difficulties I have been through, I am sure you will admit that I did my best.

In my letter of last Monday evening I told you that I had not yet decided on a definite course of action and that I was consigning the whole thing to my subconscious mind.

As I was gradually waking up the next morning, an entire plan of action flashed into my conscious mind. I realized that if I were to expose the Potts-Quackenbush conspiracy, I would need something more than my own unsupported story. I would need tangible evidence to prove my charges. And, as I became completely awake, I realized that I had evolved a most promising *modus operandi.* After a good breakfast I sallied forth and found a store where I was able to buy an unusually fine battery-powered, pocket-size tape recorder.

Note: I have entered the cost ($237.99) on my expense account, and I want you to notify our comptroller that this is a necessary business expense and should be passed without question.

I hired a sign painter to paint the words GYRO-EXCAVATOR COMPANY on both sides of my car. While this job was being done, I returned to the hotel, removed from Mr. Quackenbush's briefcase a couple of order blanks and filled them out to correspond to the orders I had signed. After returning them to the briefcase, I destroyed the two signed orders. I transferred to my pockets a number of credit and identification cards made out to George W. Quackenbush. And I removed all of my own personal cards and papers.

Leaving all my baggage in the room, I picked up the Quackenbush briefcase, descended to the lobby and withdrew the money bag from the hotel safe. I told the room clerk that I was leaving and might be gone for several days or even weeks. In the meantime I wished to retain my room.

I then picked up my car at the paint shop, drove to North

Harwood, New Jersey, and parked next to the office trailer of the Jones Construction Company.

I alighted from the car, carrying the Quackenbush briefcase. In the briefcase was the money bag. And in the money bag was the $5,000. The tape recorder was in the side pocket of my coat.

I knocked on the door of the office trailer. It was opened by a man I had never before seen. Unobtrusively I switched on the tape recorder. "Are you Mr. Potts?" I asked.

"Yes."

"My name," I said, "is George W. Quackenbush. If you would be so kind as to step over to yonder machinery shed, I would like to talk to you about the Gyro-Excavator."

We went to the shed and walked in beside the big ungainly machine. Mr. Potts looked at me suspiciously. "What did you say your name is?" he asked.

"George W. Quackenbush. I represent the Gyro-Excavator Company of Indianapolis. Probably you were expecting Chet Morgan?"

"Yes," he said, "I was."

From here on I followed practically the same routine that the real Mr. Quackenbush had used on me the day before. I explained about poor old Chet and his slipped disc. I gave the entire sales pitch about fluffing up the earth. I gradually worked around to the $5,000. And I explained—even more convincingly than the real Mr. Quackenbush—how this payment was a completely ethical honorarium for professional services. Mr. Potts signed the order. And when I finally produced the money, he grabbed it with unmistakable eagerness. As he started to count it, there came an interruption. Two men stepped around from behind the Gyro-Excavator.

Mr. Potts looked at one of these men with astonishment. "Why, it's Mr. Jones," he said. "What are you doing here?"

Mr. Jones seemed angry. "I had heard," he said, "that you were having a Gyro-Excavator shipped out here. I had also heard vague but unproved rumors that the Gyro-Excavator Company has a bad reputation. So I asked my friend here, who happens to be the chief of police of North Harwood, to keep an eye on things. When the machine arrived, he notified me. And today we came out here to look it over. We happened to be standing behind the machine when you came in. And we were just on the point of making our presence known when the conversation became so interesting we could not bear to interrupt you."

Mr. Potts smiled a sickly smile. "I'm so glad," he said, "you happened to hear us. Mr. Quackenbush offered me a bribe, and I pretended to go along, so as to trap him."

"And just how," asked the chief of police, "did you think you were going to trap this man? You did not know you were going to have any witnesses. So, for all you could tell, it would be merely your word against his. You would have no proof."

"Wait a minute," I said. "You are getting this wrong. It is just the opposite of what this man Potts claims. I am the one who was pretending to be a crook, so as to trap him."

"Without any witnesses, as far as you knew?"

Triumphantly I drew the tape recorder from my pocket. "I brought along a very good witness," I said. "I have here a recording of our whole conversation."

The chief was still hostile. "Give me that thing," he ordered. I handed it over. He played part of the recording.

"Now do you believe me?" I asked.

"No," he said. "This is nothing but a scheme for blackmail. If Potts decided to cancel that order or back out of his bargain some other way, you could threaten to expose him by playing the recording before a judge and jury."

"You're all wrong," I said. "If Potts wants to cancel that order it will suit me just fine. My name is not Quackenbush. And I don't represent the Gyro-Excavator Company."

The chief of police made me hand over the briefcase and the contents of my pockets. Everything he found bore the names of Quackenbush and the Gyro-Excavator Company. He even looked out the door and saw the name *Gyro-Excavator* on my car. "All right," he said, "if your name is not Quackenbush, what is it? And if you don't represent the Gyro-Excavator, what do you represent?"

I was just about to blurt out the truth when a restraining thought entered my mind. These people were so suspicious that I was sure they would continue to doubt the purity of my motives. If they found out that I am the sales manager of the Earthworm Tractor Company, they would jump to the conclusion that I had dreamed this whole thing up, had masqueraded as a Gyro-Excavator salesman in order to discredit that company and had deliberately corrupted Mr. Potts so that he could be blackmailed into buying Earthworms. It seemed to me that this was one of the occasions when silence is golden. "Gentlemen," I said, "I have nothing further to say."

The chief of police spoke to Mr. Jones. "If it's all right with you, I think I'll lock up both these characters on charges of bribery and conspiracy to defraud."

"It's all right with me," said Mr. Jones.

Even though I doubted the legality of this arrest, I maintained my discreet silence.

Potts and I were taken to jail and locked up—fortunately in separate cells. That was last Tuesday. For three days I refused to say anything to anybody. I even refused to ask for a lawyer. I just sat there like Henry David Thoreau or any of the other famous men who accomplished great things by merely remaining in jail and doing nothing. For three days I concealed my identity and thus saved the Earthworm Tractor Company from becoming involved in this ugly situation.

This morning my patience was rewarded. Mr. Jones and the chief of police entered my cell. Mr. Jones administered a blistering denunciation—which I will not repeat except to say that he made many of the same points that you, Henderson, made in your last letter.

In conclusion he said, "I don't want to get mixed up in a long and disagreeable court case, so I have dropped all charges against you and Mr. Potts. At my request the chief here is letting both of you go. We have destroyed the tape so you cannot use it for any evil purposes. We are returning your recorder, your briefcase and your filthy money. Your car is waiting for you outside. And you will remove your excavator as soon as possible."

"Thank you," I said.

"I have just fired Mr. Potts," he went on. "Never again will I have any dealings with him. I have destroyed the Gyro-Excavator order. Never again will I have any dealings with that company. And never again will I have any dealings with you."

"I will try to keep out of your way," I said.

"I am placing a large order with the Earthworm Company. And it may interest you to know that in the future I intend to deal exclusively with Earthworm."

"That is indeed most interesting," I said.

And it may interest you, Henderson, to know that as soon as I got back to the hotel here in Philadelphia I mailed the briefcase to Mr. Quackenbush, with an anonymous note asking him to send for his silly excavator. I am keeping the tape recorder. And I am sending you the tainted $5,000. With your refined sense of ethics you will know better than I what to do with it.

All best wishes,

Alexander Botts

ALEXANDER BOTTS
AND THE YOUNGER
GENERATION

EARTHWORM TRACTOR COMPANY
EARTHWORM CITY, ILLINOIS

Gilbert Henderson
Chairman of the Board
Thursday, March 8, 1973

Mr. Alexander Botts
Ripton, Vermont 05766

Dear Botts:

Once more—as I have done a number of times since your retirement as Sales Manager of this company—I want to hire you temporarily as a Special Consultant. I want you to fly out at once to Vancouver, British Columbia, and call on Mr. Andrew MacTavish, the Earthworm Tractor dealer in that city.

Mr. MacTavish has always been one of our most reliable dealers. Recently, however, right in the middle of negotiations for what looks like one of the most important sales of his career, the poor man seems to be losing his grip. In recent letters he refers vaguely to trouble he is having with the "younger generation." And he pays no attention to questions we send him about business matters. Please find out what is the matter, give him any help you can, and report to me as soon as possible.

In offering you this assignment, I feel it is only fair to advise you that our Board of Directors has recently raised strong objections to what they consider exorbitant fees charged by a number of our other

275

Special Consultants. The Board has therefore placed a limit on all moneys paid to Special Consultants of one hundred dollars ($100.00) per day, plus reasonable expenses. I trust this provision will meet with your approval.

Most sincerely,
Gilbert Henderson

ALEXANDER BOTTS
RIPTON, VERMONT 05766

Monday, March 12, 1973

Dear Henderson:

In accepting your assignment, I feel that it is only fair to advise you that it will be necessary for my wife—whom you have always known as "Gadget"—to accompany me on this trip. As you will remember, she has a thorough knowledge of the French language. In Canada, where many of the inhabitants speak French but no English, she will be invaluable as an interpreter—and for other purposes.

We are both leaving for Vancouver as soon as we can get plane reservations. We accept your terms, which we understand mean a fee of one hundred dollars ($100.00) per day for each of us, plus reasonable expenses for both. We trust this provision will meet with your approval.

All best wishes,
Alexander Botts

Thursday, March 15, 1973

Mr. Alexander Botts
Care MacTavish
Earthworm Agency
Vancouver, B.C.

Dear Botts:

As you and your wife have probably left Vermont already, I am sending this letter in care of our Vancouver dealer.

It becomes my painful duty to advise you that your impulsive action in placing your wife as well as yourself on the Earthworm payroll with full expense-account privileges has not been authorized by the company.

I cannot accept your specious reasoning that just because there are many French-speaking Canadians in the easterly Province of Quebec, it follows that you will need a French interpreter to establish communication with a man by the name of MacTavish who lives in the westerly Province of British Columbia where the population is predominantly English or Scottish.

Unless you can think up a more plausible excuse for your attempted raid on the company treasury, I shall be compelled to disallow all claims for compensation or expenses which you may file on behalf of your wife.

Very truly yours,
Gilbert Henderson

Care MacTavish Earthworm Agency
Vancouver, British Columbia

Tuesday, March 20, 1973

Dear Henderson:

Yesterday morning Gadget and I arrived in Vancouver and called on Mr. Andrew MacTavish. He handed me your letter of March 15—which, for the moment, I will ignore because I have more important matters to discuss.

From one point of view Mr. MacTavish has no real troubles; he just thinks he has. But from another point of view—as was once explained by Socrates or William James or one of those people—if a man thinks he is in trouble when he is not in trouble, that is a sign that he is in very serious trouble indeed. Good old Andy, as he likes to be called, is worried about his son. This is not unusual with fathers. But Andy thinks he has more cause for worry than most. To the end that you may understand the situation, I will now give you a much abbreviated version of his long tale of woe, together with a few remarks by Gadget and me.

"For many years," said Andy, "ever since my wife died, my chief concern in life has been the welfare of my only son—my only child—Robert Bruce MacTavish. I call him 'Bob.' As a schoolboy he was one of the finest lads I have ever known—strong, handsome, honest, friendly, intelligent, sensible, diligent in his studies, courteous and well-mannered, admired by old and young, a perfect example of the highest type of Scottish-Canadian youth."

Gadget tried to be appreciative. "A worthy son," she said, "of a worthy father."

Andy paid no attention. "I did the best I could," he said. "I loved that boy so much that I planned his whole life for him. I decided to make him the finest tractor man in all of Canada. As an infant he had toy tractors to play with. Later I took him riding on tractors. By the time he was ten years old—too young for a driver's license—I took him out on back roads in the woods where no misguided police could interfere and I let him drive some of the largest and most complicated Earthworm machines. I always sat beside him on the seat and instructed him so carefully that nothing ever went wrong."

"What a wonderful plan," said Gadget.

"And I did more. I taught him how to repair tractors—how to take them apart and put them together. I taught him how to be proud, rather than ashamed, when he got his hands dirty with good clean grease and oil. I let him travel around with my salesmen so he could learn the kind of sales talk that really sells. He worked in the office so he could learn the financial and paperwork aspects of the business. I was training him to be my first assistant and to take over the entire business when it was time for me to retire."

"You did a wonderful job," said Gadget. "You thought of everything."

"No," said Andy. "I made one hideous mistake. I decided Bob should have a better education than I had. I never went to college. I decided Bob should go."

"A splendid idea," said Gadget.

"That's what you think. That's what I thought. But wait till you hear what happened. When he graduated from high school I sent him to a small supposedly high-grade liberal arts college down in the States where he could receive individual attention from his professors. Well, he got it, all right."

"And that was bad?"

"Horrible. They just naturally brainwashed that boy. When he got home he told me that he was afraid his conscience would not let him go into the tractor business with me. This really shook me up."

"I should think it might."

"Yes. Up to this time I had not talked to him much about his studies. But after this announcement about his conscience, I really began asking questions. 'What's the matter with you?' I wanted to know."

"And what," asked Gadget, "did he say?"

"He claimed the entire capitalistic system is morally wrong. All business is crooked. He is also against a lot of other things."

"Like what?"

"He deplores the literary taste of the twentieth-century public in English-speaking countries. He even claims that most of the wholesome books I gave him before he went to college—books like the novels of Harold Bell Wright and the poems of Edgar A. Guest—are nothing but trash. It seems the only things the Professors of Literature approve of are more or less modern books by authors I never heard of, or else such out-of-date people as Chaucer or Shakespeare."

"Shakespeare," said Gadget, "wrote some good stuff."

"Sure," said Andy. "I will admit that Shakespeare is all right—in his place. But I can't see that he will be much help to my son Bob in the tractor business. You know what they did at that college? They persuaded my son to play the part of Hamlet in a performance they put on in the college theater. And Bob says he is more proud of the way he played Hamlet than of anything else he ever did. Can you imagine that? I had hoped to make him into the world's most successful tractor salesman—and all he wants is to play Hamlet."

By this time, Henderson, you will no doubt realize that the conversation was getting tediously long. Also, the conversation was getting nowhere, so I spoke up to say that Gadget and I were in sympathy with the poor man, and that perhaps the situation was not as bad as he supposed.

"Your son," I said, "is growing up. It is normal, at his age, that he should try to be independent of parental authority, and this in turn makes him temporarily unwilling to listen to your wise counsel. He has been paying more attention to his professors, largely because they are new to him. My wife and I, if we could meet him, would also be new to him. And we might be able to help him in his present state of confusion."

"I doubt if you could be of much help to Bob. But if you want to talk to him I'll ask him to fly you—in our private plane—to a big chromium mine a couple of hundred miles north of here where we are planning an important sales demonstration. Bob is a licensed pilot. You'll have a pleasant trip. And you'll have a chance to get acquainted with Bob. You probably want to go up there anyway. Mr. Gilbert Henderson said so in a letter that arrived just a few days ago."

"That's right," I said. "He wants me to help put over the sale."

"Oh, yeah? I doubt if you would be much help. It is true that Bob claims his conscience won't let him work permanently for me or any other capitalistic enterprise. But he is still working for me temporarily. So there is still a remote possibility he might change his mind. But one difficulty is this girl—"

Gadget promptly spoke up. "*Cherchez la femme*," she said—showing off her knowledge of the French language.

"This girl," Andy continued, "works as a telephone switchboard operator in the hotel at the mine where you are going. Her name is Mimi. Bob met her just recently, but she is already a bad influence. She encourages all his crazy ideas. And the crazier they are, the more she encourages them. But let us get started."

Andy led us to a room down the hall where he introduced us to his

279

son, Bob. The young man looked all right to me. He was neat and clean. And even his hair, though long, was not excessively so. Andy explained what he wanted. Bob agreed. And in less than an hour Bob, Gadget and I were in the air, headed north.

As the plane sped rapidly over the beautiful mountains of British Columbia, Bob remarked that his father had introduced us merely as Mr. and Mrs. Botts, but had not supplied much further information. He said he wanted to be helpful. And he asked politely if we would tell him the exact purpose of our visit. Naturally I did not want to say we were planning to talk him out of some of his crazy ideas. I hesitated. And right away Bob's tone of voice became suspicious.

"Are you, by any chance," he asked, "representing the Earthworm Tractor Company?"

"Yes and no," I replied, making up a plausible explanation as I went along. "For years I was employed by the Earthworm Company—first as a salesman, then as Sales Manager. Later I left the Company, and since than I have been a free agent—sometimes operating completely on my own, and sometimes as a Special Consultant. And all the time I have been a dedicated student of industrial relations. I have also been a reformer—constantly pointing out the mistakes of the higher executives of the Company."

"It sounds to me like an interesting career," said Bob. He was apparently losing his suspicious attitude.

"The career of a reformer," I said, "is always interesting."

The young man launched forth on a long list of ideas—all of which he had apparently learned from his professors—all of which he seemed to consider new and unprecedented—and all of which I had heard before.

As near as I can remember, he was against large corporations, international cartels, overgrown conglomerates, the military-industrial complex, all foreign wars, so-called free enterprise, cutthroat competition, our profit-oriented society, tax loopholes for the rich, exploitation of the masses, dehumanization of assembly-line workers, racial hatred, persecution of minorities, pollution of the environment, chemical fertilizers and insecticides, destruction of our natural resources, corrupt politicians, the degrading influence of the boob tube, public neglect of true art, music and literature, and the pernicious reliance of mankind on machinery.

"Good for you," I said. "I, too, hate machinery! What a blessing it would be if all our machines could be destroyed—all of them!"

"But I didn't say that, Mr. Botts. I don't hate machinery. I sort of like it—that is, I like to drive tractors, and I don't think all machinery ought to be destroyed. It just ought to be sort of—well—kind of controlled—sort of used more sensibly."

I changed the subject. "A little while ago," I said, "you inquired as to the purpose of my visit to British Columbia. By this time you have probably guessed the answer. As a student of industrial relations I want to observe a big sales demonstration that I understand is going on at a mine somewhere up here in the mountains. If you know anything about it, please tell me."

"I know a lot about it, Mr. Botts. I've been up here several times in the past month. My father wants me to work on a big sale we are trying to put over with the company that owns the mine. It's called Metallica, Incorporated. Its home office is in the United States, but it seems to be one of these enormous international corporations that controls mines all over the world. So I am sticking around to see what goes on and try to make up my mind if it is as immoral as I have been told it is to work for a profit-oriented business like my father's Earthworm Tractor agency and to have dealings with a capitalistic monstrosity like this mining outfit."

As Bob finished his resounding pronouncement, I decided to bring out once more my verbal big stick. "Bob," I said, "you should make up your mind right away. All the evidence shows that these great monopolistic corporations are rapidly spreading their evil tentacles over the entire world—especially over Canada."

"Well," said Bob, "I doubt if everybody in the whole United States wants to reduce all Canadians to economic slavery. When I was at that college down in the States I met a lot of good honest people. From what I have seen, most people in the States really like Canadians. And most Canadians seem to like the people down there."

"Right you are," said Gadget. "But don't I see something interesting up ahead?"

Our plane was headed north over a fairly wide mountain valley with a flat floor. Ahead of us, on the east, or right-hand side of the valley, we could see a huge hollow scooped out of the mountain wall a short distance above the valley floor. The curved, inner surface of the hollow was made up of a series of oversized steps or terraces, one above the other. It looked like the grandstand on one side of a football field—only bigger—maybe a mile long and a half-mile high.

"That," said Bob, with an instinctive air of pride, "is the great Rocky River Open Pit Mine. Isn't it wonderful?"

Gadget and I agreed.

"It's not really a pit," Bob explained. "They just call it that because it's open instead of underground. It's sort of like the mines at Bingham Canyon in Utah or at Tahawus in New York State. Just beyond the mine you can see what looks like a narrow cleft in the mountain side. That is the Rocky River Gorge—very narrow and very deep. Can you see it?"

"Yes," I said.

"A short distance up the Gorge is a dam which you can't see from here. It backs up a lake which provides water for electric power. Below the dam the river flows down the gorge and then through the middle of the company town which you can see on the floor of the main valley right at the mouth of the gorge. The big buildings down there are the crushing plant, the smelter, the power house and the company hotel. The smaller houses are the homes of company employees—also a few stores, a church, a school, and so on. The airport is just this side of town. After we land I want to take you on a sight-seeing tour of the whole mining operation."

Bob banked around, made a perfect landing, taxied to a small hangar and drove us in a company car to the company hotel. There was a small amount of late-winter snow left on the ground, but not enough to bother about.

It was now early in the afternoon. Gadget and I got settled in our rooms and then rejoined Bob in the coffee shop, where he introduced us to a good-looking girl.

"This is a friend of mine," said Bob. "Her name is Mimi. She has a job as a telephone switchboard operator here in the hotel. But today she has the whole afternoon off. And I wondered if it would be all right with you if we took her along on our sight-seeing trip."

Gadget and I agreed.

Bob drove us on a zigzag road up the mountain slope until we reached an area between the gorge of the Rocky River and the big open pit mine. Here the road divided into a series of branches leading onto the various benches or terraces. Bob explained how the inner vertical face of each bench is drilled and blasted to break the ore—known as chromite—into chunks about a cubic foot in size.

He went on to explain that up to this time the method of operation has been to use a couple of big power shovels to load the chunks of ore into a fleet of several dozen big motor dump trucks which would haul the stuff down the zigzag road to the crushing plant where it would be converted into fine particles and moved on a conveyor to the electric furnaces in the smelter.

Having described, in a rather dull, routine manner, the previous method of moving the ore, Bob became suddenly enthusiastic as he began talking about the new and improved Earthworm process. To me this was naturally encouraging. Anybody who loved tractors as much as Bob did could not be converted by a lot of mere college professors into a permanent enemy of all machinery.

"Come with me," said Bob, "and I'll show you something really beautiful."

Bob stopped the car. We got out. He led us around a bend in one of the benches and revealed to our astonishment the latest improved model of the great *Earthworm Super-Creeper*. As this mechanical marvel was assembled only a short time ago in our California branch factory, I had never seen it. And since you, Henderson, have probably never seen it either, I will now give you a short description.

At the front end of the Creeper is a magnificent crawler-type Earthworm tractor—the largest I have ever seen. Behind this machine is a train of forty—count them—forty enormous dump wagons, each slightly larger than a railroad boxcar. Each wagon travels on four wheels with pneumatic tires eight feet in diameter, and each wheel is driven, through planetary gears, by an electric motor which receives its electric current through heavy insulated cables from a powerful generator connected to a diesel engine in the lead tractor. The tractor and the forty wagons are hitched, each to each, by special double-X couplings equipped with automatic electronic controls which insure that each vehicle follows the exact track of the vehicle in front—thus enabling the entire Super-Creeper to go around even the sharpest curves and follow all the zigs and zags of the road without getting out of line.

After we had all admired the Super-Creeper for some time, Bob explained that the local manager of the mine had shut down all operations for a couple of days so that preparations could be completed for the big demonstration the next day.

"And," said Bob, "it will be a real honest-to-goodness big demonstration. You will notice that all these dump wagons are empty. Behind them are four small but fast-working Earthworm loaders. The ore has already been blasted out of the rock face, and when we start work tomorrow morning with our high-grade crew of mechanics and operators, we'll load that ore, run it down to the crushing plant, and come back for a second load so fast and so smooth that all the people around here will have their mouths hanging open with astonishment. And that's not all. His Royal Highness, the Grand Mogul himself, will be here. He is flying up in his private plane all the way from New York, and bringing his family. He will stop off in Vancouver to pick up my father. They are due to arrive late this afternoon. Tonight they will be at the hotel. And tomorrow they will be on hand for the big demonstration."

"And just who," I asked, "is this Grand Mogul?"

"He is the president of Metallica, Incorporated, the big corporation that owns mines all over the world, including this one. He is the big boss—the head man. His name—believe it or not—is Howard Randolph Hildebrand. That means his initials are H.R.H. So most of the people around here call him His Royal Highness. But not to his face, of course."

"Apparently," I said, "His Royal Highness is a typical example of the wealthy, capitalistic dictator—arrogant, intolerant and so powerful that nobody dares show the slightest disrespect in his presence."

Bob thought this over. Then he said, "Mr. Botts, I wonder sometimes if you don't love an argument so much that you just naturally take the opposite side of everything. Do you really believe that His Royal Highness is as bad as you say? After all, you have never met him."

"Bob," I said, "you are a man of keen perceptions. You have correctly analyzed my basic habits of thought. Of course I like a good argument. Of course I take the opposite side. How else can I arrive at the truth? I admit I sometimes make wild statements. But I hope you will believe me when I say that I agree with your thoughtful attitude toward capitalism, and that I agree we should wait until we learn more about His Royal Highness before we make any final judgments."

Said Bob, "Mr. Botts, talking with a man like you is a real privilege."

On this happy note our conversation ended. We turned to Gadget and Mimi, and Bob drove the four of us back to the hotel. Here Bob and Mimi excused themselves to attend a young people's party at one of the homes in town. Gadget and I sat down to a good dinner in the hotel dining room. And Gadget reported on her conversation with Mimi when the two of them were walking around together at the mine.

"It was delightful," said Gadget, "to talk to a girl who is so intelligent and yet so artless in her enthusiasms. She hardly knows me, but as soon as we were alone she started telling me all about Bob."

"She could see right away," I said, "that you are understanding and sympathetic, and that she could trust you."

"Maybe so," said Gadget. "Anyway, she told me that Bob is the finest man she ever met. He is just wonderful. They have long talks about his plans—how he will give up all thought of mere money-making, getting married, raising a family, and all that sort of dull, bourgeois existence. Instead, he will pursue his true destiny—helping to create a finer society. And Mimi says she tells Bob she agrees with everything he says."

"You mean she really believes all the hogwash that Bob puts out?"

"Of course not. She just tells him that because she's in love with him. It's perfectly natural."

"I don't believe it," I said. "No decent girl, just because she is chasing a man, would ever pretend that she likes all his silly ideas."

"I once knew a girl," said Gadget, "who was chasing a tractor salesman, and she pretended that she liked his silly tractors."

"I don't believe that either," I said. "You know very well that you never had to pretend. You have always liked tractors—especially Earthworms. And you never thought they were silly."

"Let us return," said Gadget, "to the subject of Mimi. After she had expressed her complete approval of everything Bob told her, I mildly suggested that perhaps Bob might be able to accomplish more in the way of social reform if he broke away from his intellectual professorial friends and started working for his father in the tractor business where he would be in closer touch with the common people. I also said that if he was earning a good income he would be better able to support a wife. And if he found the right girl she would be such an inspiration to him that he could carry on his work with a warmth and understanding that might otherwise be impossible."

"And what," I asked, "did Mimi say to all that?"

"She just said, in a sort of wistful voice, that she hoped and prayed Bob would find the right girl."

"What's the matter with her?" I asked. "Doesn't she know Bob has already found the right girl?"

"She knows it all right. But she's afraid to say it out loud. It seems too marvelous to be true."

As I could think of nothing helpful to add to the conversation, I pointed out that we had finished our dinner, and I suggested that we go up to our room. We did so, and I have been spending the rest of the evening pounding out this letter on my portable typewriter.

In conclusion, I am happy to report that everything is going better than anybody could have expected. His Royal Highness and old Andy MacTavish, after a slight delay, are due to arrive later this evening. They will be on hand for the big demonstration tomorrow. The sale of the Super-Creeper will go over with a bang. Bob and Mimi, largely because of Gadget's wise counsel, will complete their return to sanity. Bob will take a permanent job with his father. It will be obvious to all that, even though there has been no need for a French interpreter, I was right in bringing along Gadget. And everybody will be happy, including your highly effective Special Consultant,

Alexander Botts

Vancouver, British Columbia
Thursday, March 22, 1973

Dear Henderson:

I regret to report that the big show scheduled for yesterday at the mine has resulted in total disaster. At a critical moment our friend Bob, from whom we had expected so much, suddenly reverted to his previous state of mental derangement, tried to play Hamlet, and wrecked the entire project. The demonstration was a miserable failure. The Super-Creeper is a total loss. All chance of making a sale is gone. And both His Royal Highness and I are in a hospital in Vancouver. It seems to be a good hospital, but that is small consolation for the veritable holocaust of destruction that has engulfed us.

The doctor says I need rest and quiet. He persuaded me to stay in bed. But when he tried to prevent me from writing this letter to you, I raised such an uproar that he finally consented to bring in a stenographer—to whom I am dictating these remarks. I am afraid you may have received inaccurate reports of what has been going on. I feel it my duty, therefore, to give you the whole truth—including the fact that I am not in any way to blame for any of the misfortunes that have occurred. Nor is Gadget in any way to blame. Having made this important point, I will now try to pull myself together and give you a calm and factual account of this whole regrettable affair— starting at the beginning.

Yesterday morning up at the mine, Gadget and I had breakfast with Old Andy and Bob and with His Royal Highness, whom I will refer to from now on as H.R.H. He looks important, but acts and talks like a regular guy. Also present was a technical advisor to H.R.H.—a professor from some sort of engineering school.

After breakfast H.R.H. told us that his family—his wife and two children—who had come along mainly to enjoy the plane ride and the beautiful mountain scenery—would not be able to attend the demonstration. The children had contracted colds, and their mother would stay with them in their hotel room.

Bob told Gadget that Mimi would not come along either; she had to work at her job all morning. Then Bob brought around the company car and drove us up the zigzag road. We all got out. And the big demonstration began. You have seen so many demonstrations,

Henderson, that I will not describe it in detail—merely stating that the first round went off very well. The Super-Creeper did its Super-Creeping with precision. The loaders filled the dump wagons with surprising speed. The whole works zigzagged down to the crushing plant, dumped the ore and returned so fast that the professor from the engineering school was overwhelmed.

Turning to H.R.H., he exclaimed, "These Earthworms are the finest machines I have ever seen! They are fantastic!"

The second round began. Once more the Super-Creeper came around the bench. Once more the loaders filled the dump wagons to overflowing. The whole magnificent mechanism approached the place where it was supposed to turn off onto the zigzag road. Our little group of admiring spectators was standing nearby. We gave a spontaneous cheer.

Then everything came apart. The ground beneath our feet began to shudder and sway. Deep down we could hear the rocks groaning and growling. Cracks began to open in the solid earth. Rocks began slipping and rolling down the slopes. Far away on the mountain sides we could see the leaves on the trees shivering and shaking.

People began yelling "Earthquake! Earthquake!" And that is what it was. It was purely local. Nobody down here in Vancouver felt it. But up there at the mine it was really something. It was such a jolt to our feelings that I suppose all of us went just a little bit crazy. And we all responded, each in his own way, by trying to save whatever we loved the most.

The tractor driver jumped off his machine and ran away—probably trying to save his own skin.

The professor began a frantic search for a book that had got away from him.

Gadget and I just grabbed each other.

H.R.H. let out a yelp of agony: "That hotel is going to fall down on my family. I got to get down there and help them." He leaped into the company car, started it, and promptly smashed it into a big rock slide that was coming down the slope.

Bob just stood there like Hamlet, trying to decide what to do—and doing nothing.

Gadget began to yell at him: "Bob! Mimi is in that hotel, and it's going to fall down on her! Do something!"

Bob went into action—like a wild man. He leaped in the air and landed running. He headed down the zigzag road, veered off toward the deep gorge of the Rocky River, caught himself on the very edge, turned around, ran back, jumped in the seat of the tractor and started driving down the zigzag road at the three-mile-an-hour top speed of the machine. He could have reached his beloved Mimi quicker by running. But he was too frantic to think straight. He never stopped to unhitch the wagons, so they followed along. Almost at once the tractor seemed to go completely out of control. It lurched off the road, headed for the gorge, and plunged over the rim. Bob saved himself by jumping off the tractor at the last moment. But that whole beautiful Super-Creeper—first the tractor and then all forty wagons—disappeared in depths. And then came the final disaster. There was another earthquake shock—worse than the first. A much bigger rock slide came down the slope. Apparently something hit me on the head. And the next I knew I was on an ambulance plane on the way to Vancouver.

Gadget came along. She wasn't injured. She is with me here in the hospital. She says H.R.H. got caught in the same rock slide, and he is in another room here in the same hospital. The doctor says each of us will make a complete and speedy recovery. We are supposed to rest, so I will close with a summary of the situation:

1. Neither Gadget nor I is to blame for the earthquake.

2. As a realist, I admit things do not look good. How can we solve Old Andy's troubles with the younger generation when the younger generation has gone crazy? And how can we sell a Super-Creeper when the only one we have is a total wreck in the bottom of the Rocky Creek Gorge?

3. As an optimist, I trust that before long something will turn up. What, I don't know.

Gadget joins in best wishes.

Alexander Botts

P.S. The next day, Friday, March 23, 1973. Just as I expected, something has turned up. In fact, several things have turned up. This morning the doctor said I could sit up in bed and have some visitors, so Gadget brought in Bob, who had flown in the day before in his father's plane from the mine. He started making excuses for his recent conduct.

"Ever since I played Hamlet in that school play," he said, "I have tended to identify with the character. I have always hesitated. But I have always hoped that in a real crisis I would react with vigor—just like Hamlet at the end of the play. Well, the crisis came day before yesterday."

"And you reacted with vigor. So what?"

"When that earthquake struck," said Bob, "I didn't know at first what to do. But when Mrs. Botts mentioned Mimi my brain really began to work. I did about an hour's thinking in a tenth of a second—sort of like a computer."

"And what did you think?"

"I thought I ought to go into action, but not the way Hamlet went into action. That guy could talk all right. He was always spouting wonderful quotations. But when he actually did something, he did it wrong, and the results were terrible. I still remember the curtain call we took at the end of the play."

"This was when you played Hamlet at college?"

"Yes. Ten of us came out to acknowledge the applause. Only one—Horatio—was supposed to be alive. The other nine were theoretically dead—The Ghost, Polonius, Ophelia, Rosencrantz, Guildenstern, Queen Gertrude, Laertes, King Claudius, and Hamlet, who was played by me."

"Listen," I said. "Does all this have anything to do with your performance up at the mine?"

"Certainly. I wanted to act with vigor. But I didn't want to kill anybody. I just wanted to find Mimi. I wanted to save Mimi. So I started running down the road, and I ran so fast that I sort of skidded off the road and over to the edge of the gorge, I looked down. And there was that concrete dam—all cracked by the earthquake and shaking and starting to come apart. Water was already pouring through the cracks."

"And that's when you started thinking fast—like a computer?"

"I sure did. I knew there was a big lake upstream from the dam. I knew there was a town downstream from the dam. And I knew Mimi was in that town. If the dam went out it would be just like the Johnstown Flood that my grandfather used to talk about. For a moment I felt hopeless. Then I remembered something."

"Yes, yes. Go on."

"I remembered that book I read when I was in high school. It was *The Winning of Barbara Worth*, by Harold Bell Wright. My English professor was probably correct when he said it was wretchedly written. There wasn't a single good quotation in the whole thing. But it had a good ending."

"Better than *Hamlet?*"

"Much better. There was a flood in that Barbara Worth book. The gates of an irrigation ditch washed out, and the whole Colorado River came pouring down into what is now the Imperial Valley in California. Everybody gave up hope except one young engineer. He organized a rescue crew. They brought in hundreds of railroad freight car loads of rock, dumped them into the stream, and made a makeshift dam that saved the whole valley—including a girl named Barbara. I decided that if that young engineer could save an entire valley, I could save one little town—including a girl named Mimi.

That's why I ran the Super-Creeper into the gorge. But the man who had been driving it claims I made a fool of myself. He says that even though the dam cracked a little it would never have gone completely to pieces. So I just destroyed a million dollars' worth of machinery—and took his job away from him—all for nothing."

"He might be prejudiced," I said. "Have you heard from anyone else on the subject?"

"I asked His Royal Highness about it this morning. He's in the next room down the hall here."

"What did he say?"

"He wouldn't say anything—one way or the other. So I may be in wrong sure enough. But everything else is all right. There was no flood. The earthquake was just a local rock-slippage under the mine. It hit the mine and the dam pretty hard. But there was only minor damage to the town, and nobody there was hurt. If necessary, the old dam will be replaced by a new one—stronger and earthquake-proof, they hope."

Bob was interrupted by a new group of visitors. H.R.H. arrived in a wheelchair, followed by various people who had just been flown in from the mine—the professor, two men who were introduced as consulting engineers, H.R.H.'s wife and children, Old Andy, and Mimi, herself.

Old Andy came over to my bed and told me that he had just been talking with you, Henderson, by long-distance telephone. He said he told you that after Gadget and I had conferred with Bob and Mimi, all his troubles with the younger generation had disappeared, and everything was fine. He must have been unusually enthusiastic, especially about Gadget, because he claimed that you told him to tell me that all is forgiven and both Gadget and I will be paid in full. This pleasant news prompts me to say thank you and I told you so.

When Old Andy finished speaking, H.R.H. called to me from across the room. "Have you heard the latest news from the mine, Mr. Botts? The dam can be rebuilt. The Super-Creeper is a total loss. But it was worth it. Of course it was the property of Old Andy or the Earthworm Company, and I want them to know that our company will repay any loss not covered by insurance."

"Thank you," said Andy.

H.R.H. continued, "These two engineers who flew up to the mine yesterday have made a complete investigation. They assure me that when this young man, Bob, ran all that machinery and rock into the gorge, he blocked the stream just long enough to let the lake drain out slowly and harmlessly. Otherwise there would have been a tremendous rush of water that would have wiped out the whole town. Thus, at a cost of only a million dollars, Bob has saved many million dollars' worth of property, and what is much more important, he has saved hundreds of lives, including my own wife and children. We all owe him a big debt of gratitude."

There was a lusty cheer from all present, and Mimi stepped up and kissed her hero.

H.R.H. spoke to Bob: "Now that I have expert engineering proof of everything you have done for our company, I have come to a definite decision on the matter we were discussing yesterday. I have decided, on the basis of that short but convincing demonstration, that we are going to need two complete Super-Crawlers at the mine—just as soon as they can be manufactured and delivered. And I want you to handle the sale—partly because you would receive a good commission, which you have—in an indirect way—so richly deserved. What do you say?"

"I suspected something like this might happen," said Bob. "So I have the order here in my pocket—all made out for one Super-Creeper. That's all I expected. But I can easily change it to two. There is just one thing more." He turned to Mimi. "Do you think it would be morally right," he asked, "for me to join my father's profit-oriented business and deal with this giant multinational corporation?"

"I think," said Mimi, "it would be immoral for you to do anything else."

Bob produced the order and changed a "one" to a "two." Being careful businessmen, they both initialed the change in the margin. And H.R.H. signed his full name, Howard Randolph Hildebrand, on the dotted line. And that was that.

In closing, I am happy to report Gadget and I are leaving for home tomorrow. We are planning a cruise next June to Norway to see the Midnight Sun. And, during our absence, we are turning over our summer home in Ripton, Vermont, to Bob and Mimi for their honeymoon.

All best wishes,
Alexander Botts.

ALEXANDER BOTTS, DETECTIVE

EARTHWORM TRACTOR COMPANY
EARTHWORM CITY, ILLINOIS

Office of Gilbert Henderson
Chairman of the Board
Thursday, May 23, 1974

Mr. Alexander Botts
Ripton, Vermont 05766

Dear Botts:

Since your retirement several years ago as Sales Manager you have served the Company so well on various assignments as temporary Special Representative that I am hoping you will help us out once more.

We have just received a letter from Mike Warner, our dealer in South Gumbo Parish, Louisiana, stating that one of his best customers has just canceled a big order for Earthworm equipment, has decided to sell out his successful contracting business and invest the entire proceeds with a man Mike describes as a clever swindler who is promoting a wild scheme for building a large health resort in South Gumbo. This resort will attempt to cure rheumatism, arthritis, and almost all other known diseases by subjecting the patients to hot baths in mud extracted from the swamps of the area. Mike says he has protested violently against this scheme—in vain. He asks if I have any suggestions.

My reaction is that anybody who claims to cure almost all known diseases by smearing the victim with hot mud is obviously a crook who should be exposed. As long as one of our dealers and one of his best customers seem to be involved in the affair, it is proper that the Earthworm Company should offer as much help as possible.

I am therefore writing Mike that I am asking you to go to Louisiana and do everything you can to solve this problem. Presumably you know nothing about mud baths. But you understand people. And you have the type of devious mind that can analyze the thought processes of criminals—as was proved by your recent solving of the Mohole swindle in Vermont.

Kindly proceed to South Gumbo at once. You will receive the usual stipend plus expenses.

Most sincerely,
Gilbert Henderson.

South Gumbo Motel
South Gumbo, Louisiana
Monday, May 27, 1974

Dear Henderson:

Your letter reached me back in Ripton, Vermont, last Saturday, and I got busy at once. First of all I tried to persuade my wife, Gadget, to come to South Gumbo with me. As you and I both realize, she would have been most valuable as an advisor in the sort of delicate negotiations I shall be called upon to handle down here. Unfortunately, however, she was unable to leave Ripton at this time. As I know you will be as disappointed as I am, I will explain the circumstances in full so that you will not blame either her or me for her failure to respond. The situation is as follows:

It appears that the beautiful old Community House in Ripton Hollow has been so neglected in recent years that it has begun to decay, rot and fall to pieces. And the local citizenry has decided, quite properly, that something should be done.

In the old days there would have been a local campaign to raise funds for the repairs. But, as you are probably too old to realize, Henderson, we now live in a new age. So something called an ad hoc committee was formed. Gadget became a member. An appeal was sent to some agency in Washington. And before long the ancient Community House was declared some sort of historical monument or shrine. This, in turn, automatically opened the floodgates of Federal and State aid. And the ad hoc committee, including Gadget, is now feverishly at work trying to persuade the authorities in both Washington and Montpelier to allocate as much cash as possible. I think the committee would like a million dollars, but would probably settle for forty thousand.

And now, having explained why Gadget is not with me, I will discuss my adventures since leaving Ripton.

I was able to get a plane out of Burlington, Vermont, last Saturday—the same day your letter arrived. I landed in New Orleans on Sunday, rented a car, drove to South Gumbo, and checked into the South Gumbo Motel last night—Sunday.

This morning I called on Mike Warner, our dealer. His place of business looked prosperous. But Mike himself was in a dismal mood. Business, he said, is rotten. Inflation is ruining the economy. The whole country is going to the dogs. Greed and corruption are rampant. And he could not see any hope for the future. After he had run on for some time with his prophecies of doom, I was able to get in a word or two.

"I have been told," I said, "that one of your best customers is being taken for a ride by a swindler of some kind."

"He used to be one of my best customers," said Mike. "But not anymore. He has gone crazy like everybody else."

"Can you tell me some more about it?" I asked sympathetically.

"It's a sad case. The man's name is John Bradley. He was born right here in South Gumbo. He used to be one of the finest young men I have ever known—honest, intelligent, hardworking, progressive. Ten years ago, when he was just twenty-one years old, he started in the contracting business. At first it was small jobs. Then he got bigger and bigger contracts—mostly roads and levees. He made money on all of them. He gradually built up a big fleet of Earthworm machinery. He paid for everything as he went along. And now, at the age of thirty-one, he's going to throw it all away."

"It sounds incredible," I said.

"It's true. He is planning to sell his whole business and put everything into this fool mud-wallowing foolishness. And that's not all. He recently got married to a dizzy dumbbell from New Orleans, and she is a bad influence. She encourages him in all his crackpot ideas. The whole situation is practically hopeless."

"I must admit," I said, "that it sounds bad. But I have had a lot of experience with difficult problems. If you would introduce me to the young man, it is just possible that I might be able to talk some sense into him. When can we go?"

"You can go anytime you want. But I won't go with you. I refuse to waste any more of my time on any such brainless jackass."

"How do I find the guy?"

"Take the main highway in front of the building here. Drive south a couple of miles. You'll see a lot of Earthworm equipment parked outside a big repair shop and storage shed. A few hundred yards farther on is a white house. That's where he lives."

"Thank you," I said, politely. "You have been most helpful." I drove down the main highway, past the John Bradley construction headquarters, and knocked on the door of the white house Mike had described. The door was opened by young John Bradley himself, and I proceeded to ingratiate myself at once.

"My name," I said, "is Alexander Botts. I represent the Earthworm Tractor Company. And I am here to congratulate you on your wisdom and good judgment in recognizing the sensational possibilities of the remarkable health project I understand you are promoting—a project destined to make South Gumbo one of the outstanding health centers of the world."

As I had expected, the young man seemed pleased and flattered by my words. He ushered me into a pleasant living room and introduced me to his wife. Her name is Mary. She seems to be a nice girl. Her husband seems to be a nice guy. And almost at once I was struck by the contrasting personalities of the three people I had so recently met in this remote locality. On the one hand there was our poor old dealer, Mike Warner—dull, dismal, discouraged. On the other hand was this splendid youthful couple, John and Mary—handsome, happy, hopeful.

I decided to get in as strong as possible with John and Mary by agreeing with everything they said—thus encouraging them to talk enthusiastically and reveal all the facts I would have to know if I were to work out a satisfactory solution to the various difficulties confronting us.

"Just how," I asked, "did you people first become interested in this mud-bath business?"

Right away Mary brightened up. "It was very exciting," she said. "One day last week John and I heard a noise outside—sort of like an Earthworm tractor engine, only different. So we rushed out. It was a helicopter. Imagine that! And it landed right in our front yard."

"Yes," said John. "And a man got out and asked if he could rent one of our backhoes for a couple of days."

"The man's name," said Mary, "is Augustus Anthony. He is a very important person. He's a scientist, and also a sort of financier who develops big enterprises."

"Usually," said John, "I wouldn't rent out a backhoe to a man I didn't know. But this guy seemed to have plenty of money. He told us he was a licensed helicopter pilot, and he said he had rented the helicopter in New Orleans. Also he had plenty of identification and credit cards. So I let him store his old whirlybird in one of my machinery sheds, and he drove off down the road in one of my backhoes."

"A backhoe," Mary explained, "is a sort of power shovel—only it works backward. It's used to dig ditches and holes in the ground."

"Yes, I know," I said. "What was the man going to do with the machine?"

"He told us," said Mary, "that he was doing some scientific exploration of a confidential nature. He had to do the work alone. And he didn't want anybody following him. So we let him drive away all by himself. The next day he came back, paid the rent for the machine, and reported his explorations had been so successful that he could tell us what he had been doing."

"And what did he say?" I asked.

"As near as I can remember," said John, "he claimed he had spent the past few months making a deep study of geological maps and government mineralogical reports dealing with the presence of lithia springs in close proximity to nonacidulous, semi-organic silt or mud deposits. I hope I've got that straight. You see this Mr. Anthony is a very learned scientist and he uses a lot of scientific terms I don't understand."

"You seem to be doing fine," I said.

"He certainly is," said Mary, proudly. "John never went to college, but he has a real brain."

"I'm sure of it," I said. "From what you have told me, I assume this Mr. Anthony hoped that right here in Louisiana he might find the exact blend of mud and lithia water that he wanted. Is that correct?"

"It is," said John. "He reported that he had dug up some very promising samples and had sent them to a laboratory at the Florida Technological University to be analyzed. If the results show the proper chemical composition that is needed for effective treatment of rheumatism and arthritis, Mr. Anthony says he will build a magnificent million-dollar health resort right here in South Gumbo Parish."

"This Mr. Anthony sounds wonderful," I said. "I would like to meet him. Do you think it could be arranged?"

"I don't see why not," said John. "He is living in a small rented boat house in a clearing on the shore of a bayou about two miles from here. The hole where he dug up his sample is right next to the boat house. He flew Mary and me down there in his helicopter yesterday. And I was so impressed with everything he told me that I am trying to persuade him to let me invest in his project."

"It is a wonderful opportunity," said Mary.

"I feel the same way," I said. "I would like to invest in this thing myself. And perhaps the Earthworm Tractor Company would also be interested."

"We could drive down there right now in my car," said John. "There is a back road."

"Let's go," I said.

The three of us got in John's car and drove down through a sort of scrubby growth that I think is called a canebrake. At the boat house we were welcomed by Mr. Augustus Anthony himself. He turned out to be even more impressive than I had expected—tall, middle-aged, dressed in stylish outdoor clothing, and with a black moustache, waxed and pointed at the ends in a way that made him look like a French count in an old-fashioned movie.

We all sat down on a bench outside the boat house, and Mr. Anthony gave us a scientific explanation of the therapeutic value of mud baths.

"The idea is not new," he said. "At one time this method of treatment was accepted by almost everybody. Later it became neglected. But recently medical authorities have come to realize that many of the older practices were highly effective. One good example is the use of folk medicines such as honey and vinegar. Another is the employment of specially selected medicinal mud."

Mr. Anthony paused. We waited expectantly. And suddenly this remarkable man gave us some information that revealed what is probably one of the most incredible coincidences in the entire history of the world. And the coincidence provided such a complete answer to the problems I was trying to solve that I will now, Henderson, give you a detailed account of everything that was said. I want you to have a complete understanding of the situation.

"Last year," said Mr. Anthony, "after considerable research, I succeeded in unearthing the story of an unusual mud bath sanitarium that flourished in the early years of this century. I had already, as a boy, heard my grandfather tell of how he had visited the place, and how it had cured his arthritis. But it was not until last year that I learned the entire story of the place—a story that has been largely forgotten. As Longfellow might have put it: 'Hardly a man is now alive who remembers that famous clay and smear.' The name of the place was Mudlavia, Indiana."

At these words I sprang to my feet. "Mudlavia!" I cried, "Mudlavia! What do you mean, 'hardly a man'? I remember the place well. I was there for almost six weeks. I know all about it, the way it used to be, that is."

John and Mary and Mr. Anthony looked at me in astonishment.

"It was back in the year 1904," I explained. "I was twelve years old. I had an uncle named Zebulon B. Botts. He was my father's brother. And he suffered from what he called the 'rheumatiz.' He heard of Mudlavia. He decided to go. I was his favorite nephew. So he offered to take me along. He thought I would enjoy the trip."

"And did you?" asked Mr. Anthony.

"It was wonderful!" I was just about to embark on a long series of delightful reminiscences, when I decided to use the occasion by employing my inborn craftiness and guile for the purpose of testing the man's real knowledge of Mudlavia by asking him a number of searching questions.

"My memories of Mudlavia are vivid," I said. "But it was all so long ago that I am no longer certain of all details. Perhaps, Mr. Anthony, you can help me remember. Just how was this mud bath applied?"

"I can tell you exactly. I was able to secure an old brochure published by the institution. It states that the mud was dug from a nearby deposit—a sort of marsh that was fed by several lithia springs. The lithia, of course, was the primary curative agent—along with the heat. While the heat was drawing out the poisons from the body, the lithia was being absorbed and starting its benevolent action on the diseased tissues."

"Thank you," I said, "for refreshing my memory. I remember that old swamp perfectly—along with those lithia springs."

Mr. Anthony continued his explanations: "After the mud was dug up, it was taken to the processing room where impurities were removed. It was then heated and taken to the bathhouse where it was spread on waterproof cots. Each patient, after removing his clothes, would lie down on one of these cots, with his head on a clean pillow. An attendant would then cover him with more hot mud. And he would remain in this pack for the prescribed length of time—maybe half an hour. Then he would take a shower, followed by a nap or rest period."

"How it all comes back to me," I said. "The management was kind enough to let me take a mud bath every time Uncle Zeb did. How well I remember those happy times when I was allowed to wallow in all that hot muck and stew in my own juice. You have described it exactly. It was marvelous."

"I was wondering," said Mary. "Did it help you or your Uncle Zeb?"

"I think it cured Uncle Zeb's rheumatiz—at least partly. But of course it didn't cure me of anything. At the time there was nothing the matter with me. I just took the baths for aesthetic reasons. But I am hoping Mr. Anthony can clear up a few more points. Wasn't there a river near Mudlavia?"

"There was, indeed. The Wabash."

"Right you are. And wasn't there a song about it?"

"Certainly," said Mr. Anthony. " 'On the Banks of the Wabash, Far Away.' "

"And didn't the song mention the moon, and trees, and hay?"

"I can't remember the exact words, but I think the moonlight was fair along the Wabash, candlelight was gleaming through the sycamores, and you could smell the scent of new-mown hay—or something like that."

"And the song was correct," I said. "I remember the moon, the sycamore trees and the hay. But no candles. The sanitarium was up-to-date and had electric lights. And no wonder the dope was correct. The man that wrote the song was taking the cure at Mudlavia at the same time I was there. He was a nice guy. I wish I could remember his name."

"My researchers have covered that," said Mr. Anthony. "The man's name was Paul Dresser. He was a famous songwriter with such hits as 'My Gal Sal,' 'The Blue and the Gray' and others. Also he had a kid brother who helped with the words of the Wabash song."

"Sure," I said. "The kid brother wrote books under the name of Theodore Dreiser."

"Incidentally," said Mary, "just how did Mudlavia get its name? Did these Dresser-Dreiser boys dream it up?"

"No," said Mr. Anthony. "Apparently the man who founded the institution thought up the name. It is derived from the Middle English *mudde* pronounced mudda, and meaning mud, plus the Latin *lavare*, meaning to take a bath."

"It's just too cute for words," said Mary, smiling happily. "You go to Mudlavia and you taka da batha in da mudda."

At this point I decided to get away from the jokes as tactfully as possible and bring the discussion back to hard facts. "It has been a delightful occasion," I said. "I have deeply appreciated the way you, Mr. Anthony, have renewed my boyhood. And you have done much more. You have convinced me, by your accurate and wide-ranging knowledge of all aspects of mudbath therapy, that you are completely competent to revive this beneficent activity here in Louisiana. I hereby congratulate John and Mary on their decision to invest in this enterprise. I would like to contribute. And I will advise the Earthworm Tractor Company that your project would be a good place for them to put any extra cash that they may have lying around."

Mr. Anthony promptly replied in a way that revealed his innate honesty. "I thank you," he said, "for your expression of confidence in my enterprise. But I could not even consider accepting any money from any of you until we receive the report from the chemical analysis. If the mud contains the requisite amount of lithia, well and good. If not, the deal is off."

On this friendly note, Mary and John and I said good-bye and returned to the Bradley home. Once more I assured this splendid young couple of my complete confidence in Mr. Anthony. I then drove back to the motel, where I have been writing this report—which I have decided not to mail at once.

I know you well enough, Henderson, to realize that if you were to receive nothing more than this incomplete account of the situation here you would at once send me a lot of half-baked destructive criticism, denouncing Mr. Anthony as a criminal, refusing to admit that he should be considered innocent until proved guilty, and in general telling me nothing that would be of any help in solving any of the difficulties confronting me. As soon as I have anything constructive to tell you, I will complete and mail this letter.

Two days later.
Wednesday, May 29, 1974.

I resume my hitherto unfinished letter to announce a whole series of unexpected events. Yesterday I called at the home of John and Mary Bradley. They were in conference with Mr. Augustus Anthony. They welcomed me. And Mr. Anthony repeated an announcement he had just made to John and Mary.

"I regret to tell you," he said, "that the report from the laboratory is negative. There is no lithia at all in the sample I sent in. The mud is useless for medicinal purposes. Our hopes for a great health resort in South Gumbo Parish are gone. The project is dead."

John and Mary were deeply disappointed. "It's just too bad," said Mary. "I feel so sorry for you, Mr. Anthony. All your work has gone for nothing."

Mr. Anthony was philosophical. "Don't worry about me," he said. "I lose a few. I win a few. And I always have many more projects in process of development."

"Really?" said Mary.

"Absolutely. My activities encompass a broad spectrum. I try to emulate Leonardo da Vinci and Benjamin Franklin—men who pursued all wisdom and all knowledge—scorning to limit themselves to narrow specialties. Such men always have failures. Leonardo designed flying machines that never flew. Franklin practically discovered electricity but was never even able to build an electric doorbell."

Mary was fascinated. "And what are you working on now?"

"I am studying the economic angles of inflation."

"You mean the high cost of living?"

"I am dealing with basic causes. Inflation is merely more money and credit than is needed to buy the goods being offered for sale. The result is high prices—which cause problems."

"I'll say," said Mary.

"Shallow thinkers," continued Mr. Anthony, "try to solve these problems by foolish methods. For instance, they loudly demand wage and price controls—which never work. They demand that Congress spend less money—which is even more idiotic. Congress is just naturally set up to pour out money. How else can Congressmen persuade people to vote for them?"

"You mean," asked Mary, "that the situation is hopeless?"

"Not at all. Instead of vainly trying to cut down on the money supply, we should devise means for producing more goods."

"Such as?"

"Take gasoline. There is at present not enough. So the filling stations raise the price. And the consumers have to pay more or do without. On the other hand, take the water in this nearby bayou. There is more than anybody needs. Suppose somebody owns the bayou and tries to sell the water at a high price. Nobody needs the water at the high price. So the price remains at almost nothing. And the answer is obvious."

"If people won't pay fifty or sixty cents a gallon for this bayou water, all you have to do is convert the bayou water into gasoline, and right away the price of gasoline will go down."

"Wait a minute," I said. "All this pseudoscientific economic flapdoodle is merely for the birds, because you can't convert water into gasoline. It can't be done."

"Are you sure?"

"Certainly. If you have been in the tractor business as long as I have, you would know that gasoline is made up almost entirely of hydrocarbons—compounds of hydrogen and carbon. Lately there has been some slight success in making gasoline from garbage or almost any refuse that contains these two elements. It takes expensive machinery—but it can be done. On the other hand, water is only hydrogen and oxygen. There is no carbon."

"I see what you mean," said Mary, brightening up. "Apparently you can make bricks without straw—in spite of what it says in the Bible. But you can't make gasoline without carbon. It's sort of like that old wisecrack about the silk purse and the cow's ear."

"I think it was a sow," said Mr. Anthony, pleasantly. "But that makes no difference. The important thing is that you, Mary, have a truly scientific mind."

"Honestly?"

"Yes. You have recognized and correctly defined a problem that has occupied my mind for a long time—how to make gasoline out of water. I am happy to say that I have recently found the solution. I have constructed a simple apparatus that accomplishes the desired result rapidly and economically."

"Good for you!" said Mary. "Where is this apparatus?"

"As a matter of fact, I brought it with me on this trip. That helicopter is a regular gas-hog. So it is a real convenience to have a small gasoline factory with me all the time."

"It sounds just wonderful," said Mary. "I want to see this thing sometime. I want to watch it work. Could you show it to us, Mr. Anthony?"

"I don't see why not. I could fly you out to the boat house right now. That's where the gasoline apparatus is set up."

"Let's go!" said Mary.

"Just a minute," said Mr. Anthony. "If I am going to make a lot of gasoline, I ought to have some place to put it. Didn't I see a big tank truck out in your parking lot?"

"Yes," said John.

"Is it empty?"

"Practically."

"All right. If you will drive the truck out to the boat house I will take Mary and Mr. Botts in the helicopter. Okay?"

"Okay."

A half hour later we were all assembled in a large room in the boat house. The various components of the apparatus were arranged on a long table. Mr. Anthony pointed them out, one by one, and explained their function.

"First of all, we have this suction hose. The far end is in the bayou. This end is connected to this electric water pump."

"I see," said Mary. "The pump sucks water from the bayou and shoots it through this pipe into this big box."

"Right!" said Mr. Anthony. "You are a smart girl, Mary. And next to the water pump is this air pump——"

"Which shoots air into the big box." Mary was getting more and more excited.

Mr. Anthony continued, "The big box, with a capacity of fifty gallons, is what I call the catalysis chamber. It has several compartments containing several catalytic agents—the most important of which is chlorophyll."

Mary came up right away with another question: "What is chlorophyll? And what does it do?"

"Chlorophyll is the green coloring matter in plants. What it does is take the water that is pumped up by the plant roots and combine or catalyze it with the carbon dioxide in the air to make carbohydrates such as sugar or starch or wood."

"Wait a minute," said Mary. "Did you say there is something in the air called carbon dioxide?"

"Yes."

"And it contains something called carbon that you need to make gasoline?"

"Yes. Gasoline is a mixture of several hydrocarbons, which are very similar, chemically, to carbohydrates."

"Now I get it," said Mary, smiling with complete happiness. "A tree, with its green leaves, combines carbon from the air with water from its roots to make wood—which you can burn in a fireplace. Your magic invention, with its chlorophyll, combines carbon from the air with water from the bayou to make gasoline—which you can burn in the engine of a car."

"You have said it all, Mary, with beautiful brevity and clarity. And now, would you like to see the apparatus at work?"

We all said, "Yes."

Mr. Anthony ran a hose from the far end of what he called the catalysis chamber to a small pail outside the boat house. He threw a couple of switches and manipulated several valves. The pumps began to whir. The pail filled up with a clear liquid. Mr. Anthony stopped machinery. The flow of liquid ceased. We all sniffed at the contents of the pail.

"It smells like gasoline," said Mary.

We poured some of it on the ground and lit it.

"It burns like gasoline," said Mary.

"Why not?" said Mr. Anthony. "It *is* gasoline."

John and Mary were convinced. I was impressed. But, with my usual hardheaded skepticism, I decided to wait and see. "Maybe," I said to myself, "he had a pailful of gasoline hidden in that big box."

Mr. Anthony connected the hose to the tank truck, and started his apparatus.

We sat down to wait. And we waited several hours, while the machine whirred on. At last Mr. Anthony, after glancing at a gauge, announced that he had pumped into the tank truck a total of exactly 7,800 gallons of gasoline—almost fifteen tons, give or take a few hundred pounds.

"Holy Moses!" said John. "At fifty cents a gallon, wholesale, that means I owe you thirty-eight hundred dollars. And I don't have that much cash with me right now."

Mr. Anthony smiled indulgently. "You don't owe me anything," he said. "I was just putting on a routine demonstration. The gasoline is a mere by-product. It is, of course, nothing but reconstituted bayou water. It cost me nothing. So you may keep it."

John and Mary were overwhelmed. "What can we do," said John, "to show our appreciation?"

Mr. Anthony came back with one of his usual startling remarks. "How would you like to buy this gasoline maker?"

"You mean you want to sell it?"

"It's like this. Right now I need some extra funds to start large-scale production. When I get going, I plan to sell these things for two hundred thousand dollars each. They will be worth more than that; they will produce, in just a few days, gasoline that will sell for more than they cost."

There was a long silence. "I would like to buy this machine," said John, "but I don't have two hundred thousand dollars."

"Don't worry about that," said Mr. Anthony. "You can give me only one hundred thousand cash. And I'll take a promissory note for the rest."

There was another long silence. John and Mary looked at each other. Mary nodded her head.

"All right," said John. "It's a deal. I have enough collateral to borrow a hundred grand at the bank. And the gasoline machine will earn enough for me to pay off both the loan and the note in no time."

After I had expressed my approval, and we had congratulated each other all around, John drove Mary and me back to his home in the truck. Mr. Anthony remained with his helicopter at the boat house.

At my suggestion, John tested out his new supply of gasoline in his car and in several pieces of equipment. It worked fine. John then departed for the bank to negotiate his loan. And I returned to the motel, where I have been finishing this letter.

The great gasoline machine has now proved to be a complete success. If I were the kind of man who enjoys saying, "I told you so," I would say just that to you right now, Henderson. But I am not that kind. So I will close this letter with all my best wishes, and with the hope that you will reconsider your unjustified suspicions, withdraw your adverse opinions of Mr. Anthony, and admit you were wrong.

Alexander Botts

TELEGRAM
FROM EARTHWORM CITY, ILL.

MAY 31, 1974

TO ALEXANDER BOTTS
SOUTH GUMBO MOTEL,
SOUTH GUMBO, LA.
I DO NOT ADMIT I WAS WRONG. I HAVE JUST DISCOVERED A COIN-CIDENCE MORE INCREDIBLE THAN THE ONE YOU REPORT. YESTER-DAY IN CHICAGO I HAD LUNCH WITH PRESIDENT OF CANADIAN OIL COMPANY WHO TOLD ME OF A SMOOTH-TALKING PROMOTER WHO ACCIDENTALLY DREAMED UP A DEAL SIMILAR TO THAT OF YOUR MR. ANTHONY. THIS CANADIAN SPELLBINDER ARRIVED IN SMALL TOWN OF NORTH MUSKEG, ALBERTA, AND DUG HOLE IN MARSH, PRETENDING HE WAS LOOKING FOR RARE LITHIUM MUD TO TREAT ARTHRITIS. THIS PROVED TO BE A MERE EXCUSE FOR DIGGING DOWN TO LARGE GASOLINE PIPELINE TO WHICH HE ATTACHED SMALL TUBE LEADING TO APPARATUS HE CLAIMED WOULD TURN WATER INTO GASOLINE. THE SCHEME WORKED. THE PROMOTER SOLD HIS APPARATUS FOR SEVERAL HUNDRED THOUSAND DOL-LARS, DISAPPEARED, AND HAS NOT BEEN HEARD FROM SINCE. I SUGGEST YOU INVESTIGATE MR. ANTHONY MORE FULLY.

GILBERT HENDERSON
CHAIRMAN OF THE BOARD
EARTHWORM TRACTOR CO.

South Gumbo Motel
South Gumbo, Louisiana
June 1, 1974

Dear Henderson:

Your wire arrived yesterday, and I hasten to inform you that you are completely wrong in assuming you have discovered an incredible coincidence. As I have a quick mind, it took me only about two seconds after reading your words to realize that there is no coin-cidence at all. It would be mathematically impossible for two different people to originate independently any such complex

305

modus operandi. Hence, your North Muskeg malefactor and my South Gumbo impostor are one and the same person. There is no coincidence.

Fortunately, besides being a quick thinker, I am also a man of action. I got going at once. I leaped into my car, drove to the Bradley house and showed your telegram to John and Mary. And I am happy to report that they have minds almost as quick as my own.

"Possibly," said John, sadly, "our friend Mr. Anthony may not be as reliable as we had supposed."

"You may be right," said Mary.

"I'm afraid," said John, "that I have acted a bit hastily—and foolishly. I took Mr. Anthony to the bank yesterday. I arranged a loan for one hundred thousand dollars and asked that the full amount be credited to Mr. Anthony. This was done. Mr. Anthony then asked the cashier if he could draw out the money in cash at once."

"Oh, no!" I said. "They didn't give him the cash, did they?"

"No," said John. "The cashier told him this is a small bank. They don't keep that much on hand. It would take several days to get it from New Orleans. The best they could do would be to issue a draft on a New Orleans bank. If Mr. Anthony took the draft to this bank personally, with proper identification, he could probably get the cash right away."

"And that's what happened?" I asked.

"Yes," said John. "They said the draft would take a little while to arrange. It would be ready this morning."

"Quick!" I said. "Call the bank." We did. The cashier said Mr. Anthony had recently arrived by taxicab—not helicopter—had picked up the draft, and departed.

"Let's go," I said. "We can use my car." We rushed out. I climbed into the driver's seat. John and Mary piled into the rear. I drove along the main road, then turned into the back road leading to the boat house. Soon we passed a taxicab that had skidded into the ditch. Mr. Anthony waved frantically from the back seat. I paid no attention.

We reached the boat house. The helicopter was parked outside. We entered the boat house. There were a few tools lying around. I picked up a wrecking bar and pried the big catalysis chamber up off the table. This uncovered a copper pipe coming up out of one of the table legs—which was hollow—and passing through a valve and entering the catalysis chamber. I disconnected the pipe from the chamber. I opened the valve. Gasoline came out. I closed the valve.

"That settles it," I said. "This Anthony man must have got hold of some sort of report or map showing a gasoline pipeline extending probably from a refinery to some point of distribution and passing under the ground right past this boat house. So he got hold of a drilling and tapping tool—which I see over there in the corner where he carelessly left it—and he dug a hole and tapped in on the line."

"Look out!" said John. The taxi had got out of the ditch. It had arrived. Mr. Anthony came charging in. He was angry.

"What do you think you're doing?" he demanded.

John replied by grabbing the man in a sort of head lock, gently forcing him down on his back, and sitting on him.

"Give me that draft," said John. Mr. Anthony refused. John began using that ancient persuader known as arm-twisting. Mr. Anthony gave up. John released one of his arms. He reached in his pocket and handed over the one-hundred-thousand-dollar draft. John let him up. He ran out the door, climbed into his helicopter, and disappeared into the wild blue yonder.

"Maybe," said John, "I should have hung onto him and turned him over to the cops, but I never thought of that. I was interested mainly in saving the hundred thousand dollars. But I suppose we should report all this to somebody."

We talked it over. Then we drove to the bank and told the whole story to the cashier. The cashier notified the police. They notified the F.B.I. After notifying the Canadian authorities, they tried to track down Mr. Anthony. They worked fast, but not quite fast enough. By this morning they had learned that Mr. Anthony had turned in his helicopter at New Orleans, and had left for London on a commercial plane. He had bought, with his Canadian money, a through ticket for Saudi Arabia. So it seems he has made a clean getaway

And now, Henderson, that I have given you an account of the more exciting events that have occurred during the past few days, I will set forth the final results which I have arranged under seven headings, as follows:

1. John and Mary have their hundred thousand dollars back. They have reverted to the contracting business. They have placed a big order for Earthworm equipment with Mike Warner. And, of course, John loves Mary, and Mary loves John, so both are HAPPY.

2. Mike has that big order, so he is . . . HAPPY.

3. John has paid the oil company for that gasoline. So it must be that the oil company is . . . HAPPY.

4. The local bank is no longer worried about that draft. So the local bank is . . . HAPPY.

5. You, Henderson, helped solve our problems in spite of being wrong part of the time. So you should be . . . HAPPY.

6. Mr. Anthony is undoubtedly safe in Saudi Arabia, where he will soon tap in on one of those rich Arabian pipelines and start selling the Arabs their own oil at a price they will consider cheap, meanwhile making a big profit for himself. Thus, for a while at least, both Mr. Anthony and the Arabs will be . . . HAPPY.

7. I have done such a good job here that I am . . . HAPPY.

So everybody is happy. Hooray! Hooray!

Yours,
Alexander Botts

COPYRIGHT INFORMATION